4.22

The ROYAL
Station Master's
Daughters

Ellee Seymour is a journalist and PR professional living near Cambridge. *The Royal Station Master's Daughters* is her debut novel. Ellee was inspired to write it after meeting Brian Heath, the great grandson of Harry Saward, who was the royal station master at Wolferon for forty years from 1884 to 1924 and who the novel is based on.

The ROYAL
Station Master's
Daughters

ELLEE SEYMOUR

ZAFFRE

First published in the UK in ebook in 2021
This edition published in 2022 by
ZAFFRE
An imprint of Bonnier Books UK
4th Floor, Victoria House
Bloomsbury Square
London
WC1B 4DA
Owned by Bonnier Books
Sveavägen 56, Stockholm, Sweden

This is a work of fiction. Names, places, events and
incidents are either the products of the author's
imagination or used fictitiously. Any resemblance to
actual persons, living or dead, or actual
events is purely coincidental.

A CIP catalogue record for this book is
available from the British Library.

ISBN: 978-1-83877-457-8

Also available as an ebook and in audio

This is for my beloved brother David. And Mum and Dad. Remembering the thrill I felt during our visits to the Royal Station at Wolferton many years ago, never for a moment thinking I would one day write a book about it xxx

Chapter 1

'Roll out the red carpet. The royal train is due in half an hour and there's not a minute to be wasted.'

Jessie watched the station master bark his order, as the syllables fell from his thick lips. Her eyes were glued to the beads of sweat trapped in the bushy bristles on his upper lip, shaped like tiny sparkling diamonds. As his mouth twitched, drops of moisture fell onto his chin. He reached into his pocket for a handkerchief and mopped his broom-like moustache with a sharp flick of his wrist.

'Make sure it's in a straight line and there are no creases,' he instructed crisply, his eyes following porters Eddie and Bill as they carried the crimson carpet under their arms along the platform.

Jessie squinted under the sun's intense brightness, shielding her eyes from the glare with her arm. She caught Eddie's cheeky wink as he teetered by, straining under the weight of the carpet. She grinned at the sixteen-year-old's mischievousness. Although nine years younger than her, she mulled, he had a confidence about him and a sunny nature that could attract birds from the trees. The two lads were new to the job at Wolferton Station and had learnt quickly, taking over from Ernest and Peter, who were away fighting with the Sandringham Company.

Harry Saward pointed to the spot where the carpet was to be laid. 'It has to be in exactly the right place for His Majesty to step onto when the train draws to a halt.'

'Aye, Mr Saward.' Eddie nodded and knelt down to position the carpet where indicated, sweat covering his face with a sheen as if it had been wax polished.

Jessie knew the scenario off by heart. The carpet couldn't be laid too early else it might be stepped on, leaving dirty marks which had to be brushed off, and it couldn't be done too close to the train's arrival as Harry didn't like to rush. Driver Dobson had never once shot over it after years of practice, slickly steaming in and stopping in exactly the right spot.

Jessie was the station master's eldest daughter and had seen Harry welcome hundreds of trains carrying royal visitors from around the world. Every distinguished political leader of the day had also set foot in Wolferton before travelling on to Sandringham for an audience with the King. She admired Harry's calmness and knew everything would go as planned; it always did.

The station had never looked lovelier than on this late summer's afternoon. Flower tubs were brimming with pink, red and white geraniums. Red, blue and white bunting framed the mock Tudor timber-framed station. Jessie and her family lived opposite in the grand station master's house that went with the job and was testament to the high regard bestowed on Harry Saward by the railway company.

Jessie couldn't imagine living anywhere other than Wolferton. The hamlet was nestled on the royal estate and almost every family who lived there had someone working for the royals, either as a cook or maid, gardener or gamekeeper. The tied cottages that came with the various jobs were like gingerbread houses, built from the local sand-coloured carstone, and their inhabitants took pride in maintaining bountiful gardens that brimmed with the sweetest fruit and quality vegetables. Before the war, the produce had scooped many prizes at horticultural shows, but now it was much needed to ensure their bellies wouldn't be empty as the Kaiser raged a terrible war against them – a community that had once welcomed him with open arms when he called in to visit his cousin, King George V. Now they were cousins at war. And the cousin he had once entertained generously was now trying to starve his people by blockading food supplies coming into the country across the sea.

Patriotic villagers lined up outside the station waving Union Jacks; the blacksmith, the butcher and his wife, retired farmworkers and young housewives jostled alongside each other, while a group of children ran along the grass verge singing 'God Save the King'. These diehard loyalists never missed out on the chance to glimpse their beloved King and Queen Mary, or their cherished Queen Mother, Queen Alexandra, who had been Queen Consort at the side of King Edward VII between 1901 and 1910. For them, loyalty and devotion to their royal family coursed through their veins, and what higher price of loyalty was there than giving your life, fighting for your King and country? Most families were missing someone, two or three men even, brothers in arms who had signed up together, while the women left behind rallied together to support the war effort, and each other, when informed that their loved one would not be returning home.

Jessie glanced up at the station clock; it was precisely twenty to three. The train was due to arrive at Wolferton in eight minutes. It was bang on time after leaving London St Pancras at 12.30 and pausing at the nearby town of King's Lynn for three minutes before making its final ten-minute haul to the royal station where Harry would be waiting to greet the King. The pilot train used as a decoy for security had passed through without any ado, so everything was running smoothly, just the way Harry liked it. Visits from the King were less frequent these days, his urgent wartime duties taking him to meet troops around the country and overseas, boosting his men's morale as the war set in, so this was a rare treat for the residents of Wolferton, who had previously been used to seeing him regularly, especially for celebratory family occasions.

Jessie's violet eyes fixed firmly on the railway track and her chest heaved in and out as she panted short breaths. She wasn't sure if it was the heat or her nerves getting the better of her. She inhaled a deep breath and felt her stomach tighten like a clenched fist. Her knees buckled and she swayed slightly.

'Steady on, Jessie. You're wobbling all over the place,' her sister Beatrice commented, having just arrived, and reached forward to steady her.

'I don't know what's come over me. I felt queasy for a moment, but I'm sure it will pass,' Jessie replied softly, fanning her face with her right hand.

'I do hope so, but I can't help noticing you do look pale.'

'I'll be all right, really, Beatrice,' Jessie assured her sister.

'Come on then, it's time to for us to stand alongside Father. Look, he is calling us over. Ada is there already, and she is waving us over. She must have left little Leslie at home, and probably for the best.'

A wave of sympathy coursed through Jessie as she joined her youngest sister, who had dark rings under her eyes. She was relieved Leslie had stayed behind; he was a right handful and his fretfulness would jar on her nerves, as well as Ada's.

Only one year separated each of the three sisters. Jessie was the eldest at twenty-five, followed by Beatrice and then Ada, who, despite her younger years, had beaten them up the aisle and was now mother to an eight-month-old son, while her two older siblings were yet to find true love.

Jessie was a perfectionist, like her mother Sarah. She had toffee-brown hair and a creamy skin and preferred to blend into the background, like the tall delphiniums and hollyhocks that grew at the back of her flowerbeds.

Beatrice was the most confident of the sisters and her thick nut-brown hair and cocoa-brown eyes were inherited from their mother, who had dark features.

Ada was fairest, resembling their father the most, with wheat-coloured wavy hair, a porcelain complexion and arctic blue eyes, which were frequently puffy due to Leslie's sleepless nights.

Jessie tossed her head backwards and her eyes scanned the railway track before she followed Beatrice. She quickened her steps and caught up as in the distance billowing, spiralling smoke in the sky heralded the train's imminent arrival.

The three sisters positioned themselves dutifully alongside their father, who stood next to the blood-red carpet.

Sarah Saward swept forward and stepped alongside Beatrice, pinning back a few strands of loose hair. The steadfast wife had been at Harry's side for over thirty years. It was a love that grew after they first met in the Cambridgeshire town of Whittlesey, where Harry was posted as a booking clerk in 1878. He wooed the farmer's daughter and their romance continued after he was promoted and posted to stations in nearby towns, being appointed station master for the first time in Fordham near Newmarket in May 1884. Within weeks, Harry spotted an advertisement for the post of royal station master at Wolferton. It was the most coveted railway job in the country and he couldn't let it slip through his fingers. Encouraged by Sarah and his family, he applied for the job – and beat 120 eager applicants, many with vastly more experience. By September 1884, Harry had married Sarah and the newlyweds settled in Wolferton. Although he was only twenty-five, he took his meteoric rise in his stride. His competence had impressed railway chiefs, who could see how respected he was by staff and passengers alike, recognising that his modesty and unpushy manner would stand him in good stead when greeting royals on his platform.

Jessie had heard him chuckle many times, 'Who would have thought it, all those years ago when as a thirteen-year-old lad, and the third of ten children always begging my pa to let me work on the railways with him, that I would end up working with the King! It goes to show that nothing is impossible if you set your heart on it, and work hard and do the best you are capable of.'

Harry had started off as a probationary telegraph clerk in Audley End, never thinking for a moment that he would proudly welcome no fewer than 645 royal trains at the station in his first twenty-seven years of service. Why, even Queen Victoria had set foot on the very same platform in Wolferton, bringing with her her trusted Scottish servant, John Brown, who drew curious glances in his kilt and sporran, an unusual sight for Wolferton. Queen Victoria's aunt, Queen Adelaide, was the first British royal to travel by rail in 1840, a mode of transport now favoured by royals, particularly the King, who travelled speedily around the country to inspect troops and visit factories and hospitals. The train's former elaborate furnishings had been replaced with practical fittings, including a bath to accommodate the royal household during extended trips.

Sarah wore a stern expression, her arms folded across her breast. She leant forward to glance at Jessie, shaking her head. Jessie knew she would face her mother's wrath later, having not returned to the royal retiring rooms earlier to assist her with any last-minute jobs. She knew her mother expected her to wait on the King and his party on arrival if required, but today she had found herself in turmoil as she anxiously awaited the train's arrival – and one passenger in particular.

She knew what was to come and dreaded her mother's comment, '*Don't make pretend you didn't hear me.*'

Those words cut through her like a knife slicing through butter. It pained her to be reminded of the hearing impairment she had suffered as a child and had stayed with her following a terrible virus; she tried her best to shrug it off and live a normal life like her sisters.

Her strong emotions took her by surprise and she needed time alone to still them – before the train pulled in. She avoided her mother's questioning gaze, turning the other way. For once, she was not going to jump to her mother's bidding.

'It's respect, a sign of respect,' Harry had explained, insisting that his daughters should always be at the station to greet His Majesty. 'How many station masters can claim the King steps onto his platform?' Harry would remind them, not boastfully, but in a good-natured way.

Suddenly, the porters shifted their luggage trolleys into position, their eyes focused down the track, as the engine's belching smoke wafted overhead, the train inching closer and closer.

Jessie's heart thumped against her ribs. She noticed Beatrice giving her a quizzical glance and she brushed it off. She ran her slim fingers down the front of her pale-blue dress, decorated with a delicate cream lace trim around the neck and sleeves, pleased she had chosen to wear it that day, knowing it flattered her tiny waist.

At her next heartbeat the train screeched to a halt. She recognised driver Dobson in his cab wearing his black cap; he knew the Wolferton line like the back of his hand and she saw him nod to the station master as he pulled in. The royal party had arrived.

Harry removed his peaked cap as he strode forward to open the carriage door. He bowed low as the King stepped onto the carpet and they exchanged a greeting, no doubt Harry enquiring if His Majesty would like refreshments in his retiring rooms before travelling on to Sandringham. The bearded King narrowed his eyes and shook his head.

Jessie inched forward slightly, watching the King's lips as he told her father, 'Thank you, Saward, but there is no time for that today. We are going straight on to Sandringham.'

Jessie's heart sank. Having calmed her nerves, she had hoped the King and his party would stay awhile and she would be able to serve them refreshments. Jessie watched her father follow the King out of the station where his gleaming Daimler and a chauffeur were waiting. Behind them were the King's trusted valet, Richard Howlett, a distinguished-looking army officer and a younger man in a bowler hat, precariously clutching two bulging briefcases in his arms. His private secretary was in attendance too.

Richard Howlett was on good terms with Harry and godfather to his grandson Leslie, the station master having gained the trust and respect of the royal household. The King paused for a moment before entering his car and politely enquired after Harry's family, having briefly acknowledged Sarah and her daughters on his way out of the station.

The army officer had a brusque manner. He was not one for pleasantries and he strode briskly as the heavily laden young man sprinted behind him. Jessie also recognised the King's sombre-looking private secretary, Lord Stamfordham, whose only son John had been killed just three months before on the Western Front while serving with the King's Royal Rifle Corps. She lowered her eyes as he passed her, imagining the pain he must be feeling but couldn't show in public, keeping the stiff upper lip.

Jessie observed Eddie and Bill leap into action and load the bags from the train onto their trolleys; these would be delivered to the King's home at Sandringham by horse and cart. He resided at York Cottage, close to the Big House, the name which locals used when referring to Sandringham House, where his mother still lived, and would continue to do so until she drew her last breath. The home had been gifted to him and Princess Mary by his parents when they married in 1893, and five of their six children had been born there.

Once the King's car had moved off, Beatrice made her excuses to return to the post office where she helped her mother when she was not attending in the royal retiring rooms. Ada also had to leave for her concert rehearsal at the church.

Jessie remained at the station, her eyes anxiously searching in all directions for sight of the one passenger she had been most looking forward to seeing. She quickened her pace along the platform, peering into the royal carriage. It was unlike any other on any train that steamed into Wolferton. The distinctive caramel and cream coloured carriage was pulled by a black engine and had the royal crest emblazoned across the front for all to see. She never failed to be in awe of the luxury of the walnut and satinwood fixtures and the plush royal-blue upholstery that matched the carpets and curtains.

She watched the Daimler glide past the front of the station on its three-mile journey to Sandringham, the crowds waving and cheering, calling out their patriotic allegiance.

She'd grown up hearing stories of the comings and goings of a vast array of royalty at Wolferton Station as the royal family had married into royal houses across Europe. Before the war, it was quite a normal occurrence for Queen Alexandra to welcome her brother, the King of Greece, or her sister Dagmar, the Tsarina of Russia, here at Wolferton, where there would always be a great fanfare.

These days it was khaki-dressed servicemen who packed the platform on their way to the trenches and battlefields, waved off by their loved ones, mothers and sweethearts weeping, not knowing if and when they would see them again.

Her thoughts returned to the one person on her mind as her search continued.

'Jack. Jack. Jack.' She whispered the name softly, picturing in her head the man who made her so giddy.

She had been in this light-headed state since the evening before when she overheard Harry tell Sarah that the King's Messenger would be arriving in Wolferton today with the King. Her face reddened at mention of his name and she felt a stirring sensation welling inside her.

'Poor Jack,' Sarah had commiserated. 'He's had so much to bear.'

Jessie had hoped to catch Jack's eye in the King's retiring room. She was anxious to see if he showed any signs of returning her feelings. She was always unable to resist the fluttering in her heart when she served him in the royal retiring room with the King, her face turning crimson and her hand shaking as she poured out their drinks.

Her feelings towards him had grown in the last two years. She'd seen him brush away a tear from his cheek in the royal retiring rooms and Sarah had instructed her not to trouble him. Later she explained he was grieving following the tragic death of his beloved wife and baby in childbirth. Sarah, who heard this from the vicar's wife, had told her how the baby boy had looked perfect, but was stillborn, and nothing could be done to save his poor wife, who bled to death.

Jack had been inconsolable and Jessie sensed his pain from the haunted look behind his eyes as she observed him grieving. She had seen him tramping through the woods, giving way to buckets of tears. Now, with the passage of time, she noticed that he seemed to be healing. He was starting to smile again and taking time to speak to her when they met. He always talked slowly so she could follow his words, knowing that she had trouble with her hearing, showing her a kindness that touched her heart.

Beatrice had encouraged Jessie to be bold. 'He's had time to come to terms with his grief. How will the poor man know you have a fondness for him if you don't give him a sign? Just be friendly, catch his eye and smile. Be yourself, the lovely person you really are, and he will be captivated,' she had advised.

'I could never be that forward. It's all right for you, Beatrice,' Jessie had replied. 'You are beautiful and bright and confident. Everyone likes you, while I am—'

'You are pretty and kind and would be a treasure for any man,' Beatrice interrupted firmly, before her sister could refer to her affliction.

But now, with the King going straight on to Sandringham, and no sign of Jack, Jessie's hopes of spending a brief moment with him had evaporated.

She was sure that by now all the passengers had disembarked. With a heavy heart she turned to leave. As she began walking away, she paused and turned to look behind her one more time, just in case. Her heart suddenly pounded as she spotted him.

Jack Hawkins stood just a few feet away, stepping off the carriage. He didn't appear to see her, but then he turned and the joyful expression on his face was enough to confirm what she wanted to know. She stepped quickly towards him and then stopped suddenly.

Without uttering a word, Jack turned his back on her and took hold of a dainty white gloved hand, helping its owner off the train and onto the platform.

Stunned, Jessie saw that the hand belonged to an elegant young woman with the sweetest smile. She held firmly on to Jack's hands as she alighted onto the platform.

Jessie suddenly felt foolish and awkward. Without warning, the green-eyed monster filled every fibre of her body. She couldn't tear her eyes away from Jack's companion and immediately assumed their close familiarity could only mean he was courting her. She was the prettiest woman Jessie had ever seen, two or three years younger than her, with clear peachy skin. Her perfectly coiffed blonde curls were pinned back stylishly in the latest fashion and she was dressed exquisitely in lilac. Jessie watched them smiling and chatting together, throwing their heads back in shared intimacy. Why hadn't Jack come over to her? Her throat clenched and she decided she couldn't bear to wait for Jack to introduce her to his beautiful new lady.

Jealousy burned inside her, flames of fury that could not be extinguished. The sight of their closeness felt like a stab to the heart and, without thinking, she ran off, brushing against Jack's arm in her haste to flee. She saw his startled expression as his head turned towards her and felt his eyes boring into her back as she hurried off the platform, lifting the latch of the wooden gate and stumbling into the path. Panting, she turned left. Panting, she turned left.

Within two or three minutes, she had almost reached her house and she stopped with a jolt. Her attention was drawn to the sight of two unknown women standing just a few feet away by the gate, one older and the other about sixteen years old. They were shabbily dressed and seemed to be having a heated discussion. Jessie watched as the younger woman began lifting the latch on the gate, but was stopped abruptly by the older woman who appeared anxious. She watched them, unobserved, as they exchanged words animatedly. The younger girl suddenly threw her arms in the air and stomped off, the older woman trailing after her as quickly as she could, limping slightly.

Jessie's curiosity was roused by their strange behaviour at her home and she resolved to follow the women, who appeared to be on the same path she had intended to take. She trailed behind them for a short distance along the stony track that led to the church where Ada would be holding her concert rehearsal very soon.

As they turned a corner, the women disappeared from sight. Jessie paused, unsure whether to continue following them or take the path on her left up into the woodland planted by King Edward VII when he settled in Sandringham, so it was a relatively young wooded area planted around fifty years ago. She decided to take the path, making a mental note to inform her parents about the strange couple later that evening. She picked up her skirt and then followed the track behind the church. It was the same gravely track she had seen Jack take when he wanted to be alone. She followed it until it became a slight upward incline. She scrambled up the stony path until she was surrounded by pine and oak trees, which provided her with the cool, healing sanctuary she sought. The warm air was filled with a heady scent from the pine trees and she stumbled clumsily over the hard dusty ground, broken twigs and bracken, pausing only to ensure she did not tear her skirt and being careful not to spoil her shoes.

Staring straight ahead, she continued scrambling along the winding path for ten more minutes until she reached higher woodland where she paused to catch her breath. The view from here was breathtaking on a perfect cloudless day such as this, heathland and bog stretching out for miles to the Norfolk coast and she could faintly make out the sea on the horizon.

She trudged on for another five minutes, spotting familiar landmarks to guide her, recognising the small, shady clearing where she and her sisters had picnicked as children, or the spot where a huge branch still lay on the ground, after being ripped off in a storm, like a limb separated from its torso, that they would sit on and exchange gossip.

Eventually, she reached an oak tree on a slight rise that was perfectly formed in the centre of another clearing. She walked around the huge trunk, tracing her finger on its deep ridges in search of the initials, which they had carved into the bark. Sure enough, the letters were there – J.S., B.S. and A.S. – enclosed in one big heart, still there after more years than she cared to remember, joining the three Saward sisters together.

This spot had been her childhood hideaway. It was where she would come to sit alone if upset. Sometimes she would play hide and seek with Beatrice and Ada and they delighted in scaring each other by making up stories of forest ghosts.

She looked around for the path that led to the folly, which had been the favourite shooting lodge of King Edward when he held his famous shooting parties. This turreted woodland building soared higher than any other she knew of and had a wrap-around balcony on the first floor giving panoramic views in all directions. It had been built as a shooting lodge for the royals to enjoy and she felt drawn towards it. She had heard mutterings in the village that it was haunted by the ghost of Prince Eddy, who had tragically died young, aged only twenty-eight, from pneumonia. She'd heard that he had enjoyed the mysterious atmosphere of the folly too, and it was where some of the royal family's more exotic animals shot by his father on trips to India were kept. Although it was twenty-three years since he had died, his heartbroken mother had left his room at the Big House untouched. In her grief, Queen Alexandra had turned his room into a shrine to him, even having the fire lit. Jessie wasn't sure if she imagined it, but she often felt a shiver run down her spine, a chill in the air, a darkening mass filling her head, when she spent time there. She wondered if the ghost of Prince Eddy was here in the folly. He had been born to be king, but after his early death the crown passed to his younger brother George.

Jessie couldn't resist peering through the windows of the folly in search of the wide open jaws of tigers and other wild animals Prince Eddy brought back from his travels in Nepal. The collection of animals shot by his father and grandfather was kept on the first floor. If she let her imagination get the better of her, she could imagine these exotic creatures that she had only seen in books, roaming around inside the building. She would shudder at the thought of them springing back to life and ensnaring her in their jaws.

Thomas, the royal gamekeeper, lived nearby with his wife Phyllis, and laughingly dismissed her fears about ghosts. He would tell her with a playful glint in his eye, 'There ain't no tigers in these woods, lassie, you can take my word for that.' Nevertheless, she wasn't convinced.

Jessie loved the solitude of the place and felt happiest close to nature with only the woodland animals for company. She liked its smells too, the nutty aroma of the warm woodland and damp moss. Feeling calmer, her mind switched back to Jack, the space between her eyebrows crossing like knitting needles.

I hope he didn't notice how foolishly I behaved. I feel so stupid now. I just don't know what came over me.

She stretched her arms above her head and yawned. Emotional exhaustion had weakened her, her nerves were jangled and her eyes wanted to close. She reached up to unpin her hair, letting it tumble down her back, tossing it from side to side.

I must just rest for a while, then I'll go back home. I'll tell them the heat made me giddy.

After clearing away some broken twigs and pine needles on the ground, her eyes settled on an area of soft moss big enough for a makeshift mattress. It was spongy and perfectly positioned under the oak tree, shaded by its fanned-out branches. Her feet ached uncomfortably and her best cream shoes pinched. She untied the laces and frowned at the scuffs on them from her scramble in the woods, then placed them under a cluster of fern leaves close by. She hoped she could clean them back at home without her mother noticing.

She yawned and stretched out again, unable to resist the tiredness that consumed her body, her heavy eyelids clasping shut like oyster shells. Lying down on her mossy bed, she tossed around until she was comfortable, her body drifting off as she enjoyed the solitude of the shady dell. She was oblivious to the great spotted woodpecker that dug its beak into the branch above her, making repetititive short, sharp rapping sounds. Or the red squirrels that darted along the branches above her.

Neither was she aware of the breaking sound of twigs close by and footsteps creeping up slowly towards her.

Chapter 2

'Excuse me, miss. I'm sorry for troubling you, but are you one of 'em Saward girls?'

Although the woman's voice that interrupted her was soft, it had an urgency in its tone that made Ada stop abruptly. Clutching her music bag tightly under her arm, she turned and faced a dishevelled figure.

She was about to ask who the unfortunate-looking woman might be, but was silenced by the chiming of the church clock. Ada's jaw tightened and she felt her body stiffen. She needed no reminding of the time, that it was three o'clock and she should now be at rehearsal. Having to be at the station for the King's arrival, a ritual her father insisted on, had made her late, even though she had left as soon as she could. She frowned as she imagined how her lateness would please Magnolia Greensticks. She became flustered at the thought of Magnolia telling the choir she was not capable of taking charge, so she had no time, nor the inclination, to dally and chat to a stranger.

The woman shuffled closer, preventing Ada from passing by. 'I apologise for the intrusion, miss, only it's important.'

Ada, her face flushed, recoiled as if stung by a bee when the woman lightly touched her arm. Her eyes widened as they fixed on the woman's face. Who was this strange unkempt individual that knew her family name and stared at her so intently? Her large sunken eyes were veiled with a sad expression, fixed in their sockets like planets in a dark hole. They glared at Ada with an intensity that made her feel uncomfortable.

'I need to know if yer related to Harry Saward, the station master?' she persisted, tilting her head to one side. There was a slight shakiness in her tone, a hesitation as if she had summoned up courage to speak.

Ada shook herself free from the stranger and took a step back, narrowing her eyes as she tried to fathom if she knew her. The woman had a washed-out leathery complexion and her light brown hair, streaked with thin grey strands, was loosely tied in a bun that nestled on the nape of her neck. She gripped a grey shawl with fringed edges over her thin shoulders, her bony gnarled knuckles shaking slightly. Her clothes were practical and looked well worn; a white washed-out, buttoned-up, high-neck blouse that gaped around her scrawny neck and a black skirt that hung loosely around her tiny waist and brushed the top of her scuffed lace-up boots.

As Ada opened her mouth to reply she became distracted by raised voices close by. She looked over the stranger's shoulder in the direction of St Peter's Church, where a group of women stood, their voices becoming increasingly louder.

Her brows pulled in as she faced the stranger again. Hopefully, it wouldn't take long to deal with her and she could then be on her way. She looked the woman straight in the eyes.

'Yes, I am indeed one of the Saward girls, as you put it. And may I ask, how do you know my family? I don't believe we have met before.'

The stranger lowered her gaze, tucking a few stray strands of hair behind her ears. Ada noticed the woman's hands were dry and wrinkled like a lizard's skin, in sharp contrast to Ada's silky soft skin and delicate fingers. She shuddered, wondering what kind of hard life this woman had had.

A sharp voice made her spin around. 'I told yer it would be a waste of time, Ma. Them Sawards won't want anything to do with the likes of us. Why should the Sawards care about us, when they have fine lives an' royal connections?'

Ada's jaw dropped at the sight of a young girl leaping out from behind a tree. The girl rushed to the woman's side and Ada stepped back, astounded by her sudden appearance and hostile tone as she spat out her words.

'I beg your pardon? What is the meaning of this? She's . . . your daughter?'

'Yes, miss, this is my Maria.' She shot a quick warning glance at her young companion.

'Pray tell me quickly, what business do you and your mother have with my family? I am in the most frightful rush.'

The older woman spoke softly. She placed her hand on Ada's arm. 'Begging yer pardon, miss, and please excuse

Maria, she don't mean what she says, that's why I thought it best for 'er to stay out of sight. Please, I don't mean to alarm yer. I just want a minute of your time 'cos what I have to say, well, it's consequential.'

'You mean confidential, Ma. It's very confidential,' interrupted Maria, with a sigh, shaking her head, her hands placed firmly on her hips. 'That's why you should let me speak.'

'Yes, that's right, miss, it's confidential, that's what I meant to say.'

'And what confidential information could you possibly have about my family that would be of interest to me?' enquired Ada, feeling uncomfortable, keeping half an eye on the group at the church gate.

There was no doubting whose daughter the girl was. She bore a striking resemblance to the older woman, despite the weariness that showed on her mother's countenance. Both had finely chiselled cheekbones you could sharpen a knife on and Ada could see they were both good looking, underneath their shabby clothes and the older woman's worn appearance. The girl's large deep brown-black eyes reflected a strong and wilful character, an air of defiance and bravado and devil-may-care attitude that Ada was not accustomed to. Not here, in Wolferton, on the royal Sandringham Estate.

The girl was thin, but well formed for her sixteen years, and her thick, wavy hair tumbled over her shoulders, knotted like bark. It was in need of a good brush, but its dishevelled state suited her sparky outspoken manner and flushed cheeks. Ada observed Maria fidgeting with her clothing, holding her dark blue oversized skirt up a mite so it didn't drag on the ground; it clearly looked like a hand-me-down. Ada noticed that the girl was wearing a pair of scuffed threadbare shoes which she quickly concealed under the hem of her skirt when she spotted Ada glancing at them with pity.

The mother's thin voice quavered. 'I saw yer at the station earlier on, you were standing next to yer pa an' I guessed you were one of 'is daughters; I can see the likeness. I thought it best to speak to yer first. We saw yer leave the station an' stop off at yer house, but I couldn't pluck up the courage then. Maria wanted to stay there and wait for yer to return home, but I didn't think that was wise. I thought it might be too much of a shock for everyone if we turned up out of the blue, especially if Mrs Saward was there, an' it would give 'er a fair turn, I'm sure. So we kept a few feet behind yer an' followed yer here. I know it must be a shock, but if I may explain, me name is Ruth, Ruth Saward, an' . . .'

'You mean to say you know where I live? And your name is Saward? I don't understand. Who are you?'

The girl nodded, a smirk covering her face. 'Yer 'eard right. We're Sawards too. We're related, miss. I'm Maria Saward.'

'Related? How could that possibly be? I don't understand.' Ada's voice wobbled, 'Unless you are—'

'Yes, miss. I'm Ruth, Willie's wife. Yer pa knows me well an' he's been kind to us.'

Ada's cheeks burned. She felt cornered, obligated to learn more about these two people who had appeared from thin air.

'Me ma 'ere is yer grandma, well, step-grandma, to be precise, as she wed Willie Saward, yer father's pa, after 'is first wife passed on. Willie was me pa, so yer pa is me stepbrother. So ye see, miss, that makes us related.'

Ada had vaguely heard mention of Willie Saward's second marriage, but always in hushed tones. It was never openly discussed; a skeleton in the cupboard, with the cupboard firmly locked and the key thrown away. She recalled walking into the kitchen once when Harry was telling her mother, 'So there's life left in the old dog. Seventy years old and he's marrying again.'

'Related . . . I can't believe it.' The words stuck in Ada's throat, her head spinning at the revelation from these shabby strangers.

'I'm sorry, I didn't mean it to come out like that,' Ruth murmured. 'I can see it's a right shock for yer.'

Ada recalled snippets of more hushed conversation she had overheard between her parents, who had washed their hands of Harry's father after his second marriage. Her mother's contemptuous words rang in her ears. 'Folk say your poor ma was barely cold when he took that wench to his bed. She knew which side her bread was buttered. It's not decent, I tell you.'

'Well, I expect the old goat needs someone to look after him in his advancing years,' Harry had remarked when his ageing father tied the knot with his new young wife aged only twenty-eight.

'What can she see in him? She must think he has plenty of money hidden under his mattress. They've made us all a laughing stock, they have. And no doubt she was expecting too, the shame of it,' fumed Sarah. 'You'd best make it plain they are not welcome here.'

Ada and her sisters had never dared ask about them. She knew the second wife was called Ruth. Now she was confronted with her, and she was not as she imagined, a temptress, fallen woman or gold-digger. She was humble and vulnerable and appeared to have fallen on hard times.

She dreaded to think how her parents would react to their presence in their community, where Harry was admired by all and had been given the honorary title of Mayor of Wolferton by his King and the community, in recognition of his many good deeds. She could only surmise that they were in need of money, and she doubted her parents would oblige their poor relations.

Ada's throat tightened. This was not the time or place to talk about family scandal. She had no intention of airing her family's dirty linen in public and knew she must rid herself of these women as quickly as possible.

'How do I know you are telling the truth? What proof do you have of who you really are?' Ada asked.

Ruth answered softly. 'That's a fair enough question, with us turning up here without a word. But I tell yer, miss, on Maria's life, that what I say is all true, an' Willie an' I, we 'ad an 'appy marriage. Yer ma an' pa knows what we say is truthful, we have a lot to be thankful to yer pa for.'E didn't turn his back on us, not like some. 'E appreciated the care I gave Willie when 'e was widowed an' struggled.'E made me promise to keep 'is visits secret, an' I always kept me word, up until today. Now I 'ave no choice but to come 'ere because of our change in circumstances.'

'What do you mean? I have no idea what you are talking about,' Ada queried, at a loss for words.

Ruth continued, speaking more assuredly. 'Yer father, miss, 'e knows more about us than 'e's ever let on, for fear of upsetting yer ma. Harry would stop off to see us sometimes on 'is way to London, even bringing us food after Willie died.'E took a keen interest in Maria's well-being, 'e could see she was bright an' liked reading an' writing. When 'e turned up at Audley End the porters an' staff that remembered 'im starting out there with 'is pa, they shook 'is 'and slapped 'im on the back. Willie was always so proud of Harry.'

'I had no idea that Father was in touch with you,' gulped Ada.

Maria grinned. 'That was the way 'e wanted it.'E's been good to me an' can vouch for what Ma says. Then you'll have to believe that we are related.'

Ada's eyes widened at the revelation. She shook her head. 'This is all so unexpected. I'm thankful you didn't just turn up at the house unannounced. I just don't know what to say.'

After a pause, she raised her eyebrows and tossed back her head. 'Now I remember. Weren't you Grandpa's maid, helping him out around the house when he became widowed? And didn't you also work as a barmaid in a rather unsavoury drinking establishment?'

'Yes, miss, that's right. I took what 'onest work I could to earn a penny, before I married an' afterwards, when the money ran out. People had plenty to talk about, their tongues wagging, but as I say, we were 'appy enough. Willie, God rest 'is soul, 'ad a heart of gold.'E took my ma in when she was poorly an' 'ad nowhere else to go. We were blessed to 'ave two boys as well as Maria. She 'as two brothers, they are lovely lads, are me Freddie and Archie. Your pa, may the Lord bless 'im, 'e doted on them, an' they looked up to 'im.'

'This is all so unexpected, I don't know what to say.'

'So you'll speak to yer father, Miss?" Ruth pressed her. "E'll vouch for us an' say how well I looked after Willie in his declining years.'E always said we could count on him if we should fall on hard times, which we have due to circumstances beyond our control.'

Ada was at a loss for words, absorbing these revelations. Her attention was diverted towards the women shuffling their feet impatiently at the lych gate, their eyes fixed on her, their mutterings becoming louder. She could see their lips twitching and wished they would just go inside the church. She raised an arm to gesture this, but was ignored.

Maria pointed to the church and blurted, 'You see, Ma, I told you not to believe those stupid rumours. There's the church, still standing in all its glory right before your eyes.'

'What are you talking about? Of course our church is still standing,' Ada retorted, her eyes following Maria's gaze. She was beginning to feel irritated with the women for protracting her lateness – and for bringing so much information for her to digest.

'An' what a good thing too.' Ruth commented. 'A couple of fellas in the pub told us that yer church 'ere 'ad been bombed by one of 'em sausage-like Zeppelins. They reckon it ain't safe to live around 'ere, that folk are sitting ducks on account of the King living close by.'

Ada's eyes widened. 'Heaven forbid, what a terrible thing to say. As you can see that is not true, even though a bomb was dropped near Sandringham,' Ada retorted.

Maria raised her eyes to the sky, shielding them from the glare of the sun with her hands. 'I'd be so scared if I saw one of 'em Zeppelins 'overing over me. Ma was nervous coming 'ere on account of what 'em fellas said. They know Harry an' when we told them we were coming 'ere they said they wouldn't be surprised if the Huns destroyed the railway station to stop the King an' our troops moving around.'

And here they were now, close to the town that had been one of the German's targets on its first air raid on Britain's shores six months before, when they dropped bombs on King's Lynn, just nine miles away, and Great Yarmouth further around on the Norfolk coast. Now their barbaric enemy was creeping along the coast closer towards them and they lived in constant fear of being bombarded again or invaded by them. Little wonder that any stranger was regarded with the greatest suspicion – in case they were a spy.

'I'm fearful the Hun could take us by surprise by air or sea, swarming in on the beaches one night,' Ada recalled her mother saying one night, her eyebrows furrowed.

'Ah, but consider this,' her father had replied with a knowing look in his eye. 'I reckon we're safer here on account of the King's home at Sandringham and the extra security he has when he travels. We have our own brave men keeping a good watch out along the coast and the lighthouse in Hunstanton. Those blasted Huns won't get anywhere near Wolferton, you mark my words.'

Ada's thoughts returned to the impatient choir ladies. She half wished she hadn't agreed to take charge, but reminded herself that she was doing this for her beloved Alfie; she wanted to make her husband proud of her. It was also her way of helping raise much needed money for the war effort, now all hopes of a swift end had been dashed. One year after the Great War had started, nobody could tell how much longer it would last, with early hopes that it would be over by last Christmas crushed.

Ada felt a warm glow ripple and rise inside her as she pictured Alfie in her mind and her lips curled.

∽

They had married at the church here just fifteen months ago. Ada shared Alfie's passion for music. He made a comforta-ble living as an accomplished organist and choirmaster, and although he always praised her singing and pitch-perfect notes, and her mastery of the piano keys, she never felt she had earned his praise. They had only been wed just over a year when Alfie swapped his life as a choirmaster and organist for that of a soldier, signing up with the Artists Rifles, one of the London's volunteer battalions that went on to become the 28th London Regiment, attracting recruits from public schools and universities. While in London one day he'd seen a poster displayed by the Artists Rifles that offered French-speaking English gentlemen commissions in the army after four months' training. Alfie was instantly drawn to the Rifles, believing he would be among like-minded, better-educated, creative recruits. His French was rusty, but it was sufficient to pass, and within a few months he was made a junior officer and held the rank of Lieutenant, spending a spell training at the infamous Tower of London.

You should have heard the jokes we cracked about hanging on to our heads.

Ada shuddered as she imagined the horror of traitors who were tortured and executed there.

Don't worry, my sweetheart, I've kept my head! And my heart is all yours. I couldn't be with better men, educated men who are writers and musicians, we keep each other cheered the best we can. I pray I will be able to embrace you soon, and that this wretched war will be over and I'll be back in time for the birth of our child, Alfie had written, a few weeks after signing up in August 1914.

They were overjoyed when she became pregnant within months of settling into their new life in Cromer, a coastal town almost fifty miles from Wolferton. But sickness had plagued her pregnancy, forcing her to her bed, writhing in discomfort.

Feeling miserable, she had broken down in tears the day before Alfie left, unable to hide her sadness at his impending departure.

'Please forgive me, my darling,' she wept. 'I don't mean to make a fuss. I'm not the only wife who will give birth while her beloved husband is away fighting for his King and country.'

'Shush. There is nothing to forgive, my darling. I promise you I'll be home soon. I'll be back in a blink before the baby is born. Everyone expects the war to be over quickly.'

Ada had nodded, turning her head away from Alfie as he pulled her close to him. He removed the clips in her hair that was fashioned on the crown of her head, watching the hair tumble loosely over her shoulders. Her stomach felt queasy, but she willed herself to forget her nausea. She wanted them to share a tender final embrace they could both remember in the days ahead when he had gone.

She knew he loved running his fingers through her wavy hair, and she felt a thrill from watching his lips curl with pleasure and his eyes sparkling from the desires their shared intimacy aroused in each other.

He lifted her chin and gently wiped away the tears that trickled down her cheeks. She was trembling as he kissed her on the lips, a lingering kiss that thrilled her and awakened her body to her womanly desires. She clung to him, wishing it could last forever, smiling up at him as he kissed her belly with its first signs of a swelling. When he released her, she felt the queasiness return and rested on her bed.

'My sweet darling, it pains me to see you suffering so much while carrying our child. If only I could take your pain and sickness.'

Ada placed her slender finger on her husband's trembling lips to silence him, smiling weakly as he propped up two plump feather pillows behind her back for her to rest against.

'I take comfort from knowing that despite feeling so wretched, it's perfectly normal to feel this way at the beginning of a pregnancy, my darling. The doctor says it's a sign I am carrying a healthy baby, that it is taking form inside. There's a little bit of you growing inside me that I love so much already, and, all being well, the sickness will pass very soon.'

'My poor Ada. It worries me leaving you like this. I don't think you should stay here alone. I know we are blessed with our dear Mrs Trussle to look after you and the house, but it would give me greater peace of mind if you moved back to Wolferton with your parents while I am away. Beatrice and Jessie will be overjoyed too. It's really the best place for you right now. My mind is made up.'

Ada protested at first, she wanted to feather her own nest in Cromer and keep an orderly house for her husband. But Alfie persisted and she reluctantly agreed, realising it made good sense. She gazed into her husband's face filled with love for her. She knew he was concerned for her well-being, never sparing a thought for himself and the uncertain fate he faced with the war.

'Alfred Heath, I am the luckiest woman to have such a caring husband. I love you more today than ever. Our child is going to have the best father in the world,' she declared, snuggling against his chest, his arms holding her tight.

He embraced her tenderly. 'Who would have thought just two months ago when the King celebrated his forty-ninth birthday in Sandringham, with the flags flying and bells ringing, and five hundred estate workers enjoying a birthday dinner and concert in his honour, that our lives could change so dramatically.'

At that dinner loyal toasts were pledged by estate workers with customary enthusiasm, little realising that within a few weeks their loyalty would soon be tested when they were called to arms.

But the long, hazy summer days of 1914 when Ada was wrapped in her husband's arms were a distant memory as the days and weeks rolled into autumn mists, and a harsh, freezing winter followed. There was no giving up in the war and Alfie and his comrades fought on, while headlines reported the shocking deaths of thousands of British troops.

Alfie didn't return home for their son's birth as they hoped he would. Ada was thankful she had gone home to to Wolferton under her mother's watchful eye, where she continued to feel sick and infirm throughout the pregnancy. Their son Leslie had arrived eight months ago into a world torn apart by conflict. It was a long and painful birth, lasting twenty-five hours. He cried so much on entering the world that Ada thought his lungs would burst and the midwife said she had never heard the likes of it before, that it would waken folk ten miles away on the coast.

She thought long and hard about a name and settled on Leslie, meaning 'holly garden', and very appropriate as the station master's garden had an abundance of the red-berried bush that winter. She regarded this as a lucky omen and hoped the luck would mean a hasty return home for Alfie. The profuse prickly festive greenery had been used to make seasonal garlands to decorate the house. The festive season came and went and the old year rolled into a new one and spring buds blossomed. But her wish for Alfie's speedy return home from France evaporated. Instead of the longed-for peace and end of the war, the bloodied battlefields were covered with a carpet of corpses as the war took a more bitter and determined hold. Their men would not be home and those left behind listened to the repeated calls from Kitchener urging more men to do their duty and sign up.

∽

Ada wished she felt more confident about the concert. Her nerves were frayed knowing the Queen and Dowager Queen had promised to attend. At first she had been unwilling to take on the role. She feared that her youth, being only twenty-three, would cause Magnolia, who was almost twice her age, to have little faith in her abilities and cause trouble for her.

Ada felt her ears burning as she heard Magnolia call out her name and she gritted her teeth. She had put Magnolia's nose out of joint by removing her as the concert's top billing in favour of the celebrated singer, Clara Griffin, and Magnolia had not taken it well.

That had happened a week ago. Ada had avoided Magnolia since then. Now, with just two weeks until the big night, Ada was beginning to feel anxious. Today's rehearsal was important and the choir needed to present a united front to Clara, who was due to arrive later today. She needed to make it clear to everyone – particularly Magnolia – that she was in charge.

Magnolia walked briskly towards Ada, her big toothy grin and horse-like features appearing even more exaggerated than usual.

Ruth tugged on Ada's arm. 'We ain't 'ere to cause trouble, miss. I want nothing for meself, just for Maria, so she can 'ave a good chance in life, just like you and yer sisters. I beg yer, will you ask Harry to meet us? Please? And then we'll be on our way, we won't detain yer any longer.'

Ada gasped at her effrontery. It was one thing for her father to meet them on their home territory. But here? Where he was the King's station master? What would her mother say? And would he agree? How could she possibly answer such an impossible question?

'I don't think this is the right moment . . .' she stuttered, looking anxiously at Magnolia, who was quickening her step.

Within a few seconds Magnolia would be within hearing distance. Ada felt herself tremble slightly, fretting about how she would explain these strangers to her. Magnolia liked to know everyone's business and had a cunning way of discovering people's secrets.

Ada's challenger was now within spitting distance, her narrow eyes locked curiously on Ada's companions as she scrutinised their shabby clothing, a smug expression covering her face. She halted next to Ada, her thick lips twisted at the corners, her pointed nose turned up with an air of triumph.

'My dear, you must introduce me to your new friends. I don't believe we have had the pleasure.'

Chapter 3

At the age of twenty-three, Ada was happily married, had a beautiful, healthy son and the support of a loving family, all while war ripped the country and families apart. She could see how her life contrasted vastly to the hardship Maria and Ruth had endured, judging by their appearance and demeanour.

The difference in their situation pricked Ada's conscience. She felt almost self-conscious to be wearing her fine sky-blue dress with a scalloped white lace collar, which complemented her flawless complexion, compared to the threadbare clothes that hung from her newly discovered relatives. Despite the empathy Ada felt towards Ruth and Maria, she couldn't help feeling on edge at being seen with them. She was aware that onlookers would be curious to know why she was engaging in prolonged conversation with these two shabbily dressed strangers.

She winced as she observed Maria yanking her skirt down over her worn-out shoes, and, sensing her shame, hoped she had concealed them in time from Magnolia's razor-sharp eye. She was surprised to find she was suddenly overcome with a rush of warm protective feelings towards the impoverished girl and her mother. What would Magnolia, with all her fine airs and graces, who loved to ingratiate herself with the royal family at every opportunity, know about poverty? And what kind of trouble could Maria and her mother be in to arrive out of the blue like this? They must be in desperate straits.

Magnolia, her back arched, head held high and arms folded across her chest, observed the new arrivals with great interest, her eyes poring over every inch of them. Her bottom lip quivered. 'As you know, Ada, one can't be too careful about the company of strangers these days. I just wanted to check that there was nothing untoward happening, to offer my assistance if necessary.'

'Ha! Do yer think we're spies or somethin'?' goaded Maria, her eyes flashing angrily as she pushed herself forward. 'Go on then, report us if yer like.'

'No, no, it's nothing like that. You have nothing to worry about, I can assure you,' Ada interrupted hastily.

Magnolia flared her nostrils at Maria and was about to speak, but Ada stepped forward quickly. 'You have no need to concern yourself about the company I am with. I assure you I can vouch for them. Please do not let me detain you, I will join in a moment.'

'Well, if you can vouch for them, I'm sure that will have to suffice,' Magnolia retorted, her bottom lip twitching.

Maria and Ruth were transfixed by the puffed-up woman they faced. It was impossible not to stare at the large dark mole on the bottom of Magnolia's left cheekbone and the two long wispy hairs protruding from it. Magnolia's hand touched it for a brief moment, aware she was being stared at.

'Yes, I'm sure. Please return to the church and let yourself in. The door is unlocked and we have a lot to get through today. I just need another moment here.'

'Umm, well, if you insist,' retorted Magnolia, arching her eyebrows. 'After all, Ada, my dear, I'm sure I don't need to remind you that punctuality is the politeness of kings.'

Ada inhaled a deep breath and gritted her teeth. She refused to allow Magnolia's comment to rile her up. She gestured towards the church, repeating that she would join her shortly. She watched Magnolia strut off, glancing back and waving her hand in the air as if she were royalty.

'How rude, how very rude, "punctuality is the politeness of kings",' mimicked Maria, pulling a face and putting on a posh voice.

'You were very rude too,' Ada told Maria in a tone of a mock reprimand. She stifled a giggle. Magnolia's haughtiness towards these two vulnerable individuals had stirred compassion within her. She could not let this snooty woman belittle her poor relations. As a churchgoer Magnolia should bestow sympathy and kindness to those in need – not snobbery and hostility. 'We were all born with nothing, and we die with nothing,' that's what the vicar always told them. 'At the end of the day, we are all equals on this earth.'

Maria's eyes glowed with admiration. 'Cor. Yer sent her packing with a flea in 'er ear. I would never have thought you had it in yer, such a fine-looking young lady like you, who doesn't seem the kind of person to stand up to a nosy old busybody like her.'

'I surprised myself,' Ada admitted, the corners of her lips curling.

'Oh, miss, I'm sorry for any trouble we caused yer and holding you up for yer rehearsal. We ain't out to make any trouble with yer family or embarrass yer in front of yer genteel friends,' Ruth demurred.

'You've nothing to worry about on that score, I assure you. Magnolia is not what I would call a friend, exactly. She is, well, she is just Magnolia and she takes some getting used to.'

'Can you tell us yer name, miss, seeing as we are related? I heard her call yer Ada, is that right?' queried Maria.

Ada extended her arm. 'Yes, I'm the youngest, and I have two sisters, Jessie and Beatrice.'

Ruth shook her hand too. 'I wasn't sure which of the Saward girls yer were. I know yer pa wished 'e 'ad sons to pass on the engine oil to, but believe me, 'is eyes sparkle like the brightest stars when 'e speaks of 'is daughters.'

'Well, I do have a young son, my little Leslie, to carry on the family tradition, if that's what he wants to do. If Father has his way, he could be a station master too one day.'

Maria's face brightened. 'Oh, I would so love to meet yer little 'un. I can imagine 'e's the apple of yer eye.'

'Well yes, of course. I had no idea Father spoke to you about us. And while it's correct he has no sons, we all help

41

around the station in different ways. Our Jessie assists our mother in the royal retiring rooms and Beatrice helps her in the post office, too. And me? Well, I have given him a grandson he dotes on.'

Ruth's eyes shone. 'Yer've all turned out so fine. Harry deserves his good fortune.'

'He's worked hard for everything he has. I do know how well my father did to be appointed station master. Mother likes to remind us of this too, though Father doesn't boast about it.'

'Why, Willie's chest would puff up like a plump pigeon when he talked about Harry at the Fighting Cock over a pint or two, saying 'e were a natural, that he taught 'im everything 'e knew.'E was always saying it was the best station master's job in the land, greeting royalty an' heads of state from around the world.'

Maria nodded. 'Yes, that's true. Pa was always speaking of Harry, saying he 'ad a job for life, with a fine 'ouse thrown in too.'

Ada wished she knew more about her father's early life. He spoke little of it, but this was not the time to delve deeper. Observing Maria's appearance, with her olive skin and dark hair, she couldn't see any family resemblance on her father's side.

'I can see yer are a fine lady and you're in a hurry. I just ask if you could be kind enough to speak to yer father on our behalf, to ask 'im if 'e will see us. As yer can see, I'm begging yer,' Ruth pleaded, her eyes moist. She stooped as she spoke, her arm clinging to her side.

Maria begged, 'Ma's not well, yer only have to look her to see. Please 'elp us, miss. As Ma said, Harry is our relation. I only 'ope he is not too posh for the likes of us. Not like that snooty Magnolia, who has a face like an ol' 'orse that needs worming.'

Ada couldn't resist smiling. 'Now you are being very unkind about Magnolia, that's quite unnecessary. And Father, he's not like that at all, you have no worries there. I'm curious to know one thing, though. Why didn't you write to him about coming here? Why do you need me to ask him on your behalf?'

''Cause of yer ma. She made it plain to Harry that we should never set foot 'ere, and I kept that promise all these years. She looks down her nose at us and I didn't want to cause trouble, knowing you have royal connections an' all. And we don't want any money, just the chance to speak to him,' Ruth replied.

'That ain't all. Go on Ma, tell 'er the real reason. You ain't any choice, yer 'ave to,' Maria urged.

Ada's eyes narrowed. 'What do mean *the real reason*?'

After a pause, Ruth inhaled a deep breath and muttered, 'The truth is we're 'omeless, miss, as good as in the gutter, an' desperate, that's why I broke me promise. We 'ad to leave our railway cottage for a new driver to move in with 'is family, with only a week's notice. I'm planning on going to stay with me sister in Doncaster once I've settled Maria in 'ere, all being well. Me two lads are with their Uncle Gus in London, 'e's taken them under 'is wing.'

'Did I hear you correctly when you said you plan to settle Maria here? You are saying you want Maria to stay with us?'

Maria gulped. 'That's right, miss, but it ain't like I'm a stranger, and 'e said to turn to 'im for 'elp if needed. And we are in need.'E knows me an' I knows 'ow to behave proper in good company. We saw 'im at the station an' kept a respectful distance, seeing 'im so busy an' authoritative. I could scarcely believe me eyes when I saw Mr Saward greeting our own King.'

Ruth cleared her throat. 'Harry is such a credit to his pa. We arrived on an earlier train an' watched him. He wasn't 'alf busy walking up and down the platform, waving off our boys an' giving orders, everyone acknowledged 'im respectfully. We wanted to approach 'im, but kept our distance 'cos we didn't want to make 'im feel awkward. I knew he 'ad three girls and seeing as you were standing next to 'im, I watched yer leave the station an' followed yer in the hope of seeking your understanding of our circumstances.'

Ruth's knees buckled and she slumped to one side. Maria grabbed her, turning her face towards Ada. 'So, will you help us, please? Look how poorly Ma is, if yer pa says yes Ma will leave me here an' travel on to Doncaster. I can work for me keep, I'm a good, 'ard an' honest worker. After all, we're of the same flesh an' blood, us Sawards are not shirkers.'

Ada's voice quavered. 'I would like to help, if I am able to, but I cannot speak for my parents. I am certainly not in a position to make any promises of that nature.'

Maria beseeched, 'But you will ask, won't yer? Please tell yer pa about us as soon as yer get the chance.'E knows me well enough. I ain't a stranger to 'im.'

Ada placed a hand on Ruth's shoulder, concern etched across her face. 'I can see you look exhausted. I'll do what I can, but you must understand I can't speak for my father. I will ask him at the first opportunity after my rehearsal.'

'Thank yer!' the destitute mother and daughter replied in unison, the relief apparent on their faces.

'I suggest you come to our house at six o'clock. Father will be home for his tea then, and you'll have to take your chance. I believe you know where we live, in the station master's house.'

The distinctive station master's house was like no other in Wolferton, built in a mock-Tudor style with timber herringbone detailing between the panels. The unique red-brick house featured an eye-catching octagonal turret on one corner with windows on all sides giving spectacular views in all directions, across countryside at the back and the station at the front. A weathervane with a cockerel on the top was perched at its pinnacle. The bay windows at the front, like the corner octagonal rooms next to it, stretched the whole length of the detached building, and had large windows with white-painted frames. The fact that his employer, the Great Eastern Railway, had provided this for Harry Saward was a glowing testament to the high regard they held him in, and their desire for royal approval.

It looked like the kind of house that a very important person lived in, someone who had a position in the community. The property's connection with royalty was clear from studying the gas lamps at the front entrance, which were topped with an ornate gold crown and the royal crest. They were fixed on the top of two red-brick plinths and similar lamps were positioned at the station. The house was surrounded by a cast iron decorative fence atop a low red-brick wall and its immaculate garden, Harry's pride and joy, was ablaze with colourful summer blooms, which had scooped many prizes at the annual Sandringham Horticultural Show. This event, having been started by King Edward and Queen Alexandra when they first moved to Norfolk was now a popular annual fixture for residents of the Sandringham Estate and exhibits were erected in the royal park. The grounds and gardens were thrown open to the public who could view the royal kennels and conservatories too.

'It's a house fit for a gentleman.' Sarah had beamed when the family moved into the splendid purpose-built station master's house.

Maria nodded. 'Oh yes, we saw it on our way 'ere. Yer couldn't miss it. It don't half look grand. I don't think there can be a finer station master's house in all the land.'

Ruth murmured, 'Thank you kindly for your help. You're a good lass, just as your pa said.' She bent forward and spluttered, her chest heaving as she coughed. Ada rushed over and handed her a handkerchief.

'Ma ain't been well. She didn't want yer to know. That's why she wants me taken care of here, I know I'm a burden on 'er.'

'I'm sure you're not, but I can see your mother doesn't look in the best of health. I will do my best. Father has a kind heart, I'm sure he will help you if he can.'

Maria smiled for the first time. 'We'll be all right now, seeing as what yer said. We'll see yer later.'

Ruth murmured, 'I apologise for detaining yer, miss. Yes, we'll be fine now, I feel a weight 'as been lifted from me shoulders. You must go to yer rehearsal. You 'ave company waiting for yer by the gate.'

Ada thought how pretty Maria looked when she smiled, and how a good wash and some clean clothes would change her appearance completely. She bade them farewell, assuring them she would do her best. She had only walked a short distance, though, when she felt someone grab her arm.

Ruth's eyes had a fiery glint and were moist. 'I'm too proud to say this in front of Maria, but I'm begging you, miss. As you can see I ain't well. It's been hard on us since we lost Willie an' the price of a loaf of bread 'as almost doubled in the last year on account of the war. You don't know 'ow much it means to me, to 'ave my Maria taken care of proper like, to know she will 'ave a full belly an' a chance to make something of 'er life with good people like yerselves. She's 'ad it tough too, in ways yer couldn't imagine. If I can leave Maria with you, I promise I won't come back an' trouble yer anymore.'

'Please do not worry, I give you my word I'll do what I can.' She could understand why Ruth was fretful, and so desperate she had to send her children away. Ada knew only too well the cost of the war on hard-up families in its first year. The greedy well-to-do had filled their cupboards in a distasteful display of panic buying when war was announced, and traders were accused by the government of profiteering, while many poor families went hungry.

'Here, take my handkerchief. And try not to worry,' Ada offered sympathetically. 'I'm sorry to hear the terrible hardship you have suffered.'

Ruth's bony fingers dug into Ada's arm and her hooded eyes pleaded. 'I wouldn't ask if I weren't desperate. I wish I didn't have to. It breaks me heart that I'll be parted from my Maria and 'er brothers, but you needn't concern yer-self about them. I just need to know that Maria will be all right, an' not keeping with bad company. I want 'er to 'ave the same chances as you've 'ad in life.'

Maria came up then and gently took her mother's arm. 'Let's leave 'er be now, Ma, she's said she'll help us an' she 'as 'er rehearsal to get to.'

Ruth persisted, her voice croaking, 'I'm speaking to yer woman to woman, miss, as one ma to another who wants the best for 'er child. You must know what that feels like.'

Maria's face turned crimson and her eyes filled with tears. She looked away and dried her eyes.

'Of course every mother wants the best for 'er child,' she choked, so that Ada wouldn't hear, biting her lip.

'What did Maria say to you? Why is she upset?' asked Ada, bewildered by the sudden sad expression that masked her face.

'She'll be all right in a minute. I reckon today 'as all been a bit much for 'er.'

Maria sniffled, wiping her nose on her sleeve. She inhaled deeply and composed herself, assuring Ada she was fine, waving her off. 'I think I need to be alone for a while, Ma. Do yer mind?'

'No, you do that if you feel you need to, I understand. I'll find somewhere to rest and will see you later at the station master's house.'

Without replying, Maria turned and sprinted off down the lane, leaving a dusty trail behind her. She passed the church and saw Magnolia raise her arched eyebrows and the startled expressions of the women dallying by the church gate, still waiting for Ada to join them, their enquiring eyes glued on her encounter with the two unkempt strangers.

Ruth pulled her shawl over her shoulders and shuffled back in the direction of the station, reaching the corner of the station master's house, pausing now and again to catch her breath, and holding onto her side.

Ada walked briskly to the church gate and ushered the choir ladies into the church, her eyes refusing to meet their questioning gazes. She delved into her music bag and then handed out music sheets. She apologised profusely for her lateness and thanked them for their patience, pretending she didn't hear them muttering under their breath or see their sideway glances at each other. She took her place at the piano, wondering how she would get them on her side. How could she make them respect her as their leader? And how would she explain the two strangers to Magnolia, who had no doubt set tongues wagging and would not give up until she had an answer.

Magnolia's face was pinched, her voice tinged with sarcasm. 'It's so good of you to join us, Ada. Some of the ladies did wonder if I should take over the choir as you were otherwise occupied. But I said we must give you a chance, didn't I, ladies?'

Ada felt stirred by her encounter with Ruth and Maria. She found Magnolia's petty snobbery infuriating and did her best to shrug off the mounting air of dissent that she sensed, observing the women taking their lead from Magnolia with their disapproving sounds. Mustering all her courage, she stood up and walked towards them, trembling at every step.

'Ladies. May I remind you to focus your minds on the reason we are here today, which is to support our brave and selfless men fighting for our King and country by holding this concert to raise much needed funds for the war effort. It's the least we can do. If any of you are not happy with me for whatever reason, then please feel free to leave. Now!'

Ada's assertiveness drew surprised gasps as she pointed to the church door. Everyone remained in their positions, shuffling their feet, exchanging side glances and conspiratorial looks.

'Very well then, let's begin and not lose any more time,' proclaimed Ada, a triumphant look on her face. 'Magnolia, are you intending to stay?'

Magnolia's mouth twitched uncomfortably. 'Well, of course, I must. I am the Wolferton Nightingale. I think – we all think – it is reasonable to expect an explanation for the inconvenience we have endured.'

Ada didn't flinch. She had no intention of revealing any information about her new relatives. 'As you observed, Magnolia, I was detained by two unfortunate people, a mother and daughter who unexpectedly approached me on my way here. They were looking for work in the area and asked if I could make any recommendations.'

She consoled herself for telling a white lie in a place of God as it was partly true – Maria did want work – and that was all Magnolia needed to know for now.

Ada returned to the piano and spread out the folds of her skirt on the stool. As she placed her fingers on the ivory keys, she felt Magnolia's hot breath on her cheek. 'Do you take me for a fool? Don't you think I heard that grubby woman say she was related to you, my dear? How interesting. I wonder if your dear mother knows about this.'

Chapter 4

Ada bade a swift farewell to the singers at the church door, relieved the rehearsal had come to an end without any further embarrassing scenes. She had no time to loiter; she needed to make haste to the station and prepare her father for his unexpected visitors that evening.

As she walked briskly along the lane, she thought back to her earlier encounter with Ruth and Maria; what a strange couple they were. Nobody would ever think of them as being their relations, this unfortunate-looking mother and daughter. She knew that sounded harsh and judgemental, but that's how folk were, they judged on appearances and first impressions.

She decided to confide first of all in Beatrice, who she expected would still be assisting their mother at the post office. She should just be able to catch her before she left for home. A bell jangled above the door as Ada entered and she found Beatrice serving a customer. She peered over the counter into the back room and heaved a deep sigh of relief that there was no sign of her mother.

Beatrice raised an enquiring eyebrow at her sister's arrival, but her attention remained focused on her customer, a stout woman dressed in an unbecoming black skirt and shapeless jacket. Ada recognised her as the butcher's wife and concealed her disdain behind her hand. Rumour was that Percy Franks had put the price of his meat up and poor folk in Wolferton couldn't afford it and were having to make do with what they caught on the land, and even set nets in their gardens to trap sparrows to cook in pies. No wonder poaching was rife among locals; why pay up to two shillings for a rabbit when they cost only ninepence or tenpence before the war and you could get one for nought on the land?

'Thank you, Mrs Franks. You are the third customer today who has invested in a war loan. It has been a most successful appeal to help fund the war,' Beatrice informed her, raising her eyes upwards in Ada's direction as she spoke.

A large green poster by the entrance showing St George and the dragon urged. WAR LOAN. INVEST FIVE SHILLINGS AND HELP YOUR COUNTRY TO WIN.

The government's War Savings Committee was appealing to the nation for support, fund the war, and to apply at their nearest post office for details.

'Seeing as we weren't blessed with any sons this is the least I can do to help His Majesty. My Percy insisted,' she replied smugly, the light from the sun's rays pouring in through the window and settling on her upper lip.

'That's very noble of you, Mrs Franks,' Beatrice replied graciously. 'If only we had more customers like you. But, alas, it's beyond the reach of many families, with the cost of living rising by more than twenty per cent. Many poor folk have nothing left over at the end of the week and, as you know, a piece of mutton is a luxury for them.'

Her sarcasm fell on deaf ears. 'My Percy tells me it's a good business proposition. And the government needs every penny it can get to finance the war. Nobody can point the finger at us and say we aren't contributing.'

Ada tittered behind Mrs Franks' back and her eyes rested on another new poster that urged people to dig deep in their pockets. Her own parents had put some of their savings into the war loans, saying it was an investment in their country's future.

'We're just about managing now, but my Percy worries we won't have enough to fill our bellies and our soldiers' bellies if the Hun are going to bomb ships bringing in our food supplies. He's doing his best to keep his prices down, unlike some other thieving buggers, excuse my language, who only care about lining their pockets.'

Ada and Beatrice both pulled a face as Mrs Franks extolled Percy's virtues. It was more than Beatrice could bear.

'Have you seen this?' she asked the butcher's wife, holding up a leaflet in front of her startled face. 'The best parts of British beef and mutton have gone up by an average of seven per cent, whereas the cheaper parts, which the poorer people buy, have risen twenty-two per cent.'

'That's not true,' she spluttered. 'My Percy, he isn't robbing poor folk like that. He's had to put his prices up, he can't help it if supplies are short, but he's not a profiteer, he helps everyone he can.'

Red faced and fuming, the butcher's wife turned and stormed towards the door of the post office, pulling her black felt cloche hat firmly onto her head.

'There is no need for such rudeness. I shall inform your mother of this,' she declared, departing in a huff.

'Good day, Mrs Franks,' Beatrice replied with feigned politeness. Then she hastily displayed the CLOSED sign on the front door, and pressed her back against the door, sighing with relief.

'Everyone, bar her, seems to know what her Percy is up to,' Beatrice commented wryly. 'Doesn't she think it's strange that his stomach is getting fatter by the day, and hers too by the look of it, while other folk's waistlines are shrinking?'

'She's a frightful woman,' agreed Ada.

'So, what brings you here at closing time?' Beatrice asked. 'I'm afraid there is no letter for you from Alfie.'

'That's not what I came for, though that would have been a delightful surprise. I have some news, Beatrice. Brace yourself; it's going to come as a big shock.'

'You're scaring me. What are you talking about, *a big shock*? You haven't heard bad news about Sam, have you?' blurted Beatrice anxiously, referring to her sweetheart, who was away fighting with the Sandringham Company.

'Oh no, it's nothing like that. Thank the Lord!'

'Then tell me, what is it?'

Beatrice listened wide eyed as Ada recounted her encounter with Ruth and Maria, finishing with Magnolia's menacing words.

'Oh, Beatrice, they both looked so poor and shabby. My heart went out to them. And it so riled me to see Magnolia standing there all ears, desperate to pick up some juicy gossip she could spread about them.'

Beatrice's jaw dropped. 'Well, that's typical of Magnolia. But she's harmless enough, I wouldn't worry about her. I can't believe the nerve of these two so-called relatives, though. Turning up like that and expecting us to take them in. Is their intention to take advantage of us, or blackmail us even, knowing about Father's esteemed position as the royal station master?'

'Oh no, I don't think so for a moment, and it seems they are on familiar terms with Father, which was a great revelation. Oh, Beatrice, you should see them, you'd feel sorry for them too. I swear their shoes are falling apart. I saw the way Maria pulled her skirt down to cover them up.'

'And they say they are related to us? And Father knows them?'

'It seems Father has been calling on them and swore the mother to secrecy, only they are on such hard times now, she is turning to him for help. You know how Mother and Father would never speak of them, they say Father has visited them at Audley End Station, that's where his father worked and lived out his retirement – our grandpa Willie. Apparently, Maria has two younger brothers who have been packed off to an uncle in London, while Ruth, that's Grandpa Willie's second wife, plans to stay with her sister in Doncaster and leave Maria here with us.'

'I can't believe I'm hearing this. I wonder what Mother will say when she learns about it. She'll be incensed.'

'That's what I'm worried about, and it's important she hears it from us first, and not Magnolia. I suggested Ruth and Maria come to our house at six o'clock. That gives us just half an hour to warn Father and prepare Mother.'

'What a shock this is going to be. We'd better not waste time then. I'll come with you to the station if you like and we can tell Father together.'

Beatrice quickly locked up and the two sisters marched to the station just a short distance away. They spotted Harry standing on the platform talking to a waiting passenger and made their way briskly towards him. His eyebrows arched as they approached, and he stroked the bristles of his moustache.

'Well, to what do I owe this pleasure? And why do you both look so serious?'

Ada took hold of her father's arm while the passenger, an elderly man, doffed his cap, smiled at the two sisters and shuffled away. 'Father, could we have a quick word, please, in private? It's very important. And confidential. What I say will come as quite a shock.'

Harry's face creased with concern and he followed his daughters into his office, where the door was shut firmly behind him.

'What's happened? Is there some terrible news?' he asked.

'It depends how you look on it,' replied Ada, biting her lip. As she blurted out details of her encounter with Ruth and Maria to her father, the muscles on Harry's face tightened and he thumped his fist on the desk.

'Did I hear correctly? Are you saying Maria wants to stay with us? In our house?'

Ada nodded. 'Yes, that's right. Ruth says you promised to help if they should fall on hard times, and it appears they have. Oh, Father, they seem so wretched and the mother's health is not good. I watched her hobble off holding on to her side.'

'I don't understand why they would turn up like this. It's true that I did promise my father I would keep an eye on them should they find themselves falling on hard times. I have helped Ruth in the past with some money, just enough to make sure she could feed her children, but she was proud and always reluctant to take it. Ruth knows how Sarah feels about her and promised me she would never come here and I am flabbergasted she has broken her word.'

He shook his head. 'I can only surmise that Ruth's circumstances must be really bad right now, as you say they are. I think it's best your mother hears this from me, and as soon as possible. I can't believe she will take kindly to this news. We need to warn her, and quickly, before Magnolia does, if you say she has wind of this.'

Harry led his daughters out of his office and locked his door behind him. Beatrice and Ada quickened their steps to keep up with their father as he stomped along the platform and left the station, crossing the path to reach their house. Within a few minutes they were sprinting down the garden path, the neat flowerbeds alongside it filled with heavily scented lavender and sunburst marigolds.

The smell of rock buns wafted under their noses as they stepped into the kitchen. They had been freshly made by Betty Fitch, their loyal housekeeper, who the Sawards regarded as one of the family. Her fresh bakes were laid out on a cooling rack, plump and flaky and dotted with raisins. She was wiping the cream-coloured range clean so it shone, and looked up cheerily as she scrubbed the pans, her arms in soapsuds up to her elbows, as Harry, Ada and Beatrice stepped into the kitchen.

Ada's eyes fell appreciatively on the buns, reaching out to pick one up, but thinking better of it when the housekeeper tut-tutted. 'Oh, Betty, they smell wonderful. What would we do without you? Can you tell me where Mother is? We need to speak with her about an urgent matter.'

Betty dried her hands on her pinafore, her voice lowered, coughing to clear her voice. 'She isn't here, but someone else is.'

Betty cocked her head towards the corner of the kitchen where the familiar sounds of her son's laughter could be heard. Ada turned to see what Betty was bringing to her attention.

She gasped, her hand flying to her mouth. 'I don't believe it. Maria. What are you doing here so early? And why are you holding my son?'

Maria stood facing them, holding Leslie in her arms, rocking him and tickling his tummy, making him burst into giggles.

'I ain't doing any 'arm, just giving 'im a cuddle.'

Her bottom lip trembled, and she forced an awkward smile at the station master. 'Oh, Mr Saward, I am mighty pleased to see yer.'

'Well, well, well. So, it is you. Maria, this is most unexpected.'

'I'm sorry, only we didn't know where else to go.'

'So, what exactly brings you to Wolferton? And where is your mother? I believe you are together.'

Before Maria could answer Ada seized Leslie from her arms. 'I'll take him now, thank you.'

Betty looked flustered. 'I'm sorry if I did wrong, Mr Saward. I didn't know what to do. I saw the poor mite hanging around the side of the house an hour ago, when I was bringing the washing in, and she looked so hungry. She asked if there were any jobs she could do for a bite to eat. I didn't think you would mind as she said she knew you. That girl is a natural with young 'uns. Poor Master Leslie had one of his crying turns and she took him off my hands and she soon had him smiling. Look at him now, as happy as Larry.'

'So I see. Where's Mrs Saward? Does she know about our visitor yet?' enquired Harry, rubbing the back of his neck.

'No, sir,' Betty spluttered. 'Mrs Saward had to go out unexpectedly, else she would have been with the little 'un, taken him out for some fresh air; she does love taking the little fella out for a stroll at the end of the afternoon. She's gone to see Aggie Greensticks, she heard she wasn't feeling

60

too good. She took her a lovely bunch of carnations from the garden.'

Harry frowned, his eyebrows meeting in the middle. He knew Sarah would not take kindly to Willie's second family stepping foot inside their house. And she was likely to hear about it from Magnolia. He hoped Maria had a good explanation. 'Are you and your mother in some sort of trouble?'

Maria shifted her feet, twisting her hands in front of her, and mumbled, 'Yer could say so. I'm mighty sorry, Mr Saward, if I did wrong coming 'ere before six o'clock, but I was invited in by yer kind housekeeper. As she says, I weren't doing any 'arm, I was only rocking the little 'un for a while to quieten 'im as 'e was bawling so loud I could 'ear 'im outside. 'E ain't half cuddly an' 'as the sweetest little face. I 'ave a knack with little 'uns and 'elped Ma bring up me two little brothers. I'll be a willing pair of 'ands, if yer get me meaning.'

Harry shook his head. 'It's not that simple, Maria. We have to consider what Mrs Saward thinks, and she may not take so kindly to the idea. Betty here keeps an eye on Leslie for Ada when she is busy with her music, so I'm not sure we need more help. I wish I knew the whereabouts of your mother at this moment.'

Maria shrugged her shoulders, her eyes downcast. 'I dunno either. I wish I did. She should be 'ere soon as that's what we agreed. Yer won't be cross with 'er, please! She's scared at seeing yer and Mrs Saward and she ain't too strong.'

Maria's manner was meeker than when she had accosted Ada earlier and she was clearly trying to make amends. 'I apologise if I gave yer a shock, holding yer little 'un like that,' she said to Ada. 'I promise I wouldn't harm a hair on his head.'

'It was just the shock of seeing you holding my little Leslie like that, so familiar, as if you'd known him for a long time,' Ada murmured. 'I'm afraid he doesn't always have the sweetest temperament, not like his father. I barely have a peaceful night's sleep with all of his bawling.'

''E's a lovely little fella and just likes a nice little cuddle.' Maria's eyes darted to the kitchen table. 'I don't suppose any of those buns are ready for eating? I could gobble one up now with a cup of Rosie Lee. My stomach ain't half rumbling.'

Betty glanced at Ada. 'The cheek of the girl! I've already given her a jam sandwich, now she wants more. I've never seen anyone gobble their food so quickly.'

'I think we could all do with a cup of tea. And there's no harm in giving her a bun.' Harry nodded, stroking his bristly moustache, deep in thought, his eyes fixed on Maria who reached out eagerly for a bun. Betty passed her a plate and some butter.

'When you have finished your tea, Maria, and caught your breath, I would like to have a quiet word with you in the parlour. We can wait there for your mother and Mrs Saward and I hope you will feel able to confide in me about what misfortune has befallen you that brings you here so urgently.'

Ada and Beatrice fixed enquiring gazes on him, which he ignored, knowing he showed a softer side to his daughters than Sarah did, who ruled the house strictly. Was he going to show his softer side to Maria now?

Mrs Saward would complain, with a glint in her eye, 'You let our girls twist you round your little finger, Harry Saward.'

'There's surely no harm in indulging your daughters from time to time,' Harry would reply benignly, with a twinkle in his eyes.

Betty fussed about, pouring the steaming tea she had just made into cups that were already laid out on the table. Maria nodded and gobbled the warm buns ravenously, her mouth full of crumbs. 'I'm hoping me ma will be here very soon, it might be better coming from 'er. I know she'll want to thank yer for yer past kindnesses towards us.'

Maria glanced up at the clock on the kitchen wall as it struck the hour. Mr Saward checked the time on his pocket watch and confirmed the clock was spot on. Fifteen minutes ticked by and Maria's eyes narrowed. 'I ain't seen Ma since this afternoon outside the church. I ran off and left 'er an' wish I 'adn't now. I'm worried about 'er. Why ain't she 'ere?'

Betty tried her best to console her. 'There, there, try not to fret, my dear. I'm sure she'll be here any time now, if that's what she said. But tell me, how come you parted company?'

Maria glanced down into her lap and said nothing, her lips trembling.

Harry looked wistful. Tension was beginning to rise within him. 'This is a fine to-do, on top of everything else, with the war and our work at the royal station.'

'Well, if that's how yer feel I'll be on me way. I ain't staying where I ain't wanted,' Maria whimpered, wiping the crumbs from her mouth with the back of her hand.

'Wait. Can you hear that? It's those humbug sausage airplanes again.' Betty shushed them suddenly, looking out of the kitchen window.

'Oh no, I don't want to die,' wailed Maria. She began shaking as an eerie throbbing sound could be heard overhead. The room felt silent. Betty clutched her chest with her hands and Harry leapt up to look outside the window.

'Blast, and dammit! They're out again. And it's not even fully dark.'

'My poor heart can't take it,' warbled Betty. 'They're going to come for us, I can feel it in my bones.'

'Over my dead body!' Harry declared, thrusting his jaw forward. 'They won't touch us.'

Maria's moist eyes widened and her mouth dropped open as she raised her eyes upwards from the window and watched the gigantic grey airship hover overhead. It had been designed to carry air passengers, but was now a weapon of war carrying bombs. The ominous sight and sound of it filled her with fear.

'Is it going to kill us? I shouldn't 'ave come 'ere. I'm scared. I want me ma,' shrieked Maria.

'Every time they fly over, I think we're done for. Thankfully they haven't dropped any more bombs since that terrible night in January, they just float about up there. But I hate it. I feel sick inside and all shaky at the thought of what they could do,' replied Betty, making the sign of the cross on her chest as she spoke.

Harry's fingers twitched over his moustache, his brows wrinkling. 'Dammit, where's Sarah? I don't like her being out on her own with that monstrous thing hovering over us. There could be spies out as well, sending signals from their car headlights, that's what they think happened before.'

'She's a sensible woman. Try not to fret, Mr Saward. 'She'll be taking cover till it's passed,' Betty consoled.

Beatrice glanced around the room. 'She isn't the only one missing. Where's Jessie? Why isn't she home? Has anyone seen her since the station this afternoon?'

Everyone shook their heads, their eyes showing concern. 'Well, this is a fine to-do,' Harry said once again, his eyes creasing anxiously.

Beatrice's eyebrows furrowed. 'Jessie is sensible. I expect she has called in on a friend or taken cover somewhere safe and is waiting for this monstrous thing to pass before returning home.'

Maria froze as her eyes fixed on the sky and she watched the Zeppelin vanish from sight. 'I don't like it. I hope me ma's all right, what if one of them drops a bomb on 'er? And yer good lady, I 'ope she's somewhere safe. I wouldn't want 'er to come into 'arm's way.'

The commotion made Leslie splutter and bawl in his mother's arms, his face turning crimson. His piercing screams made Ada wince. She held her infant at arm's length. 'Nothing I seem to do quietens him. What's the matter with him?'

Maria stepped forward. 'If I can be so bold, that noise outside would've given 'im a terrible fright and maybe 'e can sense when yer on edge. That's what me ma used to tell me if she had the blues or 'er nerves got the better of 'er, an' she takes them pills for it, Dr Cassell's Tablets for Paralysed Nerves. She reckons it helps bodily weaknesses, as she calls it, an' that's when I would 'elp out with little Freddie an' Archie. I was more of a mum to them than a sister an' helped bring them up. They are twelve and thirteen now, and no one could have done a better job, even if I say so meself.'

'I believe you could be right, Maria. Oh, my poor little lamb. I expect Leslie is teething as well, look how his cheeks are burning.'

''Ere, give 'im to me. I'll settle him for yer if yer like,' Maria offered.

'Well, if you really think you can quieten him then your arrival here is a true blessing.' Ada passed her wailing infant into Maria's outstretched arms.

The agitated child stared into Maria's face as she rocked him gently, stroked his moist cheek with a light feathery touch and whispered soothing words until his cries faded, as if hypnotised. The next moment his eyes closed and he was dozing, breathing softly.

Ada gazed in disbelief. 'That's astonishing. How did you manage that? I can see you really do have a natural way with him and one day you will be a wonderful mother.'

Maria drew in a sharp breath at this and bit her lip. Tears shimmered in her eyes as she passed Leslie back into his mother's arms.

'I'm sorry, did I say something to upset you?'

Maria's lips quivered, her voice wavering, as she turned her head away. 'It's just, I want me ma. Where is she? I don't know what to do. I ain't got nowhere to stay, no 'ome of me own.'

'I'm sure my parents won't turn you out on the streets at this time of day. Oh, Father, please say Maria can stay awhile?'

Harry rubbed his moustache as he contemplated his dilemma. He felt conflicted, wishing to keep his word to his father Willie, seeing quite clearly the state Maria was in and no doubt her mother too, while needing the blessing of his wife.

'You know I can't make any promises without speaking to your mother. I also need to speak to Ruth. Try not to fret, Maria. I'm sure your mother is well and will join us very soon, just as she said. And Mrs Saward too. Shall we step into the parlour now while we wait for them?'

Maria nodded and wiped her eyes. She glanced at Leslie who was settled peacefully in Ada's arms, his eyes still closed and his lips parted slightly. ''E looks like an angel. Sweet dreams, little angel.'

Ada's lips reached down to kiss her son's slumbering face. 'He's exhausted, bless him. Betty, I was wondering, do you know exactly when Magnolia told Mother that

Aggie was feeling poorly? I wonder why she's been out for so long.'

'I believe she stopped in to see Mrs Saward at the post office straight after the rehearsal. She mentioned something about Magnolia being flustered, and made an odd remark about strange goings-on under your nose that would make your hair stand on end.'

Ada looked anxious. 'Oh no. I bet she's told Mother about Maria and Ruth. I imagine that's what's happened. Mother will be furious!'

Beatrice's hand flew to her mouth. 'You're probably right, knowing what a nosy busybody that woman is. I dread to think what state Mother will be in when she returns.'

'There's still no sign of Jessie either. I'm really getting worried now,' said Harry, his bushy eyebrows furrowed.

'Now you mention it, Mrs Saward asked if I'd seen her when she called in earlier and was not too happy, saying she couldn't be found,' Betty recalled.

'Beatrice is probably right. She's probably stopped off to call in on a friend, so let's not worry unduly,' Ada suggested.

Maria followed Harry to the front parlour and five minutes later the sound of the latch being lifted on the back door alerted the household that someone had returned. Beatrice dashed into the parlour to warn her father, having heard her mother's voice enquire after him. Maria sat on the dark green squashy sofa, sniffling and dabbing her eyes dry. She clutched Harry's white handkerchief with the letter H embroidered in the corner. He sat next to her, patting her arm in a comforting gesture.

'Mother's home, I've just heard her asking Betty where you are, Father.'

'And Ma? Is she 'ere too?' asked Maria.

'No, I'm afraid not, and there's no sign of Jessie either.'

Sarah opened the door at that moment, her jaw clenched, a stony expression fixed on her face and her hands tightly fisted together.

'So I see we *do* have a visitor. Magnolia Greensticks was right!' Her tone was hostile. She stared directly at Maria, her lips quivering.

'A relative! That's what Magnolia said. Why does she know about our so-called relatives turning up out of the blue before me? I've never felt so humiliated in my life.'

The veins on Sarah's throat pulsed in fury. Harry walked towards her, speaking softly to calm her, but she pushed him away. Although Sarah was sometimes prone to flying off the handle, he was usually able to soothe her. But she was having none of it now.

Sarah shook her head, her jaw clenched, and turned to Maria. 'May I ask, what is the meaning of your visit? Here you are, sitting like a right little madam, as if you belong, but you certainly don't!'

Beatrice gasped at her mother's harsh tone, spoken with a ferocity she had never witnessed before, her jaw clenched.

Maria bit her lip and cautiously approached the station master's furious wife. 'I'm sorry for intruding like this, ma'am. I know we 'aven't met before, an' yer 'ave every right to be angry seeing as me ma broke her promise that we wouldn't darken yer doorstep, but the truth is I'm a Saward too, even if it don't suit yer. I'm Maria Saward. I'm Willie's daughter, I'm as much a Saward as yer own daughters.'

'How dare you make such an insinuation!' retorted Sarah.

Maria trembled at Sarah's hostility. She held her head high and continued. 'I don' mean to be rude, but I 'ave to speak up for meself as Ma ain't here. I 'ave the same blood coursing through me veins as Mr Saward does as Willie fathered us both. It should be remembered that me an' Ma, we nursed Willie when 'e was in a bad way till 'e passed on. We're good 'onest people. An' it's an 'onour to make yer acquaintance.'

Maria smiled weakly. She held out her shaking hand to Sarah, who recoiled, stepping back quickly, ignoring the offer as if it had been a venomous snake she was being invited to take hold of.

'Please, ma'am. I know it's a shock to yer. But Mr Saward 'ere, he said he would look out for us if we were in need, an' . . .'

'He said what?' exploded Mrs Saward.

Maria glanced anxiously at Harry.

'Now, dear, I think you should calm down,' he said to his wife. 'What Maria is saying is true. I had no choice. When my father was nearing his end, I was at his bedside and he made me promise to keep an eye on them. I could

70

hardly refuse. I never imagined they would turn up here like this, unannounced.'

'I don't mean to cause trouble. I want the chance to be genteel like yer daughters. I can 'elp yer 'ere with jobs to earn me keep, I'm a good worker,' entreated Maria.

'Really, young lady? You expect me to believe that and to entrust you with our grandson? Is it money that you want? Is that the real reason you are here?' accused Sarah.

'No, it ain't. I knew yer'd think that. I didn' want to come 'ere in the first place, it was me ma suggested it, an' now she's missing. I shouldn't 'ave left 'er an' I'm worried if she's fallen ill somewhere 'cos she ain't that strong. An' I'm scared of 'er out alone with those Zeppelins flying in the sky, she won't know what to do or where to go.'

Maria's eyes filled with tears. Ada rushed to comfort her. 'Oh, Mother, can't you see how upset she is? Maria is worried about her mother's whereabouts and has nowhere to go. I've seen how good she is with Leslie and I'm sure Betty would appreciate some extra help with him. And, whether we like it or not, well, she is related to us. It's going to take some getting used to. Please let her stay. At least give her a chance.'

Sarah crossed her arms, still visibly fuming, her cheeks puffed out. 'Her mother has obviously dumped her daughter on our doorstep and cleared off. How can you not see how scheming they are?'

Harry spoke gently to his wife. 'Now, Sarah, my dear, there's no need to get so het up. I can't believe you would have such an uncharitable thought in your head. It seems to me they are here because they are in a dire situation. I think Ada is right, we should give her a chance.'

'You can't be serious?'

Maria sniffled. 'Please give me a chance, else what am I to do? I ain't got nowhere to go.'

'Don't think you can fool us with your fancy tales and crocodile tears,' snorted Sarah.

'Very well, I know when I ain't wanted, yer've made that very clear. I'm orf. I'll make meself a bed in the forest with the leaves. I know just where to go too.'

Beatrice stepped forward. 'Oh no, you couldn't possibly allow that. Mother, imagine what Magnolia would say if she knew we threw someone in need out of the house to sleep in the forest? That would be regarded as very unchristian and hard hearted. Oh, couldn't we let Maria stay a night or two? She could sleep in the attic.'

Harry raised his eyebrows enquiringly. 'Well, what do you think, Sarah? Just for a night or two until we get to the bottom of this? As Beatrice says, we can't just turf her out on the streets and set tongues wagging.'

Sarah's body was arched stiffly. Inhaling a deep breath, she glanced at Maria. 'I feel you are all forcing me to agree to this when I need time to think. I can hardly be expected to make up my mind on the spot. This has come as a big shock. And heaven knows what your mother will have to say when she turns up.'

'I promise yer won't regret it if yer give me a chance, Mrs Saward. My ma will be that pleased. I cross me 'eart

I won't be any trouble. I'll do anything you want around the 'ouse to earn me keep.'

'Well,' she hesitated, her eyes glancing at everyone's encouraging expressions. 'Very well, as long as you don't get carried away. It's just for a couple of nights. I suppose you could sleep in the attic.'

'That's very generous of you, Sarah, thank you,' Harry said, his lips curling at the corners. 'Now that's settled, I suggest we make the most of the situation forced upon us. I expect Betty could do with help around the house, she is no spring chicken and sometimes I wonder if we expect too much of her. As Maria says, she can earn her keep by doing some chores and helping with Leslie.'

'I'll work ever so 'ard. I won't be any trouble. I swear on Ma's life. And on the lives of Freddie an' Archie too,' gushed Maria.

'And pray, who are these people you are referring to?'

'They be me little brothers, I 'elped bring 'em up, and they're staying in London with our Uncle Gus. They won't trouble yer 'ere.'

'I see, and what do you know of this Uncle Gus?' asked Sarah, casting a doubtful glance in Harry's direction.

'He's ma's brother and 'e's a rag an' bone man an' glad of their help. Poor little things, rather them than me. I know 'e'll expect 'is pound of flesh from them, even though Ma is paying for their keep too. They are only young 'uns, just twelve and thirteen, and not big for their age either, but they ain't shirkers. I can't help but fret about 'em, and I know Ma does too.'

73

Sarah softened her tone. 'Well at least they have a roof over their head. Beatrice and Ada will find some clean clothes for you and give you a bowl and water to wash with. They'll help settle you in the attic, though I can't say how comfortable you will be.'

'Thank yer, Mrs Saward. And thank yer all kindly. I'll be more than comfy. Being 'ere, well, it's like being in a palace, not that I know that one of 'em looks like. All I need now is for me ma to turn up; she'll be that pleased. I won't be able to sleep not knowing where she is.'

Beatrice cocked her ears at the sound of the front gate being opened and peered through the net curtains. Could it be Jessie returning home? Or was it Maria's mother?

'That's strange, it's Eddie,' Beatrice said. 'He has a letter in his hand. What purpose does he have here at this time of day?'

Chapter 5

Beatrice dashed to the front door, quickly followed by Ada. Eddie would normally have walked round to the kitchen door at the back of the house, but Beatrice had pointed him towards the front when she spotted him from the window, her curiosity strongly roused by the letter he was bringing at this late hour.

The porter stood on the step, framed by the carved wooden archway in the porch. He removed his cap, clutching the letter in his hand.

'I apologise for coming round at this time of day, but I gave my word.'

'What are you talking about?' asked Ada, stepping forward.

'Is there someone here by the name of Maria?'

Maria pushed herself forward. 'Who wants to know?'

'I have a letter here for a lady by the name of Maria Saward, and instructions to give it to her in person after six o'clock this evening. I would have come earlier, but . . .'

Harry and Sarah jostled their way to the front door. 'Well, good evening, Eddie. What brings you here at this hour?' asked the station master, his eyebrows raised.

'Good evening to you, Mr Saward. I'm on an errand and a promise I made earlier today. I was accosted by a woman, a stranger she was, at the station this afternoon afore she boarded on the train this very afternoon. And she gave me very precise instructions.'

'Well come in, boy, come in and tell us more about this woman,' Harry urged, beckoning him inside.

'It must have been me ma. I'm Maria Saward. Give me the letter,' she demanded.

'You're Maria Saward?' queried Eddie, eyeing Maria up and down, his jaw dropping. 'Well, bless my soul.'

'One moment, Maria, we need to be sure about this. Eddie, what else can you tell us about this woman?' questioned Harry.

Eddie struggled to find the right words, blurting, 'No offence intended, but it's just that you don't look like a Saward and you speak—'

'I can't 'elp that, can I?' interrupted Maria, her face reddening.

Harry intervened. 'I'm sure Eddie means nothing by it, Maria. We need to be find out what's happened. Eddie, what else can you tell us about this woman?'

'I never set eyes on her before. I don't mean to be rude about her, but she seemed a bit shabby-like, and tired with heavy eyelids. She stopped me and asked if I would deliver this letter here by hand after six o'clock precisely. As I never heard of a Maria Saward, or mention of one before, that puzzled me, and then she jumped on the train and I got called to assist a passenger with her luggage. That's all I can tell you.'

'That's me ma you saw. Give me the letter,' Maria demanded, snatching it from Eddie.

'Well, she's not one for good manners, that's for sure,' Eddie chortled, shaking his head. 'Not even a word of thanks for my trouble.'

Maria ignored Eddie's caustic comment and held the envelope in front of her. 'It is from Ma, I know 'er hand-writing. But why 'as she written to me?'

Ada pressed Eddie for some more information. 'When did this lady come to the station? Can you recall what time it was?'

'That were around four o'clock, I think. She seemed a bit out of sorts. She was fretting, like, looking all around.'

Pausing to remember more, Eddie continued, 'She said what a grand station it was, how pretty with all the flowers and flags hanging up for the King, and how if there weren't so many young men in uniform coming and going you wouldn't know a war was going on.

'She spotted the royal train on the platform and asked if she could look inside. I thought there's no harm in that, and it clear blew her away. She said, "I ain't seen anything so marvellous in my life. It's just like a little palace on wheels. Oh, my Willie would have been proud to see this." I had no idea what she was talking about.'

'Willie's my father . . .' declared Maria. 'And he's . . .'

'That's enough, Maria,' warned Harry, shooting her a cautionary glance. 'Pray continue, Eddie. What else did the lady say?'

'She said what a grand job the royal station master was doing, she knew you by name. I said, "Oh, you know him, do you?" and she said she knew him a long time ago. Then, when I pointed you out across the way on the upside platform and said she could speak to you herself, she went silent and stiffened like and said she wouldn't trouble you, that you were far too busy and important for the likes of her.'

Maria only half listened to Eddie. She had ripped open the envelope and her hungry eyes devoured every word that leapt from the page. Eddie's gaze didn't leave Maria's face. His cheeks reddened when she returned his stare.

'That will be all, thank you, Eddie. I'll see you at the station tomorrow,' said Harry, hurriedly closing the front door on the porter.

'Well, what does she say, Maria?' enquired Ada gently. 'Is everything all right? Can you read all the words?'

'I might not be posh, or speak nicely like yer, but Ma did 'er best to make sure we 'ad some schooling. Mr Saward knows I am a good school scholar with me reading. He said I was a quick learner. I ain't without something up 'ere,' Maria retorted, pointing to her head.

'Did he now?' enquired Sarah, flashing a haughty glance at the station master.

'Later, my dear, I'll explain all later,' Harry assured her.

'Very well. I have the feeling that I may not be fully informed about this situation and would appreciate being told everything. You know how I don't like surprises.'

Scanning the lines on the notepaper, Maria's lips moved as she read the words in front of her. Looking up, her voice faltered. 'Ma's not here. She's gone to London to see Freddie and Archie, she says she has business with Uncle Gus, and then she is going to stay with her sister in Doncaster.'

'Doncaster?' queried Harry, his eyebrows creeping together.

'Yes, Doncaster. She has an older sister there called Freda. She's gone to stay there for a while to build up her strength. I don't understand it, but it seems she's gone off just like that, without even saying goodbye.'

Ada commented, 'Well, Ruth mentioned earlier that she was planning on going to Doncaster, but it slipped my mind to tell you. I certainly never expected her to leave without saying farewell to you, Maria, or meeting my parents as she said she wished to.'

'She must 'ave 'ad her reasons. I reckon she counted on yer taking me in. Please, don't make me go away. I'll end up in the workhouse an' never have the chance to make something of me life. Please let me stay.'

Sarah shot a glance at Harry. 'Very well, it looks like you will be staying here for a while – at least until we get to the bottom of this. We can't have a Saward in the workhouse.'

Maria sighed with relief. Harry deliberated, 'Sarah's right. Nobody is going to send you there, but we do need to talk this through properly tomorrow, and you must tell us everything. We don't want any more shocks.'

'Umm, we'll leave it at that for now. What a strange evening this had turned out to be. There's still no sign of Jessie, though. Whatever's happened to the girl?' asked Sarah, peering through the curtains. 'She did appear to be rather distracted today.'

'I was thinking the same,' replied Ada. 'I've been worried this last hour as it's not like her, especially as she was out when the Zepps were flying over us. What shall we do?'

Her mother commented, 'Ah, now I think of it, Aggie did say that Jessie seemed out of sorts this afternoon, uncharacteristically upset. She said she called out to her, but she flew past and almost sent her flying, without even stopping to pass the time of day.'

'Maybe she didn't hear Aggie, you know how Jessie struggles with that sometimes, but it's certainly not like her to be impolite,' Ada pondered.

Beatrice pricked up her ears. 'Was that the back door? Yes, I can hear someone in the kitchen.'

They all made their way through to see who it was and were confronted by Jessie in the kitchen, her hair loose and bedraggled around her shoulders and her dress crumpled.

'Why, Jessie . . .' her mother exclaimed. 'Where on earth have you been all this time? You've had us worried sick.'

'I'm sorry, Mother, I didn't mean to worry you. It's just that, well, I was overcome by the heat this afternoon. The crowds at the station were just too much and I needed to get away. I suddenly had an urge to go up into the woods where we spent time as children and I dozed off. The eerie sound of the airship passing overhead woke me. I was terrified, the Huns might see me. All I could do was take cover under some bushes and pray I would be safe, that's why my hair is in such a mess.'

Sarah's expression changed from a scowl to one of concern as the family fussed over Jessie, commenting on how lucky she was and how worried they had been about her. Maria sat quietly in the corner of the room, her eyes fixed on her new relative. She buried her face in her hands.

'We have some news for you, Jessie,' Ada announced. 'This is Maria, and she's our relation.'

'What are you talking about? How can she be related to us?' asked Jessie, staring at the girl.

'Yes, indeed, she is. She's Willie's daughter from Audley End, and she's staying with us for a day or two.'

Jessie raised an eyebrow. 'Really? I can't believe it. How has this come about?'

Ada filled Jessie in about Maria's sudden arrival and Maria noticed how Jessie's eyes never left her sister's lips. She rose and walked towards Jessie holding out her hand.

Jessie took Maria's hand. 'Well then, Maria, welcome to Wolferton. What a lovely surprise this is. Forgive me if I don't always hear you and you need to repeat things.'

Maria faltered. 'I'm very pleased to meet yer, Jessie. And I assure yer there ain't no need to apologise about yer hearing on my account.'

Beatrice commented, 'We were just going to sort out some bedding in the attic and spare clothing. Maria only has the clothes she's standing in, and I don't think they'll be seeing the sunshine anymore.'

'I'm sure I have a skirt and couple of blouses I can share with Maria too,' added Jessie, glancing over at Maria's shabby garments.

Her eyes fell to Maria's feet and she gasped. 'What are you wearing on your feet?'

The room fell silent. Jessie lifted Maria's skirt. 'My shoes. You're wearing my shoes! I saw them peeping out from under your hem.'

'What on earth do you mean? How can she be wearing your shoes?' asked Beatrice.

'That's a very good question. They disappeared this afternoon when I took them off to rest. I placed them under some ferns and walked a few steps away when I closed my eyes for a few minutes, but when I opened them, they had gone.'

Maria squirmed, her fingers fidgeting with her skirt, pushing Jessie's hand away and pulling it down over the front of her shoes. Jessie stared at her in disbelief.

All eyes turned to Maria for an explanation.

'What is the meaning of this, Maria? Is it true? How can you explain wearing Jessie's shoes?' demanded Harry sternly.

Maria lowered her eyes, twisting her fingers in front of her.

Jessie grabbed hold of Maria's skirt and yanked it up. 'See for yourself.'

Ada looked closely at the girl's feet, her eyes incredulous. These were not the scuffed unstitched black lace-ups she had seen Maria wearing that afternoon. These were cream buckled shoes; they were Jessie's best pair.

Maria stuttered, her eyes moist. 'I'm sorry, Jessie, I did take them, only . . .'

Jessie's cheeks burned. 'So you admit it! What explanation do you have for your actions?'

'I don't expect you to understand. And I mean it when I say I am sorry, but I were desperate. I didn't know they belonged to you.'

Shocked gasps filled the room. Maria pleaded with Ada. 'You saw the state of me shoes earlier. Will you tell 'em what they were like? As soon as I left yer the soles almost came off.'

'Do we want a thief staying here?' snapped Sarah, a triumphant *I told you so* expression covering her face.

'Please, let me explain,' begged Maria. 'I ain't a thief.'

'Let's give her a chance to explain,' pleaded Ada. 'Tell us, Maria, why did you take Jessie's shoes? And please, tell us the truth.'

The girl took a deep breath and spoke slowly, describing how she had run into the woods after meeting Ada and climbed up as high as she could until she found a shaded spot away from prying eyes. She stumbled across Jessie's shoes left under a cluster of ferns, but saw nobody nearby and thought they had been abandoned for some reason.

'I didn't see yer there, Jessie. I would never have taken them if I 'ad. I swear on me life.'

'So you stole a pair of hardly worn shoes, thinking they had been left for you to find. You are like a common thief,' Sarah snorted.

Tears gushed from Maria's eyes. 'No. I tell yer I ain't no thief. I didn't see Jessie or anyone else. I never thought about why they were left there like that, I just thought me luck was in. 'Ere, you can 'ave them back.'

She unclasped the cream shoe on her right foot and lifted her heel and pointed to two fat juicy blisters on her reddened, inflamed foot.

'See, this is why I took 'em. And yer'd have done the same in my situation. I couldn't walk any more. My shoes 'ad barely any leather left under the soles, I was walking on 'oles and they were split at the side. Me feet were burning from the pain.'

'Oh, Maria. Those blisters look very painful. But leaving Jessie in the forest with no shoes, didn't you think about how she would manage to get home?' asked Ada.

'I didn't see 'er. I swear it, else I've never 'ave touched them. Do yer knows what it feels like to walk on soles so thin that yer can feel every twig an' stone underneath you?'

Turning to Jessie, she pleaded, 'I'm sorry, please forgive me. I swear I didn't know they were yer shoes. I acted on impulse. Ma always says I act first and think later, an' it's true. But look at it this way, no 'arm's been done, you got 'ome all right.'

'Well, you have a cheek, that's for sure,' retorted Jessie. 'As chance would have it, I was lucky. I searched all around for my shoes, and then fortunately I saw Thomas the gamekeeper in the distance and called out to him. He went back home and lent me his wife's boots, for which I am so grateful.'

Sarah rose and stormed out of the room, her temples throbbing. 'Well, I think I've heard enough. I succumbed to my better nature by giving this girl the benefit of the doubt, but she is clearly taking us for fools.'

Chapter 6

The station master paced around the parlour shaking his head, his arms folded behind his stooped back, his eyebrows furrowed. He paused in front of the brass-encased oval clock that had pride of place in the centre of the oak fireplace as it struck eight times. He checked the time against the silver watch that was secured by a chain in his waistcoat pocket, nodding.

Sarah had been persuaded to return to the room and sat by the window staring out at the garden in stony silence, her lips pursed and her sturdy arms crossed under her generous bosom. How could they now trust Maria to stay under their roof? And what would their community think about her sudden presence?

Jessie was seated on the sofa, her head spinning at the day's revelations. She pitied Maria for being in such desperate need, but she found the girl's justification for helping herself to her shoes hard to fathom; what if Thomas hadn't passed by in her hour of need? Could she believe Maria's claims that she hadn't seen her? Surely Maria must have realised that shoes of such quality would not have been abandoned.

As these confused thoughts swarmed around her head, her heart twisted in agony as she remembered Jack and the emotional way she had reacted to seeing him that afternoon. What would he think of her running away from him like that?

Beatrice stood by the fireplace, her chin cupped in her hand, her eyebrows furrowed. Her thoughts drifted too, to her sweetheart Sam Peters. How she longed to hear news from him. She was surprised at how much she missed him and each day she eagerly searched the mailbag when it arrived at the post office for letters from him.

Harry broke the silence. 'Can anyone tell me where Maria is now?'

The mere mention of her name made Sarah shudder. She glared daggers at Harry. Beatrice ignored her mother's steely glance, answering, 'I think she's in the kitchen with Ada, who's trying to calm her down. Maria's beside herself with worry that we're throwing her out on the streets.'

'That's no less than she deserves,' snapped Sarah through pencil straight lips.

Beatrice shook her head. 'I know what she did was terrible. But what would people say if we showed her the door? Could we not start afresh and get to know her properly?'

'What would folk say if they knew the truth about her? They'd say good riddance to her!' scowled the station master's wife, still fuming, her brows knitted together.

Harry turned to Sarah. 'My dear, Beatrice is right, we should start afresh. I know you are not going to like this, but I don't see that we have any choice. We should let Maria stay for a day or two while we sort out this mess, especially now Ruth has gone on to Doncaster.'

∞

Ada persuaded Maria to return to the parlour. She was red eyed.

Jessie glanced at Maria. 'I've thought on this long and hard and it was clearly a misunderstanding. Let's put this behind us now I have the shoes back and no damage has been done. There are far more important things to worry about right now.'

Sarah continued her objections while Harry spoke persuasively to make his case using his most diplomatic skills until Sarah had calmed down. 'Very well, I'll agree on one condition – even though it goes against my better judgement – that this will be her last chance. I'll be watching her like a hawk. I'll ask Betty to keep a good eye on her as well. And if she steps one foot out of line, she will be shown the door. There will be no more chances.'

'Of course,' agreed Harry, breathing a sigh of relief. 'Those are my sentiments exactly. Thank you, Sarah. I knew I could rely on your charitable wisdom.'

Beatrice's face broke into a smile. 'I'm pleased to hear this. Thank you, Mother. Despite the shaky start Maria has had, I hope we can put this disagreement behind us and show her some kindness. Just look at the different lives we've had. We should consider how privileged we have been compared to her. We have many blessings to be thankful for, and I can't imagine the kind of hardships Maria has faced.'

A look of relief washed across Maria's face. 'I'm so ashamed of what I did, and now yer being so kind to me like this. I promise yer won't regret it and I thank yer from the bottom of me 'eart. I 'ope we can be on good terms from now on, Mrs Saward.'

'The correct pronunciation is *h*ope, and you must pronounce the letter "h",' instructed Sarah. 'I hope you will make an effort to improve your use of English while you are here. Just listen closely and copy how we speak, and then you will pick it up.'

'I will, I can promise yer that, I mean, I promise *you*, 'cause I want to speak better. Thank yer Mrs Saward ... oops, I said it again, it just slipped out, I mean, thank *you*.'

Ada smiled. 'I'm so pleased that's settled, and I've no doubt the way you will be speaking the King's English very soon. Ma is very strict about correct pronunciation, and I can help you too, if you like.'

'I would like. Thank *you*, Miss Ada.'

'That's perfect, and just call me Ada. I think Maria will pick up our way of speaking admirably. As we all know there are far more important things for us to worry about anyway. What news is there from Captain Beck and the Sandringham Company?'

Harry stroked his moustache. 'I'm afraid there's still no news. But Captain Beck is a fine man; there's no better. He'll be doing his utmost to safeguard Sam and the others.'

At this, Beatrice stood up and threw herself into Harry's warm arms, her eyes welling up.

'Now, now, what's brought all this on?' said Harry, concerned.

'Oh, Father. I was thinking of Sam. I can't help but worry about him.'

She rested her head against her father's chest, listening to his pocket watch ticking away. He smelt faintly of tobacco and it was a comfort for her to feel the warmth of his chest swelling with his deep breaths. Just picturing Sam's mischievous face in her mind's eye gave her an aching feeling in the pit of her stomach.

'I should be there with him, with Captain Beck and the boys,' muttered Harry under his breath. 'I shall regret not going till the day I die. I should never have listened when they said I was past it.'

'Oh, Harry, don't be ridiculous. At fifty-five you were far too old to join up,' retorted Sarah.

'Yes, that's as may be. But Frank was only a year younger. And there's none fitter than me,' the station master replied solemnly.

∽

Harry had had an active role with the Territorials before the war, a proud and distinguished record as sergeant in the Sandringham Company of the 5th Battalion in the Norfolk Regiment, which had been formed in 1908 at the request of King Edward by his loyal land agent, Frank Beck. Harry had taken part in the drill nights, training and manoeuvres, some at Wolferton, in preparation for the threatened outbreak of war. When war was declared in August 1914, over one hundred men mobilised from the royal estate – gardeners, gamekeepers, grooms, dairymen, estate office workers, farm and engineering staff, joining recruits from all over North Norfolk, with companies raised by towns from Great Yarmouth King's Lynn with their headquarters at to Dereham.

There wasn't a soul who didn't believe Captain Beck would guard the well-being of their sons as if they were his own. His two nephews, Second Lieutenant Alec Beck and Captain Evelyn Beck, stood shoulder to shoulder with their uncle, Frank, as they marched to war. Frank could not be dissuaded from going, arranging for his brother Arthur to act as agent until his return. No man was more highly regarded by both estate workers or the King than Frank Beck. Though small in stature, he was a giant among men. He had taken over as Sandringham agent from his father, Edmund, who had died following a carriage accident on the grounds in 1891. As well as running the vast estate, he was invited to attend formal royal occasions as a courtier, not just in Sandringham, but also at Buckingham Palace.

Shortly before the Sandringham Company left, the King sent a personal telegram:

My best wishes to you ... on the eve of your departure for the front. I have known you all for many years and am confident that

91

THE SAME SPIRIT OF LOYALTY AND PATRIOTISM, IN WHICH YOU ANSWERED THE CALL TO ARMS, WILL INSPIRE YOUR DEEDS IN THE FACE OF THE ENEMY. MAY GOD BLESS AND PROTECT YOU.

Captain Beck replied on behalf of his men, thanking the King and expressed 'their one desire is to prove themselves worthy of their King'.

Harry saw the boys off from his station, with Frank Beck leaving behind his anxious wife Mary and five daughters. The boys grinned happily, chanting popular songs, their cheery rendition of 'Roll the Old Chariot Along' still ringing in his ears as the train chugged off, huffing and puffing, its thick smoke billowing overhead in the cloudless sky, the sound of their loved ones hollering, 'Godspeed and come back safely.' Before they left, Captain Beck had made a moving speech to their families, many in tears, on the immaculate lawn at his house in Sandringham, promising he would return them home safely from the conflict. Captain Beck and his men then turned and marched away to the cheers and cries from estate workers. But how many would return? And when would that be? Nobody could say.

∽

'And who would run Wolferton Station if you were away, Father?' asked Beatrice now.

Beatrice withdrew from her father's embrace and babbled, 'Sometimes I think I'll never see my Sam again. The

92

papers are full of reports about the terrible battles, of men dying, now we hear gas is being used in Belgium to kill thousands of our men. I can't bear to think of it. We live in fear of being invaded and that monstrous balloon flies over us and bombs us and we're surrounded by spies.'

'We have no choice about it, as awful as it is. We are fighting for our freedom; no Huns are going to set foot on British soil, though they keep trying to land their boats on our coast. Just think of Ada, and her Alfie fighting in France. He hasn't even seen the sunshine on the face of his firstborn son. At least you were lucky to hear from Sam yesterday. These are terrible times and we have to be patient and pray that he and all our other lads will return home soon, and Alfie too. We can't let the damned Huns win.'

Beatrice sniffled. 'You're right, Father. I don't know how Ada bears it. She is so strong. I wish I was more like her, but I'm not. I hate this wretched war.'

Sarah rose from her chair. 'I won't have self-pitying talk like that in this house. We are Sawards, servants of the King and Queen, and loyal to them to our dying breath.'

Beatrice's face was flushed. Her eyes flashed with anger, but she held her tongue. Her parents didn't share her reservations about war. Beatrice thought it unfair that wars were made by egotistical men who left it to women to pick up the pieces after countless lives had been shattered by the losses.

At the beginning of their two-year courtship just the sight of Sam, with his wide smile, honest, open face and mop of dark hair that she loved running her fingers through, was enough to give her butterflies in her tummy. His skin had a ruddy glow from his outdoor work at the royal stud caring for the King's magnificent racehorses, following in the footsteps of his fathers. But the intensity of those feelings had faded, though she had shielded this from him as he packed his bag for an unknown land, realising her fondness for him was more as a brother than lover.

Beatrice reached into the pocket of her skirt and unfolded an envelope. She took out the letter that had reached her yesterday and read it again. It was dated 28th July 1915.

Dearest angel Beatrice,

By the time this reaches you, we will be on our way to foreign soil. We will be taking a ship from Liverpool and are told it could take a week to reach our destination. I've never been on a ship before. I only hope I have good sea legs and that the water is balmy. I would hate to be sick and make a fool of myself in front of everyone.

Our training at Watford was tough. Other battalions were there too, and I tell you we couldn't have been treated better by the town's kind folks, who took us in to their homes. We have made many wonderful friends here with hearts of gold. I told my landlady Gladys and her family all about you and, God willing, I said I would invite them to our wedding when this war is over, and you will see for yourself the kindness people have for us.

Beatrice, I carry your beautiful photo in my chest pocket. It's always close to my heart, making it beat faster when I think of you. I am so proud to be with Captain Beck's boys in the Sandringham Company. Do go and see Betsy and High Cloud if you have a chance to pop over to the stud. I miss riding them and hope they will remember me when I return.

I worry about Ma and her poor heart, and you know how she worries all the time. I know I can count on you to keep an eye on her and Florence and the two boys. They can be little rascals and fair wear Mum out. I feel truly blessed to have your love.

Farewell for now, my love. I will write again when I can.

With fondest love, forever, my angel,

Sam

Sam's tender words caused a pang of guilt in Beatrice as she replaced the letter in the envelope. If only Sam knew, she was no *angel*. She hardly dared confess her change of heart to him at a time like this, when he needed to count on her love more than ever. He was good through and through and she resolved to remain loyal to him and keep up the pretence.

∽

At the end of the evening, they made their way to bed, the Saward sisters having made the attic room as comfortable as possible for their unexpected guest. When Maria reached the room it was in darkness. Public warnings forbade any light in the room that would catch the enemy's attention. She rubbed her eyes and a moment later, after they had adjusted to the darkness, she glanced around and caught sight of the small iron bedstead and a large metal chest on the floor to store clothes. A marble stand with a floral water jug and bowl were placed against the wall. There were two small windows at the height of Maria's head, enabling her when standing on tiptoe to see the night sky and give her a good view over the front and side of the house. She heard an owl hooting and looked up into the sky, reassuring herself that the monstrous Zeppelin had moved on as she drew the curtains tightly shut.

The air in the low-ceilinged room was stifling. After unbuttoning her blouse, Maria flung herself onto her bed and sobbed. So much had happened that day and now she was here, in the station master's house under the care of her new-found relatives who were, in reality, no more than strangers.

A few minutes later, Maria slipped into the crisp white cotton nightgown that had been laid out on the patchwork bedcover. She sat on the edge of the bed, her fingers fumbling for the silver chain that dangled around her neck.

What would the Sawards think of her if they knew her secret? How could she tell them of her shocking past?

Still sniffling, she slid under the sheet and closed her eyes, her hand clutching the chain. As she drifted off, she saw her mother's kind face and her two brothers playing mischievously at the railway station where they grew up at Audley End and felt a bitter sweetness, loving them so much, while saddened that they were forced by circumstances to live apart.

She saw herself proudly pushing a big wheeled perambulator with a gurgling blond-haired baby boy sitting up propped against a fluffy pillow. Chatty women stopped to admire his chubby face and sparkling blue eyes, complimenting her on his good behaviour. The baby gurgled when faces bent down and stared at him, pinching his cheeks and poking him, yet he barely cried, not like Ada's little Leslie.

She twisted and turned in her bed, an intense pang of longing rising up within her, an aching that burned to her core.

'I'm gonna make yer proud of me, Joey. I promise yer, on my life.'

Chapter 7

The morning sun burst through the kitchen window, marking Maria's cheeks with three golden streaks as she devoured her breakfast. She circled her finger around the bowl, licking every speck of porridge until it was clean. She gulped down a glass of milk and wiped her mouth with her sleeve.

'That's as good as me ma makes, Betty. I'll wash up, if yer like. Oops, I mean, *my* ma, and if *you* like.' She grinned, pleased as punch at correcting her pronunciation.

'It looks like you already have,' chortled Betty, pointing to Maria's spotless bowl.

'That's a compliment from you, Betty. Where is everyone this morning?' enquired Maria.

'Well, you've had a bit of a lie-in, young lady, and Mrs Saward said we shouldn't disturb you. She has a kind heart once you get to know her. Mr Saward is at the station and Mrs Saward and Beatrice are at the post office. Ada is still in bed, bless her, as the little 'un kept her up in the night and they are now both sleeping it off. She must be exhausted. She's rushed off her feet with all the preparation that needs doing for the concert.'

'But I shouldn't be lying in while everyone else in the house is working.'

Betty handed a pinafore to Maria. 'I have a job for you as I hear you are keen to help. I want to see if you are as good as you say you are. And you don't want to get that frock dirty.'

Maria rolled up the sleeves of the blue dress that Ada had lent her and tied the pinafore around her waist. 'Oh, you won't find fault with *my* work,' she replied cheerily, taking up the challenge.

'Mrs Saward is very particular about how she likes her washing up to be done, but a smart girl like you will soon get the hang of it. First of all, fill the bowl with hot soapy water and be sure to wash it off with hot water in another bowl. Be sure to wash the glasses and any fine china first, leaving the china out to drain on the side while you dry the glasses.'

Maria pointed to the wooden drainer next to the sink. 'That's simple enough. I've washed up many a time before.'

'That's as I would expect, so you'll know not to wash up while the cake of soap is still in the water.'

Betty handed Maria a block of Sunlight carbolic soap and pointed to the copper in the scullery where she could fill her washing up bowl with hot water.

'Of course I know that. I'll show *you* I'm up to it. Just leave me to it.' Maria grinned.

'Very well then. You certainly learn quickly, if the way you have caught on to proper speaking is anything to go by. I'll start upstairs and change the beds. But try not to make too much noise and disturb Ada and the babe.'

Maria felt surprisingly refreshed after her sleep. She was desperate to win everyone's approval so that maybe, just maybe, the Sawards would let her stay longer than a couple of days and she would become a fine lady just like Ada, Jessie and Beatrice. She imagined herself holding her head high and wearing a beautiful gown, like Wolferton's most respected women. Magnolia Greensticks would see her, but fail to recognise her as the shabby, coarsely spoken girl she had turned her nose up at. Unaware of her real identity, Magnolia would ingratiate herself with her – and then Maria would experience the thrill of seeing her shocked face when Magnolia realised she was none other than the Sawards' poor relation.

'I will have a fine dress of my own one day. I won't wear anyone else's cast-offs anymore. I'll show them I'm as good as them,' Maria promised herself, getting stuck into her cleaning.

∞

Having finished the sink full of breakfast crockery, she scrubbed clean the sturdy oak table and then, hovering low over it, her elbow swinging backwards and forwards over the surface, she rubbed in beeswax until it shone.

She then turned her attention to the pantry just off the kitchen, two steps lower with a stone floor. The room was cool and she eyed the shelves laden with a few jars of neatly labelled home-made jams and chutneys that

Betty had cleverly made by adjusting the ingredients to overcome any shortages. At the end of the shelf was a tin containing recipes cut out from a magazine. They advised on war-time alternatives. Maria picked up the top one, a French recipe for blackberry jelly without sugar, and gawped in disbelief. 'Carrots, lemons and sugar beet in place of sugar? How can *that* taste like blackberry jelly?'

Delving underneath, she found a recipe for nasturtium pickle to have on the plate with cold meats or a piece of cheese. Maria had no doubt that Betty's magic hands would whip up the tastiest pickle using nasturtium seeds, shallots, cloves, allspice, vinegar and seasoning. The garden was abundant with bright yellow and orange nasturtium petals along the back wall, so Betty had a good supply of seeds.

There was a green enamel storage tin labelled flour, a precious commodity as its price was rocketing, and some loose vegetables, potatoes and carrots from Harry's vegetable garden, laid out neatly in a wooden box. Some runner beans had been sliced and put in a jar and covered in salt to preserve them. Mixing bowls, pie dishes, a chopping board and rolling pin were piled on the middle shelf within easy reach. A small meat safe – a wooden square box with wire-mesh sides so the air could circulate and keep flies off its contents – contained a portion of cold meat pie and a few slices of gammon, as well as a bowl of Betty's dripping. Maria's mouth salivated as she dipped a finger in the pie, licking the delicious gravy flavour. She savoured the taste, forcing herself not to dip her finger in the dish again. How she missed such tasty food, having to make do with soup made from potato skin and any scraps from the butcher.

A dainty lace cover, its edges weighted with colourful beads, covered a dish of butter placed next to the white enamel bread bin. An enamel jug contained the fresh milk from Blackbird Farm, run by Beatrice's friend Lizzie.

Maria washed the wooden shelves down and ensured all the produce was neatly returned to its original place.

'Good morning, Maria. I trust you slept well.'

Maria looked up to see Ada peering into the pantry, her face tired with heavy shadows sinking under her eyes. 'My goodness. You have been busy, lots of elbow grease there, I can see. And the kitchen table is gleaming. I can see you are a hard worker.'

Maria stepped out of the pantry and thanked Ada, grateful for her kind words. She cocked an ear. 'Ah, it's little Leslie, he's woken up, bless him. Shall I bring him down for yer, I mean *you*? I hear he gave you a bad night again.'

'Oh, yes please, if you're sure you don't mind,' replied Ada, rubbing her eyes. 'And you're right, I was up with him most of the night.'

Maria disappeared upstairs and returned to the kitchen carrying the wriggling infant. She sat him on her lap and bounced him up and down. The corners of Maria's mouth were turned up and her eyes danced.

Ada reached over to stroke her son's chubby cheek. 'Look how good he is with you, he's all smiles and contentment, he's no longer a screaming scamp.'

A wave of tenderness welled inside Maria. 'He's a dear little boy. I like to think I have a way with little 'uns. You see, Ma hasn't been too good these last five years after having pneumonia and bronchitis; she was never her old self again afterwards. The doctor didn't think she would pull through. I nursed her, sat up with her at night mopping her brow when she became feverish and making a light beef broth like I'd seen her do to help build up her strength. So it was only natural that I became like a mother to our Freddie and Archie when Ma wasn't able to cope.'

'Oh, Maria. If we had known about you and how bad things were we could have helped,' said Ada.

'Pa, he was worried sick, and he was getting on and did his best, but it got too much for him. He would sit in front of the fire, his head buried in his hands, crying like a baby. He didn't know I saw him, he tried to keep it from me. I'll never forget the joy on his face when Ma finally pulled round after she had been poorly for a month with a pneumonia that really knocked the stuffing out of her. When he could see she had turned the corner, he kissed her hand, grabbed hold of me and kissed my cheek too, thanking the Lord for saving her. That's why I'm fair worried about Ma. She ain't strong, I mean, she *isn't* strong, I'm worried it might be her chest again.'

'Maria, I'm lost for words. I'm so sorry, you've had a terrible ordeal. Your ma was blessed to have such a loving daughter care for her. I hope your mother will recover soon now she is with her sister. If I speak to Father, maybe you can stay a while longer; as long as there is no trouble from you. Mother will be pleased to see your pronunciation is already greatly improved. I've noticed, well done, Maria.'

'I'm trying really hard to speak properly. It's not that hard once you put your mind to it,' replied Maria slowly, emphasising each word clearly.

'I want to get on with Mrs Saward. If you could speak to them, I promise I'll speak good and proper and won't cause trouble. I feel like a weight has already been lifted from my shoulders, being able to talk you like this from the bottom of my heart,' stammered Maria, her eyes filled with a sad expression.

She glanced down at her feet, twisting her hands in front of her, her face scrunched.

'I sense something is amiss. Is something else worrying you, Maria?' asked Ada.

Biting her lip, Maria nodded. 'It's my brothers. I can't help but fret about Freddie and Archie. They are so young and I worry that Uncle Gus is working them to the bone.'

Ada nodded. 'I promise you we will find out how they're doing after you've settled in a bit.'

Maria put Leslie down on the floor and he played contentedly with his soft clown. She clutched Ada's hands and kissed them. 'Thank you, Miss Ada, I mean Ada. You've no idea how much that means to me.'

Ada laughed, shaking her head. 'There's no need for this, silly. Now come on, let's give Leslie his breakfast before he starts yelling for it.'

'Just two eggs for us, Maria, we are saving as many as we can for the Egg Collection,' Ada instructed, referring to the appeal for citizens to donate eggs for the benefit of servicemen being treated in hospitals in France and Belgium.

Maria collected two fresh eggs from the pantry and added them gently to the small egg pan that she had filled with boiling water. The pan was a creamy white colour on the inside from the hard scale that had built up from the boiled water; every house had a separate pan for boiling eggs. While they bubbled away, she thinly sliced some bread and smothered it with butter.

Ada devoured her breakfast as keenly as Leslie, whose mouth opened like a baby bird being fed a plump worm when Maria popped the sliced bread with gooey egg yolk into his mouth.

'He eats well, and even though he is only eight months old, he is growing into a strong little boy.' Maria smiled.

'You're doing a grand job with him there, Maria. And I'm sure Betty is grateful to have an extra pair of hands to help around the house. She always complains about her knees when she bends down to make up the fire or wash the floor.'

'I don't mind doing that. Anything! Betty and I will get on like a house on fire. I've taken to her and won't let you down,' Maria replied eagerly.

Once Ada had finished her breakfast, she stood up and stepped into the hallway. She patted her hair in front of the mirror. 'I have to leave soon. I'm hoping to meet our star singer for the fundraising concert. We are very fortunate to have secured Clara Griffin as top billing, thanks to her being good friends with Hettie, whose husband Hubert Harrington is organist at Sandringham Church.'

'Not *the* Clara Griffin?' exclaimed Maria, her eyes widening. 'Oh, she is so beautiful and dainty and has the voice of an angel. I hear people want to cry when they see her sing, it makes them shiver so. I know that sounds silly, but, I'm sure I would too. I can't believe you know such a star as her.'

'Oh yes, and you may get the chance to meet her, Maria. From what I hear she's such a lovely person too. I want the concert to be a great success. I want to make my Alfie proud of me and raise lots of money for the war effort.'

Maria gulped, her expression incredulous. 'Me? Meet Clara Griffin? Bloomin' 'eck. I shall pinch myself. And you mustn't fret so Ada. I know you will make your Alfie proud. You couldn't be doing a better job. I'll knit some socks for the troops too and make lavender bags to sell. I'll bake cakes. I'll do anything I can to help.'

Ada cocked her head at the sound of the front door knocker being slammed down. She opened the door to see the two haughty Greensticks sisters standing on the front step. Ada's arm swept wide open to invite them in. They spoke in hushed words that Maria couldn't hear, then followed Ada into the kitchen.

Magnolia thrust back her shoulders, her lips quivering as she addressed Ada. Maria's eyes were fixed on her tombstone teeth and distinctive mole.

'My dear, we called in at the post office this morning and Mrs Saward informed us about the arrival of your new relative, so we felt we must welcome her to Wolferton. I feel we may have got off on the wrong footing yesterday. I was only concerned about strangers in our midst and the lateness of the rehearsal.'

Maria's jaw dropped in surprise.

'I don't believe we have been introduced properly. My name is Magnolia Greensticks and this is my sister Aggie and we are delighted to meet you,' Magnolia continued. 'Maria, is it? We want to assure you that any relatives of the Sawards are friends of ours too.'

Ada's eyes widened in amazement; she was as stunned as Maria and shot her a look that urged her to speak.

'You've really come to see me? I don't understand . . .' Maria choked on her words.

'I apologise for any confusion and understand you might not be expecting our hand of friendship after yesterday. We were rather harsh. I hope we can start afresh.'

'Well, yes . . . I would be delighted. Thank you kindly for calling in to welcome me, Miss Greensticks.'

Maria spoke slowly and carefully, pronouncing all her vowels and consonants.

'You may call me Magnolia.' She grinned.

'And I'm Aggie,' added the younger sister, stepping forward.

Maria had never encountered two stranger-looking sisters. They were almost identical in appearance, both tall and big boned, with coarse dark brown hair, long

107

horse-like facial features, parrot-shaped noses and big yellow teeth. Their hands were large too, like men's, she noticed.

'Yes, I was born with this scar on my face,' murmured Aggie, touching the crescent-shaped red mark on her forehead. Maria hadn't mean to stare.

Magnolia's hand instinctively flew up to stroke the mole on her face.

'I'm sorry, I didn't mean to be rude,' stuttered Maria, her face turning crimson.

Both sisters shared a taste for dressing flamboyantly, wearing almost identical gowns. Magnolia's purple creation had a heart-shaped lace neckline with pink bows down the front of the bodice and Aggie's burgundy gown was the same, even down to the pink bows. They wore matching felt hats perched perkily on the sides of their heads, which complemented their gowns and had three pink bows each added to the front.

Maria was unsure whether to offer refreshments to the guests, but remained silent, listening as Magnolia loudly proclaimed what a wonderful job Ada was doing with the concert.

'You think I'm doing a good job?' gasped Ada incredulously. 'But I thought . . .'

Magnolia shook her head. 'I shall not cause any more trouble, we shall be allies in constructing the best fundraising night that Wolferton has ever seen. And I am naturally delighted to share the billing with Clara Griffin as Wolferton's Nightingale. That's if you want me to.'

'Of course I do. And your support means a great deal to me, thank you, Magnolia.'

A moment later, Leslie's deafening cries from the floor filled the room.

'I'm so sorry, Ada. I only wanted to squeeze his peachy cheeks. He looks so like his father, my dear,' Aggie babbled nervously, crouching over the child.

'You never did have a way with babies. Perhaps it's time we left,' intimated her sister. 'I'm sure Ada is very busy.'

'Oh, but you are wrong, Magnolia. I adore babies. If only . . .'

Aggie appeared flustered as Ada escorted them to the door. As Magnolia passed Maria, she pronounced, 'My dear, you can confide in me at any time you wish. Believe me, we all have skeletons in our cupboards. I'm sure we'll get used to your charming ways. The important thing is you are a Saward. I can't help noticing that you seem different today, more well-expressed than our first encounter.'

After they'd left, Ada declared, 'I'm flabbergasted. I can't believe the change in those two women. They are usually such snobs, though I admit it is pleasing to see them climbing off their high horses and being so uncommonly kind towards you. I was pleased they noticed a change in you.'

'Me too, but what a bloomin' cheek to mention me in the same breath as skeletons in the cupboard like I'm some horrid secret that's come crawling out from under a stone with dark secrets to hide,' protested Maria.

'Well, they'll just have to keep guessing, won't they? Maybe they have a skeleton or two of their own.' Ada grinned.

Leslie's cries ceased and his eyes followed Maria as she walked around the kitchen.

'Look how he can't take his eyes off you,' Ada said. 'Could I ask a favour of you? Could you look after him this afternoon while I see Clara? Betty usually does, but she has a pile of ironing to catch up on, and you do seem to get on so well. There is some new music we need to discuss before our next rehearsal. I'd be so grateful.'

'Oh, Ada, I'd love to. I'll take the greatest care of him, as if he were me own, I promise you, cross my heart.'

∽

After Ada had left on her bicycle for Sandringham, Maria returned to the kitchen and slumped into the Windsor chair, scooping up the infant from the floor and cuddling him on her lap. She stroked his blond curls and bonny face and hummed a nursery rhyme that Ada sang for him, bouncing him up and down on her lap. Instead of Leslie's face she saw another one in his place. The more Leslie laughed, the quicker her actions became, speeding them up to the words she chanted louder and louder. 'One potato, two potato, three potato, four, five potato, six potato, seven potato more.'

Her head began to spin and she was oblivious to Leslie's cries. All she could see in front of her was a beautiful baby boy, and she was never going to let him go, not again . . .

110

She snapped back to her senses when she heard Betty's angry voice shouting at her. 'Stop it this minute and give the child to me. What on earth has possessed you?'

The housekeeper grabbed Leslie from Maria's tight grip. Maria looked as shocked as Betty did. Leslie's face was red from screaming, his little chest panting for breath as his chubby arms and legs thrashed.

'Look what you've done to him. The poor little thing. I've never seen him so upset.'

Aghast, Maria's eyes widened and filled with tears. 'I thought it was ... I'm sorry Betty, I'm so sorry. I don't know what came over me. Please, yer won't say anything to Ada, will yer?'

Betty's brows snapped together. 'How could you ask such a thing? You looked as if you were off your head. How can I keep this from his mother? If anything happened to Master Leslie I would never forgive myself.'

'I didn't mean any harm. I promise yer, I was only playing with him and lost myself for a moment. It were only a game.'

Betty shook her head. 'That's a funny kind of game, if you ask me, making him cry like that. And I thought you were meant to have a motherly way with him.'

Maria's mouth gaped open and her eyes filled with scalding tears. 'You don't like having me here, do yer? Yer're just jealous. Yer're jealous of me good work an' want to turn the Sawards against me. I think it's best I leave. And I ain't ever coming back!'

Flinging open the back door, Maria ran down the path and out outside the house, oblivious to the figure that slipped out from round the side of the house and followed her shadow. Tears streamed down her cheeks, her heart pounding. She paused to catch her breath and spun around at hearing the quickening crunch of heavy footsteps behind her, but they stopped suddenly. There was no one in sight.

She shrugged her shoulders and carried on. A moment later, she looked over her shoulder and the corner of her eye caught sight of a shadowy figure darting behind a hedge. She felt a chill along her spine and a sense of unease. She paused for a moment to see if there would be any further movement. Her eyes were drawn across the path to the station, which heaved with activity, a big black engine hissing and the shrieking sound of the guard's whistle giving a final warning to passengers.

'All aboard,' he yelled. She didn't glance up as the engine pulled out of the station, carrying day trippers to the red-and-white-striped cliffed coastal town of Hunstanton, the final destination.

She sniffled, mortified how she had lashed out at Betty who was a good soul, and how she had let her nerves get the better of her and make her forget her proper pronunciation. 'Where should I go now? I'm just trouble wherever I go.'

Picking up her skirt, her legs unsteady and her heart heavy, Maria fled to the one place she felt safe, wearing a pair of sturdy shoes that Beatrice had kindly given her, she ran along the stony path, finding her way through misty eyes.

Chapter 8

Maria's hasty departure did not go unnoticed.

'And there we were, Aggie and I, just crossing the path to come here and tell you, Mrs Saward, how we had called at your house to welcome your new relation to Wolferton when, blow me down, our eyes almost popped out of our heads.'

Sarah rolled her eyes. 'I am rather busy today. If there is anything you need to say, please do so quickly.'

Magnolia continued. 'We were beginning to warm to her, knowing she is a Saward. But it appears something untoward seems to have happened since we left a moment ago as the girl stormed out of your house and disappeared around the corner. She was very flustered and appeared to be crying. She seems very highly strung, Sarah, to say the least, not at all like your own well-bred girls.'

Beatrice gave her mother a quizzical glance. Sarah folded her arms, her lips pursed. 'I haven't the faintest idea what you are talking about. I'm sure it's nothing to worry about, but thank you for letting us know.'

Magnolia sniffed. 'Yes, well, we will be on our way. I must say, she looked a little, how can I put it delicately, in need of charity.'

'Well, they say charity begins at home, so she's in the right place as we are distant relations. We think she will settle in very well,' Sarah retorted stoutly, surprised at her defensive feelings towards Maria.

Beatrice's eyes glinted approvingly at her mother's reply. Slinging her canvas postbag over her shoulder, she added, 'Yes, Mother's right. Us Sawards stick together. Was there anything else you wanted, Miss Greensticks?'

The Greensticks sisters shuffled out, their chins raised upwards, having been put firmly in their place. 'What a pair of nosy busybodies those two are, always meddling in other people's business,' Sarah commented once the door had shut behind them.

'I was proud of you, Mother, for standing up for Maria. What you said is true, us Sawards will stick together.'

'Let's hope I won't regret it. I do hope nothing's amiss, to make Maria run off like that,' Sarah replied, brushing off the compliment. 'Now, do you have the letter for Sam's mother? I hope it will please her and bring her some comfort. And there's a letter for the vicar as well. They'll be anxious for news of their boy, Piers. You'd best be off now. And please give Edith my best wishes.'

'Of course I will. I'll stop off at her cottage at the end so I can chat with her for a while, and I'll tell her my news from Sam, and about our new guest too.'

The bell jangled on the post office door at that moment and two elderly ladies stepped inside, Mrs Biggs and Miss Hawkins. They expressed concern that food parcels they had posted to their men on the front line had not arrived.

114

Mrs Biggs declared, 'Bertie would have mentioned it in his last letter. He's always so grateful. And I put in a packet of his favourite tobacco too.'

Miss Hawkins nodded, saying her nephew hadn't received his parcel either.

Sarah shook her head, perplexed, and assured the two women that the parcels had been sent off along with the other post.

'Maybe they'll arrive soon. Just give it another week or so. This is a time of war, after all.'

Beatrice recalled a similar report had been made two weeks earlier, and again, they had brushed off any concerns thinking the parcel was on its way. She made a mental note to check with the family. As she stepped outside, she raised her face to the sun for a moment, listening to the sound of birdsong, then looked around her. The sight of a widow and her daughter dressed in mourning, the absence of young men in the streets, were reminders of the impact of war in her community.

She could barely face reading the news now. Every Friday, when she opened the pages of the *Lynn* Advertiser she saw notices announcing the deaths of their men.

Some had letters posted from the front, but there was little news from Gallipoli, the Turkish peninsula that her Sam had been sent to under Captain Beck. Other families in the community were desperate for a letter too. The occasional one did land on a doormat, making those still waiting for news all the more anxious. Even though letters from the troops were heavily censored, lest they fall into the hands of the enemy, just a few words on an Army card was enough to confirm to their loved ones that they were still alive.

With a heavy heart she pulled her straw boater firmly onto her head and straddled her bicycle, which was propped up against the wall, and flung her grey canvas postbag across her shoulder.

Within seconds of setting off, she spotted Jessie at the end of the station platform, about to step onto the path, having just finished her cleaning duties in the royal waiting rooms. Beatrice braked alongside her sister and told her how their mother had magnificently stood up for Maria. She also recounted what she had been told by Magnolia about her sudden disappearance.

'I wonder what could have upset her,' Beatrice pondered.

Jessie thought for a moment. 'Umm, I wonder. I do have a hunch. Perhaps she has gone to the woods again. Maybe she is drawn there for solace when her mind is troubled, like me. She might need time on her own to think. After all, she is going through an enormous upheaval right now. She must be missing her ma dreadfully, what with her going off as she did without saying goodbye, and being separated from her younger brothers too.'

Beatrice placed her feet back on the pedals. 'With all this hullabaloo, Jessie, I haven't had a chance to ask you about Jack. How are things? Did you get a chance to speak to him at the station?'

Jessie grimaced. 'Not exactly. I saw Jack step off the train with a beautiful woman, she was so pretty and they looked so happy in each other's company. I couldn't face seeing them together and ran off.'

'Oh, Jessie, you silly thing. I'm sure Jack isn't a ladies' man and there was a perfectly good explanation.'

'Perhaps you're right, but I made myself look foolish in front of him. I think it's best I put him out of my mind. I'm destined to be an old maid. You've got your Sam and Ada has her Alfie and I'm . . . I'll just be an old spinster like the Greensticks sisters.'

'Don't be ridiculous!! Any man should count himself luckier than the richest man in the land to have you as his wife. You might walk up the aisle before me,' scoffed Beatrice.

'That will never happen. Sam will never give up loving you, he adores you. It melts my heart to see the way his eyes sparkle when you are together.'

'I know but part of me isn't sure he is the right man for me. Still, I pray he will return home safely. I have a letter from him for Edith, I know it will bring her great cheer. I fear she is struggling without him, poor thing.'

Jessie went on her way as Beatrice fumbled with the elastic from the straw boater, her thick auburn hair tied neatly behind her neck in a bun and resting just above the crisp white collar of her blouse. She needed that collar today to provide cover from the sun's intense rays. As she did so her fingers brushed against a silver chain. She flicked it from under her blouse and held up a heart-shaped locket. She prised it open and gazed longingly at two miniature images looking back up at her; one showed Sam, proud in his khaki uniform that he wore with the Sandringham Company, and in the other photo his face was beaming and he was wearing his Sunday best. She remembered the day it had been taken – at a summer fete the year before. She gazed at the photos with mixed emotions, her stomach in knots. The locket had been a surprise parting gift from Sam.

'It's just like him to be so thoughtful,' choked Beatrice, showing the new locket to her mother on the day of Sam's departure. He had presented it to her on their last evening together, when she had promised to wait for him.

'I want you to do me the honour of being my wife, Beatrice,' he had said. 'Will you wait for me? I'll buy you the best ring I can when I get back.'

With Sam off to war, Beatrice had readily accepted, hoping their engagement would somehow help him pull through the battles that lay ahead. Swept away in the heady moment, she declared her love for him and his eyes filled with tears of gratitude, even though she was not entirely sure she was telling the truth.

Beatrice recalled the day Sam left had Wolferton with the Sandringham Company. He had clung on to her on the platform where families crushed against each other to wave their boys off, singing tunes to keep their moods lifted, chanting 'God Save the King', and promising their families they would be home again soon. She had watched Sam frantically waving his white handkerchief from the carriage window, and she had waved hers back at him, as she ran and jumped along the platform next to the departing train, his smiling eyes never leaving her face, until he vanished out of sight, and all that could be seen was a trail of steam fluttering in the cloudless sky, the train's hissing sound fading out into the distance.

Beatrice had wept when she had returned home, feeling a knot twisting inside her stomach. Sam was the most decent man she had ever known and she vowed she would keep her promise. This was a time of war and a girl had to stand by her man and give her hope. She brushed off her own uncertainties, burying them deep inside as she gently kissed Sam's trusting face looking up at her in her locket and clasped it shut, concealing it back under her white blouse. She hitched her black skirt up above her ankles so it didn't catch any grease from the bike chain and pushed herself along the ground with her feet, before sitting back in her saddle and pedalling away.

'Come back soon, Sam. Please, come back home soon, your family needs you,' she whispered under her breath.

Beatrice would be spellbound watching Sam work his magic with the King's racehorses, whispering in their ears and stroking their smooth coats. He understood every movement and sound they made, having learnt his skills from his father, Herbert, who worked in the royal stud. As a lad, he would trail along with him every chance he could and try to make himself useful too.

A terrible tragedy three years ago had seen Sam become a man overnight. Herbert was riding one of the horses gently when it was scared by a fox that ran in its path. He tried to rein the horse in, but he was thrown head first into a ditch and drowned.

Sam had promised to take care of his grief-stricken mother, Edith, his sister, Florence, who was fifteen, and twin brothers Roly and Ben, thirteen years old, and he was true to his word.

Sam was so good at his work that he was offered his father's job, and soon filled his shoes, both at home and at work, ensuring they still had a roof over their heads in their tied cottage. Beatrice was doing her best now to care for Sam's family while he was away. She would call in on Edith shortly, but first she had a few stops to make, first at Dr Fletcher's house on the outskirts of the village.

His house was one of the grandest in Wolferton and had a sweeping drive leading to a fine-looking brick house with bay windows on either side and a porch with stone pillars. The widowed doctor had only an unmarried daughter who lived on the south coast with an elderly aunt. Beatrice recognised her handwriting on the envelope of the letter she had to deliver and left it with Dr Fletcher's housekeeper, Gladys. There would be no heartbreaking news for the doctor, she thought ruefully.

Beatrice pedalled away and stopped off at the black-smith's forge. Jed's eyes were watering from the intense heat of the fire in his brazier he was leaning over, hammering away and shaping iron horseshoes. He stopped and mopped his brow as Beatrice handed him a letter, telling her he would show it to his wife, who could read better than he could and would be bringing him his lunch over soon. She could see from the postmark that the letter came from his son, Simon, who was serving in France in France, and she told him she hoped she was bringing him good news and that Sid was well.

She continued on her rounds for another hour, exchanging courteous pleasantries with families, all keen to know everyone's news – good and bad – so they could pull together.

Finally, Beatrice drew to a halt at Bramble Cottage. Lifting her skirt carefully as she disembarked from the bike, her mail bag, now almost empty, slung over her shoulder. The cottage was a typical two-up, two-down, close to the hackney stud and church. Edith lived in the last of the terraced cottages. It had diamond-shaped lattice windows, a small flower garden in the front filled with colourful blooms and a larger vegetable garden at the back. Fragrant lavender lined the narrow path leading to the front door, filling the warm summer air with its sweet scent. She spotted plump thrushes fighting for scraps of food on the wooden bird table that Sam had made as she propped her bicycle against a horse chestnut tree close to the front gate.

Beatrice pulled out Sam's letter from her postbag, smiling at the thought of how happy his mother would be to have news from him.

Beatrice picked up the iron door knocker shaped like a horse's head and slammed it down three times. She waited, but there was no response. That's strange, she thought, Edith usually opened the door quickly as she was always pleased to have visitors, especially Beatrice.

Beatrice peered through the front window, but there was no sign of Edith, so she decided to go to the back door. Just as she turned to walk off, she heard the front door being unbolted and creaking open. Florence beckoned her in. Her eyes were red and puffy. Beatrice stepped towards Edith and greeted her with a warm smile, holding Sam's letter out to her, hoping it would cheer her up.

'Come in, Beatrice,' replied Edith dully, her face drained of all colour. Beatrice noticed her sunken eyes were filled with a haunted look, and were puffy and reddened too, as if she had been crying.

'What is it, Edith? Tell me, has something happened?'

Edith nodded, sobbing into her handkerchief. Her shoulders were shaking. She looked up at Beatrice, trying to speak, but the words would not come out. As Beatrice reached forward to comfort her, she noticed a stout woman enter the front room from the kitchen. She recognised her as Winnie, Edith's older sister, who was married to a newsagent in King's Lynn.

Beatrice could see that her eyes were red from crying too. Her bulbous nose was almost purple. Winnie took hold of Edith's arm, leading her gently towards a chair. Edith sat there sobbing quietly, her head in her hands, unable to look up.

'You'd better sit down, Beatrice. We have some news for you,' choked Winnie.

The station master's daughter nervously looked from one woman to the other. She was afraid of what they might say.

'What is it, Winnie? Why are you all crying? Please tell me what's happened. Is it Sam?'

Winnie glanced at Edith, biting her lip, and nodded. She held up the *Lynn Advertiser* she had clutched under her arm. She took a deep breath, her chest expanding like an accordion, her voice wavering, as she spoke.

'Oh, Beatrice, come, look at this. It's terrible news.'

'What do you mean? What does it say?' asked Beatrice, feeling a chill rush through her body.

Winnie handed the paper to Beatrice. Her eyes scanned the headlines, 'What does this mean, "The 5th Norfolks. Thirteen officers missing and two wounded".'

'Captain Beck is amongst them. His name is at the top. And his nephew Alec is missing too,' Winnie murmured.

'What do you mean they are *missing*?'

'Just that, nobody knows where they are, if they are dead or alive.'

'But Captain Beck, not Captain Beck!' cried Beatrice. 'And Sam, is there news of him?'

Winnie shook her head. 'Not a word. I've read it closely, so we must be thankful for that. There's another report here about the 5th Norfolks in Gallipoli, I'm afraid it's not good news.'

Beatrice took the paper, her hands trembling as she read of the 'very severe and continuous fighting, with heavy losses on both sides'.

Her face filled with horror. Winnie placed her hand on Beatrice's arm. 'The mayor of King's Lynn is doing all he can to find out where our boys are. He's heard there are over four hundred prisoners in Turkish hands. We have to hope Sam is one of them, that he is safe.'

Beatrice reeled at the thought of their Sam in Turkish hands, and what this could mean.

'Oh, no. Oh my God. I don't understand. But I have a letter here from Sam. What does it mean *they are prisoners-of-war*? And where on earth is Gallipoli?' Nobody could answer.

Beatrice choked. 'But, I don't understand, unless he sent it before he left.'

Edith's hands shook as she took the letter from Beatrice. She stared at it, as if in a trance, before opening the envelope. Beatrice and Winnie watched as Edith read it, mumbling aloud the words in front of her, pausing after every sentence to look up at them. It was very similar to what Sam had written to Beatrice, about the kindness of the people of Watford and how hard the training had been. He promised to write to his 'Dearest Mother' again at the first opportunity, and not to worry about him.

'My Sam is the best boy any mother could have,' Edith croaked. 'I couldn't bear to lose him, not after my Herbert. Where would we live if anything happened to him? We'd lose the cottage.'

'None of this makes any sense. Are they dead or not? The papers are blaming Lord Kitchener and Churchill for misleading us,' declared Winnie. 'How could they not know where the Norfolks are?'

Beatrice concealed her own fears, but deep inside she was terrified. 'We mustn't think the worst. The report says "missing". That means they could still be alive. Maybe they have been wounded and are in hospital somewhere. I'll ask Father if he can find out anything.'

Winnie nodded gratefully at Beatrice. 'All we can do now is hope and pray for their safe return. We must pray for Captain Beck and hope he is still alive.'

Chapter 9

'All I know is that she flew out the door without so much as a by-your-leave. I've no idea why,' Betty lied, biting her lip, her cheeks flushed. 'I was planning on making a nice steak and kidney pie for lunch, but with Master Leslie here keeping me on my toes after changing the sheets, the time flew by. You'll have to make do with cold cuts. I've only got one pair of hands, you know.'

Betty slumped suddenly, reaching out to the table for support and Jessie rushed to her aid.

'Am I all right, you ask?' bleated Betty, wiping her forehead with the back of her arm, complaining about her age. She pointed to a pile of ironing in the basket that awaited her attention and paused to catch her breath.

'Why don't you have a rest for a while and I'll give Maria another hour or so to reappear. If she hasn't returned by then, I'll go out and look for her. Look, Leslie is yawning now, bless him. I'll lay him down in his cot while you have a little nap.'

'That's kind of you, Jessie, but there's so much to do. And Mrs Saward will expect all the cooking and washing to be done just the same,' she said before yawning.

'Still, I dare say a quick forty winks won't do any harm.'

By the time Jessie had settled her lively nephew down in his cot, Betty had dozed off in a comfy chair. Her nose twitched and made small snorting sounds.

Jessie could see from the housekeeper's greying hair and lined face that she was not young anymore. She had noticed her holding her back and wincing when she bent down to wash the front doorstep or down on her knees to sweep up. The family knew the time would come when she could no longer continue, but she was regarded as one of the family and they never minded if she needed a rest in the day.

Ada returned home at that moment, brimming with delight as she rushed through the door and found Jessie. 'Oh, she is so lovely. And the most beautiful singer. I could listen to her for hours.'

'Who might you be referring to?' enquired Jessie.

'Why Clara, Clara Griffin, the acclaimed singer from London who will star in our concert. She couldn't do more to help and has even suggested a new song she will perform in public for the very first time and has ordered the score and music sheets for us from her supplier in London. Isn't that kind of her?'

'It is indeed,' muttered Betty, stirring after her nap. 'And in case you're wondering, Maria has rushed off and your little lad is snoozing away.'

'My goodness, how time has flown. It's now four o'clock,' Jessie exclaimed. Noticing that Maria hadn't returned, she offered to go out in search of her.

'Just be sure you come back with your shoes on your feet,' Betty called as she left.

Jessie stepped out briskly along the path in the direction of the church. She paused, wondering if Maria might have sought sanctuary there.

She unlatched the gate and was walking along the church path when she noticed a shadowy figure around the corner, its silhouette beamed onto the path as if it had been stencilled there. It appeared to be a man's figure.

Curious to see who it was, Jessie picked up her skirt and walked softly round to the side of the church where she saw a man crouched in front of a tombstone arranging a spray of fresh lilies and roses. Her body tensed as she recognised the figure. It was Jack. Her cheeks flushed as she recalled her rushed departure from the station yesterday. Part of her wanted to flee, but her legs were rooted to the spot.

Jessie lowered her gaze, embarrassed to have interrupted him. 'I'm so very sorry. I didn't mean to intrude on your privacy . . .'

The man's face looked surprised. He drew in a sharp breath, a generous smile curving across his lips. 'Jessie?'

She nodded, lifting her head and feeling her cheeks burn. 'Jack!'

Her eyes were fixed on his lips so she could be sure of the words he spoke. 'What brings you here, Jessie?'

'I'm so sorry, Jack, I had no idea it was you. I'm looking for someone and saw a shadow around the corner . . .'

Jessie's words stuck in her throat. Once again, she felt foolish in his presence. She couldn't take her eyes off Jack's gentle face and the tenderness in his eyes. She felt giddy, her legs buckling under her and butterflies fluttered in her stomach. Just being close to Jack made her lose her senses. Her heart beat fast and a warm tingling sensation spread across the back of her neck and face.

'No, Jessie, it's me who should apologise for startling you. You find me here remembering on the anniversary of my dear wife Amy's death, and our infant son, Edwin.'

Jessie lowered her eyes again, her voice faltering. 'I'm so sorry to have intruded on your private moment of sorrowful reflection. Please excuse me, Jack, I'll leave you to continue with your contemplation.'

She was afraid of making herself look a fool again, or for Jack to see her burning cheeks. She took a few steps forward to walk around him, but Jack's arm touched her shoulders as she passed by, forcing her to stop. She felt an electrifying sensation ripple throughout her body at his touch and her mouth dried up.

'I just want to say, I'm sorry we didn't get the chance to speak at the station. I was with His Majesty and accompanying Clara Griffin, a dear friend of Hettie and Hubert's, who is staying with her friends in Sandringham. She is the star act at Ada's concert and has the most angelic voice, I gather she is most sought after. I offered to accompany her to Wolferton and the King insisted she travel with us in the royal train when he heard of her plans. He is a great admirer of her music.'

Jessie's jaw dropped. 'You mean the lady you were with yesterday was Clara Griffin? *The* Clara Griffin, who is singing at Ada's concert! I had no idea she was friends with the Harringtons. I thought you and she might be . . .'

'You thought we might be companions? Romantic companions?'

Jessie averted her eyes and nodded, feeling foolish. Her pulse began to soar as she realised she had jumped to the wrong conclusion. 'She is so beautiful, I could understand it if . . .'

Jack gazed at her, his lips smiling. 'Clara is beautiful, it is true, and she does have many admirers, but I am not one of them in that sense. Her heart has already been taken. She is a delightful and accomplished musical artiste who is very popular with the King and in great demand in London. She will travel anywhere to support people in raising funds for our troops, and jumped at the chance to sing at the concert Ada is arranging.'

Jessie felt the colour draining from her face and wished the ground would open up and swallow her. Despite feeling elated at Jack's reassurances, she stood awkwardly, shifting from foot to foot. 'Will you be there, Jack, at the concert?'

'I'm afraid not. The King and I leave tomorrow. I hardly ever stay in a place for a day or two before moving on, that's how it is these days, until the war is over.'

Jessie turned her head away, a huge wave of disappointment sweeping through her body. She gasped and shivered in excitement as Jack hesitated and then gently took hold of her chin and turned her face towards his. Her heart raced as she gazed directly into his dancing eyes, watching his lips speak to her. 'There is something I would like to say before I go, Jessie.'

Her body tingled at his light touch, feeling his breath as he spoke. 'What is it, Jack?'

He paused, taking a breath and looking deep into her blue eyes. 'Please forgive me if I am too bold, but time is not on our side with this war. What I would like to ask, if it isn't presumptuous, is if I could cherish hopes of seeing you when I return.'

'Well, yes. I will be seeing you at the royal retiring rooms on another day, I'm sure.'

'No, Jessie. That's not what I meant.' Jack paused for a moment, his eyes holding her face steadily in his gaze. 'I wondered if I would be able to see you again as more than a friend.'

Jack's cheeks were flushed when he finished speaking, searching Jessie's countenance for a response.

A smile spread across her face and her heart pounded so loudly she thought he would hear it. 'Did I hear you correctly, Jack? Are you saying you would like us to walk out together? You are asking me to wait for you until after the war?'

Jack blushed, standing back. 'I apologise. I should never have asked. I can see I have offended you and made a presumption that may not have been welcomed by you.'

Jessie's eyes shone, and the words spilled out. 'Oh no, Jack. You haven't offended me. My answer is yes. Of course I will wait for you. I had no inkling you shared my feelings!'

Taking both of her hands and clasping them in his, Jack declared, 'My dearest Jessie, you have made me the happiest man. I have so longed for this moment, for us to be alone so I could share my innermost feelings with you. I haven't stopped thinking about you since we spoke during my last visit. Whenever I see you at the station or out walking I've wanted to approach you, but haven't known what to say.'

Jessie's eyes widened. 'Oh, Jack. You don't know how much it means to me to hear you say those words. Such sweet words.'

Jack's eyes glowed with love and sincerity. 'And it gives me great joy to know you share the same feelings for me. I'm so glad we had this chance encounter, Jessie, my dearest. I was hoping our paths would cross, for us to have time alone. I wasn't sure you returned my feelings, but now I shall cherish the memory of this moment when I leave.'

Jack gently pulled Jessie towards him and embraced her, enveloping her tightly in his arms. She enjoyed the warmth of his strong chest pressing against her body, feeling it rise up and down, as if they were joined together.

She looked up at him. 'Oh, Jack. When shall we see each other again?'

He gently caressed her soft hair, his finger moving slowly down to her arm. 'I cannot say for sure. When I am with the King I do not know where I will be or when I can return to Sandringham. But wherever we are, I shall see your lovely face in my mind every day, sweet Jessie. I promise to write when I get the chance.'

He lifted her milky delicate hands to his lips and kissed them gently, his slate-grey eyes narrowing as his gaze fixed upon her pale complexion. Jessie allowed his lips to linger on her silky skin, enjoying the electrifying sensation that burnt through her. She knew in an instant that she never wanted another man's lips to touch her. She longed for him to press his lips against hers. She knew one day she would give herself to him that way.

She felt her heart pounding as she slowly withdrew a hand, holding it close to her cheek, her eyes lowered and head slightly tilted to one side in a show of modesty. She suddenly felt overcome by embarrassment, wondering if she had been too forward.

Jack looked concerned. 'I apologise if I have detained you from your intended purpose, but I couldn't let this chance with you pass today.'

Jessie shook her head. 'There is no need to apologise. But yes, I am passing through here for a reason.' She blurted out everything about Maria and her search for her.

'I've not seen a girl of that description around here. Poor Jessie, it certainly sounds like you have your hands full at the moment.'

'I'm sure I will find her very soon. I wish you and His Majesty Godspeed, my dear Jack.' She could see only goodness facing her and impulsively pecked him lightly on his cheek. She blushed at her forwardness and turned to leave.

Jack tilted her lips towards his and they pressed together in a soft lingering kiss.

When she pulled herself away, flushed with burning desire, Jack reassured her. 'I have the highest regard for you, my beloved Jessie. I ask that you to remember that at all times.'

'Oh, dear Jack, my love, how could I ever doubt that?' she murmured as she bade him farewell.

'I shall leave tomorrow with a lighter heart, knowing I have your affections to return to,' Jack vowed. 'I pray I will return with Godspeed.'

After Jack had vanished from her sight, she repeated his words over in her mind, calling the exhilaration she had felt when he had called her his 'beloved'. Her heart was singing. Jessie could think of nothing else as she made her way to the back of the church and followed a path until it reached the wood.

She forced her thoughts to return to her search for Maria. Her instincts told her to retrace her steps to where she had rested and Maria had taken her shoes. Distracted by the fluttery feeling inside her and Jack's words of endearment ringing in her ears, she almost missed the path she needed.

Within a few minutes, she was clambering along the track, inhaling the aroma of sweet pine from the trees. She found the stony path, the one she had taken the day before, stopping at a high clearing to admire the clear view that stretched to the North Norfolk coast where she loved scrambling on the beach for cockles, which they then feasted on. Betty would boil them up with a cup of water and add a splash of white vinegar, cracking open the shells so they could scoop out the orange cockle flesh. She found the shells too pretty to throw away and used them as decorative features in a corner of the garden at home.

Jessie barely paused for breath, feeling intoxicated and giddy with Jack's words spinning around her head. She longed to return home quickly to share her good news with Ada and Beatrice and hoped her parents would be thrilled for her.

She stood by the familiar ancient oak tree where the sisters' initials were carved into the bark and looked around her. Among the spruces in front of her for as far as the eye could see, there was no sign of Maria. She cupped her hands to her mouth and called out Maria's name. There was a faint echo that she picked up. She walked around the tree and called out again in her loudest voice.

A tap on her shoulder made her jump and she spun around, gripping her chest with relief when she saw Maria standing in front of her.

'Maria, it's you. What are you doing here? Everyone's worried about you.'

'I didn't mean to alarm yer, but I seem to cause nothing but trouble. I shouldn't 'ave run off like that when you've all been so kind to me. I just needed to be alone for a while to think. And I love it up here in the woods. It's peaceful and full of mystery.'

'I like it up here too, it's where I come if I need time on my own to think. It's such a special place with wonderful woodland sounds and smells. There was no need to run off without telling anyone though.'

Maria looked shamefaced. 'The past, it 'as a way of catching up with yer. I realised that today. Ma always says so and it's true. There's things I can't escape from, bad things. I try me best to fit in, but I ain't sure I'm cut out to talk posh.'

'If you wish to, you can improve yourself, I'll help you. We all will. You must not let your past worry you. You have a new life here now. You just need time to settle in,' Jessie reassured her.

'Maybe yer right, I mean *you* are right. Very well, I'll try my best to speak proper again, if you're sure *you* haven't given up on me.'

'Of course we haven't. We already share something in common, being up here in the woods close to nature.'

'There's something very special about being 'ere, I mean *here*, that's magical. I like the quietness and the shadows from the trees. And down there I came across the most lovely house – over there.'

Maria pointed towards the Folly and Jessie told her the story of Prince Eddy, the son of the Dowager Queen Alexandra.

'Prince Eddy would have been our king, but died of pneumonia, just as he'd become betrothed to Princess Mary, who after he died married his brother, our present King George, and is now our Queen Mary.'

'That's so sad. But it's a queer thing too! Fancy marrying your brother's intended after he kicks the bucket.

I thought our family was a funny lot!' Maria chortled. 'There's me and your pa, we're half-siblings with a thirty-eight-year age difference. How strange is that!'

'It certainly is, especially when you consider that makes me your niece, of sorts!' Jessie grinned. 'Imagine if Magnolia knew, she'd be beside herself.'

They both threw back their heads and roared, a side-aching belly laugh. 'You certainly have a funny way of putting things, Maria. We should be going home now. Everyone will be wondering where we are.'

Maria bit her lip, her eyes downcast. 'I told Betty I weren't going back. I don't think she likes me.'

Jessie reassured her otherwise, 'Put those daft notions out of your head. Of course Betty likes you, if you give her half a chance. And you have me on your side. We are Sawards, remember, and we stick together.'

Chapter 10

'This letter came for you. I just found it on the front mat.'

Maria had just returned from the woods and blurted out a hasty apology for her disappearance, which was accepted, much to her relief. She took the letter from Sarah's hand. Puzzled, she said, 'But nobody knows I'm here, except Ma. And it's not her writing.'

The atmosphere in the room was heavy and Maria could sense that something was very wrong. She felt nervous, thinking she might be the cause, but quickly realised it was because of something much worse and placed the letter in her pocket for later.

Betty's plump arms were wrapped around Beatrice's shoulders. Her eyes were red from weeping. Ada sat in the winged armchair rocking Leslie in her arms to quieten his cries. Sarah returned to the table, a half-empty cup of tea in front of her, her head in her hands.

The front page of the local newspaper was laid open on the table and Maria shuddered as she read the headline, the Sandringham company disappeared. Harry entered the room and Beatrice rushed over to him.

'Oh, Father, what if they are all dead? I tried to be brave for Edith, but a part of me thinks, what if they never come back? What if they're dead?'

Harry's eyes drooped, his jaw clenched and he choked on his words. 'I can't believe it. Not our Frank, and all our boys from the Sandringham Estate. I wonder if Frank's wife has any other news, or anyone at the House. Someone must know what's going on.'

Maria walked over to Ada, vowing from now on to speak less coarse. 'Here, I'll take the little 'un for a while if you want to spend time with your sisters. I know this is hard for you too, with your Alfie away in France.'

Maria shot a glance at Betty, to see if she could gauge from her expression if she had told Ada about the earlier incident, but the housekeeper avoided meeting her gaze, her lips pursed. Ada acted as normal and gladly handed over Leslie to Maria, who sighed with grateful relief, cooing and smiling as she held him in his arms. She guessed the housekeeper hadn't told Ada anything and mouthed 'Thank you' to her under her breath. Betty shook her head. She had mulled over in her mind the best course of action and didn't feel this was the right time to add to the family's woes, promising herself to keep a closer watch on Maria.

∞

Usually, the family would have ravenously devoured the cold cut ham that Betty had baked and served for dinner, followed by her milky rice pudding, but nobody had an appetite that evening. Ada was content for Maria to bathe Leslie and prepare him for bed.

The family talked and talked about the war until Ada pulled herself away to the front parlour, her head spinning and her stomach churning. She tried diverting her attention to cross-stitching, threading her needle with colourful strands to stitch a thatched cottage and the surrounding garden, but gave up in despair. A brooding silence filled the air.

Her parents joined her, her mother taking up her cross-stitching sampler while Harry reread the paper.

Ada broke the silence. 'The concert couldn't be happening at a better time. I hope it brings people together and lifts their spirits a little – if that's even possible.'

'It will be an honour to have our Queen Mary and Dowager Queen with us too,' Sarah commented. 'The concert will unite us all. You are right, Ada, it couldn't have come at a better time.'

Maria entered the room and Ada offered to teach her how to cross stitch, but Maria appeared distracted, staring out of the front bay window. 'Perhaps another time,' she demurred.

Maria's hands fidgeted with the collar of her dress and, pushing her hand down the front of it, she brought out a silver chain, her tense expression softening to a look of tenderness as she held it close to her face.

'Is that a locket?' Ada enquired. She walked towards Maria. 'Whose pictures do you have in it? May I see it? I have one with my beloved Alfie's photograph in it and

Beatrice wears one for her Sam,' she said as she took out her own locket and held it towards Maria.

Maria gazed at Alfie's smiling face. 'Oh, he's so handsome. What a fine gent. But he doesn't have a moustache here, like in your wedding photo?' she queried, pointing to the framed picture of her nuptials on the mahogany chiffonier.

Ada stifled a giggle. 'Ah, that's because I was never fond of it. So, one night, when he was asleep, I snipped it off! I asked him to have a new photo showing his clean, handsome face before he left. I think he looks so much better without it. So, Maria, come on, tell us. Do you have a sweetheart?'

'Oh no, it's nothing like that,' stuttered Maria awkwardly, her face reddening as she clasped her locket shut and tucked it under her blouse.

Ada raised an eyebrow and shrugged, but didn't press Maria, sensing her discomfort on the subject.

'I think I'd like to go upstairs, if I can be excused,' said Maria. 'I'm rather weary.'

Once she had made her way upstairs to the attic room, Maria recalled the letter and fished it out of her pocket. On the front of the envelope in large spindly letters was written 'Maria Saward, care of Mr Harry Saward, Station Master, Wolferton, Norfolk'.

'Well that certainly is strange,' she muttered, feeling uneasy again. Who would possibly be writing to her care of the station master? No one knew she was here, apart from her mother. And it certainly wasn't her hand.

Maria's hands trembled and she rocked slightly as she opened the envelope and read the letter. There was just one line on the page, '*Don't think you can hide from me. I'll be watching you.*'

Her hand flew to her mouth and she dropped the paper as if it were a red-hot poker. She swayed, staggering to the edge of the bed, her breath coming fast. Her muscles tightened and she gripped the bedcover.

Even though the note hadn't been signed, only one person could have sent it. The thought filled her with dread. 'He knows where I am. He knows I'm staying with the Sawards. Oh what am I to do? I can't let him ruin my life – not again.'

She forced herself up, stumbling across to the window and peered out across the front of the house, casting her eyes in every direction.

'What if he's watching me now? Has he come here to blackmail me?'

A thought occurred to her. Maybe she hadn't imagined someone following her earlier. Maybe it had been him.

She reeled as nausea filled her body and she felt her fingers and toes tingling. She gazed around the room, wondering if this would be her last night here. Should she leave tomorrow now that he knew where she was?

She remembered the letter and resolved. 'I'm not running off like a criminal. I'm not afraid of anyone. I'm a Saward and I belong here.'

Although the room was stuffy and airless, she was grateful to have a roof over head in such a fine house.

She undressed, carefully folding the dress that had been loaned to her and put it in a tin chest at the bottom of the bed. She rubbed the back of her neck. She poured cold water from the jug into the matching bowl and splashed it over her warm skin, enjoying the cooling sensation.

She slipped into her white cotton nightgown and brushed her hair. Sitting up on her bed, she felt for her locket again and unclasped it, chiding herself for her carelessness in bringing it out in front of Ada. Her heart melted as she gazed lovingly at the innocent face looking up at her, the dimples on the baby's cheeks and his sparkling blue eyes. She tenderly brushed her lips on the picture and kissed it gently, whispering a loving endearment under her breath before clasping the locket shut and tucking it out of sight.

She lay on the firm mattress and pulled the sheet up to her chin. Although her tired body was ready for sleep, her exhausted mind remained active, reliving the terrible news of the Sandringham Company and the threatening letter.

When her eyes finally closed and she drifted off, she slept fitfully. Her vivid dreams showed a little boy in danger. She stood close to him and held out her arm, but he couldn't reach her and she was rooted to the spot. She could only look on helpless, paralysed with fear and sensing danger. The sound of a piercing scream, followed by blackness, confusion and the cries of people running towards her, made her cry out.

She awoke and bolted upright, her eyes wide open. Her face was beaded with sweat and her body shook. She racked her brain, trying to make sense of the dream, and vowed to guard Leslie closely with her life, fearing her nightmare might be a terrible foreboding.

∾

The next morning the family commented on the dark shadows under Maria's sunken eyes, which resembled deep muddy puddles. Ada looked washed out too and stifled a yawn.

Sarah enquired about Maria's letter from the day before, but Maria was relieved when Beatrice interrupted her by addressing Jessie. 'Have you told them yet about Jack? It will be good for them to hear some uplifting news.'

Sarah raised an eyebrow at the two sisters, their heads turning to Jessie. 'I was going to tell you, all in good time, but I wasn't sure if this was the right moment, after everything that's happened.'

'I'm in the dark here. What are you talking about, Jessie?' her mother asked.

'It's Jack, I bumped into him quite by chance yesterday, and . . .'

'Oh yes?' Ada asked, raising an eyebrow, her lip curving slightly.

'I was walking through the churchyard and saw Jack there, tending to his wife's grave. I stopped and we talked for a bit. I knew for sure then that I have a genuine fondness for him, and, I'm so happy to say he returns my affections.'

Jessie's eyes shone and she turned to her sister. 'Oh, Ada, I felt weak and giddy just from being close to him. Is that how love makes you feel? Jack is the kindest, most gentle, most patient and understanding of any man I have met. He put me at my ease and we talked awhile. I could barely believe my ears when he . . .' Jessie paused, her eyes bright.

'When what? What happened next?' urged Ada.

'He asked me to be his sweetheart,' Jessie blurted.

Ada gasped with delight. 'That's wonderful news, Jessie. I'm so pleased for you. Jack is a wonderful man.'

'Ah, well, you might think I don't know much about affairs of the heart, but I'm not blind,' retorted Sarah, a smile curling on her lip. 'This comes as no surprise to me. His wife's death was a big shock, but I've long thought Jack had a sweet spot for you. I saw the way he looked at you when he was with the King.'

'I can never take his wife's place, but there is a bond between us, I can feel it. I promised to wait for him, till after the war. I hope to catch sight of him later at the station as he leaves today with the King, though we may not have a chance to be alone.'

'Perhaps you should go now. I'll just change into my shoes and come too.' Sarah smiled.

'Thank you, Mother. I only want a minute alone with Jack. I don't know when we will meet again.'

Jessie rushed out quickly before her mother could change her mind. Her father was already at the station and Beatrice had left too. A moment later Sarah bade farewell to Ada and Maria. Ada watched Maria tend to Leslie in his wooden highchair as he beamed at her.

'He certainly has his father's charm this morning,' commented Ada.

Leslie reached up with his arm and caught hold of the chain around Maria's neck that had slipped out from underneath her blouse. He held on to it tightly, chuckling as if they were playing a game. Maria's expression darkened as she yanked it from his grip and concealed it under her sleeve. Leslie bawled and kicked out his arms and legs, turning away from Maria's outstretched arms.

'What's got into you, Maria? You're upsetting him,' Ada asked incredulously.

Maria's chest began to heave with small sobs that she was no longer able to contain and she burst into tears. Ada stared at her, shaking her head. 'I don't understand you, Maria. I saw you grab that locket from Leslie. And you wouldn't show me last night. Why don't you want us to see it? What are you hiding from us?'

Maria's voice wobbled. 'I want to tell you, but don't know how. I wish I could, 'cause it's tearing me apart.'

'What is it, Maria? What's caused you so much distress?'

Maria sniffled. 'If I tell you, please don't judge me too harshly.'

Ada reached out for Maria's hand. 'Of course I won't. There's only the two of us here, and Betty won't be back for a while, so you can speak freely, and in confidence.'

'Oh, Ada, you are the kindest person I have met. From the first moment I met you, you've been so good to me. You wouldn't understand the bad things that have happened to me. I ain't had an easy life, and I don't seek trouble, but somehow it finds me.'

Maria gulped, her moist eyes narrowing.

'What do you mean *bad things have happened to you*? What kind of trouble *finds you*? I don't understand.'

Maria twisted her hands in front of her, her voice unsteady, 'I wish I could say, but it ain't easy. I ain't told anyone before.'

'But, Maria, if you are in any sort of trouble, we will help you,' Ada said softly, placing an arm around her shoulder.

Maria turned her face away. 'I carry a big secret. It's a burden and too big to keep to myself. I only hope you won't think the worst of me for knowing, that you won't disown me.'

'You're a Saward, Maria, you must always remember that. We stick together through thick and thin. Please trust me, tell me everything while we are alone. I promise you will feel better if you unburden yourself.'

Maria followed Ada to the kitchen table, while Leslie played happily on the floor. Ada gently took her hands in hers.

'Very well. I'll tell you going back to how Ma and Pa met,' Maria said, taking a deep breath. 'Ma used to work at the Fighting Cock. It was a rowdy pub near the railway and popular with thirsty railway workers. Pa used to go there sometimes, she could see he wasn't like the others, he was respectful and kept himself to himself. When Pa's first wife, Mary, became poorly and the end of her life was close, Ma saw that he struggled and she offered to help out and nurse her. She cooked broths and kept the house nice.

'Pa was heartbroken when Mary died. I was told that she was such a sweet lady, but then Pa began courting Ma. He was lonely, I guess, and wanted someone to care for him and he offered a fine home near the station. As you can imagine, none of his family approved of Ma, being as she was so much younger than him – by around forty years, with Pa being seventy and Ma only twenty-eight.'

Maria paused as she noticed Ada's eyes widen as she absorbed everything she heard. She continued. 'I know. I can see why the family wasn't happy about it. Ma told me Willie was a lonely man and asked her to stay on as his housekeeper. He missed having a woman around the place, and they got on well enough. She had a roof over her head and the security she needed.'

'And then?'

'Ma got in the family way with me and then Freddie and Archie were born later. They are lovely boys; they were the apple of his eye. Them being born set tongues wagging, saying he was too old for them to be his. But they were, Ma swore on all our lives that she hadn't been with another man.

'People couldn't believe he still had it in him, after fathering ten children with Mary. Ma says none of Pa's children wanted to see him again after he wed my ma, and your ma made this clear in no uncertain terms as they have royal connections due to your pa being the royal station master. But Pa was always so proud of Harry and talked of him every day.

'Pa promised that he would never make any demands on him, except for one. He asked Harry to promise to care for us if we ever became desperate after he'd passed on. Of course, Harry agreed, even knowing how important it was for him to maintain dignity and not bring shame on the family 'cause of connections to royalty.

'Money was tight after Pa retired and we moved into a tiny cottage right next to the tracks that the railway company said we could use for a while. The whole place shook when trains passed by and it were covered in filthy smoke. I swear there was one engine driver who did his best to smoke us out.'

'Maria, that sounds unbearable. I wish you had come to us for help earlier.'

'We have our pride, you know. Pa loved spending the afternoon in the garden, smoking his pipe, watching the trains go by, waving to his old pals who tooted the horn to him as they drove past. In the evenings Pa would go to the Fighting Cock and knock back a pint or two and play cards, talking about the old days on the line.'

Maria paused again for breath, carrying on when Ada gave her the nod. 'Then Pa died and we were shunned by everyone. Soon all the money were gone and we were told we had to move out of the cottage. Ma was beside herself with worry and didn't know which way to turn. She heard a barmaid was needed at the Fighting Cock and went back there.

'Every penny Ma earned went on keeping that roof over our heads. I wanted to help out and Ma asked the landlord if he needed another pair of hands. He said he would find me work during busy times. It never occurred to us to ask Harry for help then. We thought we would manage, but we were wrong.'

Maria closed her eyes for a few moments and took a deep breath.

'In your own time, dear Maria. I understand how upsetting it must be for you to relive these painful memories,' said Ada gently.

'It is hard, but I'll carry on now I've started. I didn't want to go to work in the pub. I had just turned fifteen and wanted to train as a dressmaker. I'm good with my hands; can turn any material into a pair of curtains or a skirt. Ma said we couldn't afford to wait for an apprenticeship, she said I should be grateful for this chance and she needed the money now, that my time would come later.

'I didn't have any choice. I could see how tired Ma was, always bending forward and holding her back with her hand. She seemed to turn into an old woman overnight. It was then she packed Freddie and Archie off to London to stay with Uncle Gus, promising to send what she could for their keep.'

'I'm sure she did it for the right reasons. When did you last see your brothers?' asked Ada.

'Not for nearly a year now, and I do fret for them, 'cause Uncle Gus is a horrible man who thinks only of himself. I don't know what money Ma sends him now, if she is able to, and if her money has run dry I fret that he is taking this out on the poor helpless boys.'

'Oh, Maria, we can't allow that to happen. I'll speak to my father. I'm sure we can arrange for you to see them or get news of how they are.'

Maria choked, a tear pricking the corner of her eye. 'That would mean the world to me. I thank you from the bottom of my heart for your kindness.'

'Well, we must do something. What if they are in danger of being bombed? London is a target.'

'I worry about that every day. And I will go there, at the first opportunity. But I have other big pressing worries that weigh me down.'

'There's more?' queried Ada, raising her eyebrows and holding her throat. 'What more can there be?'

Maria threw herself in Ada's arms, her eyes filling with tears.

'You poor thing, you've suffered so much. But no more, I promise you that. You are safe here with us.'

Chapter 11

It took considerable gentle coaxing from Ada to persuade Maria to continue. Her sobs cut through to Ada as she tried to imagine what terrible trauma this poor girl had experienced.

After dabbing her eyes dry, Maria stepped back and unfastened the top of her blouse. Her thin fingers fumbled with her locket while Ada's eyes never left her face. 'In your own time, Maria. Please don't feel you have to say more if it is too painful for you. Though Ma always says it's better to share your troubles if you can.'

After breathing in deeply and summoning up some courage, Maria raised her head, her voice steadying. 'I want to unburden myself, but I ain't sure how you will take it. It ain't for fair hearing really. I keep forgetting to say, *it's not*, instead of *ain't*.'

Ada rested her hand on Maria's arm. 'You can tell me anything. And don't worry about saying "ain't", I really don't mind, it takes time, that's all. In fact, it's marvellous how quickly you've mastered speaking "proper", as you call it.'

At first Maria's words stuck in her throat, but with Ada's patience and gentle coaxing she began again, watching Ada's eyes widen with incredulity as her words tumbled out.

'The trouble started when this new landlord took over the pub by the name of Walter Jugg. A fouler man on this earth is impossible to imagine. He was Satan in disguise.' She shuddered, screwing up her eyes and wrapping her arms around her shoulders. 'I took an instant dislike to him, with his smelly breath and sweaty face, which was always too close to me for comfort. He would spit on his thick grubby paws every time he handled money and smirk when I gave him a look to show how disgusting I thought he was. That only made him laugh, and I would scuttle off as far away from him as possible.

'His face, you never seen anything like it, Ada. It was covered in yellow scabs from smallpox and he only had four teeth in his mouth; he bragged how they had been knocked out in a boxing tournament – that he almost killed the other fella who never walked again. I shiver at the thought of him.'

Maria's voice quietened and Ada moved closer so as not to miss a word. 'Ma warned me not to be on my own with Walter. She'd given him the benefit of the doubt at first, but not for long, seeing how wild he became after he had had a few drinks.

'She soon regretted going back to work there and getting me a job. She did her best to stand up to him, but was scared of making too much fuss and losing the work. She needed every farthing she could get. I once saw Walter pin her against the wall in the yard and force his full weight against her. I picked up a shovel to belt him, but she shot me a pleading look warning me against doing anything, so I dropped it.

'Walter heard it fall to the ground. He turned around and grabbed me by the throat, staring right into my face. Ma threw her arms around his neck to pull him off me, but he just pushed her away. I tell you I thought I was a goner then. When he released his grip around my neck I crumpled to the ground, gasping for breath. He stood there laughing, saying he liked a girl with a bit of fire. I pleaded with Ma for us to leave our jobs at the pub, but she begged me to give him one more chance, and swore that we would leave straightaway if anything like that happened again.'

'And did it?' asked Ada, taking hold of Maria's hand and clasping in between hers.

Maria nodded, her stomach in knots. Her eyes were misty with tears. Small sobs travelled up her throat. She bit her lip, forcing out the words.

'The next day Ma had a terrible fever. She was too weak to stand and her skin was burning. She was soaked through with sweat and pleaded with me not to go to the Fighting Cock alone, but I thought I could stand up to Walter, having seen him at his worst. I knew we needed the money for Freddie and Archie and I couldn't let Ma worry more than she already was.

'I didn't know it was Walter's birthday that day. He had turned sixty and was blind drunk, falling about all over the place on both sides of the bar when I arrived at six o'clock. He was laughing loudly, throwing back his head, smacking his thighs and making smutty jibes not fit for ladies' ears. He kept topping his tankard up and belching when he couldn't get the ale down quick enough. It were disgusting!'

Maria shuddered, shaking her shoulders. Ada gulped, 'I don't know how you could face such a monster again.'

'I had no choice. I kept my eyes down and avoided Walter as much as possible. I cleared the tables and washed up, keeping an eye out for him all the time.'

Suddenly, Maria paused, sensing they were no longer alone. They had been so engrossed that they hadn't heard the front door opening and the footsteps coming down the hallway and into the kitchen.

'The wicked scoundrel. Just tell me where he is. I'll see to that man!'

Harry's face was purple with rage, his mouth quivering and his moustache slanting down the side of his face. He slammed his fist down hard on the table. 'He will not get away with his despicable behaviour. Where can I find this loathsome villain?'

'Father, please, you are scaring Maria,' cautioned Ada. 'And now Leslie is bawling.'

She bent down and scooped Leslie off the floor, wiping away his tears and stroking his fair skin.

'Maria, why didn't you tell us this before?' asked the station master.

Maria became agitated. 'How could I? You don't know what he's like. It's best you just leave matters alone. I'm scared of what he might do.'

'He will not get away with such abominable behaviour against my family. You have no need to be afraid while you are under our roof,' he thundered.

'I know you mean well, Mr Saward, but please. I don't want to stir anything up and bring you trouble.'

'I've heard enough to know that scoundrel has harmed my family. And I intend to see him punished for it.'

Maria's eyes filled with tears. 'Please, I beg you, Mr Saward. You don't know what he's capable of. You would never get the better of a man like Walter Jugg. Why, he almost killed a man once!'

'I'm not afraid of him. All the more reason to track him down and hand him over to the police. I had no idea your mother had fallen on such hard times. She should have told me. I would have helped.'

'But would you have helped? It's all well and good for you to say that now. Mrs Saward didn't want anything to do with us, if you remember. My ma is a proud woman and felt guilty for bringing me here after the promise she made not to do anything that would bring shame on you, 'cos of your job, your connection with royalty and all that.'

Ada intervened, cautioning Maria to calm down. 'Father has offered to help, Maria, we can't change the past. But he can help you now, we all can, if you will let us.'

Harry lowered his voice. 'I can see how upsetting this whole business is for you. I'm thankful I needed to come back home for some paperwork and overheard your conversation.'

Ada turned to Maria. 'I think you said there was more. Are you able to carry on now? Please trust us.'

Harry raised an eyebrow. 'There's more?'

Maria nodded bleakly, feeling she had no choice but to tell them everything. She held her head up. 'Yes, I'm afraid there is.'

Ada took her hand in hers and made encouraging signs.

'It ain't easy for me to speak about this in front of you, Mr Saward, as it's of a delicate nature, but having heard some of my pitiful story, it seems only fair that you hear the rest of it.'

'I want to hear it all,' Harry told her. 'In your own time, of course.'

Maria gripped Ada's hand as she spoke, her breath shallow. 'Very well. As I was saying, it was Walter's birthday and he was more than worse for drink. I tried to keep out of his way, staying in the back room to wash up the tankards. I heard him calling out my name from the front and ignored him as I saw him falling over.

'Then he fell again and pulled himself up, his eyes fixed on me as he staggered towards me, swearing oaths under his breath. I smelt the ale seeping out of his pores – he were belching and knocking into things.

'I was scared rigid. I was about to run away when I felt his grip on my shoulder. I could feel and smell his breath on me. I'll never forget how disgusting it was to the day I die.'

'I'll see that that man gets the punishment he deserves,' cried Harry.

'Shush, Father, can't you see, you're upsetting Maria? Do you want to stop now, Maria? I can see you are upset, and I can understand that,' Ada consoled.

Maria continued through steaming tears. 'No, it's all right. I want to finish now I've started. Walter is not the kind of man you would want to cross. He's built like a bear and smells like a pig. I stood there, unable to move and could barely breathe. I was terrified, remembering how he had nearly strangled the life out of me the day before.

'He put his hand over my mouth so I couldn't cry out. I tried to bite it, but he clipped me round the head and lifted up my skirt with his other hand, telling me to shut up, or else . . .

'He had tried to force himself on me once before, but I gave him a good kicking in his shin and ran off. He told me I owed him for that, and pressed against me so hard I could scarcely breathe.'

'That man is a monster!' roared Harry.

'Yes, that's exactly what he is,' croaked Maria. 'He said if I made a sound he would do the same to my mother, just to show me what he could get away with. The thought of him forcing himself on my poor ma again was too much for me to bear. He hissed into my ear, telling me not to make a fuss, and it would all be over quickly.'

'That's enough. I don't want to hear any more. That man will pay for his disgusting behaviour,' Harry exploded.

'It will be my word against his, that's what he said. Believe me, I tried to scream, but nothing came out. I was afraid of what he would do to Ma.

'I tried to push him away, but I was no match for him. He lifted me over his shoulder and carried me to the coal shed and threw me on the ground. I was screaming and thumping him the hardest I could, but nobody heard.'

'Oh, Maria. My poor Maria,' cried Ada, choking on her anger.

'That man isn't going to get away with this,' thundered Harry, his face puffed out with rage.

He rose and paced around the room, visibly shaken. 'I have to return to the station now, but will give considerable thought to what you have told me. Your poor mother, how is she? If there is anything I can do, please do not hesitate to ask.'

Before he left the room, he turned to Maria. 'By the way, you can call me Harry from now on. You are my stepsister, after all, strange as it might seem with our age difference. No need to keep up the formality.'

Maria's face brightened for a moment. 'That's much appreciated, thank you, Mr Saward, I mean Harry. I were used to calling you Harry before, but I'll continue to refer to your missus as Mrs Saward as I sense that's what she'd like.'

'I think so too,' Harry agreed.

When he left, Maria's face crumpled. Tears shimmered in her eyes, and her upper lip quivered. Ada reassured her, 'You did right to tell us, Maria. Father will see to this. He'll know what to do. You are safe here.'

'Ada, there is something else, of great consequence, only I couldn't say it in front of Harry.'

'More? What do you mean? Don't hold back. Tell me what it is that is causing you so much distress.'

Maria turned her face away, her fingers fumbling with the chain around her neck.

The words stuck in her throat. 'It ain't easy to talk about this, this is the hardest part for me.'

Ada's eyes showed concern. 'What is it? Whatever it is, I can see it weighs heavily on you and you will feel better if you unburden yourself.'

Maria held her stomach as if in pain. She rocked slightly and raised her head, her voice wobbly.'I had a baby. A baby boy, just like your Leslie.'

Ada's jaw dropped to the floor. 'A baby boy? You have a son? But how? And where is he?'

Maria stammered. 'I called him Joey. He was my Joey. Walter put me with child, but the baby died, Ada. It were God's way of punishing me for Walter's wickedness. I only held him for an hour afore he turned blue and went cold like marble. Then the midwife took him away.'

'Maria, it wasn't your fault. I'm so very sorry for the loss of your son,' Ada whimpered, moved to tears.

She held Maria in her arms as the girl's high-pitched pitiful cries filled the air. They were cries of agony from the very pit of her stomach, as tears cascaded down her cheeks.

'I'm scared Ada. I think Walter's here in Wolferton.'

Chapter 12

The royal train stood majestically on the upward platform as railway workers shovelled spades full of chunky coke into its furnace. They were all sweating profusely.

Jessie spotted the train as soon as she left home and walked briskly towards the station, the heels of her shoes clicking along the path. She reached the platform within a couple of minutes and her eyes scanned hordes of families jostling shoulder to shoulder. She recognised most of the faces from Wolferton; local people waiting to travel into King's Lynn on market day on the upside platform. The shocking news about the unknown fate of the Sandringham Company from the day before had shaken them; their dark puffy eyes and sad expressions tugged at Jessie's heart as she heard people asking each other anxiously if they had any news. They shook their heads sadly, some sharing embraces and wiping away tears, and continued on with the day.

Jessie brushed past Eddie, catching him by his shoulder. He was uncharacteristically gloomy too, his head lowered, as he pushed his trolley along the platform.

She paused and turned to face him. 'What time does the royal train leave, Eddie? There's someone with the royal party that I need to speak to before they leave.'

'My apologies, Miss Jessie, I didn't see you. I can't see anything straight at the moment. My head is filled with that news. What's happened to 'em all? All our lads.'

'Oh, Eddie, if only I knew. But not even the King can tell us. When is the next train due?'

'At ten thirty on the dot, that's in only eight minutes. You know how His Majesty doesn't like to be kept waiting, so you'll need to be pretty quick. They're not here yet.'

Jessie's eyebrows furrowed. She thanked Eddie and trotted to the King's retiring room. Sarah had just arrived as well and stood in the middle of the room snorting oaths under her breath. 'He's to blame for all this, the Kaiser. How could he turn against his own cousin like this?'

Without waiting for an answer, she continued uttering profanities against Kaiser Wilhelm, who had frequently alighted at Wolferton Station and been most welcome while visiting his royal relatives in Sandringham.

'I know folk say they could never warm to him. That man has a heart of Satan and one day I hope he will pay for his wickedness, either in this world or the next,' Jessie replied.

She glanced into the mirror and pinned back a couple of loose strands of hair from the side of her face; she wanted to look her best for Jack. She smoothed down her blue dress, wondering how long it would be until he appeared, when she felt a light touch on her shoulder that made her jump.

'Jessie. What a wonderful surprise. I'm so pleased to see you. How are you?' asked the man's voice.

She hadn't heard his footsteps approaching, but the closeness of him next to her made her feel giddy. She saw Sarah discreetly walk out of the room and stand at the doorway.

'Oh, Jack,' she gasped, turning to face him. 'I was hoping to see you before you left. Where's the King?'

Just looking at his kind face, which was filled with tenderness, and the gentle smile that curved his lips, ignited the flickering embers of love that burned inside her.

He took her delicate hand in his. 'He's talking to your father for a moment. I was hoping for a few minutes alone with you too.'

She pressed her body against his chest and melted in his rapturous embrace. He tenderly stroked her cheek, wishing the moment would never end. She knew their time together was brief and gazed up towards his face. 'Oh, Jack, we're all in a terrible state of fear not knowing what's happened to the Sandringham Company. Poor Beatrice is afraid that Sam is dead and Ada is desperate for news from Alfie. When is it all going to end, Jack? What does the King say? I'm so afraid.'

'I wish I could tell you, my dearest Jessie. We are doing everything in our power to find out more. The King has asked at the highest level to be kept informed about Captain Beck and his men from the estate.'

Jack tilted her chin up. 'I can hear footsteps outside. I must go now. I can't say when I will see you again, my darling Jessie, but I want to let you know I meant everything I said yesterday. I wanted to ask; can I still count on your feelings for me?'

'Jack, of course you can, without any shadow of a doubt. I shall wait for you to return. Please come back. Please stay safe.'

Jack's lips curled and his eyes creased. 'I promise I will write when I can, my love, but now, I must go. I can hear His Majesty outside with his private secretary, they are ready to leave now. Farewell, my beloved.'

'Farewell, Jack, my love, take greatest care, wherever you go,' Jessie whispered, her heart pounding.

His gaze never left her face as he tenderly lifted her hands to his lips and kissed them gently, his lips lingering on her pale skin, his deep blue eyes fixed on her adoring gaze. He then swiftly touched his mouth on Jessie's lips, surprising her and taking her breath away. She felt herself become giddy, intoxicated with the passion of their embrace, her cheeks turning scarlet as he pulled away.

A few minutes later, he joined the King's party on the platform, and she watched as they entered their royal carriage. She felt a warm glow inside her tinged with sadness as the guard blew the whistle and she watched the train steam off, leaving a trail of smoke in the sky.

Her mother stood next to her. 'Don't worry about Jack. He's got a good head on his shoulders. He'll be back when he can.'

Jessie nodded, gulping. 'I know that, Mother.'

'Come on, chin up, there's my girl.'

Jessie forced a smile and inhaled a deep breath, stroking the folds of her skirt.

She had begun dead-heading wilting geraniums in the tubs on the platform when she saw a shadow next to her. It was Eddie. He appeared nervous, shuffling from one foot to the other.

Jessie straightened up. 'How are you, Eddie? And your ma?'

'We're both well enough, Miss Jessie, in the circumstances. And you? Did you get to see who you were hoping to meet?'

'I did indeed. It was such a relief too. Is there something on your mind?' she enquired.

Eddie narrowed his eyes, speaking hesitatingly, close enough to Jessie so she could read his lips. 'Aye, there is, but I don't quite know how to say it, Miss Jessie.'

'Well, try me, what's on your mind?'

'That young girl I saw at your house when I dropped off the letter, Maria Saward, I believe she is called. Is she still staying with you?'

'She might be, Eddie. Maria is a distant relative and she is helping Betty around the house and caring for Leslie while Ada's time is taken up organising the concert.'

'Ah, so she's really a Saward then? That's what I heard.'

Eddie's cheeks turned crimson under Jessie's inquisitorial gaze. 'Have you taken a liking to her, Eddie Herring? I do declare you have!'

Eddie shuffled his feet and bashfully affirmed Jessie's question. 'Nothing gets past you, does it, Miss Jessie? Yeah, I admit she caught my eye. I could see she has a bit of spark about her. I hope you don't think I'm too forward, but do you think I have a chance of winning her affections?'

Jessie smiled, reaching out to touch Eddie's arm. 'Why not let her know you have feelings for her? You have to be bold at times like this, what with the war and everything, but I'm afraid I can't speak for Maria's heart; we are just starting to get to know each other.'

'Oh well, Miss Jessie, no harm in hoping,' responded Eddie. 'I must go now, if you'll excuse me. The 10.45 to Lynn is just pulling in and I'm needed elsewhere.'

'We must all keep hope in our hearts, Eddie, and grasp at any chance of happiness we can during these difficult times.'

∽

The day's mailbag was heavier than usual and Beatrice hung on to her handlebars extra tightly to stop her from swaying. She was dressed smartly in her post office uniform which was not flattering – a black shapeless skirt, a plain white buttoned-up blouse and sensible stout black shoes. Her straw boater with a band around the crown completed her summer attire. Magpies soared overhead, sometimes low in front of her, as she swerved to avoid riding into scurrying rabbits that dashed across her path.

Beatrice's first stop was back at the vicarage. It was one of the largest houses in the village, set back from the track and surrounded by woodland and a low carstone wall. She braked sharply in front of the gate, inhaling a lungful of fresh air perfumed with sweet peas that the vicar's wife, Jane, prided herself on growing. The delicate blooms were easily a match in quality with the fragrant pink roses that twisted high up the trellis in Harry's garden at the station masters' house, which had won many plaudits in local garden shows where they often competed against each other.

Beatrice admired Jane for her tireless devotion to the poor, doing her utmost to keep families together and out of the workhouse, and even offering them a night or two under her own roof. Jane looked up from the garden where she was kneeling by one of the flowerbeds. She was a slim lady with delicate features and high cheekbones and Beatrice imagined how lovely she must have looked in her youth; her almond-shaped eyes still had a sparkle and she held herself with an elegant poise.

'Good morning, Mrs Rumbelow. I have a letter for you,' Beatrice called out.

She could see from the envelope that it had been posted by the army post office in France. 'I think it's from Piers,' she added.

Jane leapt up, brushing soil off her skirt, her face beaming as she quickly walked down the path and eagerly grabbed the letter that Beatrice held out.

'I hope Piers is well. It's so lovely for you to hear from him.'

'Oh, Beatrice, I've been praying for news from him. We are stunned after hearing about the terrible news about the Sandringham Company. My husband is out visiting the soldiers' families, he is taking them prayers and words of comfort. I shall be calling later as well. We must all support each other during these terrible dark and uncertain days.'

'Oh yes, we must, and our Queen Alexandra sets a fine example in that respect, always making time for bereaved wives on the estate,' agreed Beatrice. 'I hope that Piers is safe, he is such a lovely young man. I have very fond memories of him.'

Jane barely seemed to hear Beatrice's words as she ripped open the envelope. A few seconds later, she lifted her face from the page she had scanned quickly, her eyes shining. 'I thank the Lord he's still alive, Beatrice, but he says the fighting and conditions are terrible.'

She quoted from the letter. '"We've had a very rough time over this last week. We lost a few men, the stretcher bearers ducking not to get shot in the head. I heard we killed over two thousand of them in one day. They came in on us in masses, but our boys cut a line through them. If they keep coming like that the war won't last for long."'

'He's so brave, they all are,' sighed Beatrice.

'Can you believe this?' Jane continued. 'One of his comrades, Private Perkins, was saved by having a Bible in his left breast pocket when the bullet struck him. He says it was a miracle, it went right through his tunic and Bible, and then it turned off his body. Oh, I just hope and pray Piers has the Bible his father gave him before he left.'

'I'm sure he does, I mean, he would, wouldn't he? Being a vicar's son.'

'He says it breaks his heart when he can't save an injured comrade, and he tells me . . .'

Jane choked back her tears and pointed to the words on the page, speaking falteringly. 'My dear, darling boy, he tells me not to worry about him and that he will be home with Godspeed. He says we must be brave at home and stay strong for each other and to know he constantly thinks of everyone in Wolferton with the fondest memories.'

'Oh, that's so touching,' choked Beatrice, moved by the words of Jane's beloved son.

Jane dabbed her moist eyes with a handkerchief. 'I wish he'd stayed at home, he's such a sensitive soul. But my husband said people would speak badly of him if he didn't go.'

'May I?' asked Beatrice, pointing to the letter, which Jane then handed her to read. Her fingers danced along the lines, which detailed the desperate shortage of medical supplies and the heroism of the brave men Piers treated in water-filled trenches while sniper bullets flew overhead. He had refused to take any leave as medical skills were badly needed. Beatrice choked as she read his final line, urging his family not to worry about him. It was so typical of Piers, just like her Sam.

Jane placed the letter back into the envelope, gulping back sobs, tears of relief that he was still alive. 'There isn't one family in the country who isn't suffering. It's a war for mothers, too, who carry the most terrible burden if their sons don't come home.'

Beatrice bit her lip, choking on her words and sharing Jane's sheer emotional relief. 'That's very true, Mrs Rumbelow. I hope Piers will be home on leave soon, at the very least.'

Beatrice felt huge relief. Piers was alive! He had been a medical student at Cambridge University when war broke out. His mother pleaded with her only beloved child to stay home and join the clergy instead, but Piers was determined to use his medical skill to save the lives of those who fought so bravely for their country.

Beatrice's thoughts turned to Edith, imagining the pain she felt awaiting news from her eldest son. She bade farewell to Jane and continued on her rounds, offering a listening ear to two more mothers after delivering letters from their sons, in one case reading it to the mother who had never been taught to read.

Finally, she headed for Bramble Cottage, wondering how she would find Edith, and how her jangled nerves were coping. As she lifted herself over the saddle and placed her bicycle against the fence, she caught sight of Florence, Sam's younger sister, in the front window peering out. She then flung the front door open and ran down the path, throwing her arms around Beatrice's waist.

Her words gushed out and sounded urgent. Beatrice could see she had been crying, her eyes were red and puffy. 'Oh, Bea, I've been waiting for you. It's Ma, she's in a terrible state. I don't know what to say or do for the best.'

Beatrice stroked the girl's long fair hair, which hung loosely over her shoulders, and wiped her eyes dry.

I know what a nervous disposition your mother has, but as far as we know Sam is still alive. We must remain hopeful until we have more information, Florence. After all, Sam has Ted with him. Do you remember? You gave him to him as company.'

Florence sniffled, a small upward curve on her lips. 'Oh yes, I do remember. I told Sam that Ted would always be there if he was ever in trouble – and he promised they would both come home together.'

'That's right. Let's remember that,' comforted Beatrice, with a faint smile. 'Who would have thought a tortoise would go to war?'

Sam's pet tortoise had been given to him by his father when he was a lad. 'I remember seeing Sam's face when you gave Ted to him as he marched off to war.'

Florence nodded. 'I thought of it at the last moment and put Ted in a biscuit tin with some lettuce and ran with it to the station platform where Sam was waiting for the train and placed it in his hand.'

'I think he was too surprised to say anything,' chuckled Beatrice.

'I said Ted would bring him luck. All his chums laughed and slapped him on the back. I can still see Sam's face as he promised that he and Ted would be back before I could blink.'

'It was a lovely gesture. I'm sure Ted will bring Sam good luck.'

Beatrice looked at the girl's moist eyes, and the innocence that shone from her face. 'I'm always here for you, Florence. If there is anything you, Edith and the twins ever need, you only have to ask.'

Beatrice couldn't help thinking how different Florence was to Maria, even though there was only a year or so in age between them. You could read Florence's open face like a book, while Maria's, on the other hand, illuminated a defiant spirit and strong character but a sense that she was holding something back.

One similarity between both girls, however, was an eagerness to please at home and their deftness with domestic chores as they cheerfully rolled up their sleeves to carry out tasks. They were also both caring towards their mothers and protective towards their brothers.

Beatrice followed Florence into the cottage, wondering how she could lift Edith's dwindling spirits which had sunk to a new low since her last visit. She gasped when she saw her feeble figure, her shoulders slumped, sitting in a winged armchair in the corner of the room, her eyes shut as she rocked to and fro.

'I don't know what to do with Ma. She's been like this ever since that terrible news. I can hardly get a word out of her,' Florence stammered.

'Call for the doctor. I'll stay with her,' Beatrice instructed.

172

Edith remained in a trance-like state, gripping a photograph of Sam close to her chest, her eyes wide open and staring upwards.

'Please Lord, give Edith strength. This war is not going to claim another innocent life.'

Chapter 13

Ben and Roly rushed home grinning from ear to ear. The thirteen-year-old twins had been out hunting for rabbits and held up a brace that Lizzie Piper, a local farmer, had told them they could keep.

Beatrice and Lizzie had been childhood friends. She guessed Lizzie had turned a blind eye to the boys poaching. Beatrice was in awe of Lizzie's courage in taking on the running of Blackbird Farm. It had been left to her when her father dropped dead suddenly in 1913. She thought she could take charge of it, and shrugged off scornful comments from those who thought that, as a woman, she wasn't up to it.

Two years later, she married Wilfred Piper, who ran a smallholding near Hunstanton, but he soon made it clear he only married Lizzie to take charge of her farm, insisting she register it in his name. 'Over my dead body,' she told him.

Beatrice discovered this much later, after seeing the delight on Lizzie's face when Wilfred went off to war. 'I don't care if he never comes back. In fact, I hope he doesn't.'

Lizzie then confided in Beatrice the truth about her marriage, delighting in describing how Wilfred's hopes of avoiding signing up on the grounds of being exempt as a farmer came to nothing after Lizzie told the tribunal that she had a replacement, a farmhand by the name of Sid Bucket, who was medically unfit to sign up due to his wheezy chest.

'She's another Mrs Cresswell,' muttered the chairman of the tribunal, referring to the tenant farmer on the royal estate who had been a thorn in the side of King Edward VII by objecting to damage that resulted from his shooting parties. The outspoken woman farmer fearlessly stood her ground for as long as she could. But Mrs Cresswell could only hold out for so long, eventually unable to pay her rent, producing poor crops and given notice to leave. Beatrice hoped Lizzie, also a tenant farmer on the royal estate, would fare better than her predecessor. She was concerned too as she had heard rumours that Sid Bucket had a fondness for drink and was work-shy, but she kept these concerns to herself.

When the boys entered the room, they looked concerned at the expressions on everyone's faces, and Beatrice hastily explained the situation.

Florence returned with Dr Fletcher and he examined Edith, a grave expression on his face. After he had finished, he spoke to Beatrice and Florence, asking if anything had upset her.

'The war, of course, and the missing men in Gallipoli,' Beatrice mentioned.

'That's very true, but I think there might be something else troubling her,' muttered Florence.

'What would that be?' queried Beatrice, her eyebrows raised.

Florence bit her lip, her voice quavering. 'It's that man at Blackbird Farm, the new manager. He came here yesterday and scared Ma.'

'You mean Sid Bucket?' asked Beatrice, her eyebrows arched.

'He told her he's set his sights on getting Bramble Cottage for his cousin who lives up north and works with racehorses. He said it was as good as promised if Sam doesn't come home, that it's only a matter of time. Poor Ma, she's been in a terrible state ever since,' Florence spluttered, her eyes filling with tears.

'That won't happen, will it?' pleaded Roly.

'Absolutely not,' Beatrice snapped. 'Sid Bucket has no right to say anything of the sort. He is a greedy opportunist striking fear in your hearts and I shall get to the bottom of this.'

'Someone clearly should,' added Dr Fletcher. 'No wonder Edith's nerves are shot to pieces. I've left something to calm her; she needs a good rest. I think a change of scene would be good for her as well, to bring some vigour back. Is there anywhere she could go for a few days? A distraction from the likes of Sid Bucket will improve her delicate disposition. God knows she has enough to worry about without this.'

'Oh no. I don't think Ma would go away. She'd be worried about the house and what Sid said,' croaked Florence.

Beatrice told Edith firmly, 'I think she should go. It's an excellent idea. And don't worry about Sid Bucket. I shall see Lizzie and we will confront him about this.'

After the doctor had left, Beatrice reassured Edith that Sid had no claim to her home and mentioned the doctor's suggestion that she go away for a change of scenery.

'I'm not sure.' She shook her head, twisting her hands in her lap. 'What if Sid bursts in and takes over my home when I'm away? I'll be fretting all the time.'

'Shush, calm yourself, Ma, else you'll make yourself ill again,' soothed Florence, kneeling down at her mother's words and taking hold of her hand.

'I promise you nothing like that will happen. I'll be sure to keep an eye on the house, and if Sid Bucket tries to set foot here, I'll gather what men we have left in Wolferton and boot him out,' Beatrice promised.

Edith thought for a moment. 'Well, perhaps it would do me good. I could spend a few days with my younger sister Joyce in King's Lynn. You could come with me, Florence. You know how Aunt Joyce enjoys your company.'

Florence muttered under her breath. 'More likely she wants to put me to work on her sewing machines.'

She threw a pleading glance towards Beatrice, who then recalled the reason for Florence's lack of enthusiasm; she'd heard that the aunt owned a successful dressmaking business and was a hard taskmistress to her seamstresses, frequently making them work late into the night with poor lighting.

'I'm sure it won't be for long,' Beatrice consoled her. 'I'll come and visit.'

'I know how you feel about your Aunt Joyce,' Edith said. 'And I know you would prefer us to stay with Winnie, but she doesn't have the space for us. We can always arrange a visit as she lives close by. I promise it won't be for long, just a week at the most.'

'We can look after ourselves,' piped up Ben. The twins both had Sam's easy nature and had done their best to step into his shoes and look after their mother when he went to war. They had hearts of gold and, like Sam, had grown up quickly after their father's sudden death and were mature beyond their thirteen years.

'It wouldn't be right to leave you on your own. No, I couldn't do that,' blurted Edith.

Beatrice thought for a moment. 'I'm sure Lizzie at Blackbird Farm could do with some extra help seeing as Wilfred is away. I've been hearing troubling rumours about Sid Bucket too, how he is a lazy good-for-nothing who doesn't turn up some days, and when he does, he isn't fit to work. I don't know how Lizzie manages. I'll have a word with her.'

Ben and Roly nodded eagerly. 'We love it there. And you can be sure we won't let Sid Bucket get the better of us.'

'Well, that could be the answer,' Edith replied hesitatingly. 'If Lizzie doesn't mind, that is.'

'Lizzie will be delighted to have the company and has plenty of room,' Beatrice said enthusiastically. 'The twins are fit and strong and she'll give them their keep in return for their help.'

Florence nodded her approval, and Edith agreed. 'Very well, if you can make suitable arrangements with Mrs Piper I would be most appreciative. I'll write a note to Joyce now asking if Florence and I can visit, and maybe you would be kind enough to post it for me.'

Edith stood up shakily, grabbing hold of Beatrice's arm to steady herself as she did and was led to the table. Florence produced some writing paper and a pen and ink and, in her scrawly handwriting, Edith wrote to Joyce and asked if she could arrive in two days, with her daughter. Florence groaned when she saw that her mother had offered her dressmaking services during their stay.

Once the letter was ready, Florence accompanied Beatrice outside, and they walked side by side along the path.

When they reached Beatrice's bicycle, Florence grabbed hold of her arm, her cheeks flushed. Beatrice reassured her. 'There's no need to worry about Edith. I'm sure she will be fine after a good rest.'

Florence shook her head, her cheeks turning pink. 'No, that's not what's bothering me, though I am cheered to hear it. There is something else. It's of a delicate personal nature.'

Beatrice's eyebrows raised, her face showing concern. Florence didn't have a bad bone in her body and she loved her as her own sister. 'Why, whatever is the matter?'

Florence shifted from one foot to the other, fumbling with her fingers. 'There's someone I like, and . . .'

'I see. Is it someone I know?'

'Well, yes. I wondered . . . do you know if Eddie has a sweetheart?'

Florence remained silent, biting her lip. Her cheeks reddened.

'Ah, I see, you're sweet on him. Am I right?'

Florence blushed, lowering her eyes. 'Do you think he might like me too?'

'Oh, Florence, any boy would be proud to have you on his arm. But don't you think you are too young to be courting? What would your mother say?'

'I'll be sixteen in two months,' she retorted. 'I saw him at the station last week when I came back from King's Lynn with Ma and he was very attentive. He was whistling and I caught his eyes as I passed him and he smiled at me. It made me feel quite giddy and I was struck dumb. I couldn't say a word and now I can't stop thinking of him.'

'Oh yes, that's Eddie. He is very friendly and can be a charmer, but I believe he has a kind heart too.'

Beatrice had seen him wink at female passengers while pushing their luggage, it was just his friendly way. She could see why Florence found Eddie appealing, but could not speak for where his affections lay.

'I'll see what I can find out,' said Beatrice, deciding that was the fairest thing to do. 'But I'm not making any promises.'

The answer seemed to satisfy Florence. As the station master's daughter picked up her bicycle and was getting ready to mount the saddle, her eyes were drawn to some brown paper stuffed into the privet hedge a couple of feet away. Her curiosity roused, she screwed up her eyes and walked towards it. She thrust her hand into the thick of the hedge and pulled out a sheet of screwed-up wrapping paper.

Florence looked baffled. 'What on earth? How did that get there?'

'That's very odd. I'm sure it wasn't there when I arrived, else I would have noticed. It looks like someone has deliberately stuffed it in your hedge. I wonder why.'

Beatrice turned the paper over in her hands. The name Private Fred Topping was written clearly on it. She knew Fred, a likeable eighteen-year-old woodcutter serving with the Sandringham Company. He lived with his widowed father in the nearby village of Dersingham.

Beatrice unfolded the paper and, screwed up inside, she found the remnants of wrapping from a Fry's chocolate bar and packet of tobacco. This was the remains of a parcel intended for Fred that had never made it to him.

'Not a word about this to anyone,' she cautioned Florence. 'Do you understand? I will deal with this.'

Florence nodded meekly. 'Do you know who could have left this here? Why are you so upset, Beatrice?'

'I believe this parcel was intended to be posted to Fred, but it's been stolen, the contents used and then dumped. I would like to keep it for evidence.'

'Oh no. That's wicked. Why would anyone do that and why was the packaging left here? Nobody in our family would do such a terrible thing. I feel sick just at the thought of it. Poor Ma, this would really push her over the edge if she knew of it.'

'Don't worry Florence, and I think it's best not to tell your ma. It looks very suspicious to me.'

'Who on earth would do such an awful thing?'

'I don't know, but I intend to find out.'

Beatrice waved goodbye to Florence and then pedalled off, fuming, her head in a spin. She thought back to yesterday when Mrs Biggs and Miss Hawkins were complaining that their parcels hadn't been delivered to their men on the front line, and also the parcel missing from even before then. Could these disappearances be connected? She needed to find out. And if they were, who could have carried out such a wicked act?

As she spun left down Primrose Lane, braking to take a corner, she saw some more brown paper, a larger piece this time, protruding from the hawthorn hedge. She screeched to a halt, her pulse still soaring, and gently laid her bicycle on the grass verge. The branches of the hedge were prickly and she carefully prised them apart. She pulled out the scrunched-up bundle of brown paper, her mouth dry.

Just as before there was a name written on the paper, this time it was Corporal Timothy Watson, and it included with it his regimental address in France. Beatrice's knew the discovery had to be more than a coincidence.

Without any doubt there was a thief in their midst! She couldn't imagine who would sink so low. These were parcels sent by local families to their beloved boys who were putting their lives on the line. She realised the post office would come under scrutiny. Who had collected the parcels that day? It must have been either Eddie or Robbie Bucket, Sid's son, who helped out a few days a week.

Deep down she didn't believe it could be either of them, but the finger of blame would be pointed in their direction. She had known Eddie all his life and he was as honest as the day was long, and Robbie was a meek and timid lad who wouldn't say boo to a goose. She crumpled to the ground, pondering on the impact this could have on her parents as well. They could face accusations of carelessness, neglect and lack of diligence in their running of the post office.

She glanced further along the hedge and gasped when her eyes picked out more remnants of wrapping paper peeping out from the leaves. She walked over to them and pulled out another two sheets of discarded brown paper, reading the names of Corporal Jeremy Hinds and Lieutenant George Forsythe.

Her eyes scanned further along the hedge and, scarcely believing it, she saw more discarded brown paper with chocolate bar wrappings and tobacco paper concealed behind a rock. In all she estimated that at least six parcels had been stolen, and it seemed likely that Mrs Biggs' and Miss Hawkins' parcels had been stolen too. Were there others?

She flung her hand to her mouth and gasped at the enormity of her discovery. Her body shook, enraged at the thought that someone could behave in such a vile way.

Beatrice tucked the folded packaging into her post-bag and decided to return home to report on what she'd found, her heart racing as she mounted her bicycle, careful not to get any grease from the chain on her skirt. After a few seconds, she groaned and pulled to a halt as she felt the absence of air in her back tyre.

Bending down she saw a thorn embedded in the rubber and had no choice but to push the bike the remaining mile back to the post office, hoping Eddie could fix it for her as he had done once before.

She had sent parcels to Sam – his favourite tobacco, some home-made biscuits and a pair of socks she had knitted. Had he received them? She didn't know. She paused briefly to mop her moist brow with the back of her arm when she passed the church, deciding to head straight to the station first to see what she could discover there about the matter. But as soon as she set off again she stopped dead in her tracks; there in front of her was some scrunched brown paper underneath a rock.

Staring in disbelief, she stifled a cry as she read the name on the wrapping – 'Piers Rumbelow'.

Chapter 14

Beatrice arrived breathless at the station, dragging her bicycle alongside her. She found Eddie in a shed at the back polishing the lamps. She burst in and poured out everything, mentioning the disappearance of the earlier packages too and how it all tied together.

She reached into her postbag and thrust the evidence in front of him.

Eddie's face paled. 'I can't believe it, Miss Beatrice. I can't believe such wickedness exists here in Wolferton.'

'Neither can I, Eddie. May I ask, who collected the parcels today? Was it you or Robbie?'

'Oh, it were Robbie today.' His eyes widened. 'But he's not the thieving sort, Miss Beatrice, I can't believe for a moment he had anything to do with this.'

'Those were my thoughts exactly,' retorted Beatrice.

'I don't mean to be unkind, but he doesn't have all his wits about him, not since . . .' Eddie added.

Beatrice agreed, conscious that Eddie was referring to Robbie's mother abandoning him when he had been ten years old. Mollie Bucket had loved her son dearly, but her husband was a cruel man. One day, after sending

Robbie off to school, she had covered her bruised face and said she was heading to the market. That was the last time Robbie had set eyes on her. No word had been heard of her since, and appeals by police for information came to nothing.

Folk noticed the decline in Robbie's appearance and manner since his mother disappeared. He became more withdrawn and skipped school, taking up poaching and skinning rabbits instead. Sid Bucket was known to be callous and heartless to Robbie, telling him his mother had run off because she didn't want him and threatening to throttle the last breath out of her if she stepped foot in Wolferton again. Robbie never believed him, he knew his ma was good, and clung to the hope that one day she would come back for him.

'I know what's happened to Robbie is terrible, but we should tell Harry about this, he'll know what's best to do,' Eddie suggested.

'Yes, we must inform Father as soon as possible. I don't want to land Robbie in any sort of trouble with that brute of a father of his. You've seen the marks on the poor boy. But if it wasn't you, and neither of us believe Robbie was behind it, then who could the thief be?'

Eddie shrugged his shoulders. 'After what happened last month to the two young lads up before the beak for doing the same thing, how could anyone be daft enough to try it? You must have seen it in the papers. They were from good homes too. It beggars belief.'

'Oh yes, I do remember,' she said. 'They were sentenced to six strokes of the birch; you would have thought that would put anyone off trying the same thing. I recall that the father of one of the boys told the court his lad suffered from asthma and wasn't strong enough to take the whipping. But the court insisted it went ahead and a doctor was was called to be present in case he had breathing difficulties. The doctor asked them to stop halfway through and he took the boy's pulse, the poor lad almost passed out, but the beating carried on to the end. It was a harsh punishment, even though their crime was dreadful.'

'It were terrible. What are we going to do, Miss Beatrice?'

'Let's speak to Father first. In the meantime, please keep a careful watch on all parcels that Robbie picks up. We need to get to the bottom of this. But please don't breathe a word to anyone else. My parents have enough to worry about right now and I'm afraid this could bring terrible shame on the post office.'

A loud cough from the doorway made them swing around. The station master stood there. 'I've been looking for you, Eddie, there's plenty of work to be getting on with. And what are you doing here, Beatrice? What's going on that Eddie feels I should know about?'

Their surprise showed on their faces and Beatrice's hand flew to her mouth.

'Will someone please tell me what's going on?' the station master repeated, his voice tinged with impatience.

At that, Beatrice told him everything and felt immense relief when she had finished. 'Do you think Robbie could be behind this?'

Harry stroked his moustache. 'Now you mention it, the boy isn't back from lunch yet. He's an hour late. I was getting riled about it as I will not tolerate lateness without good reason.'

Beatrice looked worried. 'Oh, Pa, do you think something could have happened to him? It's surely out of character.'

Her father replied. 'I really don't know. I must admit I've had my own concerns about Robbie. There was an occasion where he failed to turn up for work, and when he did he seemed cowed in some way. He kept pulling his sleeve down and during an unguarded moment I saw bruising there. When he saw me looking he scurried off.'

Eddie chipped in. 'I remember that. I saw the bruises too, but Robbie's too scared of his dad to say anything that would get him in trouble.'

Beatrice looked thoughtful. 'I have this funny feeling that Sid has something to do with this. I might be wrong but there's only way to find out for sure. Why don't we call on them?'

'I think we have to,' Harry commented, stroking his moustache as he always did when deep in thought. 'We have to be careful before making serious accusations. You know what kind of man Sid Bucket is. I think we should inform Police Constable Rickett straightaway as well.'

Beatrice shook her head. 'Not yet, Father. Of course, we must let the police know, but I wonder if it would be more prudent to visit Sid's house first and be sure of our facts.'

Harry scratched his head. 'Very well. I certainly want to hear what Robbie has to say for himself. But you must go home, Beatrice, this is man's business. It's no place for a young woman. Eddie and I will go together.'

'But, Father, I want to come. Please! I promise I won't interfere, but I feel I should come. I feel a responsibility as I found the packaging. Also, a softer woman's approach can sometimes help in difficult situations.'

Harry tried digging his heels in, but finally agreed. 'Very well, but on the condition that I do all the talking. And if we discover either Sid or Robbie are in any way responsible for these despicable acts, they will be immediately reported to Police Constable Rickett. Is that agreed?'

'Oh yes, Father, that's right and fair,' Beatrice readily agreed, hoping that their visit would clear Robbie of any wrongdoing.

Harry informed his staff that he had urgent business to attend to. Flanked by Eddie and Beatrice, they turned right outside the station, following the twists and turns of the dry stony path, just a whistle away from the Three Magpies pub, an establishment Sid Bucket was frequently thrown out of when drink got the better of him.

They reached Sid's cottage and shuddered at the neglected state of the front garden. It was overgrown with waist-high weeds. A broken cart and some rusty old tools were dumped in abandoned flowerbeds. A few marigold blooms and a spindly red rose bush was the only sign that flowers had once been tended there.

Beatrice drew a sharp intake of breath as the hinges of the wooden gate squeaked when she opened it tentatively, afraid the sound would alert Sid to their presence if he was home.

They walked softly up the cobbled path, which had large tufts of grass sprouting between some of the cobbles. Pausing, they glanced around, but there was no sign of Sid as they tiptoed to the front window, its glass covered in dirt and grime, its faded curtains open just enough so they could peer into the front room. Their eyes fell on a pile of grubby-looking men's clothes strewn over a high-backed Windsor chair. There was ample evidence of Sid's drinking; a stoneware jug and a pewter tankard lying on their sides on the stained tablecloth that was little more than a rag.

Beatrice screwed up her eyes and stared hard, then reeled backwards as she spotted some scrunched-up wrapping on the sideboard. She recognised it as being from a brand of shortbread biscuits that she knew to be Piers' favourite. Her heart skipped a beat when she saw some crumpled parcel paper on the floor below it. Could it be the evidence they needed? She pointed it out to Eddie and her father, and they all tramped to the back of the house to investigate further.

The back of the house looked even more dilapidated than the front. Beatrice ducked to avoid catching her hair in the cobwebs hanging down from the wooden lean-to which had been added at the back door. The stench from the outside primitive lavatory, nothing more than a bucket in a covered outbuilding with a wooden bench across it and a hole in the middle for sitting, made Beatrice feel nauseous. Her stomach heaved and she leant forward to hold back the rumbling of sickness so she did not vomit. She covered her mouth with one hand and pinched her nose with the other, unable to breathe, waiting for the nausea to pass.

Eddie picked up a rusty tin bucket that caught his eye. He peered inside to see a pile of dead birds – sparrows that had presumably been trapped using the net he spotted nearby. He guessed they had been killed to provide a meal for Sid and Robbie, though once the feathers were plucked and the innards removed with a teaspoon, there would be little flesh on the birds to feast on.

Harry pointed to a couple of rabbit skins pinned out on a board. Sid Bucket was a shrewd poacher, there was no doubting that. A bucket of freshly dug potatoes and a few onions were stored by the back door.

To their surprise, the back door was ajar. They stepped tentatively inside. Harry called out Sid's name. The kitchen had the stench of tobacco, stale beer and a burnt dinner. There was no sign of Sid, but plenty more empty stoneware bottles, dirty boots and unkempt clothes scattered around. The cause of the burnt dinner smell was quickly discovered when they spotted remnants of a frazzled kipper in a rusty, burnt frying pan. Unwashed greasy crockery and cutlery with food stuck on it were dotted around the table.

'Poor Robbie. I had no idea where he lived was quite this bad. And there's no sign of Sid,' exclaimed Harry, shaking his head as his eyes scanned the room.

Beatrice ran her finger along a shelf with a couple of tins on top. It was thick with dust and cobwebs dripped down from the corners of the room. She shuddered and headed to the front room and picked up the ripped wrapping that she had seen through the window and the parcel wrapping from the floor. She examined the wrappings closely, smoothing out the fragment of torn parcel paper. It was stained with some sort of dark liquid, most likely beer, splattered over a name she couldn't read. Her heart sank.

Picking up the shortbread wrapping, she commented, 'I'm sure this belongs to Piers. I was at his house once when he packed his bags for Cambridge and he joked about how pampered he was when his mother slipped a packet of this shortbread in, saying it was his favourite.'

'The villain!' exclaimed Harry. 'To think he could stoop this low. It must be him and not Robbie. Can you see anything else? I think we will need more evidence than this to nail him.'

Beatrice scanned the room, her eyes dropping to the fireside hearth where she spotted some fragments of paper that had been burnt. She could make out some writing.

Picking up the paper, she shook her head. It was part of a letter and had Piers' name on written on it. It was the crucial evidence they needed. They had to find Robbie and make sure he hadn't had any part in the thefts.

A muffled sound caught Beatrice's ear at that moment. It seemed to be coming from behind a door inside the room. She stiffened, pointing to the door and held her ear close to it. 'Shush, I can hear something. It sounds like it's coming from behind here.'

Harry strained his ears. 'You're right. It looks as though that door goes down to the cellar. Stand back and I'll open it.'

'Oh, be careful, Father!' cried Beatrice. Harry lifted his finger to his lips and the room was hushed as he lifted the latch.

'Blimey, it's not budging. It's locked, but where is the key?'

The sound from behind the door became louder and more frantic. A boy's voice could be heard calling for help.

Eddie's fingers stretched along the mantelpiece. He picked up an old rusty tobacco tin and shook it. Hearing what sounded like a metal object inside, he opened it up. Inside was a rusty key which he handed to the station master.

Beatrice pleaded, 'Please be quick, Father, it sounds like someone is crying.'

As soon as Harry unlocked the door, a dazed-looking teenage boy stumbled almost straight into his arms. His eyes were moist and he opened and shut them as they became accustomed to the light. His body shook and his face was flushed with signs of a red, burning mark on his right cheek.

His frightened eyes searched each of the faces in front of him in disbelief. He gasped. 'What are you doing here? Pa will be back soon, and he'll have the hide off you for letting me out.'

Beatrice placed a comforting arm around Robbie's shaking shoulders. 'You're safe now, Robbie. You have no need ever to worry about your father again. He can't treat you like this anymore.'

Robbie's lower lip trembled. 'He'll think I've dobbed on him. You don't know what he's like.'

'I think we have a good idea,' Harry replied. 'Why did he lock you up in the cellar? And what is the meaning of this? What do you know about this wrapping paper?'

Robbie spluttered, 'He wanted me out of the way. I can't say anything, I'm too fearful. I'm sorry, Mr Saward.'

'This is a very serious matter,' said Harry, staring directly at Robbie's terrified face. He explained about the discovery of the stolen food parcels and Robbie's eyes filled with fear. He sobbed, his chest shaking and gripped Harry's arm tightly, his voice croaking. 'He made me do it. I'm so ashamed, Mr Saward. He made me take them and give them to him, else he'd beat me black and blue. He said he'd lock me in the cellar and throw away the key and nobody would ever find me. I'm scared of the dark down there, with rats and . . .'

Harry's eyes flashed in anger. 'That man will answer for this. He's one of the most wicked and despicable monsters I've had the misfortune to meet. I believe you, Robbie, but I must inform Police Constable Rickett. And we need to find your father.'

Robbie, his face thin and gaunt, red on one side, clung to Harry, his eyes blazing like a scared animal. Robbie was young for his age and had always struggled at school and been kept in classes with younger children. Beatrice had heard that once Sid had given him such a sharp clip around the ear that he sent him flying across the room, and he'd never been the same since. He was a bit of a loner and was bullied by other lads, who threw stones and taunted him for being different.

Beatrice felt a wave of sympathy wash over her as she gazed at Robbie's thin body.

'You poor lad,' muttered Eddie. 'You should 'ave told me, Robbie lad, we could have done something.'

'Do you know where your father is now?' Beatrice asked him gently, holding his thin hand in hers. It was cold and shaky.

Robbie spoke falteringly, 'He saw you coming from the front window and . . .'

He paused, the words sticking in his throat. Beatrice encouraged him to take a deep breath. 'Then he walloped me across the face and said it was my fault, that I led you here. He pushed me in the cellar and warned me not to make a sound, else I'd be in for a thrashing. I'm scared of him, Mr Saward. What's going to happen to me now?'

'I think we should get you out of here before your father comes back. We can think then what's best to do. What a brute that man is,' Beatrice seethed.

'You can come and stay with me, Robbie, I'm sure my Ma will agree,' offered Eddie.

Robbie gulped, 'You're all so kind to me. I don't deserve it after what I done. I ain't no thief. I'm ashamed and I'm scared.'

Harry walked to the back door. 'It's my guess Sid won't be too far away. He's probably watching us now, waiting for us to leave. He'll come crawling out soon enough when he wants a drink.'

They returned to the station where Harry called the police. Police Constable Rickett arrived promptly, thanking Harry for informing him of the crime, and thanking Beatrice for the crucial evidence she'd gathered. It was agreed Robbie could stay with Eddie during the police investigation due to how badly he had been treated by his father.

Sid remained on the loose for another twenty-four hours. Word soon spread about the theft and people were alerted to search their outbuildings. He was captured in a barn on the outskirts of Wolferton. His cover was blown by the keen-eyed blacksmith who had seen him lurking suspiciously and kept watch at a distance, sending word to police of his whereabouts.

Police Constable Rickett didn't mince his words as he hauled the scowling, swaggering thief from his hiding place in a trailer, a sack covering him.

'You filthy, disgusting, thieving devil. You deserve everything you get coming to you.'

The blacksmith spat in Sid's face as he passed him, handcuffed to the police officer. 'That's from all those lads you've robbed. May you rot in hell.'

Chapter 15

'Is there any mail for me today?' asked Ada, calling in at the post office a couple of days later.

'No, I'm afraid there's no news from Alfie today,' replied her mother. 'Maybe tomorrow.'

'I'll write to him again later today. I know how my letters cheer him.'

Each day's post was handed out in the trenches with the evening meal, and Ada could imagine Alfie ripping open the envelope and hungrily devouring her news, a more welcome treat than his bully beef ration.

'Why, you'll never believe what I read in the paper. One soldier in the trenches sent in a letter saying he was lonely and would appreciate people writing to him, and he was swamped. He was sent three thousand letters, ninety-eight large parcels and three mailbags of smaller ones. He must have filled up his field post office.'

'That's extraordinary, but heartwarming that so many kind people responded. By the way, I'm also expecting an important package, the sheet music that Clara Griffin so kindly requested on my behalf. She placed an order a few days ago and Fortescue & Son promised it would be sent by return of post.'

Sarah shook her head. 'No, I've seen nothing of the kind with a London postmark. I'll keep an eye out for you. There's a letter here for Maria, though, if you could give that to her. Beatrice was going to drop it off later, but you may as well give it to her now.'

Ada noticed the envelope was postmarked Doncaster. It was bound to be from her mother and Ada hoped it wasn't bad news. She didn't want to lose Maria now, seeing how patient she was with little Leslie; she was thankful this freed up her time to devote to her music and the concert, which she so desperately wanted to succeed.

She had been relieved when it was agreed that Maria could stay on indefinitely. Betty had vouched for her, saying she was turning into a really good helper. She had reluctantly agreed not to say anything about Maria's earlier incident with Leslie, and since then Maria had rolled up her sleeves and worked even harder around the house to show her gratitude to the kindly housekeeper.

'I may have to eat my words. It seems that Maria is turning out to be better than I gave her credit for,' Sarah commented.

'She's surprised us and can't do enough to please us all. Why, today she is taking a cake and flowers to Magnolia for her birthday. In fact, Maria was invited to join me for tea with them. I was planning to go, but I'm very busy with the concert and have made my excuses. The Greensticks sisters really seem to have taken a shine to her.'

'Yes, indeed. I am a little surprised to see how they have taken to Maria, Magnolia in particular. Did you tell Maria about their little family?' Sarah asked, her lips curling into a smile.

'I did hint at something in their house that would amuse her, but not the whole story. I wouldn't want to take that pleasure away from the Greensticks.'

∽

Back at the station master's house, Betty wrapped the cake in greaseproof paper.

'Who would 'ave thought you could bake a tasty cake with powdered eggs, seeing as our eggs are going to injured servicemen. It's unbelievable what you can do if you put your mind to it.'

'Ah well, Maria, when needs must, that's what you do. And you soon get used to adding beetroot to your cake mix instead of sugar when it's scarce, and margarine instead of butter isn't so bad.' Betty grinned. 'Our boys need all the eggs we can send them; we can't begrudge them that.'

Maria enjoyed baking too and could whip up a tasty meal from whatever ingredients she could lay her hands on in the pantry. She commented on the delicious aroma and asked Betty for her recipe, which the housekeeper rattled off without pausing for breath. 'You simply boil the brown sugar with the raisins, cinnamon, ground cloves, butter, or lard or shortening if you prefer, as well as some water, let it simmer away for three minutes and then let it cool. When it's cooled add the flour, baking powder and baking soda and give it a good mix. Then pop it in the oven, and that's all there is to it.'

Jessie had cut a spray of pink roses, white lilies and blue delphiniums for Maria to give Magnolia for her forty-fifth birthday and she set off with them and the cake tin under her arm, curious to see the mystery family that Ada had referred to.

She found their home as instructed at the furthest end of the village. It was a semi-detached picturesque cottage built from red-brick carstone, similar to many others in the village. She walked down the cobble path and chuckled as she stood in the porch and read the name above the front door: 'Kitty Cottage'. What a curious name it was.

Magnolia answered the door and greeted Maria with a warm toothy smile, ushering her in quickly and closing the door firmly behind her.

'Just being cautious, my dear. You will see why soon enough.'

Both sisters were dressed in identical royal-blue dresses, decorated with different coloured satin bows around the waists – yellow for Magnolia and red for Aggie – with large spotted bows tied around their necks. Their hair was piled up in curls, held in place with tortoiseshell combs.

'It's very kind of you to invite me,' Maria said, smiling. She held out Magnolia's gifts.

Magnolia's bottom lip curled slightly. 'I am looking forward to getting to know you, we both are. Please, do come in.'

Maria stood frozen on the spot. Her eyes swivelled around, taking in every inch of the wall covered with photographs of cats, some of them even dressed up like people. Every spare surface on the fireplace and mahogany chiffonier was also covered with porcelain feline figurines of all colours and descriptions.

'I hope you're not allergic to cats, my dear.' Magnolia grinned.

Maria spoke in her poshest voice. 'Not that I know of. This is a sight to behold. I swear I haven't seen anything like this before. You don't 'arf love your cats, don't you?'

Maria's ears pricked at the chorus of cats meowing from the next room.

'We certainly do. Would you like to meet our little family?' Magnolia asked, taking the cake and flowers from Maria and passing them on to Aggie, who scurried out to find a vase.

'Your family? Are your cats your family?'

'They are indeed. Come and meet them.'

Maria's eyes almost popped out of her head and her mouth gaped wide open, as Magnolia led her through to the back sitting room.

'There's Oscar and Jasper, Helena and Maud – named after the youngest daughter of our King Edward, God rest his soul, and Queen Alexandra. You'll soon get to know them.'

Maria raised an enquiring eyebrow, her eyes incredulous as she took in her unusual surroundings.

'Surely you've heard of our Maud, Maria? Why, she's the Queen of Norway and stays at Appleton House on the Sandringham Estate every year, war permitting.'

Maria feigned knowledge of the queen, making a mental note to educate herself about the royal family's many cousins and relatives spread across Europe; maybe Betty or one of the Saward sisters could explain it all to her.

She looked on in awe as the sisters fussed over the four cats who they seated in high chairs around the table, just like children. Their seats were wooden boxes, with lace-edged cushions placed inside for comfort, their initials embroidered on the covers. The cats each wore bibs and made soft meowing noises, their moist noses twitching, their whiskers flickering and they licked their lips as they eagerly watched Aggie cut up small inch-size pieces of cake and feed it into their open mouths, one at a time. One of the cats opened its mouth wide and yawned, then shook its head and licked its paw, while another sneezed a couple of times.

'People never know what to say at first. They think it's quite strange, but to us it's perfectly normal to love cats as if they are your own offspring,' Aggie murmured, stroking Oscar, who purred delightedly and nuzzled his head against her hand.

'Well, I ain't seen anything so sweet before in my life!' gasped Maria, her eyes fixed on Oscar, the plump ginger tomcat, Helena, his chubby black and white furry companion, and Maud, a beautiful white feline with deep green eyes, each poised on their own seats alongside Jasper, the tortoiseshell tabby.

'My dear child, you mean, "I haven't", not "I ain't". Do you mind if I correct you?'

'Oh no, I don't mind one bit. I keep trying 'cause I wanna be posh like you so folk respect me. Mrs Saward and the sisters are helping me speak proper too,' she blurted, with a grin. 'Only now and again, me old way of speaking will slip out. See what I mean, I mean *my* old way. It takes time to change a lifetime's way of speaking.'

Magnolia informed her, 'I can assure you we are not posh in the slightest. We have more in common with you than you realise. We believe that regardless of a person's background, it is within everyone's ability to speak properly – if they want to, of course. It's especially important to speak well living here in Wolferton as one never knows when one will bump into royalty. You can't say "ain't" in front of our royal family.'

'Well, I do know that, that's why I want to speak properly,' declared Maria, wondering what Magnolia could have meant by them having more in common than she realised.

An awkward silence followed as Maria tried to make sense of what Magolia had told her about having more in common with her than she realised. Oscar placed a paw on the table, and Aggie gently removed it.

'Now, now, Oscar. We have a guest for tea.'

Maria stifled a giggle and sat transfixed, watching the cats slurp up the milk that had been placed in saucers in front of them, licking their lips and their paws and purring contentedly. After a few minutes they became restless, trying to jump down, but were restrained by Magnolia. Helena tried to stand on the table. Aggie scolded her, wagging her finger. Helena snarled and Aggie became flustered and removed her bib. The remaining cats jumped out of their seats and then they prowled around the room, stretching out their limbs and rolling on their backs as the sisters stroked their tummies.

Having settled their feline family, Magnolia and Aggie returned to the table. 'Naughty cats! They are usually much better behaved. I think it's because they're not used to you, Maria. Your presence has excited them,' Aggie explained.

Maria looked pleased at this and pulled a face at the cats, as if to say 'be on your best behaviour'.

'Now let's have some of this wonderful cake. I do enjoy Betty's cakes,' murmured Magnolia, as she slid the cake slice through it.

Maria stifled a giggle, not wishing to appear rude. She watched how Aggie held her teacup to her lips, making sure her little finger was also crooked upwards, though for the life of her she couldn't make sense of why it was etiquette to do so. She heaped praise on the Greensticks sisters, telling them she couldn't wait to tell her ma and brothers all about their extraordinary cats and their kindness to her.

'The thing is Maria, we believe you should never judge a person by their appearance, as we have discovered with you. And the same goes for, well, how you think of us.'

'I couldn't have put it better, dear sister.' Aggie nodded, brushing the cat hairs off her dress.

Maria screwed up her face. 'You're really not what I expected, and seeing you here, in your own home with your little *family*, has taken my breath away. I'm that pleased I have to pinch myself. And your cats, well, they are almost like humans. I can't believe how they act, and what I've seen. How did you train them to sit at the table?'

'Well, my dear, I must confess Aggie takes all the credit for that. She has the patience of an angel and spent hours training them, bribing them with their favourite nibbles, no doubt, though today they were not at their best.'

'I think they are wonderful. You must have lots of patience,' Maria said admiringly.

'They give us much joy. They are our babies, as we have not been blessed in that way.' Aggie smiled. 'Next time you visit I'll introduce you to those who have passed on, but stay for ever in our hearts. Did you see their photographs on the wall in our parlour?'

'You mean, every one of those pictures belongs to a different cat you once owned? Were they all like these that you have now?'

'Oh absolutely. It started when our dear little mischievous Bertie would spontaneously jump on an empty chair at the table and sit there while we ate. And then Freda sat next to him and did the same. They were the most perfect, best behaved cats ever. Magnolia suggested putting bibs on them and having them as our babies,' explained Aggie.

'I know it can seem peculiar, but they have far better table manners than many people I know,' simpered Magnolia, as she wiped her mouth, exaggerating every movement with a flourish.

'Sometimes we take them out for a walk. We have a special lead, but once our little Princess slipped her collar and ran off. She was hit by a train,' Aggie continued, dabbing her moist eyes with her lace-edged handkerchief.'So now we only take them out one at a time. It's a sensible precaution in case there are any dogs around. We wouldn't want to scare them.'

Once they'd finished eating and spent more time chatting, Maria stood to leave. As she did so she spotted four exquisite wooden cots filled with soft bedding for each cat, their names carved in the front. Aggie explained they were always placed in front of the stove at night so they would be warm.

'Who made these for you? They are so beautiful!'

'Well, that is a strange thing. That Robbie Bucket made them, the one who folk say is a bit, how should I put it delicately, on the simple side. The poor boy, he's had a troubled life since his mother disappeared and thanks to his good-for-nothing father. One of his schoolteachers told us he was gifted with his hands and could make anything. We commissioned these little beds and were astonished when we saw the quality of his work.'

Magnolia added, her voice low, 'That is the reason my sister and I have resolved not to judge people on first impressions, though I must confess I was shocked to hear he was involved in the scandalous theft of food parcels. Mrs Saward mentioned it in the post office when I called in earlier today. It must be his good-for-nothing father behind it.'

Maria agreed and profusely thanked the sisters for their hospitality and a tea party she would remember for the rest of her life. She felt elated as she left Kitty Cottage, promising herself that she too would not make harsh judgements on first impressions, as she had done with them.

The Greensticks sisters chuckled as they closed the door behind Maria.

Magnolia scooped up Maud as she nuzzled her head around her ankles, stroking her smooth fur. 'I've rather taken to the girl, you know,' she told Aggie. 'There's something about her, her spirit, that I find appealing. If only I could have been like her at that age, possessed that kind of courage and forthrightness.'

'Now my dear, it doesn't do to look backwards. It will only make you maudlin.'

'Maybe you're right. But it's easier said than done at times. Come on, Maud, time for another saucer of milk,' Magnolia replied, stroking her friendly moggy in her arms.

∽

Back at the station master's house, Maria was bursting to tell everyone about her day. 'Who would have thought I would one day have tea with two posh 'uns like the Greensticks sisters and their family of four cats. I don't know whether to laugh or feel sorry for them.'

Maria had Ada in stitches as she recounted her tea with the cats and how well behaved they had been.

'They ain't so bad. I mean, *they are not so bad*, once you get to know them.'

'They are certainly eccentric, and we are used to their strange ways here. By the sound of it you'll soon be posher than them,' laughed Ada.

Suddenly remembering the letter her mother had handed to her earlier for Maria, Ada retrieved it from her pocket.

'I have something here for you. This came earlier and I forgot to give it to you. I hope all is well with your mother.'

Maria seized the letter and turned her back on Ada as she tore the envelope open. 'You mean to say you've had it all morning?'

'I'm so sorry, it slipped my mind, with so much else happening.'

Maria buried her face in the page.

'I'll leave you alone to digest your news,' Ada added, observing Maria's anxious manner. 'It's a lovely afternoon. I think I'll take Leslie out for some fresh air while he's quiet.'

Maria barely glanced up and mumbled an acknowledgement. Her eyes hungrily devoured the words in front of her.

My dear Maria,

I hope you can forgive me for leaving the way I did, but it were for the best. I pray for you every night, and for the first time in many months I can sleep knowing you're in good company with a roof over your head. Mr Saward has done good for us afore and I knew he wouldn't turn you out with nowhere to go.

When Freda she clapped sight of me she said, 'Oh my gawd! Is that really me sister Ruth? You look like a bag of bones.' I were that shaky when I arrived that all I could eat were 'er beef broth, but each day I get stronger and last night I ate a couple of mouthfuls of her suet pudding. I shall soon be as fat as a goose if she 'as her way. I still feel a pounding on me chest sometimes and can't catch me breath still, but don't you fret about yer ma. I'm on the mend.

As I feared your Uncle Gus is making Freddie and Archie work all hours. I had to stop off in London afore I came to Doncaster to give him more money. The sight of me boys being worked to the bone broke me heart. The scoundrel makes them work on his rag and bone rounds for a few pennies instead of sending them to school. He even had the cheek to ask me for more money for their keep, he wants more all the time. I fear he spends the money I give him on drink and then he makes out he's had nowt. I hope to be strong enough soon to take in some laundry to earn a few more shillings for them to keep that wicked man quiet. I'll turn me hand to pot washing, anything, to have some peace of mind.

When I left I promised Freddie and Archie I'd be back for them as soon as I could. With the Lord's will, I hope it won't be too long.

You must be wondering about young Joey. He is a fair 'un and growing bonnier by the day. He has a sweet smile that warms the cockles of me heart. You can be sure he is well looked after and Freda couldn't have found a better wet nurse in Annie. She is a sensible gal and don't ask questions, grateful for the money and happy with what I give, though I am skint now. Freda has kept her word and Joey stays 'ere, with Annie coming in to take him for fresh air. He ain't gone into any workhouse, and never will. I swear the little fella is getting fond of me and he looks the spitting image of you.

I must rest now and will give this letter to Freda. I pray one day soon we will be together, all of us.

Your loving Ma

Maria turned her head as her eyes welled up. 'Oh, Ma, how I miss you. How I miss holding my Joey. When will I see you both again?' Scalding tears poured down her cheeks and her chest pounded with heavy sobs. Her heart ached to see her baby boy again and her stomach twisted into knots from sheer agony, imagining his sweet face, at only six months old. She didn't need cats to be her pretend family, like the spinster Greensticks sisters. She had a baby of her own, he wasn't dead at all, despite what she had told Ada. And she had a mother and brothers who needed her too. It tore her apart having to care for Leslie, who was the same age as her own child, wishing she could reach down and kiss her own Joey's soft cheeks and put him to sleep at night.

She had considered getting rid of the baby to spare her family the shame. She had pulled her shawl over her face as she followed a path to a cottage that stood alone at the end of her village. Everyone knew young girls who walked through Widow Gaskin's door were in trouble. She greeted Maria with smiles, wiping her dripping hooked nose with her sleeve. She assured her she could take care of everything and nobody would be any the wiser. Maria peered through her house into the back room and shuddered when her eyes rested on a range of medical implements. A rubber pipe and white enamel bowl were laid out on a table next to a grubby-looking bed covered with a crumpled sheet. She wondered how many desperate girls in her situation had lain on that bed and the fear they must have experienced. She stroked her stomach, imagining the tiny life that was growing inside her, and vowed that her baby would live to see the light of day. Without speaking, she had run out of the house, her chest throbbing. The following week she heard Widow Gaskin had been charged with manslaughter after two girls died during botched abortions.

'That could have been me. Thank God I had nothing to do with her. Somehow, we'll manage,' she had cried to her mother, wiping away a tear. 'Those poor girls, what must they have gone through.'

Now, she rubbed her cheeks dry with the sleeve of her dress and sniffled. She felt wicked, too, for telling the

Sawards her little baby boy was dead, justifying her lies by telling herself that everything she did now, trying desperately to improve her standing in life, was to benefit him, so he would one day be proud of his mother.

She patted her eyes dry and composed herself, tucking the letter away in her pocket. Hearing the back door open, she forced a smile onto her face. She scooped Leslie into her arms and rubbed her nose against his cheek, his laughter a bittersweet reminder of Joey. When Ada returned a few moments later, Maria tried to hand him over, but the infant clung to Maria.

Ada's eyebrows creased and she let out a wishful moan. 'I honestly don't think he likes me, Maria. Look how he prefers your company. Whatever I do doesn't seem to make any difference.'

Maria's face turned red and something inside her snapped. 'Stop it. Stop complaining about him all the time. You don't know how lucky you are to have such a beautiful son.'

Ada appeared shocked at Maria's outburst. 'I'm really am so sorry about your baby, Maria. Does it upset you to be with Leslie? I would understand if it did.'

'Oh no, I love being with him. He's such a joy and I have to put my sadness behind me. I shouldn't have spoken out of turn like that and I'm sorry. I feel so foolish, and selfish. I ain't got a sweetheart or brother in the war to worry about, but I hate that I am parted from my own, those what are closest to me.'

∽

Maria wasn't ready yet to share her big secret. The shame of having a child out of wedlock gnawed at her. She fretted about her younger brothers and their poor treatment with Uncle Gus. She fretted about how much longer they could rely on Freda's kindness and continue paying Annie to look after Joey, knowing that every penny her mother could spare from Willie's inheritance had been used up.

Aunt Freda was the only family member aware of her situation.

When Joey was born at Aunt Freda's house, Maria soon forgot the excruciating pain of giving birth, a labour that had lasted eighteen hours, and immediately felt an outpouring of love for her son. She marvelled at his perfect features and melted inside when his innocent wide-eyed face looked up at hers. She smothered his cherubic cheeks with kisses, her heart aching with a deep love that made her shiver and pressed him tight against her chest. She treasured every moment she spent with him, remembering how he greedily clasped his hungry mouth to her breast until his stomach was filled.

Aunt Freda warned Maria. 'Don't get too attached to 'im, lass, remember yer've got to give 'im up. Yer're young, you'll have more babies. There'll be a good family that can take him in, or someone else who can 'elp yer for a small fee.'

Maria was distraught. Having saved her unborn baby from the murdering clutches of Widow Gaskin, she was being asked to give him up to strangers and never see him again. How could she? Her mother had tried to convince her during the pregnancy that this was the best course of

214

action, but once the moment had come, she couldn't face parting with him.

Maria's heart was filled with dread when she thought about giving up her precious newborn. She recalled the horrendous crimes of Amelia Dyer, the evil child murderess who preyed on vulnerable women, taking in their unwanted babies in exchange for money and the promise they would be cared for. They trusted the woman, who had advertised her services as a baby nurse She was a trained nurse and soon raked in a fortune. But unbeknown to those poor women, Amelia Dyer was an infamous baby farmer, taking babies or infants into her care and promising to look after them in exchange for payment, and later strangling them or allowing the poor souls to die of neglect or starvation.

Her monstrous crimes came to light when the body of a baby girl was recovered from the Thames and traced back to her. Dozens of distraught women came forward to say they had given their infants to Amelia Dyer, but they could not be found, and several more babies were recovered from the river, each with white edging tape wrapped around their tiny necks.

'She could have killed hundreds of babies, that's what the papers are saying. I ain't giving my baby to the likes of her,' Maria cried, her eyes filled with fear. 'Never, ever while I still have air in my lungs and a mouth to speak my mind. As long as I have breath in my body, I shall keep him. I'll manage somehow, whatever it takes.'

Chapter 16

Beatrice and Ada scanned the week's edition of the *Lynn Advertiser* for updates on the war. Ada pointed to a cartoon showing a portly middle-aged man resembling a country squire pointing his walking stick at a pipe-smoking young man out walking with his sweetheart. The caption read, 'Look here, my lad, if you're old enough to walk out with my daughter you are old enough to fight for her and our country.' Behind them was a sign pleading, 'Enlist Now, 100,000 men wanted'.

The large broadsheet newspaper was spread across the kitchen table. It featured pictures of handsome local soldiers proudly wearing their uniforms. The accompanying text was announcing their deaths, followed by a list of other deceased servicemen from the area. They left behind so many broken hearts.

Ada next pointed out a letter from a ninety-year-old vicar fuming at a lack of Christianity, complaining about empty church pews. He moaned:

In the villages and towns of Norfolk there are more people who seek their own pleasure on the Lord's

Day than care anything about the honour of God. It is sad to see how many wait for the opening of the alehouse on the Sabbath morn and never enter the House of God.

Should fathers and mothers who have sons at the front be seen leaving the alehouse on the Sabbath and never seen in church or chapel? Oh, that the many millions of the nation would turn to the God whom they have forsaken, then this cruel war would end and the nation would have a happy and prosperous peace.

She shook her head at the vicar's miserable rantings, muttering under her breath that vicars should be showing understanding and forgiveness to their errant flock, continuing to turn the pages.

The delicious aroma of Betty's flavoursome lunch filled the kitchen. The Sawards were grateful that her thrifty ways were now paying dividends, that she could be economical with food, bulking up stews with lentils, and for being able to count on Lizzie at Blackbird Farm for milk and a chicken from time to time.

It only took ten minutes for Betty to make Trench cake, which required no eggs, using vinegar and baking soda instead, and a pinch or two of spices and dried fruit. Plain flour, margarine, cocoa, brown sugar and milk were used too, and although it was less moist than the usual fruitcake, the Sawards knew it would survive the journey to the battlefields after being posted to Sam and Alfie for Christmas 1914, and it had been favourably received by them both.

Harry, Sarah, Jessie and Maria came in then and joined Ada and Beatrice, taking their places at the large oak table. Ada appeared irritable, struggling to placate a wriggling Leslie, and plonking him in his high chair.

Betty's mutton stew was being served for lunch. Using less meat and thickened with extra onions, potatoes and carrots and flavoured with fresh rosemary from the garden, it was always a favourite. A creamy milk pudding followed, washed down by a steaming cuppa. Betty made the cream herself by pouring milk that came straight from one of Lizzie's cows into a tall enamel tin and giving it a good shake, leaving it to stand for a day, after which time she would scoop a thick layer of cream from the top.

There was one subject besides the war on everyone's lips – the shocking theft of food parcels and the forthcoming court case. Sarah put down her knife and fork and told them, 'Poor Mrs Rumbelow, she called in at the post office this morning and was in a very bad way about it. She dropped off another parcel that she'd made up for Piers with his favourite shortbread biscuits and Fry's chocolate cream. At least that wicked Sid Bucket can't get his thieving hands on it now. You can't help but feel sorry for Robbie though, having to stand trial too. We must hope the court will see it was Sid's doing.'

Ada glanced up from her plate. 'Poor woman, my heart goes out to her. I bumped into her this morning and she told me how much she is looking forward to the concert. She said everyone is talking about it, how it will bring families together, from those that live in the manor houses to small farm cottages; their hearts beat the same and we're all in pain.'

Sarah enquired how plans for the concert were progressing.

Ada looked rueful. 'I'm still waiting for some sheet music that Clara kindly ordered for me from Fortescue's in London to arrive in the post. She's keeping the music a mystery until the sheets arrive as she wants to surprise us all, but they should be here by now. I hope and pray they come within the next couple of days in time for our final rehearsal. What will I do if they don't? She'll consider me a laughing stock, I'll be a failure.'

'You? A failure? Never! They'll turn up, you wait and see,' Maria blurted. 'I believe in you.'

Maria gently pushed small spoonfuls of mashed mutton into Leslie's mouth, followed by the pudding, which he devoured ravenously. 'I bet it raises lots of money too. I can't wait to hear that Clara. I hear she's a real songbird.'

'Oh, Maria, I hope you are right. I hope we don't let her down and the music score arrives in time. Mother, will you please give the package to Beatrice as soon as it comes? I won't be happy until it arrives,' Ada pleaded, her eyes moist.

'How about putting on something for the young 'uns here? Something to give them some cheer?' Maria pondered.

'What do you suggest?' asked Ada, raising her eyebrows.

'Well, how about having a circus? I love a circus, with all those exotic animals. And we can have the galloping horses too, that's my favourite roundabout. It wouldn't half cheer up folk too,' she said excitedly.

'What do you say to that then, Harry?' enquired Sarah, with a slanted smile.

He caught her gaze. 'I'm not so sure a circus would be a good idea, not after last time!'

'What do you mean, "not after last time"?' quizzed Maria. 'I think the young 'uns would love it, and it would raise lots of money. Oh yes, let's have a circus show, with all the animals and the acrobats.'

'Can you imagine how difficult it would be to transport wild animals here to Wolferton?'

Jessie grinned. She knew the cause of her father's reservations, and she stifled a giggle. 'It's a good idea, Maria, but maybe we could have a circus without the animals? Just have clowns and acrobats, perhaps? That is, if we can find any. They may have volunteered for the war.'

'I never thought of that. But a circus wouldn't be the same without exotic animals, that's what everyone wants to see,' Maria protested.

'Perhaps I had better explain,' Jessie said, shooting a sideways glance at Harry. His lips curved and his eyes twinkled as he nodded to Jessie.

'I have a story about the circus coming to Wolferton. Father used to love telling us about it as he had only been here a few months when it came. The famous Sanger Circus rolled up here, in Wolferton. Isn't that right, Father?'

Harry confirmed this, his eyes twinkling.

Maria was all ears, her hands cupped in her chin, elbows on the table. Sarah rose, saying she had to get back to work, and Harry checked his watch and said he had to leave too, but let Jessie recount the story.

'Ooh, how wonderful. Go on then, Jessie. What happened?' egged on Maria.

'It was all part of Prince Eddy's celebrations for his twenty-first birthday, and a right do it was too. There were such huge festivities and celebrations in Sandringham, with a ball in the evening for a thousand guests, so Father was rushed off his feet at the station.'

'You mean a circus came here, came to Sandringham, especially to perform for the Prince's birthday? Is this the Prince who died before he could become King?'

'Yes, that's the one, it's true. Every word of it. The Prince was the apple of his mother's eye. He looked so like Queen Alexandra. She doted on him; anyone could see that. She would have given him the moon if he asked for it.'

'Go on, Jessie, what happened? Tell me now while Leslie is quietly settled with his toys,' Maria entreated.

Jessie chuckled. 'It wasn't just for royals and their guests. The big top was set up on Sandringham Park and labourers on the estate, two hundred and fifty of them, were invited to a command performance to mark the Prince's coming of age. The whole show arrived by special trains to Wolferton. It was a real spectacle. Then one of the elephants suddenly decided to go walkabout and stretch its legs just as he was being loaded into a carriage-truck.'

221

'What? It just wandered off?'

'That's right. The porters were trying to load a large elephant into a carriage-truck, but he wouldn't budge.

'The elephant stood rooted outside the station and dug his heels in deeper, blowing his trumpet loud in the air and swinging his trunk around. It must have been heard as far away as the Big House itself.

'Someone had the idea of tying the elephant's chain to a lamp post to restrain it; but the elephant was having none of it. After making the loudest trumpeting sound you can imagine, he uprooted the lamp post and walked off with the lamp post still attached to him. Father was petrified of it running amok in the station.'

Maria exploded with laughter. 'I can't imagine it. Oh, what a sight! Poor Harry. And the poor elephant. What happened next?'

'There was chaos everywhere, with people flying around in all directions. Nobody knew what to do in case he ran off and went on the rampage.'

'I can't believe it. An elephant, here on the rampage,' squawked Maria, holding on to her sides.

'That wasn't all. He then demolished the station gates and threw them into the middle of the street outside. Poor Father ran after him. Then, much to everyone's surprise, he walked into his truck, as calm as could be, and the door was quickly slammed shut before he could change his mind, and the circus continued on its journey to Sandringham. What a to-do that was!'

'I've never heard anything like it!' exclaimed Maria.

Harry chortled as Jessie continued. 'The show went off as planned. In all, two thousand inhabitants from the area came to see daring acrobats climbing three high and tigers in their cages, and the elephants perform. It was certainly a night to remember.'

Maria listened agog. 'Cor, what a sight that must have been. I would love to see the circus. Can't we have it here again?'

'I don't think so, not after that. You'll need to think of something else.'

'Now there's a tale to tell my ma and brothers when I see them next,' Maria exclaimed. 'Freddie and Archie will love that yarn.'

'So now you know why it's not a good idea to have the circus back here. I don't think Father would be happy about it.'

'I can see that, so I'll just have to think of something else then. I did enjoy that story. It makes me wonder how different life must have been here before the war. Are there any more stories you can tell me about those days? I can write to Ma about them, and Freddie and Archie too, that won't half tickle 'em.'

Ada piped in, 'I remember some of the stories Mother told us about merrier times here before the war, during King Edward's reign.'

Maria cupped her hands under her chin, eyes wide open, all agog as Jessie recounted her tales.

'There is one I recall, it sets a pretty picture in your mind. One winter there was so much snow, it completely upset the shooting programme for His Majesty and his guests who were here for Christmas. On this particular afternoon the sun shone brightly like a summer's day and the keen wind made the weather very cold, so the Queen and the ladies of the house party did not venture out to join the men for lunch.

'Instead their mother was joined in the afternoon by the two young princes, Eddy and George, and she took them for a sleigh ride down here to Wolferton. I've never heard laughing like it, they were enjoying themselves so, and even their tutor looked a picture as the sleigh swept into the station yard. The tutor needed to depart by train for London. Mother says the princes had rosy cheeks, bright eyes and happy faces and it was a joy to see. The sleigh was pulled by a couple of greys, and their mother was wrapped with a warm coat with fur around the collar and a fur muff. When the tutor left, the princes jumped out and threw snowballs, slipping and sliding about just like ordinary lads.'

Maria gulped wide eyed. 'Ooh, that sounds wonderful. I would love to ride in a sleigh, through the white country lanes and the woods looking so pretty too, just like a fairy tale.'

'It sounds like a pretty picture. And to think that the little prince George is now our King. There were so many big parties at the House in his father's day. We do miss those days, all the well-dressed guests from big houses around the country that arrived here at Wolferton. And Caesar, of course, you must have heard of Caesar.'

'No. Who, or what, is Caesar?'

Ada grinned. 'I thought everyone knew Caesar. He was the former King's faithful dog that went everywhere with him.'

Maria shook her head. Jessie laughed. 'Do tell Maria about Caesar. How he went for Father's trouser legs.'

'He did indeed. On more than one occasion as he didn't like the smoke and sound from the steam engines. And it wasn't just our father who had his trousers bitten. Caesar might have been a fox terrier, but he was treated like royalty himself; he was His Majesty's most loyal and constant companion. He even had a footman assigned to him to clean him and was allowed to sleep on an easy chair next to the King's bed.'

'He never did!'

Ada's eyes crinkled. 'There was no mistaking whose dog he was. His dog collar said, "I am Caesar. I belong to the King." You had to treat Caesar with the greatest respect. When the King died, Caesar went into mourning, like a human. The poor dog refused to eat and whined for days outside his master's bedroom. Then he managed to sneak in and hid under the King's bed. He was found by Queen Alexandra who encouraged him to eat and restored him to his normal self.'

'Awww. That's such a sad story, to hear how the poor dog missed his master so much.'

Ada continued. 'Caesar was even granted full honours and led the King's funeral procession, walking behind the carriage carrying the King's coffin. He was placed ahead of the heads of state, even before our King George V and eight other kings, though Kaiser Wilhelm didn't approve of it. That shows how special he was.'

Maria sighed. 'I know of no other dog that has been so loved. He must have been a true and loyal friend to the King.'

She thought of the Greensticks sisters and their devotion to their cats. 'It just goes to show whether you are royalty or just ordinary folk, animals love you just the same.'

Ada and Jessie shared a mutual smile, telling Maria they had enjoyed recounting the stories to her.

She enthused bright eyed. 'Hearing these tales makes me realise all the more how special life is here and its connections with the royal family. It makes me even more determined to make something of my life.'

∞

A few days later, Beatrice eagerly rushed into the house. She held up the local newspaper, her eyes filled with dread. 'What does this mean?' she asked her mother incredulously. 'I don't understand, how could the Sandringham Company have just vanished?'

Sarah frowned. 'What are you saying? Soldiers can't just disappear into thin air.'

Beatrice's bottom lip quivered as she pointed to the report of the dispatch from Gallipoli by Sir Ian Hamilton, the British Commander-in-Chief. He described a fearsome battle on 12th August when fighting grew hotter and the ground more wooded and broken, the men injured, exhausted and thirsty. They retreated, but another 250 men and their officers still kept pushing forward. Amongst these were 'a fine company enlisted on the King's Sandringham Estate. Nothing was ever seen or heard of any of them again. They charged into the forest and were lost to sight and sound. None of them ever came back.'

'No, it's impossible.'

'Sam. Oh, Sam. My poor Sam. Oh, Mother, maybe they are all dead,' yelped Beatrice.

Her mother clutched the table to steady herself. 'Let's hope and pray they are alive and safe somewhere. Poor Mary Beck, how must the poor woman be feeling. There's still no news about Captain Beck or his nephew.'

'Surely they are either dead or alive. None of this makes sense,' cried Beatrice, dabbing her moist eyes with a handkerchief.

Sarah read on shakily. 'It says here that some of the officers reported missing earlier are alive. Captain Cedric Coxon has made it, he's written to his mother telling her he is safe, but wounded, and has been taken prisoner of war. Oh my Lord, he was shot in the neck, but he's pulled through. Isn't that just wonderful! He's still alive. Maybe Sam is too. And Captain Beck.'

Beatrice took the paper from her mother. Her throat wobbled. 'Oh, Mother, how can I tell Edith this? It will be the end of her.'

Sarah gulped. 'This is a black day for Wolferton. Hopefully we will hear more news soon. It says here the Mayor of King's Lynn is making exhaustive enquiries and great and important influence has been brought to bear on the mystery of the missing soldiers. Everyone is doing their best and we can only place our trust in them.'

Beatrice sobbed, scalding tears cascading down her cheeks. Sarah drew her distraught daughter close to her, stroking her hair, knowing no words of comfort that could soften the blow of this shocking news.

The paper had printed a survivor's account of how machine guns and rifle fire swept the ground and they were surrounded by Turks up on the hill: 'We went too fast and got lost, there is no doubt about that. We heard nothing but the noise of the firing and shouts of "On, the gallant Norfolks. Forward boys!"'

'The poor boys, they didn't stand a chance. Sandringham has lost its fine men,' Beatrice reflected. 'And for what?'

When Edith heard, she wanted to go into mourning, but followed the example set by Mrs Beck instead. 'Frank is still alive until I am officially told otherwise.'

Chapter 17

Word of Sid Bucket's dirty deeds had spread quickly throughout Wolferton and beyond.

'Toss him in the dungeon and throw away the key,' chorused outraged folk from the community.

'That's too good for the likes of him. He should be deported to the other side of the world and sentenced to hard labour,' demanded others, seeking revenge.

Robbie's plight divided people, drawing sympathy from some who knew the hard life he endured at home. Others thought, 'Well, the boy should have dobbed on his father. He should have told Harry about it. If any lad of mine did that he'd be in for a good leathering for sure, and then I'd disown him.'

Police took the view that both Sid and Robbie were equally culpable and that justice had to be seen to be done for them both. Sid and Robbie were charged on six counts of theft of parcels intended for servicemen: all brave men fighting for their King and country. Constable Rickett informed Harry and Beatrice of the date of their hearing, which was to be in two days' time, before magistrates in King's Lynn. Beatrice told her father she must attend.

~∞~

Two days later, Jessie agreed to help with deliveries from the post office as Beatrice took the train from Wolferton to King's Lynn and walked briskly for ten minutes into the town centre.

'Why not make the most of your time in Lynn and visit Edith afterwards?' Sarah had suggested. 'I'm sure seeing you would be a good tonic for her. And it would be good for you too to have a change of scene.' Beatrice had readily agreed.

She now trotted along the cobblestones, too deep in thought to admire the town's many fine buildings, with its prominent Custom House topped with its ornate white cupola a stone's throw away. Her eyebrows furrowed as she pondered what fate awaited Robbie.

She soon found the courthouse, located in the Guild-hall on Saturday Market Place, the town's main centre, and glanced up at the spectacular building with its distinctive black and white chequered façade. A grim cell block was located in the basement.

Harry had agreed to write a testimonial for Robbie's good character, which he gave to Police Constable Rickett to hand to an appropriate person in court on the day of the hearing. Beatrice wanted to be in court to see that Robbie was given a fair hearing.

She lifted her skirt and stepped briskly up the wide staircase and was directed to the public gallery, where she perched herself on a wooden bench in the front row; it quickly filled with other eager spectators as news of the hearing had made headlines in the local paper.

Robbie's hearing was not the first case of the day. The woman next to her expressed her disgust at the earlier defendant charged with attempting to obtain money from the War Office by false pretences. Private Albert Henley had lodged with Mrs Anna Pickford for eighteen years, but was killed on the Western Front. After his death the landlady wrote to the War Office describing him as her adopted son and sent a forged letter saying he wanted to leave all his estate to her. However, a further letter was received by the War Office saying that the soldier had left his effects to his brother.

'She got three weeks in prison, should have been three years,' the enraged woman told Beatrice. 'War can bring the worst out in some folk, greedy devils.'

Beatrice shuddered and agreed with the woman, who turned and repeated the details to a man on her other side. She glanced down and saw the court reporter scribbling away in his notebook. Constable Rickett arrived, removing his helmet before sitting on one of the benches in the middle of the room behind a stern-looking man wearing a dark suit and with large white sideburns sprouting from the sides of his cheeks. Beatrice assumed him to be the prosecuting officer.

The crowd alongside Beatrice began chanting, demanding justice for the troops and their families who had been robbed while serving their King and country. Beatrice's heart pounded, her mouth dry as her eyes scanned the courtroom for Robbie and his father. She spotted the dock, surrounded with an iron railing, where they would both stand, but there was no sign of them yet.

The rowdiness was silenced by the clerk, who was wearing a long dark gown. Clearing his throat, he commanded. 'Order. Order. Silence in court. Please stand.'

Everyone promptly rose and silence filled the courtroom. Beatrice held her breath as her eyes became glued on the three magistrates as they entered from a back room and took their places in decorative carved seats, on an elevated platform behind the clerk the centre chair being the tallest and most elaborate, resembling a throne.

This chair was filled by the unsmiling, balding chairman, Sir Ronald Hythe-Simpson. He was in his seventies and bowed slightly before sitting down. Two equally stern-looking colleagues who both looked older than Sir Ronald flanked him, one on either side. Beatrice recognised them all from the papers as leading pillars of the community.

On one side was Mr Furling, the funeral director, who had an elaborate white furry moustache that spread out across his cheeks like angel wings. He refused to retire, saying he would carry on until the day he was ready for his own box. He had a nervous twitch, which made his thin face jerk to one side in a spasm, his mouth opening to show a set of decaying teeth and gaps where some were missing.

The third magistrate Beatrice recognised as a well-to-do retired farmer with ruddy cheeks, who was dribbling down the side of his mouth. Lizzie had mentioned him, as he was partial to a cuddle with barmaids after having had a few drinks. Beatrice guessed he would go along with whatever sentence Sir Ronald saw fit.

Beatrice shuddered, sensing they were not in any mood to show mercy. They would need to satisfy the public's outrage, that was clear for her to see.

A hushed silence descended as Sid and Robbie were led into the dock up some steps from the cells underneath. Beatrice pushed herself forward as far as she could so as to be able to see better. She gasped as she saw the fear on Robbie's face, his jaw trembling and his eyes filled with terror. She spotted a smartly dressed young man in his twenties sitting in front, who turned to speak to him, holding out his arm and half-smiling as if offering a sign of encouragement. Beatrice saw him pick up some papers and hand them to the prosecuting officer; he read them and grunted, barely acknowledging them, looking ahead to address the magistrates. She could see the young man had a kind face and she hoped he would be speaking up for Robbie.

Sid turned his head upwards to face the public gallery, glaring defiantly with his eyes wild, showing no shame or remorse.

The charges were put to them both by the clerk and loud angry demands for justice could be heard from the public gallery when they pleaded guilty to them all, including the theft of parcels sent by Mrs Biggs and Miss Hawkins. Robbie spoke so softly that he was asked to speak up. He turned slightly and looked upwards, smiling faintly when he recognised Beatrice in the public gallery when she raised her hand at him. She instantly felt a sharp prod in her side from the angry woman next to her, but Beatrice brushed it aside.

The prosecutor, a thin upright man wearing a pinstriped suit, outlined his case in a loud, crisp voice, describing the heartless, selfish acts of theft that were unimaginable to all civilised beings in the community. Ladies in the public gallery sniffed and dabbed their eyes when the discovery of Lieutenant Piers Rumbelow's looted parcel was mentioned. The image of the greedy thieves tucking into his favourite biscuits while he was saving the lives of his comrades wounded in a foreign land, the beloved only son of a vicar and his loyal wife who were pillars of the community on the King's estate, was too much to bear.

Angry spectators raised their fists and shouted for justice; their faces contorted.

Sid slumped in the dock, looking down at the floor as the evidence was read out. Afterwards, the chief magistrate, said, 'You have no legal representation here today, Mr Bucket Senior. Do you have anything to say for yourself?'

Sid scowled and made an inaudible grunting sound.

The young man seated in front of Robbie rose and addressed the court. He gave his name as George Perryman and said he was acting not only as Robbie's solicitor, but as his guardian too for the day after the boy's plight had been brought to his attention, as the only family with him today stood alongside him in the dock. Gasps could be heard throughout the hushed courtroom and Beatrice leant forward to hear every word.

'Your Worships, I am here today to represent Robbie Bucket, a thirteen-year-old boy who finds himself in this court on the most serious of charges. After hearing of his appalling and deplorable circumstances from another solicitor earlier this morning via Constable Rickett, who made the arrest, I offered to represent him free of charge.

'I was here today on another matter which has been adjourned when he told me about the case. I was aghast to hear the boy had nobody to speak up for him on these charges, which he now faces, and has admitted his guilt. Your Worships, I beseech you to consider the choices facing this poor boy; he was threatened with a severe beating if he did not comply with his father's wishes to steal food parcels intended for our bravest of men. He was frequently beaten by him and locked in the cellar.'

The solicitor, his kindness shining through like a beacon, turned to Robbie and asked him to raise his shirt. Robbie stood in the dock and lifted the garment. His chest and back were black and blue and covered in wheals and scars.

'Robbie never ate any of the stolen foods intended for our heroic servicemen.' Mr Perryman paused, pointing a finger at Sid. 'His father devoured everything in the parcels, every tiny crumb and morsel. He taunted his only son by holding them under his nose, while starving him at the same time, as you can see by the thinness of the boy.' He paused again while the courtroom gasped. Robbie hung his head low, his shoulders shaking.

'The only kindness he was shown was at Wolferton Station, where his work colleagues and the Saward family continue to extend this benevolence. I have a letter here that Police Constable Rickett handed me a moment ago – yes, the very same arresting officer. It is a testimonial from Mr Harry Saward, the royal station master, who knows Robbie well and can account for his honest character.'

The solicitor removed a letter from his pocket and reached forward to give it to the clerk, who passed it on to the magistrates seated behind him. There was a pause while they read its contents. It was hard to judge from their expressions if this had drawn a sympathetic response from them. Beatrice smiled inwardly at her father's kindness; he had told her not to worry, that he would look after Robbie. She was relieved the letter had been given to Mr Perryman and that it had now reached the court's attention. Surely the magistrates would give weight to her father's words as he was of such exemplary character.

'Robbie was terrified of his father and forced to comply with his demands,' Mr Perryman continued. 'He had no choice, other than to face a thrashing and be locked up in a dark cellar without food. He is ashamed of his actions, of letting down people in his community and very much regrets not confiding in Mr Harry Saward, fearing he wouldn't believe him. Your Worships, I ask you to take Robbie at his word and show him compassion and clemency for his acts, which, granted, were dishonest in the eyes of the law, but the law isn't black and white.'

The lawyers, scribes, police and public hung on to every word that fell from the solicitor's lips in the hushed courtroom. The magistrates scratched their heads, their jaws wide open. As they prepared to leave to consider their verdict, George continued to state his case. 'I implore you, sirs, to show mercy on this boy and use the wisdom you are bestowed with to see that in order for justice to be served, it need not be applied with harshness in exceptional cases like this, especially if true remorse is shown. It is clear who the real perpetrator is here, and the wicked father should carry the higher level of guilt for the threats he inflicted on his son to make him obey his orders.'

'Hear, hear!' cheered Beatrice, her cheeks flushed and eyes flashing as she stood to applaud the eloquence of George's speech.

'Sit yer down,' chorused the glowering women on either side, yanking at her skirt impatiently.

All eyes stared up at her and Beatrice felt her cheeks flush as she sat down. Only someone with a heart of stone could fail to be moved by the rousing speech from Robbie's defence counsel.

The magistrates rose and retired to an adjoining chamber to consider their sentence. Beatrice leant forward and tried to catch Robbie's attention, but he didn't look up, his eyes fixed on his lap. She thought he looked a pitiful figure, little better than a street urchin. He tried to move his seat away from his father, who snarled at anyone that looked in his direction, their fingers pointing at him.

Beatrice was relieved to see Robbie's legal representative speaking to him and placing a comforting arm on his shoulder. The chattering in the public gallery became louder as they all agreed that Sid deserved what was coming to him, and his sentence couldn't be harsh enough, while believing mercy should be shown to Robbie.

The reporter scribbled away furiously, looking up for a moment at the two figures in the dock, then returning to his notes and scribbling some more. Within ten minutes the magistrates returned.

'All stand please,' ordered the court clerk brusquely. Sid and Robbie both stood and looked straight ahead as the three magistrates returned to their seats. Sid rose with a swagger and Robbie twitched nervously as they awaited their sentence. Beatrice's heart was thumping hard as Sir Ronald looked straight at them, his voice loud and firm.

'Sidney Arthur Bucket and Robbie Reginald Bucket, you have both admitted six charges of theft of the most atrocious nature that I have heard in my forty years on the bench. There is no doubt, as Mr George Perryman so eloquently pointed out, that the real villain is you, Sidney Bucket, and you are a disgrace as a father.'

The chairman pointed an accusing finger at Sid, his small currant eyes looking as if they would burst from his face, as he continued. 'You are sentenced to a total of six months in prison, that is one month for each charge of theft to run consecutively. Jailer, take him down.'

Sid was roughly pushed down the stairs to the cells by the court police officer as spectators cheered.

'Now it is your turn, Robbie Bucket. We have given serious thought as to how we should sentence you. Our decision takes into account your plea and the fact you were bullied by your father into stealing. We take into account the written testimonial given by Mr Saward – you are, indeed, most fortunate to have such a generous and supportive employer, and for these reasons we are showing you compassion.

'However, we have to send out a clear message that we will not tolerate behaviour of this kind and our sentence must serve as a deterrent and be a clear lesson to anyone who is tempted to do the same.'

Beatrice flung a hand to her mouth and she saw Robbie look up at her with fear etched across his face. The reporter's hand flew across one side of his notebook and back again, quickly flickering over his pages to take down every word. Beatrice knew this case would make big headlines in the newspaper tomorrow, and her heart went out to Robbie, fearing that whatever the result, he would forever be dubbed a thief.

'Robbie Bucket,' continued Sir Ronald, his chubby cheeks puffing out as he spoke, 'you are sentenced to six strokes of the birch.'

'No! Oh no! You can't do that, it's not fair,' yelled Beatrice, rising from her seat, her nostrils flaring. All eyes swivelled up towards her. She shook her head, gazing down at Robbie, who was fighting back tears.

'Silence in court,' thundered the clerk, slamming his wooden hammer down on his desk. 'The court demands silence.'

She saw the solicitor look up at her, pressing his finger to his lips, urging her not to say any more.

'Madam, that is the decision of the court,' replied Sir Ronald coldly, in a tone that made her spine tingle. 'Law-abiding citizens expect to see justice being served for what is a most despicable act of theft.'

'But . . .' she began, and then clasped her lips shut as George looked up at her again with another warning glance.

'Silence in court,' bellowed the clerk. 'This is your final warning. The court has made its decision. If there are any more outbursts`, you will be arrested for contempt of court. All stand.'

The magistrates swiftly stood, grunting as they rose, and swept out of the court. Beatrice watched as Robbie was led down the steps in the dock by a burly jailer, throwing a pleading look at his brief. She pushed her way past spectators, whose tongues were wagging approvingly at the sentences handed down, with some narrow-eyed women declaring Robbie got off lightly.

Beatrice couldn't wait to escape from the courtroom, feeling frosty glares boring into her back as she ran down the stairs, looking out for George Perryman to ask if there was anything he could do to help Robbie. A court official told her he was down in the cells with Robbie and she decided to wait for him in the corridor.

She paced up and down the hallway and half an hour later the court official pointed her out to the solicitor as he emerged. He walked towards her and she noticed he had a limp. His expression was solemn and he was clutching his briefcase under his arm. Beatrice introduced herself and choked as she spoke. 'Please, please, please. Isn't there anything you can do to spare him the birch? If you had seen the conditions the poor boy lived in, it would break your heart.'

The solicitor shook his head. 'I'm so sorry, I wish there was something more I could do. The clerk told me the bench were considering sentencing him to twelve strokes, and if it hadn't been for the visible signs of cruelty that Robbie suffered at his father's hands, or the testimonial from your father, that's what it would have been.'

He handed Beatrice a handkerchief as she cried out, her eyes burning with tears. 'Is there nothing you can do?' she asked.

'I can request a doctor is present to tend to any wounds as I expect the punishment is intended to leave its mark on the poor boy.'

Beatrice choked. 'His body won't take it, he's so thin. He doesn't deserve this. But I thank you for speaking on his behalf.'

'Robbie is very lucky to count you and Mr Saward as friends who are willing to speak up publicly for him and defend his honour. I greatly admire your courage, Miss

Saward. I promise I will continue to keep a close eye on him. I only wish there was more I could have done for him today.'

Through moist eyes Beatrice looked into the solicitor's kind face. His eyes crinkled in the corners and his fair curly hair gave him a boyish look. She felt a slight giddiness in her stomach.

'Oh, please call me Beatrice,' she murmured.

'I'm delighted to make your acquaintance, Beatrice. And you must call me George.'

'May I please ask, if it's not too impertinent, but your limp . . . ?'

'Ah, you've noticed my gammy leg. I'm afraid it's the result of childhood polio, but it's a small cross to bear. Although it means I am unfit for war, I count my blessings that I am here to help poor souls like Robbie. Now, if you will please excuse me, I must return to the office. Here is my card. If I can ever be of assistance in the future, please do not hesitate to contact me. George Perryman at your service, ma'am.'

Beatrice took the card and curled her lips in a faint smile. She tucked it into her purse and stepped out into the street, watching George limp around the corner.

His kindness had touched her heart. His good deeds towards Robbie, when he desperately needed help and had nobody else to turn to for advice, had stirred warm feelings within her. She berated herself for allowing such thoughts, especially while Sam was still missing, his fate unknown. She could see that George Perryman was the perfect gentleman, and for all she knew he was either married or betrothed.

Feelings of foolishness and guilt suddenly overcame Beatrice and her face flushed. She quickly dismissed thoughts of Mr Perryman from her head. 'You're engaged to Sam, Beatrice Saward. Before you know it he will be coming home. He's coming home to marry you.'

Why did this thought not excite her? she pondered, twisting her fingers in front of her, unaware of busy court officials pushing past her in the corridor.

Chapter 18

Beatrice's head was still spinning, her mind resolutely determined to be loyal to Sam when he set foot on Norfolk soil again, as she walked down the street. Her feet made tapping sounds as she strode over the cobblestones. Ahead of her was Nelson Street, a winding lane which led to the river and was lined with pretty timber-framed homes dating back to the seventeenth century. It was named after the naval hero, who had local connections, having been born nearby on the north Norfolk coast.

Beatrice needed to turn right where some smart-looking three-storey town houses stood. Within a couple of minutes, she found the address that she had scribbled down. A brass plaque on the wall confirmed Beatrice was in the right place. She pulled the doorbell, giggling at the words engraved on the sign, MRS JOYCE THIMBLE, SEAMSTRESS OF THE MOST FINEST GOWNS.

She stood on a scrubbed doorstep, flanked by white Roman-style pillars. The elegant house had large sash windows on either side of its royal-blue door and stood in a winding crescent where professionals ran their businesses or the well-to-do lived.

A maid answered the door. She had dark hair swept into a white mopcap, pale features and large saucer eyes. The maid showed Beatrice into the parlour, her eyes remaining glued to the floor.

'May I offer you refreshments, ma'am? Mrs Thimble is with a client at the moment. I will let her guests know you are here. Please take a seat.'

Beatrice gladly accepted and sank into the soft plum-coloured upholstery on the spoon back chair placed in front of the large bay window. It was positioned next to a small round table covered with a lace tablecloth and an identical seat was placed on the other side. The room was elaborately furnished with a fine mahogany chiffonier and the curtains on either side of the window were made from a heavy damask in peacock blue and gold.

The maid returned carrying refreshments and Beatrice gulped down the tea, the warm wetness soothing her parched throat. Within a few moments, the door opened and Edith shuffled in, followed by Florence. Florence's face lit up and she rushed to Beatrice, who stood up and opened her arms.

Florence threw her arms around Beatrice's waist. 'I've missed you so much. Tell me your news.'

'I will tell you everything. But first, Edith, how have you been?'

Edith joined Beatrice by the window. 'I did right to come here. I feel stronger day by day. The doctor says I need to rest another week or so as my nerves are still jangled, and then we'll be back in Wolferton.'

'Well, that's wonderful news. I can see you have some colour in your cheeks again. The rest has done you the world of good.'

'I tell her not to read the paper, it distresses her to read news about the war and our boys who have been killed,' Florence commented. 'I can't wait to go home.'

Beatrice noticed Florence's downcast gaze and her lips trembling. 'Is everything all right?' she asked.

'Ma wants me to stay on here, but I would rather die!' she blurted, biting her lip.

'Hush, child. How can you say such a thing at a time like this? After everything your Aunt Joyce has done for you,' her mother scolded. 'You should be grateful that she has offered you a needlework apprenticeship.'

'I am most grateful for the offer, but my heart is in Wolferton. I come alive when I am out in the country lanes or in the thick of the forest, or running down to the marsh, when I am with my family. And I should miss you, Beatrice. I would desperately miss everyone in Wolferton.'

Edith threw an exasperated glance towards Beatrice. 'Well, I can't admit to understanding how you could turn down such a good chance as this,' Edith replied ruefully. 'But it would be a hard-hearted mother who made her daughter stay somewhere if it made her unhappy. And I would miss you, too.'

Florence thanked her profusely, adding, 'I'll do anything you wish, other than stay here. There must be a position for a companion or maid in Wolferton, or even at the Big House in Sandringham.'

'We shall have to see,' said Edith. 'But in the meantime, do tell us about the court case, Beatrice.'

Beatrice recounted details of her morning in court. Florence and her mother listened open-mouthed.

'I always knew that Sid was good for nothing,' retorted Edith, slamming her fist on her knees. 'What chance does that poor lad of his have with a pa like him.'

'Poor Robbie,' Florence commented. 'I can't believe he's a thief. He used to be so withdrawn. I often saw other boys laughing at him. They would throw rotten apples at him on their way home from school, or roll him in the snow to make a snowman out of him. It was cruel.'

'His solicitor says he has to take his punishment. Eddie's family have kindly said they'll take him in afterwards – for now at least. There is nothing we can do, and the people in that court, they wanted their blood, I tell you.'

As Beatrice was leaving, she promised to call in and see Ben and Roly at the farm and inform them of their mother's progress. Florence showed her to the door, gripping Beatrice's arm as she stepped onto the path.

'Oh, Beatrice. I hate it here. Aunt Joyce makes me work until nine o'clock at night. She says I have to work hard to earn our keep, and I don't want Mother to fret, so I don't tell her anything about it. I couldn't bear to stay much longer.'

Beatrice's jaw dropped. 'Why the . . .' she began. 'Where is your aunt? Let me speak to her about this. How dare she take advantage of you like that!'

'No, please don't. I don't want to make any trouble. I just want to go home as soon as possible. I want to see Eddie too, I can't stop thinking about him,' Florence stammered, her body shaking and her eyes pleading with Beatrice for reassurance.

'Oh, Florence. I'm sure Eddie feels fondly towards you, but with the war going on, I have a feeling his heart is not searching for romance.'

'How can you be sure? I can't wait for this damn war to finish so we can all be together, a family again, with Sam and the twins. Oh, Beatrice, when will we hear from Sam? The silence is tearing me and Ma apart.'

Beatrice pulled Florence close and hugged her. She felt Florence's racing heart and her stomach churned with pangs of guilt for allowing herself that earlier fleeting thought of George.

She fished out a handkerchief from her skirt pocket, gently wiped Florence's tear-stained cheeks and whispered, 'I wish I knew, sweet Florence. I wish I knew.'

On her way back to the station, she paused outside a boarded-up shop. She shook her head in despair. The owners had been forced out of the town due to their German nationality. Fitz and Helga, and their daughter Hannah, had lived above the shop, a successful jewellery business, and she encountered them after they stopped at Wolferton Station to visit an acquaintance in the area. They had engaged Beatrice in conversation outside the post office asking her for directions and she had begun a brief friendship with Hannah, a bright-eyed blonde-haired studious girl a year or so younger than her who always had a book in her hand and wanted to be a schoolteacher. 'It's best you cut ties with Hannah for now. We can't take risks,' Harry had declared.

A week or so later the jewellery shop had been attacked and ransacked one night by angry nationalists in their community. Hannah and her family escaped with whatever possessions they could grab. She often wondered what had happened to them and hoped they were in a safe place.

∞

Beatrice boarded the train at King's Lynn and squeezed into a seat next to an elderly woman in black who was weeping over the loss of her grandson on the French battlefields. She was being comforted by her niece, a gangly girl aged around seventeen with cropped shiny hair and a wide mouth. Beatrice could see the brave face she was putting on for the sake of her distraught elderly relative, her own eyes deep with sorrow.

'We are going to Hunstanton to visit my aunt's sister for a few days. I thought the sea air would do her some good,' the girl told Beatrice between sobs, dabbing her eyes dry. 'Poor cousin James, he's the second one we've lost in the last month. We are all in pieces.'

Beatrice gasped at the enormity of their loss and wished them a pleasant stay at the coastal resort. The Sawards had enjoyed many visits there, admiring the grand Sandringham Hotel, which was owned by the railway company, so splendid it could rival the Ritz or Savoy any day, and skipping along the promenade joyfully and enjoying the seaside attractions and its small iron pier. They were happy childhood memories. If only a dose of fresh sea air was all that was needed to cure the agony of loss, the pain, grief and heartache for these two heartbroken souls, it would be bottled up and sell like hot cakes.

The train steamed into Wolferton and Beatrice's companions still clung to each other as she left the carriage, wishing them courage and fortitude.

Betty commented on Beatrice's ashen face when she returned home and insisted she sit down and have a cup of tea. She was soon joined by Maria, Sarah and Jessie, with Ada due to return shortly from her rehearsal. They listened in astonishment as Beatrice described the courtroom scenes, of George Perryman's heartfelt defence that fell on deaf ears, but which had aroused a strong desire within her to stand up and speak for Robbie.

'You were lucky not to get yourself arrested, speaking out like that in court,' rebuked Sarah, shaking her head. 'What will your father say when he gets to hear about this? We have the Saward name to consider, as you well know.'

'I know what I want to say, and that's *bravo*, Beatrice. Poor Robbie was forced to steal.' Maria beamed at Beatrice, her face shining with admiration. 'It was very kind of Mr Saward to send a note speaking up for him. The lad deserves a second chance. Everyone does. Sometimes life isn't black and white, only for those who don't have any worries.'

'I think that's enough of that, Maria. Stealing is stealing. It's wrong, and that's all there is to it. Didn't your mother teach you that?' demanded Sarah.

Maria's eyes flashed and she opened her mouth to speak, but stopped herself as Jessie pressed her hand on her arm and threw her a warning glance.

'Of course she did, and I didn't mean otherwise,' Maria stuttered. 'I apologise if my words angered you. It's just, I'm feeling out of sorts. I've written to Uncle Gus enquiring after Freddie and Archie, but haven't heard back. I'm worried to death about them.'

Maria paced around the room, rubbing her hands together. 'What am I to do?' she asked in a shaky voice.

'Well—' started Sarah, after a pause and raising a finger to emphasise her suggestion before she was interrupted by Jessie.

'I think you should visit them and see for yourself. I'm sure it could be arranged and Father would help you with the rail fare. What do you think, Mother?'

Maria's eyes shone and her mouth curved into a smile. 'Would he really? I fret that Uncle Gus is working them down to their bones to make them earn their keep. Ma says at least they have a roof over their heads, and I I'm not to interfere. If there is a Lord up there, I hope he's looking down on them. They haven't done anyone any harm.'

'That seems like a sensible idea,' Sarah approved, much to everyone's surprise. 'Do you reckon it would be easy enough for you to find the little lads?'

'I'll come with you too, if you like,' offered Jessie.

Sarah shook her head. 'I'm not so sure that's a good idea.'

Seeing the disappointment etched on Maria's face, she told her, 'Well, seeing it's on your mind so much, but only if Mr Saward approves.'

'Thank you both for your kindness. I can't wait to see Freddie and Archie. I'll go after Ada's concert.'

Betty offered, 'You're a good girl. And I'll bake you a nice cake to take them when you go.'

∞

The early evening was warm and mellow and the sweet scent of honeysuckle filled the air. Maria counted her blessings as she stepped outside the station master's house, feeling quite grand that she was walking out of the front door as if she belonged there, nodding at a couple of young lads loitering nearby.

She was on her way to the church to see Ada to offer any help she could for the concert. As she approached the church, she spotted Ada by the gate talking to the vicar. She quickened her step and offered to relieve Ada of her overflowing armful of sheet music, which was at risk of slipping to the ground. Ada's face showed concern and a trickle of the choir ladies bade farewell as they passed them by.

'If the music from Clara doesn't come within the next couple of days we will have to change our programme. I feel so sorry for Clara, I don't know what to say to her.

She has set her heart on this music,' Ada told the vicar. 'I can't make sense of it. The shop insists it was dispatched days ago.'

Ada finished speaking to the reverend and joined Maria to walk back home, telling her how anxious she was about it.

'Don't worry about it. I'm sure it will turn up,' Maria said, trying to cheer Ada up.

'I hope you're right, Maria. Anyway, how was your day?'

Maria told Ada what she'd heard from Beatrice about Robbie's court case and Ada expressed admiration on hearing of Beatrice's outburst in support of Robbie.

When they had almost reached the station master's house, a raised voice made them look up. They saw a man clip two boys around the ears before they ran off.

'What an awful man,' commented Ada, pulling a face. 'I don't know who he is. He is a stranger to these parts.'

Maria's eyes remained fixed on the unknown man as they continued walking towards the house. He was lolling against a tree, rolling up a cigarette. A sense of unease welled up inside her as they got closer and her stomach tightened, as if the strings of a corset were squeezing her in. There was something about the way he moved his bulky beer belly that looked familiar and alarmed her.

'I can't say he looks the friendly type,' shuddered Ada, when they were within spitting distance of the stranger.

Maria froze as her worst fears were confirmed.

'What is it, Maria? Do you know that man? Why are you looking at him that way?'

Maria's face turned scarlet and her heart pounded. Her throat clenched as the man drew hard on his cigarette, inhaling in every last puff of tobacco, and flicked it down, stamping on it and grinding the butt slowly into the ground. His face fixed hard on hers, his intense expression making her shiver.

She took a sharp intake of breath as the stranger stepped forward, nodded at her, then turned his back and walked up the path towards Sandringham.

'Maria. What is it? You look as if you've seen a ghost.'

'Oh, Ada, it's worse than that. I've seen the devil himself.'

Ada shook Maria's shoulders. 'What do you mean you've "seen the devil"? Who is he? Oh no, is he . . . ?'

Maria choked, 'Yes, it's him. That's the man who forced himself on me. That's Walter Jugg!'

Chapter 19

Beatrice clutched the telegram in her hand. Her hands were shaking. 'Oh no, not Piers. It can't be!'

She shot a desperate glance at her mother. 'I'm afraid so. It just came in this afternoon, so you'd best get over to the Rumbelows' straightaway.'

Beatrice shook her head and felt a lump rising in her throat. 'Oh no, poor Mrs Rumbelow. It will finish the poor woman off.'

Beatrice placed the envelope carefully in her bag and slung it over her shoulder. It was almost four o'clock when she pedalled off carrying news that she knew would break the hearts of Jane and her husband, people who dedicated their days to offering comfort and support to his parishioners.

Larger post offices had telegram messengers to deliver the most painful news, but smaller communities, like Wolferton, did not always have these 'Angels of Death', as they became known, it was down to the postman to be the bearer of bad news. While an officer's next of kin was informed by a telegram that was telegraphed over to the post office, the next of kin of other ranks received their terrible news by standard post, in brown envelopes with the letters OHMS – On His Majesty's Service – printed on the top, so Beatrice would have no idea of its heart-breaking contents as she delivered the post, until she heard the anguished cries from inside the house after she had left, alerting neighbours that there had been another terrible loss.

Piers had been a serving medic and a junior officer. As Beatrice pulled up outside the vicarage gate, her heart filled with dread and her mouth dry. Mrs Glossop, the ageing housekeeper, answered the door, and Beatrice enquired if the vicar was at home. The housekeeper confirmed that he had just returned from his calls and was in his study.

Mrs Rumbelow appeared at the door clutching a bunch of freshly picked roses.

'Good afternoon, Beatrice. What brings you here?'

She glanced down at Beatrice's hand and swayed when she what she was holding.

'I'm so sorry, Mrs Rumbelow,' Beatrice muttered softly, handing over the telegram, her lips trembling.

'Oh no. Not my Freddie,' she cried, gripping the telegram. The flowers fell from her hands to the ground, scattering over the hallway carpet. Oh my God. Please don't say . . .'

Her husband rushed to her side as she tore the envelope open, then let out a piercing scream. 'No, no, no. My son, our beloved son. He's dead!'

Beatrice hung her head, knowing there was nothing she could say. She felt like an intruder in their private grief as the vicar ran to his wife's side and held her in his arms as she cried inconsolably.

The vicar bit his lip, trying to fight back his own tears, but he gave way to them and fell to his knees, letting go of his wife and holding his head in his hands.

Jane pulled him up and pummelled his chest with her fists. 'Don't tell me there is a God. I don't believe a kind God would take such a wonderful son as ours.'

Beatrice crept away, shaken to her core by the raw emotion she had witnessed. *If God can take the vicar's son, what chance have lesser mortals like Sam and Alfie? Praying isn't going to save them, that's for sure.*

The atmosphere at the station master's house that evening was sombre.

Beatrice's voice trembled as she described the agonising scene at the vicarage. Betty placed a comforting arm around her shoulders.

'What is this world coming to? Our men are dying. And for what? What good is going to come of it?' sobbed Beatrice.

'You know what for, Beatrice. We are not going to let the Huns run our country and get rid of our King. Look what's happening in France; they are gassing our lads. If we don't fight back, we are lost,' muttered Sarah.

'But what if Sam is dead too? And we haven't heard from Alfie for weeks,' Beatrice whimpered.

Betty soothed Beatrice until her rapid breathing slowed down. 'Each day is getting worse. I was going over to Blackbird Farm to see Ben and Roly, but I can't face it

257

now. All I can hear is Jane's cries in my head. The poor, poor woman.'

The next day, Beatrice was resolved to be strong and not give in to feelings of despondency. When she arrived at the post office, Sarah held up a letter that had come for Ada.

'You'd best take it over to the house now. Ada will be desperate for news of Alfie.'

Beatrice packed the rest of the letters in her bag and set off, relieved there appeared no brown envelopes with OHMS on the front for her to deliver that day.

∞

Ada eagerly ripped open her letter with a yelp and her eyes danced excitedly along the lines. Her hand flew to her chest, her face creasing into a worried frown and then changing to a smile as she absorbed his words.

My darling Ada,

I hope this letter finds you well and our beloved Leslie brings you joy each day. How I miss you all, but we must get our job done.

We are now billeted in a chateau in beautiful countryside along with a number of exceptional men from other regiments posted here for officer training in which I assist. It would be wonderful under any other circumstances and I have been lucky enough to get a tiny room with another Artist, so we have more privacy than ever before.

I count my blessings that I survived my spell in the trenches last month, having marched for several miles from our previous location in heavy rain, our boots dragging in mud. The trenches twisted and turned in all directions and we stayed there through the night, with rain pelting down on us, crawling out in front of barbed wire entanglements to hear the listening posts. We were so close to the enemy, but the heavy artillery couldn't do much in case they hit their own men.

I go to services when I can. They are popular with the Artists and sometimes a bishop will officiate and we sing with all our hearts and souls. I always pray for you and our beloved son and beg you not to worry on my account as we are here fighting for a just cause. I am proud to be serving our King and await the day we can be reunited and I get to hold our precious son.

Your parcels and letters are always a joy. Could you send me writing paper and envelopes in your next dispatch?

I send you my heartfelt love.

Your darling, Alfie

Ada's eyes shone as she recounted Alfie's news. 'I'll write to him after the concert. I can't wait to tell him all about it.'

Her face saddened. 'He'll be devastated to hear of Piers' death. He was very fond of him.'

'I know he will, my heart goes out to his parents. But I'm so happy for you, Ada, it's such a relief to know he is well,' Beatrice replied, her voice tinged with despondency.

Ada placed an arm around her sister's shoulder. She noticed her looking downcast. 'I hope you have news soon from Sam too.'

'I hope Alfie and Sam will be home very soon with Godspeed.' Betty groaned, bending down to pick up a basket of clean laundry.

Maria jumped up saying, 'I'll do that.'

'I don't mind if you do. All this bending, it makes me feel my age. And mind you put everything in its right place.'

Maria had put away the laundry a few times, saving Betty a breathless walk up the steep stairs. She knew which drawers she needed for Sarah's white cotton nightwear and petticoats and Harry's socks and underwear. She was careful to hang the station master's crisp white shirts in the large walnut wardrobe so they didn't crease. She paused to look out of the turret window, giving her a bird's-eye view across to the station. She rubbed her eyes and watched as Eddie stopped Beatrice, who had just left the house to continue on her rounds. They engaged in conversation and she could see he was anxious. She liked Eddie, she could tell he was a good sort, and she wondered what had caused him to appear fretful.

Her mind turned to Walter and her head began to spin. *So where could he be?* She pressed her face against the window, her eyes flashing anxiously in all directions, recalling the menacing words he had written in his note, '*Don't think you can hide from me. I'll be watching you.*'

She didn't know why he was in Wolferton but it couldn't be good. He'd want to blacken her name and ruin her life and she didn't know what to do. She had asked Ada not to tell anyone else that they'd seen him, just in case she was wrong, so as not to cause unnecessary alarm.

She stood up and smoothed the bedcovers, taking in a few gulps of air. Her head was still in a spin as she began walking out of the bedroom. Her eyes were lured in the direction of a drawer still ajar and she went over to close it. She peered in and saw Harry's tie pins and cufflinks neatly laid out in their boxes. Her eyes fixed on a distinctive-looking rectangular beige box with the word Fabergé embellished across it.

Intrigued, she opened the drawer fully and gently lifted it out. The name Fabergé stood out. The look and feel of the box made her think that she was holding something special that might be worth a lot of money. She racked her brains, whispering the name under her breath, unsure how to pronounce it.

Her curiosity roused, she opened the lid. Staring up at her was an exquisite gold jewelled pin. She was no jewellery expert, but she could sense that what she was looking at was very special. She removed it from its satin casing and turned it over, noticing the crowns engraved on it.

'Blimey. I ain't seen anything so grand as this before.' She gawped wide eyed as she stepped to the window to scrutinise the pin in the sunlight. 'I bet it's worth a bob or two.'

Her fingers itched and tingled at the touch of the golden pin. As she went to replace it in the drawer a thought struck her. *Take it and run, before Walter gets to you.*

Another voice in her head reasoned, *Put it back, Maria. Don't be foolish. Think of what happened to poor Robbie. Think of the many kindnesses you have had from the Sawards.*

Maria's fingers continued to twitch as she wrestled with her conscience. She shuffled from foot to foot, her heartstrings tugging as she imagined her darling Joey being placed in a workhouse now that the money her mother had given for his keep in Doncaster had run out. She imagined Uncle Gus's cruelty to her two innocent brothers when he realised he had bled her mother dry. And now, for some unknown reason, Walter was hot on her heels, unnerving her and making her look over her shoulder whenever she went out.

'I'm sorry,' she whispered guiltily, her skin tingling as she fingered the precious pin. 'I don't see as if I have a choice. I'll just borrow it. Just in case I need it. Maybe I can pawn it and then somehow get it back later. I'll get a job somewhere, anywhere, to buy it back.'

The temptation too strong to resist, she slid the shiny pin into the pocket of her skirt, leaving the empty box inside the drawer so as not to make it too obvious that something was missing.

She slid into her attic room and threw open the chest, carefully concealing the pin between clothing, resting it on top of a blue blouse which she folded over four times. She fished deep down into the chest and retrieved Walter's letter. She placed this in her skirt pocket, intending to destroy it. She returned downstairs, her face flushed, dismissing the guilt she felt at her impulsive act.

However hard she tried, her stomach churned and tightened and her nerves jangled. She busied herself scrubbing the front porch step and sweeping the hallway carpet, avoiding chatter and eye contact with Betty.

'You fool. You stupid, ungrateful fool,' she whimpered to herself. 'What have you done?'

Maria immediately regretted her reckless actions. She was determined to replace the pin and could think of nothing else. Her mind was in a daze as she resolved to put right her terrible deed as soon as she could. But whenever a chance arose to slip into Harry's bedroom unseen, she was suddenly sidetracked by Betty.

She planned to seize her moment when everyone was seated for lunch.

Beatrice arrived home first. 'Have you heard the news? Robbie is back. Eddie mentioned it earlier when I bumped into him,' she blurted out.

'Now how would I have heard any news? I've been here all morning,' retorted Betty, dishing up braised liver with potatoes and runner beans.

'Blimey, that was quick. How is he?' enquired Maria, grasping the fact that the boy would have had his severe punishment.

'He's at Eddie's, he told me this morning. Eddie's neighbour Bernie Figgs brought him back in a cart first thing from Lynn. He'd been keeping an eye on things and made enquiries at the court.'

'What do you mean, he's at Eddie's?' asked Maria, her eyes incredulous.

'He had nowhere else to go. Eddie says he's in agony, in terrible pain from the strikes, and he doesn't know what to do. Father said he could stay with him today as he has another lad helping with portering.'

'The torturers didn't waste their time then.' Maria spat her words, reminding her of the temptation she had given in to that could have terrible consequences for her if discovered. She wished more than anything to be rid of it now.

'Why, Maria, what's gotten into you to speak so fiercely?' asked Betty.

Maria avoided her gaze and bit her lip. ''Cos it's not fair. It's not right. People make mistakes when they're desperate,' she choked.

'Well, I dare say they do,' Beatrice chipped in. 'And they suffer for it too. By all accounts the poor boy has the most awful wheals stamped across his behind that are red and sore and bleeding still, as if he had been branded like a lamb. Eddie is hopping mad. He says no decent human being would treat an animal like that.'

'The poor lad. He must see a doctor, otherwise those sores could turn nasty,' Betty commiserated. 'How about I bake a cake for when he gets his appetite back?'

'That would be a welcome treat, I'm sure. It's so touching to see how caring people can be, in spite of the cause of his affliction,' retorted Beatrice. 'Eddie told me he sent for Dr Fletcher straightaway and he came over within a shot. He showed him how to bathe the wounds with salted water and put camomile on afterwards. But it stings and pains Robbie so much that he can't help screaming when he is touched there. Eddie asked if I could call in and see him later. He says he wants to thank me for speaking up in court.'

'I imagine he is very thankful for that was a wonderful thing you did,' Maria said, her voice faltering.

Beatrice's voice was wistful. 'If only I could have done more; could have stopped it.'

'I doubt anyone could have done that, not from what I've heard,' soothed Betty.

'But you tried, didn't you? You spoke up for him, you were like a guardian angel,' Maria retorted, her eyes shining in admiration.

Beatrice blushed. 'It was the least I could do. Nothing I said, nor his solicitor's pleading, made any difference. They wanted their pound of flesh and it broke my heart to see Robbie's pleading eyes looking up at me. Giving him a whipping with the birch is barbaric and should be banned.'

Beatrice winced as she imagined the pain of the forceful lashing landing on Robbie's bare skin as he knelt down. She hoped a doctor had been present as the cluster of thin birch branches was bound together, looking much like the head of a broom, to inflict the utmost pain. The first stroke inflicted a mild pain, building up to a more intense pain with each subsequent stroke.

'Poor Robbie, taking such a beating for what his father put him up to. The court should have shown mercy on him. It's Sid Bucket who should have had the birch,' declared Maria, rage sweeping through her body.

The rest of the family arrived home and were seated at the table. The subject changed and Harry beamed with pride as he boasted about his splendid climbing roses, the best he could remember, and Sarah mentioned that some ladies from the choir had dropped off eggs at the post office for the National Egg Collection.

Maria barely heard a word. She could think only of Harry's Fabergé pin hidden in the chest in her room and reflect on the enormity of her actions. Would Beatrice speak up for her in court if she ended up there? Would she be birched too?

'I must return it before they notice it's missing,' she vowed under her breath.

Beatrice's question caught her off guard. 'Oh, who was your letter from Maria? The one left on the doormat? Not bad news, I hope.'

Maria fumbled in her pocket. The hairs on the back of her neck tingled and she realised with a feeling of dread that she didn't have the letter anymore. It must have fallen out. She ignored the question, jumping up from the table quickly and clearing away the dishes.

Chapter 20

'What a morning it's been. I must admit I am that tired now and could do with forty winks while Robbie's cake is baking,' murmured Betty, stifling a yawn.

'You sit down, Betty, I see how you wait on us all day,' Maria replied. 'I'll make you a cuppa and finish cleaning up while you have a rest. God knows you deserve it.'

'Well bless you, girl, aren't you the kind one,' Betty replied appreciatively, rubbing her eyes. 'It's just, I'm not as young as I used to be and I must admit I do like having an extra pair of hands around the place to help, especially cleaning the kitchen floor. I'm not so good on my knees anymore, and they don't half ache when I bend down with that broom.'

Maria propped a cushion behind Betty's back and watched her close her eyes. She planned to seize the moment to return the gold pin to its satin-lined box in Harry's drawer before he noticed it had gone. She crept upstairs after the dishes were cleared away in search for Walter's letter too, to no avail. Puzzled, but shrugging it off, she retrieved Harry's treasured pin from between the folds of the blouse, placed it in her pocket and stepped quietly downstairs to the landing below. She felt inside her pocket again to reassure herself it was still there, her fingers running along its edges. Whatever monetary value it had was small in comparison to the kindness and generosity the Sawards had shown her. Now she had to replace it and find Walter's letter. She didn't want anyone else to find it first and start asking questions.

She placed a shaking hand on Harry and Sarah's door handle while taking the pin out of her pocket and holding it in her other palm. It felt clammy.

'Maria!' a voice called out.

She froze. Her heart pounding. Hearing her name called a second time she turned around. Jessie stood at the bottom of the stairs.

Maria's face turned crimson and her eyes widened. She had been caught red-handed about to enter Jessie's parent's bedroom, the precious pin still burning in the palm of her hand, which she clenched tightly shut.

Maria's throat tightened, her legs shaking, and she weakly acknowledged Jessie, guilt plastered across her red face.

Jessie walked halfway up the stairs and Maria met her halfway down, quickly returning the pin to her pocket without Jessie noticing.

'What is it, Maria? What are you doing outside my parents' bedroom? You look startled. Only Betty should tidy up there. It looked as if—'

'As if what?' croaked Maria, awkwardly. 'I was just checking the beds were aired.'

'I'm sorry, Maria. Forget it. I was looking for you. Beatrice wondered if you would take a cake round to Robbie's house later. She called in to see him after her rounds this morning, but he was sleeping, and she has to go to Blackbird Farm after work to see Ben and Roly.'

'Of course, I'll go,' replied Maria. 'But first I have to finish my jobs here.'

Maria had no choice but to follow Jessie downstairs. Fired by feelings of immense guilt, she washed the lunch dishes with extra vigour until they sparkled, her elbows flying in the air as she scrubbed the pots and pans. She swept and scrubbed the floor on her knees to save Betty the chore she struggled with.

With Jessie still in the house, Maria didn't dare risk trying to step a foot inside Harry and Sarah's room again. After finishing the chores, and hearing Jessie leave the house, she climbed into her attic bedroom and undid the chest, where she placed the pin between the folds of her blouse once again, planning to return it to its rightful place when she returned from seeing Robbie. Then she made her way back downstairs.

Refreshed after her snooze, Betty opened her eyes. 'Well, upon my soul!' she exclaimed. 'I only closed my eyes for a minute and when I wake up I see the house fairies have visited us.'

Maria said meekly, 'I hope it's all right. Only I know how particular you are, Betty, and Mrs Saward is, too. I just wanted to do something, to be worthy of all your kindness for having me here.'

Betty shook her head, laughing. 'Is it all right, my child. Why it's more than all right. It's really good. I can't fault it. You'll be doing me out of a job if I'm not careful.'

Maria blushed. 'Oh no, I would never do that. Nobody cooks and bakes like you, Betty. I just wanted to help. I would never want to upset you.'

Betty winked at Maria, her face beaming. 'Come here, you silly thing. Of course I'm glad of your help. You'd soon have an earbashing from me if it didn't meet my exacting standards, even if I need the odd forty winks now, I promise you that.'

Maria's face glowed at such high praise as Betty wrapped the cake in greaseproof paper. Jessie gave her directions to Eddie's cottage and Betty held out a basket with the delicious cake and a slice of cold rabbit pie left over from lunch. Before she left, Maria smiled at herself in the mirror, turning her head from side to side. The deep green dress she wore brought out the colour in her hazel eyes, making them seem more luminous. She was beginning to feel like . . . well, like one of the smartly dressed Saward sisters. It felt good.

As Maria warily stepped outside onto the dusty path, her head spun around in every direction, her eyes protruding as she searched everywhere for Walter.

Feeling relieved that he was nowhere to be seen she breathed a sigh of relief and tightly gripped the basket, waving at Sarah, who was standing on the step outside the post office. She was talking to Eddie. Maria paused and glanced at him sideways, seeing him through different eyes. For the first time, Maria's stomach churned and she felt fluttery inside as his gaze fell on her face. Perhaps it was because she had learnt of his kindness to Robbie, and this ignited a flame inside her. She blushed when he grinned at her. She nodded her head to Sarah and rushed over to speak to her.

Maria felt herself redden even more under Eddie's direct stare as he introduced himself and complimented her on her dress. She lifted up the cloth covering the food to show him the tasty fare she was delivering to Robbie, explaining that she was going on behalf of Beatrice.

'Robbie will be pleased of your pretty company. He was feverish last night, sweating, and could hardly sleep from the pain of his beating. So, if he don't have an appetite for what you are taking, please don't be offended.'

Maria felt a pang. She was moved by Eddie's thoughtfulness towards Robbie, and her cheeks flushed pink at his compliment.

'So you really are related to Harry Saward then?'

'I am, but it's a long story.'

Sarah made her excuses to go inside, saying she had her work cut out and couldn't stand idle and chatter.

'What does she mean by that?' asked Maria.

'I just stopped off here to inform Mrs Saward that the head housekeeper from Sandringham House will be inspecting the royal waiting rooms the day after tomorrow, a message just came though to Mr Saward about it.'

Maria was aghast. 'But that's no notice at all. Poor Mrs Saward, she'll never have time to clean it all through from scratch.'

'Oh, she'll be fine. I'm sure it's nothing to worry about, knowing how Mrs Saward is very particular and likes everything to be just so. I don't get to look in, us common folk ain't allowed in there. I believe Jessie was there a couple of days ago going over the furniture with her duster and polish. And she's been working in the garden too, so everything should be in order. We get used to these royal commands here, you know.'

'I'm sure you do.' Maria grinned. 'I'll be on my way now.'

'Can you tell Robbie I'll be home as soon as I can, but with our troops coming and going all day, I can't say when that'll be. I only wish I was a Tommy too. I can't wait for that day when I'm old enough fight alongside them. I'll show those Huns.'

'Oh Eddie, no!' Maria blurted out, surprising herself with the strength of her reaction. 'I mean, of course you must, but that won't be for a while, will it?'

'Why, would you miss me?' Eddie teased, out of Sarah's hearing. Maria's cheeks flushed. 'I might only be sixteen years old, but I'm ready to take on the Huns. They don't scare me!'

Maria gulped, her body tensing and her cheeks flushing again under his intense gaze.

'Why, you are a brave one,' Maria said.

'Really? You think so? You've made my day.'

Maria raised her chin and arched her back. 'Get away with you, Eddie Herring. You don't know the first thing about me.'

A slow smile spread across her flushed face as she gazed at the goodness etched on Eddie's. It was the first time she had looked at him closely and her eyes lingered on him appreciatively. Eddie made his excuses as the guard's shrill whistle rang in her ears to announce an imminent departure. She felt a warm glow course within her body and savoured a sweet shimmering sensation. Her face reddened again. She hadn't felt that way about a boy before and she smiled inwardly as she reflected on how despite his youthful years, he was blessed with a wise head on young shoulders.

She quickly shrugged off any hopes of her romantic notions coming to fruition, asking herself what Eddie would really think of her if he knew she had a bastard son and had just given in to temptation and taken something that wasn't rightfully hers. However hard she tried to justify her actions, she could barely bring herself to say the word 'stealing'. Eddie would be shocked, like all decent folk. *What respectable boy would want anything to do with her?* she asked herself. She was soiled goods in any man's eyes.

She looked over her shoulder as she continued walking, nodding politely as she passed older folk of Wolferton busily tidying their gardens, their backs bent as they hoed their flowerbeds, some digging them up, like Eddie's family, to replace them with vegetables. A couple of ladies in their seventies, their thinning white hair tucked under mobcaps, gossiped together over their garden fences, their heads turning to watch her as she walked by. They quickly turned their backs on her and she heard one of them mutter, 'Aggie

Greensticks was only saying the other day that the Sawards had a relative staying with them, that must be her.'

Maria recognised Eddie's cottage at the furthest end of the lane from the directions she had been given. Rows of green runner beans with sprouting orange flowers twisted around tall canes. The wooden gate creaked as she lifted the rusty latch and pushed it open and she followed the cobbled path to the side of the house where a large tin bath hung on the wall.

The back garden was filled with lettuces, tomatoes and potatoes. Her eyes were drawn to a chicken house fitted with wire mesh around and above its perimeter to keep the hens from straying. They bounced their heads up and down, gobbling up discarded potato peelings and food scraps. The house backed onto the railway track, but was far enough away from it not to be engulfed in engine smoke when a train steamed past.

Maria knocked tentatively on the back door and pressed her ear against it. Nobody answered. She knocked again, and after not getting a response, she cautiously lifted the latch, putting her head around the door and calling out, asking if anyone was at home. A woman's voice replied telling her to come in.

She stepped into the kitchen and glanced around, looking for the woman who spoke. A bowl of water stood on a sturdy oak table covered with newspaper. A wet flannel lay on a dish next to it. There was also a pile of freshly dug potatoes and a few runner beans ready to be cleaned. Maria placed her basket on the table and called out 'Hello!'

'I'm in the parlour, come through to the front,' the woman's voice instructed.

Maria gasped as she heard groans, followed by a pained cry that pierced the centre of her heart.

The wooden door creaked as she pushed it open and she stepped into the front room. The room was darkened as the curtains were drawn. It was small with a low ceiling and was stifling hot, almost as bad as her attic room. She blinked, her eyes becoming accustomed to the darkness. She gasped, her hand flying to her mouth, as her wide eyes rested on Robbie. He was lying on a mattress on the floor face down and she glimpsed his bare rump. It was covered in thick swollen lines raised above the skin. They looked so sore that she winced, having never seen such painful wounds before; bright red and inflamed, the stripes of the birch clearly visible. Maria balked, turning away, tears springing to her eyes.

A woman who was tending to his wounds quickly pulled Robbie's nightshirt over him. 'Whoever did this would get a taste of their own medicine, if I had a say. And who might you be? I was expecting Beatrice. Are you that lass staying with the Sawards?'

Maria introduced herself to Eddie's mother and showed her the food she had brought.

She smiled. 'Ah yes, my Eddie has mentioned you.'

Maria blushed, wondering what Eddie would have said about her. Her eyes followed Mabel Herring as she stooped over the boy with her lean body, her sleeves rolled up showing her slender arms. She had fine bones in her face and Maria imagined she would have been a beauty in her day. She spotted the resemblance to Eddie's honest deep blue eyes.

Maria winced and looked away as Mabel lifted the nightshirt again to bathe Robbie's searing wounds, dabbing a muslin cloth in warm water and gently patting them. 'Didn't our Eddie warn you? Oh, you poor thing. I'm sorry he didn't tell you.'

Robbie clenched his teeth, screwing up his face and turning his head from side to side when his skin was touched, even though Mabel could not have been gentler. Maria felt mildly embarrassed at seeing him in this undressed state and was conscious this might play on his mind too.

'I'd no idea how bad he was. Poor Robbie,' she mumbled, biting her lip.

Robbie cried out again, his body stiffening. His face looked the other way and she could only see a mop of black hair.

'What can I do to help? There must be something we can do to ease the pain,' Maria exhorted.

Mabel pulled Robbie's nightshirt down and stood up, drying her hands on a towel hanging over a chair. She rubbed the back of her neck where a vein rippled, her eyes narrowed.

'I think he's running a temperature. I'm going for the doctor. He can't take that salted water, it's too painful for him and I don't like the look of those wounds. They may become infected. Could you stay here with him while I go?'

Maria readily agreed, her heart pounding. 'It breaks my heart to see him like this.'

'I'll be as quick as I can. Let's hope the doctor's in. That Sid Bucket wants shooting for getting his poor boy in this kind of trouble. If only his mother were here, none of this would have happened.' Mabel shook her head, picking up a blue shawl and wrapping it around her shoulders.

'What do you mean "If only his mother were here". I just assumed she was dead.'

Mabel beckoned Maria over. 'She may as well be dead. Folk haven't heard sight nor sound of her since she disappeared three years ago. I knew how Sid beat her, she couldn't hide them bruises from me. But I was still shocked when she upped and left.'

Maria's hands flew to her face. 'Oh poor Robbie. He must miss her dreadfully. I'll take good care of him, Mrs Herring, I promise.'

Mabel lent over and spoke softly to Robbie, assuring him that he would be left in good company with Maria and promised to return with the doctor as quickly as she could. Maria stepped slowly around the mattress, taking in what she had been told about Robbie's mother. She felt a pang of sympathy for his suffering. She observed Robbie's pained face, crimson red. It was clear to her he was raging a temperature. One of his eyes was wide open staring up at the ceiling, his right arm dangled down the side of the mattress. She gently touched his forehead and recoiled, feeling the heat from his skin. She took the bowl of water to the kitchen and refilled it with fresh cool water from the bowl on the kitchen table.

Robbie was only thirteen-years-old, still a child, the same age as Maria's brother Freddie. The thought of her brother being beaten in such a cruel way, suffering so much pain because of the sins of his father, made her rage inside at the injustice of it all. The sight of Robbie's appalling injuries pricked her conscience again, making her all the more determined to return the jewelled pin as soon as she returned home, and she vowed never to steal again.

'Oh, you poor boy. Now listen to me, Robbie Bucket. You're gonna get better, do you hear me. On my life I promise that you will be well again,' she whispered reassuringly.

Her heart tugged as he groaned, his face twisting, then tilting his head slightly towards her. His eyelids flickered open a little, and then closed.

'Shush,' she murmured, mopping his burning brow with the dampened muslin cloth. He flinched at every touch, biting his lip and screwing his eyes tight shut.

'I'm being as gentle as I can. I don't mean to hurt you. I'm gonna care for you just as if you were my own brother.'

She saw his eyes open again and his lips curl slightly. 'You two would get on like a house on fire, I know you would,' Maria told him. 'One day you will meet each other, I can feel it in my bones.'

She raised her head at the sound of the back door being flung open followed by rushed footsteps. Mabel had returned, flushed and breathless. A man was behind her. Mabel pressed her hands against her chest and pointed to the pitiful figure of Robbie. The doctor, a tall man, ducked low as he walked through the door. He went straight over to Robbie's side and Maria jumped up quickly and stepped into the kitchen, saying she would wait there while he was examined.

Maria winced as she heard Robbie's moans followed by a yelp. She heard the doctor speak. 'Give him some of this laudanum three times a day, ease the pain. Here is some camomile lotion for his wounds, it is gentle and healing for him. I'm afraid it will take time, a long time. I just pray they haven't become infected.'

'But, Doctor, I'm afraid I don't have money to pay for these,' protested Mabel, swallowing hard.

'That's taken care of. No need to worry. I'll call in and see Robbie again tomorrow.'

'What do you mean it's taken care of? Are you saying we don't we have to pay you, Dr Fletcher?' asked Mabel, her brows knitted.

'That's right, as I said, it's all taken care of. There's no need for you to concern yourself on that account. I bid you farewell. Until tomorrow . . .'

Mabel showed the doctor out, shaking her head at such generosity, and returned to Robbie's bedside. 'Well I never. Who would have done such a thing?'

'I'm learning fast that there are some very decent people here in Wolferton,' Maria replied, stroking Robbie's hand.

Maria told her about all the hard work being done for the forthcoming concert. 'The strange thing is that the sheet music Ada had ordered from Fortescue & Sons in Bond Street hasn't arrived although it was posted almost a week ago. Clara is beside herself with worry, she's the star singer who's come from London specially and is desperate for it.'

'Sheet music?' came a pained whimper from the mattress on the floor.

Maria and Mabel spun their heads around and watched Robbie move his lips slightly. Maria pressed her ears against the boy's face and repeated his faltering words. 'Hidden ... home ... under ... mattress ... sorry ... Father took them.'

His eyes filled with tears, and he repeated his apology.

'I can't believe it. Did Robbie just say the sheet music is hidden at his home?' Maria asked.

Mabel nodded. 'He did, I'm sure he did. He said that wicked father of his was behind it. He said you will find it under the mattress of his bed. I bet he thought it was worth a bob or two, but was arrested before he had a chance to flog it.'

'I'd best get home quickly and tell Ada,' spluttered Maria. 'She'll be over the moon.'

She hastily bade farewell, promising to return another time. As Maria passed the station, she paused for a moment as she recalled what Eddie had told her about the inspection of the royal waiting rooms in two days' time.

Maybe it's my turn to help Mrs Saward, to show how much I appreciate what she has done for me, Maria thought wistfully. *But first I must tell Ada about the sheet music.*

Chapter 21

On hearing the news, Maria sprinted to the post office and recounted it to Beatrice. Together they tore to Sid Bucket's cottage and quickly found the sheet music, as Robbie had mentioned, under his father's stinking mattress.

Back home, Ada was overjoyed it had been found and inspected the crinkled brown envelope with the name Fortescue & Son stamped on the front. She was desperate to peek inside, but was mindful that Clara had insisted the music was to be a surprise for the night of the concert.

Her fingers itched as they toyed with the paper, and Beatrice raised an eyebrow. 'Don't spoil her surprise, if it means so much to her,' she cautioned.

Ada pulled her finger back. 'I'm so curious, but very well. I'll take it to her now. That is if you wouldn't mind looking after Leslie, Maria, while I cycle over. I won't keep Clara in suspense a moment longer. I can't wait to see her face when I show her.'

'Of course I'll stay here with him. We can go out in the garden.'

Ada clasped Maria's hands. 'Thank you, Maria, you are an angel for finding out about this. You have become such a treasure to us. I don't know how we would manage without you now.'

A tear pricked the corner of Maria's eye and she bit her lip. 'I can't wait to see the concert. I know it will be a great success. All the posh people there, and royalty too; Ma will be so impressed.'

'And Alfie will be so proud. You can write afterwards and tell him all about it,' added Beatrice, placing an arm around Ada's shoulder.

Maria reached into her pocket for a handkerchief and withdrew her hand in a flash, suddenly remembering the jewelled pin that she had placed there in a moment of madness and was still concealed in the chest in her room. Her face reddened and she swallowed, looking at the happy faces around her. The Sawards had accepted her with open arms and their kindness was more than she could ever have hoped for. She could not let them know of her wicked deed.

She bit her lip, nervously pondering when she would have a chance to return the pin to its rightful place. She smiled weakly as she watched Ada cycle off, with the music placed securely in the front basket hitching her skirt up to prevent it catching on the chain.

Beatrice then took Maria's arm in hers as they walked into the garden, where Leslie was already playing.

'Maria, seeing as you've helped save the day for Ada, you're welcome to have your pick, within reason, mind you, of anything in my wardrobe that you would like to wear for the concert. We'll do it later, because first I must go to Bramble Cottage. I just heard that Edith and Florence are due to return home this afternoon and I want to air it for them.'

Maria nodded gratefully, her mouth dry as her mind swirled with the enormity of her fate should her heinous misdeed be discovered. 'I ain't ever been to a concert before. Wait till I tell Ma!'

'I'll introduce you to Sam's sister Florence. I think you'd like each other and it would be good for you to have a friend your age if you stay on here.'

Maria felt a lump in her throat as Beatrice left. The kindness bestowed on Maria deepened her feelings of guilt and made her all the more determined to prove her worth. She glanced around and saw Leslie shuffle off across the lawn on his bottom, then yanking himself up on all fours, swaying as he steadied himself. She scooped him up in her arms and playfully tickled his tummy, her eyes diverting to a gap in the fence in the corner.

As she playfully rocked the infant in her arms, she pressed her face into his chubby cheeks and smothered his soft milky skin with kisses. A warm tenderness that only a mother knows consumed her and her stomach fluttered.

'I wonder if my Joey is loved. He needs a mother's love. Oh, Joey, I do love you. When will I see you again? I can't wait much longer.'

∞

Beatrice knew where Edith kept a spare key in the back yard at Bramble Cottage and was relieved to find it still concealed under a sack in the outhouse. Once inside the house, she flung open the upstairs windows and dusted quickly. Everything was in order in the downstairs rooms and before she left she picked a bunch of marigolds and cornflowers from the garden and arranged them in a glass vase on the table in the front room.

Beatrice returned home quickly to pick up a basket of provisions that Betty had thoughtfully prepared for their return, then raced to the station, arriving at six o'clock, just as passengers were disembarking from the train. She spotted a few soldiers home on leave being greeted by overjoyed mothers fighting back tears, and office workers who commuted to King's Lynn clutching briefcases.

Her eyes scanned the platform and she soon spotted Edith and Florence standing together. At the same time, Florence spotted her and waved. Beatrice rushed forward to greet Edith, hugging her tightly, then stepping back to eye her up and down.

'I'm sorry, there's no more news of Sam,' she told them. 'Everyone is trying to find out what's happened, but until we have official notification, we must still hang on to the hope that they are alive somewhere, as prisoners of war or in a hospital maybe.'

'It's not right that we don't know. The least the War Office can do is tell us the truth. A mother shouldn't have that terrible cloud hanging over her,' replied Edith, her chin trembling.

Beatrice agreed, commenting on the restored colour in her cheeks. The break had done Edith some good, despite the anxiety she faced. The tension in her had softened and her shoulders were no longer slumped. A new peach scarf hanging loosely over her shoulders added colour to her cream blouse and grey skirt.

'I wasn't sure if you'd get the message in time. Joyce offered to call Sarah at the post office and get word to you. I would have stayed longer, but Florence begged us to leave, so here we are, back home.'

'Welcome home, both of you. So much has happened, I will tell you later over tea,' Beatrice declared, reaching down to take Edith's case.

'I'm so glad to be back. I know we've only been away three weeks, but how I've missed Wolferton.' Florence beamed, flinging her arms around Beatrice's waist, her straw boater almost falling off.

Eddie rushed over when he spotted the group, removing his cap to greet them politely.

'Here, let me,' he offered, loading their cases onto a trolley. Florence's face turned beetroot and Eddie failed to notice her adoring gaze.

'You're in luck. Mr Figgs is still here and he offered to take you back home in his cart. Mrs Saward arranged it,' he chortled, gesturing to the waiting horse as they made their way out of the station.

'I remember Hazel.' Florence smiled, as she affectionately stroked the horse's glossy mane, pressing her cheek close to its neck.

'She's still got some life in her yet,' Mr Figgs said with a grin, as he piled the bags in the cart.

Beatrice hopped into the back and sat on the floor, alongside Florence, clutching the basket of produce that Betty had given her. Florence turned her head waving at Eddie. Beatrice took Florence's hand and spoke softly. 'There is something I need to tell you. I think it's best you forget Eddie. I'm sorry to tell you this, but I think he is sweet on Maria.'

'Oh.' Florence looked down sadly. 'Silly me. I expect Maria is much prettier and more suited to him.'

'Please don't put yourself down, Florence. One day the right boy will come your way.'

Mr Figgs trotted the horse along at a slow pace, with Edith perched beside him on the front seat, listening sympathetically as Edith told him softly, 'I'm afraid there is still no news about Sam and the Sandringham Company. People says the King is doing everything he can to find out what's happened.'

When they arrived home, once inside, Edith went straight to the dresser and picked up a photograph of Sam's smiling face. 'We must pray for news soon. This waiting is unbearable.'

Florence frowned, her face masked with a solemn expression. 'Oh, Beatrice, when will this war end? I hope Ted is a comfort to Sam and reminds him of home. Did I do wrong to give him his tortoise? Was it a stupid, foolish thing to do? I only did it . . .'

'Shush, don't say such silly things. It was a very thoughtful act and I imagine Sam and Fred are both well and waiting to come home as soon as they can,' comforted Beatrice, pulling the girl towards her and gently stroking her fair hair, which was tied back off her face.

Edith made and poured steaming cups of tea while Florence laid the table and Beatrice spread out the food she had brought with her. They munched on the chunky, crumbly rock cakes.

'A penny for your thoughts?' Beatrice ventured, raising an eyebrow at Florence.

'Well, seeing as you ask,' she hesitated, one eye on her mother, 'I've been thinking it's time I found myself a job, now Mother is much better, and the money would come in very handy. It's just, if I don't, I fear she will want me to go back and work with Aunt Joyce, and she is horrid.'

'What are you talking about? What job?' spluttered Sam's mother, clearly taken aback.

'I'm not going back to work with Aunt Joyce, so I need to find other work. I know how short of money we are. You can't keep hiding it from me. I'm old enough to face the truth and fit and able enough to find work. It's what Sam would want, I'm sure,' Florence added.

Beatrice looked thoughtful for a moment, then raised her hands and made a suggestion. 'I think I have an idea. It could be the perfect solution – for everyone.'

Florence's eyes lit up. 'What is it? Please tell me.'

'Well, I heard Mrs Glossop, who helps at the vicarage, saying a couple of days ago how she wants to retire, and would have left by now, but didn't want to leave Jane in the lurch so soon after losing Piers. The poor woman is overwrought with grief. Apparently, Mrs Glossop has a daughter in Hunstanton and she wants to move in with her on account of her arthritis and her fingers becoming so knotted and painful.'

'Poor Mrs Rumbelow, of course she is feeling it bad. Piers was always so kind, he had a lovely face and manner. We read about his death in the King's Lynn paper, and it fair shook us. I'd like to help her if I can. What do you think, Mother? If they took me on and I worked alongside Mrs Glossop for a while she could show me the ropes and I'll be able to keep a neat house for them. And I would still look after you too. I promise. Oh, please say you agree,' Florence pleaded.

Edith shook her head. 'I'm not so sure, it might all be too much for you. I had higher hopes for you as an apprentice seamstress. That is respectable employment and has far more prospects than being nothing more than someone else's skivvy. Surely you can give Aunt Joyce another chance. Other girls would jump at the opportunity to work for her.'

'No, Mother. That's not the life I want. I don't mind sewing, but I don't want to do it all day every day. My fingers are cut through from pressing on the needle. And I don't want to live away from home. I want to stay here in Wolferton with you. I'm sorry, Mother, I know Joyce is my aunt, but I would rather work on the land or in a factory than be treated like a slave by her.'

Florence's expression was defiant. Edith shook her head. 'What am I to do with you? I only want what's best.'

Beatrice shot Florence a warning glance to keep her lips sealed and knelt down beside Edith, taking hold of her hand. 'Why don't you sleep on it, Edith? I think you should consider Florence's feelings, and this way she would still be here for you. Mrs Rumbelow would treat her kindly, she would be like a companion to her, and maybe one day, when the war is over, Florence might think about being a seamstress.'

Florence's eyes lit up and she clasped her hands together.

'Well, I suppose, if you put it like that,' Edith mumbled. 'Mind you, girl, I want you to think about your future too. I admit I had my doubts about how hard Joyce was working you. It was wrong of me to ignore.'

Florence hugged her mother and then cleared away the dishes. It was agreed Beatrice would raise the matter with Jane Rumbelow before she had a chance to advertise the position.

'Ben and Roly will be over as soon as they finish on the farm. You should be proud of them, Edith, they are a real credit to you,' commented Beatrice, as she rose to leave. 'Lizzie has spoken to me of how hard they work.'

Edith escorted Beatrice to the door. 'Bless you, Beatrice, for everything. And bless the farmer lady too. And her man, Wilf. Is there news of him?'

Beatrice shook her head and told her he was not the kind of man to write back home. Lizzie had confided in her that she was glad to see the back of her no-good husband, saying he was a brute who only married her to get his hands on the farm that she had inherited. Beatrice kept Lizzie's confidences to herself, thinking that nobody knew what really went on in a marriage behind closed doors.

Beatrice saw a tear prick the corner of Edith's eye. 'Poor woman. It must be hard for her without Wilf. She has enough worries of her own. How can I ever thank her for taking my boys in?'

'Please don't give it another thought. Lizzie was more than happy to have them stay over. She says they did a good turn for her too, helping out on the farm, with Sid locked up and Wilf away. She would like them to stay on now you are back, and says she will pay, if that's all right with you, till she finds someone else to take over Sid's work.'

'Need you ask! Of course they can,' Edith readily agreed.

Beatrice's eyes burned. 'I know we want our men home soon. I have such a deep longing blazing inside me to see Sam again and pray Captain Beck is still alive and will bring them home. But we cannot surrender. We must win this war to keep our freedom.'

'Amen. God Save the King,' declared Edith.

Chapter 22

Ada flew out of the front door the next day, promising her mother she would return straight after the afternoon's rehearsal.

'Why not take Leslie to see Mrs Rumbelow when you get back?' Sarah suggested. 'I'm sure he'd cheer her up. He's such a dear little boy.'

'I'm not too sure. That might be too much for her. I'll think about it.'

Ada found Clara reading her sheet music in the front of the church. She hid it behind her back when Ada approached.

'You haven't peeked, have you?' queried Clara, her eyebrows arched.

Ada assured her she hadn't. She couldn't understand why Clara wouldn't confide in her about her choice of music.

When she had delivered the music to Clara at the house of her close friends, Sandringham organist Hubert and his wife Hettie, the day before, she had pressed the singer to reveal what the music would be.

Clara resolutely refused. 'But that would spoil the surprise for you. And I do want it to be a surprise! It's something I have longed to sing for a while now, and I promise you, it will be sensational.'

'But will you have enough time to practise?' asked Ada anxiously.

'Please do not worry on my account. I shall practise here this evening with Hubert and look forward to joining you at tomorrow's final rehearsal,' Clara replied calmly.

Ada had no choice but to place her trust in Clara, with Hubert agreeing to accompany Clara on the piano. Now, as Ada stepped into church for their last rehearsal before the big night, she felt a sense of exhilaration tinged with panic wash over her.

The sound of footsteps made Ada turn as Jessie rushed towards her. She was beaming, looking prettier than ever, her eyes sparkling.

'Well, what do you think?' she asked her sister, her hand pointing at the floral displays around the church.

'Oh they're beautiful, Jessie. Just perfect.'

Jessie had spent the morning adorning St Peter's Church with spectacular flower displays and was putting the finishing touches to them.

'Oh, my dear, Ada is right. They are quite simply fabulous. I adore them!' gushed Clara, her eyes wide with admiration.

Ada walked off to speak to Hubert, leaving Jessie with the woman she had wrongly believed to be her love rival. She twisted her fingers nervously in front of her and modestly brushed off Clara's compliment. She was in awe of this famous singer who smiled at her warmly. 'I don't believe we have met, though I feel I know you already as

Jack told me *all* about you on our journey here. If it isn't too forward for me to say, I know that Jack is very fond of you. I can see he is a very lucky man, by all accounts. I hope we can be friends.'

'What did you say?' asked Jessie, unsure if she had heard correctly. She was taken aback that Jack had spoken of her to Clara. 'May I enquire, how do you know of this?'

Clara grinned. 'I have a way of discovering the secrets of men's hearts. I could tell straightaway, from the first time I saw you at the station, that he had fallen for you.'

Jessie's face turned crimson and her throat became dry. She bit her lip, feeling foolish as she remembered the jealousy that had consumed her when she spotted Clara with Jack on the station platform and had run off in a state. How foolish and headstrong she had been jumping to the wrong conclusions.

'Here, let me show you this,' invited Clara, moving towards Jessie. 'This is the man I adore who has won my heart.'

Jessie looked in astonishment as the singer unclasped the heart-shaped locket around her neck. 'This way I always feel Edmund is close to me, wherever I may be. Have you had news of Jack since he left?'

Jessie shook her head, staring at the miniature portrait that Clara held in her tiny hands. It showed a smiling gentleman with long sideburns wearing evening dress; he had a friendly face and smiling eyes. On the other side was an image of Clara, her beautiful face tilted to one side so it looked towards his image.

Clara opened her heart to Jessie about the sweetheart she was betrothed to. Edmund, she confided, was a distinguished baritone singer who before the war toured Europe and entertained royalty, but their wedding was now on hold.

Jessie studied Clara's perfectly formed oval features, her sparkling sapphire eyes and rose puckered lips which turned up at the corners, illuminating her face into the most bewitching smile. Her pale cheeks were dabbed lightly with pink blush, giving her a healthy glow. Her blonde hair was swept up in loose curls that hung down her back. Jessie couldn't pull her eyes away; she had never seen anyone so pretty before, and close up her features looked even more exquisite.

Jessie told her, 'He looks kind, like Jack. He's so handsome too. A photograph of your beloved is a most prized possession, especially at this moment, don't you think?'

Clara agreed, gazing lovingly at the image of her fiance.

As Ada returned to join them, Jessie exclaimed, 'That's given me an idea. Why don't we ask everyone to bring a photograph of their loved ones who are away fighting to the concert with them? We all have aching hearts and this will help us feel close to our men and to talk to each other about our fears, our longings and, well, anything.'

'That's the most wonderful idea,' choked Clara, clutching the locket around her neck. 'I wish I'd thought of it.'

'We must let estate workers' families know, all those who went to Gallipoli with Captain Beck,' added Jessie.

Clara's eyes shone. 'It's going to be a poignant and painful evening for families. I've heard the terrible news from Gallipoli with so many wonderful men from here still unaccounted for. But this will bring woman and their families together. It will show how people here on the King's estate have a strong bond and that will not be broken by this terrible war.'

'That's so beautiful,' Ada replied, brushing away a tear. 'The concert will do so much more than raise money. I can't thank you enough for being here with us, Clara.'

Ada turned as she heard footsteps. Maria was approaching them, gawping at the elaborate floral arrangements.

'I ain't seen anything like this before. It's just so beautiful. Oh, Jessie, you are so clever with flowers. And this must be . . .'

Maria's eyes lingered on Clara as she gawped admiringly at the singing star. Ada introduced them. 'It's an honour to make your acquaintance. I've heard about you from Ada and it's true, you are the prettiest lady I ever saw. And I hear it said that you are the best singer in the world.'

Clara smiled at Maria. 'Thank you for your kind words, Maria. Music is my life. And if I can share the happiness it brings me with people here, and raise money to support our brave servicemen too, then I feel truly blessed and honoured.'

'Excuse my appearance,' muttered Maria, suddenly conscious that she was wearing an apron. 'Only I've been sweeping up and dusting the pews to make sure they shine nicely for the concert. I'm trying to do my bit to help too.'

Ada and Clara complimented Maria on her excellent work. It had been arranged that Betty should stay home and look after Leslie on the night of the concert, but Maria had kindly insisted that the housekeeper should attend and she would stay home with the baby. Ada saw how Betty's eyes lit up at the suggestion and she couldn't bring herself to refuse.

Ada pondered for a moment. 'Maria, I believe Beatrice had kindly offered to lend you a gown for the concert. It's very kind of you to offer to stay home so Betty can come, but I believe there is a way you can come as well.'

'There is? How can I be here if I am home with Leslie?' queried Maria, her brows drawing closer.

'It's simple. Why not bring Leslie with you? You can both sit at the back of the church, just in case he has a turn, but seeing as he always behaves well with you, it's worth a try.'

'Oh, Ada. That's a wonderful idea. I never dreamt I could come too. I promise he'll be as good as gold.'

'But you must promise that if he begins to cry or make any sound, you will leave straightaway.'

Maria readily agreed and turned to Clara. 'I ain't seen a famous singer before. It's not often I'm lost for words, but I don't know what to say. Oh, I'm cock-a-hoop. Wait till I tell Ma. It will be a night to remember for the rest of my life.'

Maria walked off cheerily to finish tidying up.

'I can see she's quite a character.' Clara commented, smiling. 'Did I hear correctly that she is a Saward?'

Ada rolled her eyes, pressing her hand on Clara's slender arm. 'It's a long story that I shall save for another time. More importantly, did you manage to practise your music with Hubert?'

'Oh yes, you have nothing at all to worry about, I assure you.' Clara grinned. 'I see the choir ladies are here. Shall we make a start?'

Magnolia stood out from the other ladies gathered together in the aisle. Not only was she the tallest woman and her voice the loudest, but her purple dress ensured she could be seen from a mile off.

The rehearsal went better than expected and afterwards Clara praised the choir, singling out Magnolia for the biggest plaudit. The Wolferton Nightingale beamed, and assured Clara that she would be wearing a very special white gown for the concert, the colour requested for all the choir ladies. 'I could never eclipse your beauty, but I must shine the brightest light I can on the night,' she quipped, to an amused Clara.

'It was like hearing angels singing,' Maria told Ada as they stepped outside the church. Magnolia could be seen talking animatedly to a group of three local women at the church gate. They were discussing a poster that read:

The star of London's music halls, Clara Griffin – Singing for our Country – joined by the Wolferton Nightingale, Magnolia Greensticks, and the Wolferton Choir. Tickets one shilling, all proceeds will be given to the Red Cross.

Ada recognised them all as women with family members serving in the war, either with the Sandringham Company, the navy or in the trenches in France. Two of them,

Nancy Gates and her sister Annie Fitch, both in their forties, wore black from head to toe. Their lips trembled and their eyes filled with sorrow.

'We'll come and support you. It's what our Billy would have wanted,' wept Nancy, referring to her beloved son who had been killed by a sniper's gun in France just two months before. When news of his death reached her, her anguished cries could be heard by all the neighbours who rushed outside to find the cause of it.

Ada placed a comforting arm around Nancy; her raw pain etched across her face. Billy never wanted to sign up, but couldn't face fingers pointing at him, the fear of being given a white feather if he stayed home. While other Tommies marched off singing patriotic songs and full of bravado, Billy's eyes had a haunted look.

'We don't even have his body,' the women cried. 'No place to mourn him and take flowers.'

Ada urged them to bring a photo of Billy with them so his name could be mentioned at the concert. He had died fighting for his King and country and was a hero. The ladies shuffled off, dabbing their eyes with a handkerchief, after agreeing to spread the word.

'My heart goes out to Nancy. Billy was her only child. We are going to unite and do our men proud; we can't let their men's deaths be in vain,' Ada commented, walking back to the station master's house.

'I know you'll make your Alfie proud and I hope one day I will meet him and can tell him myself,' Maria responded.

They made their down the path at the side of the station master's house and Harry marched towards them with a look of thunder on his face.

'I think we need to have a talk, Maria. We've just had a visitor. I can't say I took to him.'

Maria's hand flew to her mouth and she shot an anxious glance at Ada. Maria had never seen Harry so angry and her knees knocked as the penny dropped.

'I think I know who you mean, I had an inkling Walter Jugg was here. It's him, isn't it? That's the man I told you about. That's the man I told you about, Mr Saward. The man who forced himself on me. I thought I saw him here the other day. What does he want here?'

Sarah, who had followed her husband outside, held up a letter. 'Yes, that was the name he gave. I found this note outside my bedroom floor this morning addressed to you. Betty handed it to me. Is this from the person you are referring to? It doesn't appear to be signed.'

Maria spluttered, taking it from her hand and realising it must have slipped out of her pocket. 'It can only be from him. What did he want? I had no idea he knew of my whereabouts and would follow me here.'

Harry puffed on his pipe, exhaling slowly the pungent nutty tobacco. He glanced up at his wife, their eyes meeting. Sarah's lips were a straight pencil line, curling down to show her disapproval. Her eyebrows met in the middle.

Harry's eyes were glued to Maria's face. 'I won't beat around the bush, Maria. He says you stole £50 from him, that you watched him when he put his takings away and helped yourself. He says if you don't pay it back he will have you arrested and taken to court.'

Maria swayed. 'He can't do that. I won't let him. He's a liar! I ain't ever touched a farthing of his bleeding money.'

Ada spoke up. 'That's preposterous, Father. You know Maria would never do such a thing. You know what a rogue Walter Jugg is.'

Maria blurted out, her voice shaking, 'You gotta believe me. I don't know where Walter keeps his money. Never did. I swear on my life.'

'I believe you, Maria,' Ada reassured her gently, placing her hand on her arm.

Harry nodded. 'That may well be the case, but here is the problem. He has given me three days to give him £50, the money he says you stole, as well as another £10 for his trouble. Or he says he'll make more trouble. And I'm in no mood for trouble right now.'

'But I ain't got that kind of money,' wailed Maria. 'What am I gonna do?'

Harry looked thoughtful. 'He kept saying there was more information he could divulge that would interest me. What does he mean, Maria? I must admit I have never met a more loathsome man in my life.'

'I dunno what he's talking about.' Maria bit her lip, trembling, her eyes swimming with tears. 'I told you everything. I believe him when he says he'll make trouble, and he won't do it by halves.'

'But we can't give in to his blackmail!' retorted Ada, her face reddening.

'Exactly!' Harry retorted. 'Now don't you fret, Maria, when Walter returns in three days' time he'll have a surprise waiting for him; we'll have Constable Rickett here listening in. He'll collar him and send him packing for good.'

Maria's eyes welled up. 'Anything. Please, do anything you can to get rid of him. I'm so scared.'

'You need have no fear of that man while you are under my roof.' Harry reassured her. 'In the meantime, I still have relatives around Audley End. I'll get word to them to enquire about Mr Walter Jugg of the Fighting Cock and see what mud we can stir up about him.'

'So you believe me, that Walter Jugg's a liar and I never touched a farthing of his money? I swear to God, I swear on my mother's life, that Walter Jugg is a lying bleedin' monster.'

Sarah reassured Maria, frowning at the use of her coarse language, but letting it pass. 'I believe you, Maria. Let's leave this to Harry. No scoundrel such as Walter Jugg is getting the better of us Sawards.'

Maria dried her eyes. 'Thank you, Mrs Saward.'

Ada took Maria's arm. 'You are right, Ma. We'll show that no-good blaggard Walter Jugg that we are more than a match for him, and he will rue the day he set foot in Wolferton.'

Maria desperately hoped that would be true, but deep inside she knew Walter was bitter and vengeful and wouldn't be happy unless he made trouble.

Chapter 23

'Why don't you wear your Fabergé pin at the concert tomorrow? It's so distinguished,' suggested Sarah. 'I'll lay your clothes out on the chair tonight in case they need an airing.'

'That's an excellent suggestion, especially as their Highnesses will be there,' Harry agreed.

Sarah had beamed with pride when Harry was given the exquisite pin designed by the House of Fabergé, named after the renowned Russian jeweller favoured by the Russian and British royal families. The pin was very distinctive, featuring a two-headed eagle crowned with two imperial crowns, topped with a third larger crown and ribbons. The work of art had been presented to Harry by the Dowager Empress Tsarina of Russia as a token of her appreciation for his unfailing courtesy and devotion towards her during visits to Sandringham. He attended to her every need with charm, professionalism and discretion on her arrival at Wolferton Station, and particularly while she was resting in the royal waiting rooms.

It was a gift that Harry treasured; he was well aware that the Dowager Queen Alexandra and Bertie were great admirers of Fabergé's exquisite work and had commissioned a collection of delicate flowers and models of animals from the estate farm from the famed jewellery maker. The precious collection of intricately created flora and fauna was breathtakingly beautiful and unique, so extraordinary in its detail. Harry and his family had been honoured to see the collection at the Big House when it was put on display, and it made him all the more proud of the honour bestowed on him to be given this precious gift.

Sarah entered their room and opened the walnut drawer. Her lips curled when she saw the rectangular box with the name Fabergé. She pictured the pin being fixed onto the lapel of Harry's smart dark suit and the admiring glances it would attract. Who would have thought, she pondered, that a farmer's daughter from Cambridgeshire would have ended up married to a royal station master who was honoured by royalty and had precious gifts bestowed on him, such as this exquisite Fabergé pin. It filled her with immense pride whenever she saw it fixed to his lapel.

She smiled as she recalled how Harry had courted her after they met at a country dance in Whittlesey where Harry worked. He knew her family from church and she finally agreed to have the last dance. Since then they never looked back and they were overjoyed when a new more prestigious turreted station master's house was built in 1898, fourteen years after moving to Wolferton. Nobody doubted that tough-talking Sarah with her high standards was key to Harry's success. Although he appeared to have a more benign nature and natural charm, he was still, nevertheless, as rigorous as his wife in meeting, if not exceeding, all professional expectations. Sarah would not allow anyone to put their reputation at risk, she liked to manage all situations and did not take kindly to surprises, especially the kind that Maria had dropped on them.

As Sarah gently lifted the box out of the drawer she paused, hearing a rustling sound behind her. She turned and saw Maria standing outside their bedroom door. Maria looked edgy, her eyes narrowing.

'Ah, it's you,' commented Sarah.

'I'm sorry, I didn't mean to disturb you,' Maria replied nervously.

'Try not to worry yourself about that unpleasant business, I'm sure Mr Saward will sort it out. Seeing as you are here, Maria, do come over, there is something I would like to show you, the likes of which you've never seen before. It proves how highly regarded Mr Saward is.'

Maria tried to excuse herself, but Sarah insisted, her face glowing as she gushed. 'How many people do you know who have been given a beautiful gift by the Russian royal family? Mr Saward is so revered and admired for his utmost professionalism, loyalty and high standards. He is so much more than just a station master; he is respected by royalty from all over Europe for his gracious manner and courteousness.'

Maria's chin trembled and her cheeks flushed as she watched Mrs Saward open the lid of the box. 'I'd better just check on Leslie, I thought I heard him cry out,' she stuttered, fingering the pin in her deep pocket. She had planned to return it to its box at the moment, but Mrs Saward beat her there by just a few seconds.

She shrunk as Sarah yelped, 'It's not here. Why isn't it in its box?'

She called out to Harry from the top of the stairs and Harry rushed up. She flung the empty box onto the bed and cried, 'It's not there, Harry. It's missing. Look, the box is empty.'

'What's missing? What are you talking about?' asked Harry, picking up the box. Looking at Sarah, he exclaimed, 'Oh no, not my Fabergé pin!'

His eyes were wide in disbelief as he held the box, turning it over in his hands and then searching inside the drawer in case the pin had fallen out.

'I've already done that,' snorted Sarah. 'When did you last wear it? Did you put it back afterwards?'

Harry raised his voice, 'Of course I did! I put it back in the box and then in the top drawer. I haven't worn it this year, it didn't seem right with the war on to show it off.'

'That's what I thought,' declared Sarah. 'So where is it?'

Harry scratched his chin. 'Calm down, there must be a perfectly reasonable explanation.'

'Oh, Harry. Let's hope you haven't lost it. It was given to you by the Russian Empress, she'll expect to see you wearing it if she visits again.'

Harry looked bewildered. 'I honestly don't know what can have happened.'

Maria pressed her back against the wall, her heart racing, deciding that she must continue hiding it for now.

She crept up to her room, flung open the chest and concealed it in a stocking.

Sarah joined Harry downstairs; she was fuming. 'I can only think of one explanation. It must be the girl. She could see it was valuable. She's probably already sold it to pay off that man who called round earlier demanding money from her, accusing her of stealing fifty pounds from his takings. And to think I had started to believe her.'

Harry soothed, 'Shush, my dear, we don't want Maria hearing these unfounded allegations against her. I know you're upset, but I really don't think Maria would do such a terrible thing, and I certainly don't believe a word that scoundrel says. You must have proof before casting such aspersions. And there is no proof that I am aware of.'

Maria's heart raced, nearly exploding. How was she to know the Fabergé pin had been gifted to Harry by the Russian royal family? How could she confess to Sarah she was right, that she was hoping to pawn it for a few bob? It was unthinkable. They would think her so wicked and hand her over to PC Rickett.

She saw all her dreams of a new life disappearing. She faced being thrown out onto the street, and had nobody to blame but herself unless she acted quickly.

Maria wiped away a tear as she considered her next steps, 'I'll return the pin and take what's coming to me.'

Sarah held her head in her hands and grumbled. 'My head is splitting with all this drama going on. Life used to be so peaceful before Maria came along.'

'Try not to fret, Mother. You know I'll help you,' soothed Jessie, leading her mother to the Windsor chair in the kitchen. 'And I'm sure Father's Fabergé pin will turn up in a blink.'

'Let's hope you are right. I'm all done in and my nerves are shaken up. I can't think about it anymore. I just want to close my eyes for forty winks, otherwise I'll be no good for the concert tomorrow. I feel I have one of my bad heads coming on, and you know they can leave me out of sorts for a few days. And now, of all times. How am I supposed to give the royal waiting rooms a good going over before the housekeeper's inspection the day after the concert?'

Sarah groaned, her face contorted in pain. She rested her head on the back of the chair, grousing about the short notice. 'Oh, but there's so little time, and I do like everything to be perfect. It's what's expected. The worry of it, on top of everything else, is making me feel giddy and has given me a thumping head.'

Jessie knelt down next to her mother and took her hand. 'You must put it out of your mind until you feel better. Mrs Inglenook has never found fault before. She always sings your praises, so I'm sure you have nothing at all to worry about.'

'Please, let me help.' Maria offered nervously. 'I'll do anything to make the rooms look good for you.'

Sarah held the side of her head. 'I think not, Maria. You are not allowed to set foot inside those rooms.'

'Shush, Mother, don't upset yourself,' Jessie whispered, stroking her mother's forehead.

Jessie told Maria, 'Mrs Inglenook is very particular about who sets foot inside those rooms and staff have to be personally approved by her. These are royal rooms used by the royal family and only my mother and myself are approved for cleaning duties there. I will help her tomorrow. So thank you for your offer, but it's all in hand, and I think in the circumstances we should leave it there.'

'It would give me peace of mind, if you could put your head in the rooms now, Jessie, just so I have an idea of anything that needs my attention later,' said Sarah.

Maria looked down at her feet. At that moment a seed was planted in her head. Her mind fizzed as the plan took shape and she determined to help however she could. But first she must return the pin.

As Sarah dozed and Jessie left for the royal retiring rooms, Maria walked towards the stairs. She could hear Ada and Beatrice upstairs discussing gowns they would be wearing for the concert.

She heard Ada tell her sister, 'I don't need these clothes any longer, I'm sure Maria could use them. I might as well take them up to her room.'

Ada climbed up the stairs with two blouses and a skirt hanging over her arm, gasping for air as she entered the attic. It was stifling hot up in the rafters and cramped, with little space to walk around. She lifted the lid on the chest where Maria's clothes were kept and shifted a few garments around to make room for the new clothes when she felt her hand suddenly rub against a solid object. Curious, she fumbled among the clothing, picking up a stocking. She saw a shiny object fall out.

'I don't believe it. It's Father's Fabergé pin. So Maria *did* take it!'

She rushed downstairs and found Beatrice in the pantry. She showed her the pin.

Beatrice smiled. 'Father will be pleased. Where did you find it?'

'Oh, Beatrice, this is going to come as a shock. It was in Maria's room, hidden in amongst the clothes in her chest. She's deceived us all.'

Beatrice jerked her head back. 'I can't believe she would be so false, after everything we've done for her.'

'Neither can I, but what other explanation can there be?'

Jessie, now back from the station, appeared at the door then and stared at her sisters' anxious faces. 'What's happened? Why do you both look so shocked?'

Through deep gulps of breath, Beatrice and Ada explained what had happened. 'We must at least give her a chance to defend herself. This is a very serious matter,' Ada insisted.

They stepped into the kitchen and were confronted by Maria. The atmosphere was fully charged and the sisters looked at each other.

Maria asked nervously. 'What's happened? Why are you staring at me like that?'

Harry walked in then. 'What's going on? I can tell by looking at you that something's amiss,' said the station master.

Beatrice frowned, her brows knitted. She held up the Fabergé pin, staring straight at Maria's face.

Maria's legs buckled and she stumbled, her eyes filling with tears.

Harry took the pin from Ada's hand and gasped. 'Why, that's my missing Fabergé pin. Where did you find it?'

The Saward sisters remained silent. Beatrice tilted her head. 'Maria, is there something you would like to tell us?'

Maria's eyes darted between them all. A muscle in her jaw twitched and a pink flush spread across her face. Taking a deep breath, she raised her chin and stuttered, 'Please, let me explain. I know what it looks like, but . . .'

Harry's face turned scarlet. 'No, not Maria. Tell me it's not true, that you didn't steal my pin?'

Maria's fixed her eyes on the floor and her body shook as Ada recounted how she found the pin concealed in Maria's chest.

Sarah who had entered the room after being woken by the commotion, was informed about the pin's discovery. She looked furious. 'We took you in as one of us when you turned up on our doorstep in need of help, and now you have betrayed us in this way. That is unforgivable and you leave us no option. We must report this to police.'

'Let's not be too hasty,' urged Harry, placing an arm on his wife's arm. 'We need to think about this. We don't want a scandal now, do we?'

'But . . .' stammered Sarah. 'What are we to do with her then? Perhaps we should send her packing off to Doncaster to join her mother and wash our hands of her.'

'I understand how you feel,' Harry replied. 'But I would like to get to the bottom of this before we make any hasty decisions.' He turned to Maria, his voice softening. 'Can you tell me why you took it? I don't want to believe you are a thief, but that's how it looks. What is your explanation?'

'Oh, Mr Saward, I'm so ashamed,' Maria cried, throwing herself into the station master's arms. 'I couldn't see any other way.'

Sarah snorted. 'There, I was right. I told you she took it.'

Harry cleared his throat, holding Maria away from him. 'Of course you had a choice. There's always a choice between doing the right or wrong thing,'

Maria shook her head vigorously, her eyes darting around the room looking at each of the Sawards whose expressions conveyed disappointment, a pleading expression on her face. 'But you don't understand,' she whimpered.

Harry replied. 'What don't we understand? You really must explain yourself.'

'Of course. I know I done wrong, but I had a reason. A good reason.'

'Really?' enquired Sarah, her voice tinged with sarcasm. 'And what reason would that be?'

Maria trembled and her voice wavered. 'My Joey. I did it for my Joey.'

'Joey? Your son Joey? But he's dead. You told me he died after he was born,' Ada blurted.

311

'I know I did, but the truth is he's alive. My baby boy is alive,' Maria cried out. 'He's with my aunt, Freda, in Doncaster. That's why Ma is there.'

'You mean to say that you have a son? A living son?' Sarah kept shaking her head, throwing questioning glances at her daughters, whose expressions showed their surprise.

Maria covered her face with her hands and nodded.

'You told us he had died. Now you tell us he's alive. For God's sake, can someone tell me what's going on?'

'I'm sorry I deceived you. I didn't know any other way, but now I can see I was wrong. You've been kind to me and trusted me and I've brought you so much trouble. The least I can do now is tell you the truth and then I'll leave. I'll be out of your lives forever.'

Chapter 24

The station master paced to and fro, his arm behind his back, shaking his head and deep in thought.

The Saward sisters stared at Maria in disbelief. Sarah bit her finger and shook her head. Harry cleared his throat and faced Maria. His expression was stern and his voice firm. 'Very well, we will hear you out. But you must promise there will be no more lies. Is that understood?'

'I promise on my life to speak only the truth. I promise on Joey's life,' she murmured. 'I ain't ever gonna deceive you anymore.'

'As if you know how to do that!' blurted Sarah. 'After telling us he was dead.'

'You have every right to be cross with me. It will be a weight off my shoulders to tell you everything.' Maria gulped. 'My ma said not to say anything about Joey as you'd think I brought trouble and shame on myself seeing as he was born out of wedlock, and you too, seeing as you have connections with the royal family.'

'Carry on, Maria, tell us about Joey,' encouraged Ada.

'I was only fifteen years old, there's no way I would allow a foul, stinking old man like Walter Jugg to lay a finger on me. You've seen him, you know what he's like, how disgusting he is. I was brought up respectable. What I told you about him and how he forced his way on me was true, every single word. I thought about getting rid of the baby, but I couldn't face the thought of killing my unborn child. And I was too scared to put him up for adoption, in case he was killed, like those poor mites that ended up in the river after being dropped off with the baby farmer Amelia Dyer.'

Sarah raised an eyebrow. 'What does any of this have to do with you stealing Harry's pin? You could surely see it was valuable.'

'I'm sorry I did it and I admit to that, but I swear I didn't know it's value. Only Annie, she's the wet nurse that looks after my Joey in Doncaster, she demanded more money. Food prices keep rising and she says she don't earn enough for her lodgings and she's worried she'll be thrown out. My ma ain't got no more money to give her. She's had all our savings and now we are skint.'

Maria began sniffling again, wiping her eyes dry with the sleeve of her blouse. 'My Joey, he's six months old now, and a bonny little boy by all accounts. That's why I love your little Leslie so much, Ada, they're the same age, or thereabouts, and every time I hold your Leslie in my arms I think of my Joey, the softness of his skin, the smell of his hair, his sparkling blue eyes, his playful chuckles and his smile.'

'Ah, now I know why you are so good with babies. It's not just because you looked after your young brothers, but because you're a mother yourself,' Ada spoke softly.

Maria nodded, tears streaming down her cheeks. 'I've been more of a mother to your Leslie than my own Joey and it breaks my heart. I feel a gnawing pain deep inside when I hold your little 'un. I'm worried too in case Walter gets wind of Joey's whereabouts and goes after him. I'm sure he must know about him.'

Tears streamed down her cheeks as she turned to Harry. 'Please forgive me, Mr Saward. You've got your pin back now. I had no idea it had such a special connection with the Russian royal family and was trying to return it, knowing I'd done you wrong.'

'What did you plan to do with the pin? Sell it, I suppose?' jabbed Sarah, her arms folded across her chest.

Maria cast her eyes to the floor, her words trickling out. 'At first I did think I was gonna take it to Doncaster with me to pawn, but I changed my mind and was going to put it back, but never had a chance. I swear to God that's the truth!'

Harry's face reddened. 'You were going to pawn my Fabergé pin – the pin that was given to me by the Russian Dowager Empress! I don't know what's worse, the lies you have told us or your plans to pawn something so precious to me!'

Beatrice held her father's arm and pleaded. 'You have your pin back, Father. Maria has owned up and apologised.'

Maria's body shook, her words sticking in her throat. 'You ain't been on hard times like us. You have your comforts here. Ma is beside herself with worry about Freddie and Archie, too. She has to pay more to Uncle Gus for their keep or I fear what will become of them.'

'So you mean, you are expected to give money to your Uncle Gus, as well as your mother?' quizzed Harry.

Maria pushed back loose strands of hair that were damp with tears. 'That's right. Ma hasn't asked, but I know how anxious she is about it and I want to help. Uncle Gus took what he could from Ma for their keep, but always wanted more and bled her dry. Ma saw him before we came here as she fretted so much over Freddie and Archie, only he had sent them out to work and she waited and waited for them to return, and had to leave without clapping sight o' them.'

Maria paused, glancing at the concerned expressions around her. 'Ma gave him her last farthing when she saw him. He were always saying 'I ain't a bloomin' charity' – excuse my language. Now I worry the boys will be thrown out on the streets as Ma is skint. He told her as much. He looks on Freddie and Archie as two useless weaklings, as useful as a lame horse, them are 'is words, but they ain't shirkers, they just ain't big and strong like some lads. Ma thinks he might be selling drink on the black market too since pubs have to shut early. Ma's worried about the wrong 'uns he's getting them mixed up with.'

'What a scoundrel,' thundered Harry. 'You should have told me about this earlier. You know I will help. I gave my father my word to keep a lookout for you all.'

'You've already done so much. We had no inkling that's what Uncle Gus was really like, and Ma thought you taking me in was more than enough to ask. We're proud people you know, we ain't used to begging.'

316

Sarah looked thoughtful. 'Having considered what you told us, I can understand your situation better. This explains why you stole Mr Saward's pin. You needed the money for Uncle Gus and the wet nurse and saw us as easy pickings.'

Maria sobbed, her shoulders shaking. 'Of course I didn't. But yes, Mrs Saward, that's my situation. I'm so sorry and ashamed. If only could have returned it before you noticed gone.'

Harry scratched his head while Beatrice, Ada and Jessie expressed words of sympathy, to Maria about her desperate plight that led her to steal. They acknowledged their more privileged upbringing had spared them the kind of hardship she had been forced to endure. Maria's eyes filled with tears and huge sobs spilled from her mouth. She rested her head against Beatrice's chest, and stammered, 'I don't deserve your kindness.'

Harry cleared his throat and placed an arm around Sarah. 'Yours is a sad story, Maria. Perhaps I could write to your uncle and arrange for my brother Ronald who lives in London to call in and see them. If he says your Uncle Gus is up to no good and mistreating the boys, I will make other arrangements for them.'

Maria broke down again, slumping into an armchair, crying big blobs of tears into a handkerchief that Beatrice held out. 'I wanted to go and see them myself, but if he could go, I would like that.'

'I'll see to it. Uncle Gus won't be able to mess about with Roland, he'll take no nonsense from him.'

'Thank you! Thank you so much. Your kindness is more than I deserve, after what I did. All I seem to say to you is 'thank you' and 'I'm sorry', but I mean it from the bottom of my heart. What's gonna become of me?' she stammered. 'Should I leave tomorrow?'

Harry shook his head. 'I think we'll sleep on it. There's no need to make any rash decisions. And I do have my Fabergé pin back now, so no real harm has been done.'

'I'll never let you down again, I promise, on me Joey's life.'

'There's no need to make promises of that nature. I will write to your mother tomorrow and send her £5 for Joey's wet nurse,' Harry continued. 'We have to keep her sweet, and she's right about rising food prices.'

Beatrice threw her arms around the station master's chest and praised him for his wisdom and generosity of spirit. Even Sarah's pursed lips curved into a faint smile and her eyes shone with a proud glint.

The sisters gathered around Maria, firing questions at her about Joey. 'We don't want to upset you by talking about him, but we would love to see him one day. After all, he is family. He could be friends with Leslie one day,' suggested Ada.

Maria felt a lump rising up into her throat. Overcome with emotion, her hand shook as she flushed out the locket tucked inside her blouse. Opening the clasp, she gazed down at the cherub-like face of Joey and showed it to Ada.

'Here he is, bless him. My Joey. Just one month old.' Maria's eyes moistened and her voice quavered.

'He's a handsome young boy. He looks the image of you,' Ada said.

'It worries me that he'll grow up taking after the brute who fathered him. But there isn't a day goes by that I regret my decision to keep him. After I insisted on having him, I went to Doncaster. Ma's sister made all the arrangements there with a midwife around the corner so folk back home didn't know I was in the family way.

'Aunt Freda was kind, but she scared me with her tales of how she lost two babes at birth. They both turned blue when they came into the world, fighting for breath. I was that glad when I heard little Joey holler. I loved him instantly, from the first moment I looked down on his sweet face and he gripped my finger in his little hand. He had an angel's face that melted my heart. Then I suckled him and the bond grew stronger. It felt so right, so natural and I knew I could never give him up.'

Ada's eyes moistened as she listened to Maria. 'Oh, he is so lovely, Maria. I can see that it must break your heart being parted from him.'

Maria nodded, wiping away her tears. Her voice wobbled, the words sticking in her throat. 'Oh, Ada. Mr Saward . . . I thought you would say he were a bastard boy and you wanted nothing to do with him.'

Mr Saward shot an enquiring glance at his wife, whose lips were firmly shut, and the disapproval painted across her face again. Ada broke the silence. 'None of it was your fault, Maria. Or Joey's. Was it, Father, Mother?'

'I'm doing my best to get used to this news. It's going to take some time, so you must be patient with me,' murmured Sarah. 'What a day it's been. My poor head.'

Harry spoke softly. 'Give her time, Maria. And rest assured, we don't use that "b" word in this house. We are all family. And that wicked man will pay for his actions, you mark my words.'

A knock on the door alerted Sarah to see who it was. She returned to the room, shaking her head.

'That's strange. Nobody was there, but I found this note on the floor. It's addressed to you, Maria. Do you think it's from him?'

Maria tensed as she recognised Walter's handwriting on the envelope. Her face paled she mumbled the words staring up at her: '*I'll be back for me dues soon, else I'll be telling everyone about yer bastard son and what a slut yer are.*'

Chapter 25

The day of the concert arrived and Ada was the first one up at six o'clock. She had barely been able to sleep in the days leading up to it, her nerves jangling as she fretted anxiously.

She drew open the floral curtains and gazed at the pale golden sun, the promise of another beautiful day. Leslie was still asleep and she slipped downstairs quietly.

A moment later, she was joined by Maria. 'You've nothing to worry about. It's going to be a cracker, you wait and see.'

Ada crossed her chest. 'I have to say I think it will be a very special evening. And may I ask, what are your plans today?'

'I was thinking of looking in on poor Robbie again, maybe take him a thin slice or two of ham and nasturtium pickle if Mrs Saward can spare it. Eddie's ma seemed right pleased with what I took over before.'

'I think that will be fine, as soon as Betty's here, of course, so she can keep an eye on Leslie while I see to the finishing touches in the church.'

Maria dashed off as soon as the housekeeper arrived. When she passed the station she glanced across at the platform where passengers were alighting from a train and spotted Eddie cheerily whistling as he pushed his trolley.

She carried on and reached the Herrings' cottage in five minutes. She noticed the back door was ajar, but thought it polite to knock first and slammed the knocker down.

Mabel answered, her face weary, and she gratefully accepted the ham and pickle that Maria held out. 'Betty's so kind, all the Sawards are. You'll have to take us as you find us. There's scarcely been time to catch up with chores these last couple of days.'

Maria glanced around at the heap of dirty plates and pans piled up on the draining board. She noticed a bowl of half a dozen freshly laid eggs that Mabel had collected from her hen house for the egg collection.

'I offered Robbie a nice fried egg this morning,' Mabel told her. 'But he would have none of it. He says he doesn't deserve it, wants his egg to feed a wounded soldier, 'cos their needs are greater than his.'

Maria was moved by Robbie's kindness, seeing how little he had and yet was willing to give up.

'I can drop them off at the station for you,' Maria offered. 'And how is Robbie today?'

'The lad had a fever all night. Eddie stayed up with him for a few hours, but I could barely sleep, so I got up and sent Eddie to bed. He's a working boy and needs his rest. I think the laudanum must be doing its job.'

Maria peered into the front room and saw Robbie lying on his front and tossing his head from one side to the other and spreading his legs in different positions to find a comfortable spot.

'I hope you don't think I'm speaking out of turn, but you look all done in, Mrs Herring. Why don't you have a nap while I sit with Robbie.'

At first Mabel resisted, but finally she agreed. Yawning and rubbing her eyes, she staggered up the stairs and Maria returned to her patient, sitting on the three-legged stool next to his makeshift bed. He was now facing towards her, still lying on his chest. She listened to his heavy breathing and was relieved to see he was no longer feverish.

She couldn't resist stroking his forehead and gazing at his pale face. One of his eyes flicked open, then closed again. She moved back, afraid she would wake him.

He blinked, trying to raise his body, looking sideways at her face. 'Who are you? Where am I?' he moaned softly, squeezing his eyes and biting his lip.

'Shush, don't move, Robbie. I came to see you yesterday, I'm a friend of Eddie's, my name's Maria. Eddie and his ma have been looking after you. Oh, Robbie, you gave us all a fright. How are you feeling?'

'He looks a darn sight better than yesterday, that's for sure,' a man's deep voice answered.

Startled, Maria looked up to see Dr Fletcher standing in the doorway. His eyes had a kindly twinkle that put her at ease.

'I can see that too, the medicine must be working. I'd best call Mabel down,' replied Maria, her eyes facing the floor, overcome with shyness. Mabel walked down the stairs having heard the doctor come in, her face filled with concern for the patient.

'It's good news. His fever has passed. The laudanum was very powerful and worked like magic on him and has made him more comfortable and helped with his healing, judging by much better he looks now. I'm pleased to say. I suggest you keep giving Robbie the laudanum for another couple of days. I'll call in again the day after tomorrow,' he reassured her.

Mrs Herring screwed her eyes up and her forehead was furrowed. 'But who's paying for all this medicine and your time, doctor? I told yer, we can't afford it.'

'As I mentioned yesterday, it's all been taken care of. Please don't worry about that.'

Maria clasped her hands together. 'Robbie must have a guardian angel. He's blessed. It's what my ma always says, that there's always goodness to be found in something bad that happens, if you look hard enough for it.'

'Well ain't that a queer saying, but never a truer word said in these circumstances.' Eddie's mother smiled. 'Thank you kindly, Doctor, and please do pass on our thanks to the kind person who has taken an interest in Robbie.'

After the doctor left, Maria adjusted Robbie's pillow that had been propped under his chest so he could raise himself onto his elbows and hitch himself up on the mattress.

'Oh, Robbie, I told you that you're going to get better. And you are! I'm afraid I have to go now,' she told him gently, kneeling by his side. 'But I'll be back soon. And in no time you'll be up and about.'

Robbie smiled weakly as he spoke falteringly. 'Thank you, Maria. Thank you for your kindness.'

Her heart melted as she gazed at his face. She could only see goodness in it and she found herself blurting out at the injustice of his birching and how angry it made her feel.

'They were only doing their duty. It had to be done as I did wrong, or was a party to wrongdoing, even though I wanted nothing to do with it.'

He winced and Maria urged him not to speak; the thought ran through her mind that she was lucky to escape such a terrible punishment for her rash acts of dishonesty. Mabel came into the room holding a bottle of camomile to treat Robbie's wounds.

'I count myself very lucky, to have Eddie and his ma taking care of me.'

Maria was moved by Robbie's humbleness, and promised to return and tell him and Mabel all about the concert, letting him know that he had saved the day by disclosing the whereabouts of the missing sheet music.

'You're a good 'un, I can see that,' Maria assured him, pleased to have seen a smile light up his face as she walked out of the door.

Mabel handed her the eggs to drop off at the station and as she passed by the Greensticks' cottage she saw Magnolia bending down in her front garden. 'Oscar,' she called out, peering behind the hollyhock's massive foliage, 'Oscar! Oscar! Where are you?'

Maria rushed over and Magnolia looked up, her eyes filled with tears. 'It's my fault. I took him out on his lead this morning while I went to see if Mrs Fisher and take her a jar of pickle. Oscar was a bit lively, meowing loudly and licking his paws. You know he loves going out. When we went into her yard he took one look at the hens roaming free and slipped his collar in a flash – it was his best royal-blue jewelled one too – and chased after them. The hens squawked and feathers were flying all over the place, and then without a by-your-leave Oscar vanished over her fence and I've not seen him since. I should have thought, but it never occurred to me. How could I have been so foolish?'

'Oh, Magnolia, please don't worry. I'll help look for him. Your Oscar will turn up, I'm sure of it. I'll mention it to Mr and Mrs Saward too. Everyone knows there is only one plump ginger cat by the name of Oscar in Wolferton.'

Aggie joined them then, her face pinched. 'I've looked around the back, but there's no sight of him. It's not the same without Oscar, and our cats are delicate and house trained, not used to being outdoors with the strays that roam around. And what if a dog . . .'

Magnolia began sniffling. 'I know people will think it's silly to be upset about Oscar going off when there's so much going on, but it's so out of character. Of all the days for us to lose our Oscar, when this is such a big day for me. How will I get through it now.?'

'You will because I've 'eard you're the Wolferton Nightingale,' Maria told her with a reassuring smile.

Maria left Magnolia to continue her search while she delivered the eggs to Eddie at the station, informing him about Robbie's improved condition and the doctor's visit, and asked him to look out for Oscar.

She cast her eyes along the dusty path looking for the missing cat as she returned to the station master's house. As she walked along the path towards the back door, she became distracted by a rustling sound nearby. She cocked an ear and listened intently; the noise seemed to be coming from the direction of the rhododendron bushes at the end of the garden. Could it be Oscar? Or was Walter Jugg on her heels? She screwed up her eyes and stepped cautiously forwards, watching the foliage swaying. When she had almost reached the bush, a shadowy figure moved quickly behind it and dashed off. The hairs on the back of her neck prickled and she froze on the spot, her head spinning around. She ran towards the bush, but stopped when she saw Beatrice unlatching the gate. She blurted out what had happened, pointing to the back corner of the garden in the direction which the intruder had disappeared.

Beatrice dashed over to where Maria signalled, and returned holding a cigarette end in her hand.

'You were right, Maria. Someone has been here. I found this discarded cigarette butt on the ground. Whoever it was trampled over the flowerbeds, and there are footprints at the back where the fence was broken deliberately. They are large footprints; they must be a man's. Father will be furious!'

Maria's face turned alabaster white. She flung her hand to her mouth and cried, 'Oh no, it must be Walter. He's here. Oh, Beatrice, what will I do? He must be watching me.'

'Or could it be a spy? Someone who wants to destroy the King's railway station or his home at Sandringham? We must be on our guard,' Beatrice shuddered.

Over lunch, Beatrice recounted the discovery of the cigarette stub to Harry and Sarah, who were both alarmed to have an intruder in their midst. The enticing aroma of Betty's rabbit pie went unnoticed by Maria. Her stomach churned with anxiety, not hunger. She was unable to shake off thoughts of Walter's ominous presence.

'How dare he trespass on my property!' thundered Harry. 'Now the scoundrel is scaring my family and putting them in fear, I shall inform Constable Rickett about his attempt at blackmail.'

Maria wailed. 'You won't tell him what it's about, about my Joey, will you, Mr Saward? I'd hate everyone to know I had a babe out of wedlock, even though I love Joey with all my 'eart.'

'Of course I won't,' Harry reassured her, pushing his chair away. 'If I leave now I might catch him at home. Just leave this to me.'

Ada piped up, 'I have some news too. I'm afraid it's rather worrying. I went to the church this morning to tend to some last-minute details and saw Reverend Rumbelow there. I caught him unawares in the vestry where he was fighting back tears. I felt very awkward and stepped back to go out but he asked me not to leave and apologised for being upset.'

'Oh the poor man, of course he's upset, his cherished only son has just died. Whatever did you do?' asked Betty.

'I told him I had seen his wife the day before and she seemed very brave and how sorry we all were. Then he looked me in the face and told me it was all an act and he fears Mrs Rumbelow is having a breakdown. He said he had to tell someone and it just poured out, how Jane has locked herself away in their son's room and cries for him, from morning till night. He looked so exhausted, and I can't imagine how heartbroken Mrs Rumbelow must feel.'

'That's so sad. The poor man, he spends all his life comforting people in distress, and who is there for him when he needs it? He's a father and has lost his only son; he's heartbroken,' muttered Beatrice.

'That's just what I was thinking when I saw him fighting back the tears,' replied Ada. 'He asked me if I would be kind enough to call in on his wife on my way home and, of course, I agreed.

'Mrs Glossop answered the door and took me to one side and told me Jane is scarcely eating. Dr Fletcher has put her on strong tablets to calm her nerves, but they don't seem to be making any difference.

'She barely knew I was there, the poor lady is eaten up with so much grief. Of course, she was dressed in mourning. She showed me Piers' bedroom and sat there clutching his clothes, his books and photographs, anything that belonged to him, just stroking it, or pressing it against her cheek, repeating his name constantly.

'I suggested we went downstairs and Mrs Glossop made us tea, but Jane barely sipped it. I then suggested we went out in the garden, as I know how much she loves it, but she said being there, surrounded by the flowers and all of nature's beauty, made her feel guilty. I asked her how that could be and she said it wasn't right that she could feel the warm air on her face while she didn't even have the dead body of her son to hold.'

'Do you think she'll be well enough to come to the concert tonight?' asked Sarah. 'If only she could come and be with other mothers and wives who are grieving too, to allow us to offer our support and friendship, our words of comfort.'

'I think she wants to be alone right now. Reverend Rumbelow told me how they had received a letter from a comrade of Piers' who said he died a hero. He went the aid of an injured soldier who was being carried over to him on a stretcher under fire. The stretcher bearer moved forward to speak to him and Piers could see a sniper behind the man and stood up to warn him to keep his head down. The stretcher bearer ducked just in time, but Piers took the shot straight through his heart. He didn't stand a chance.'

There was a stunned silence when Ada finished speaking.

'You did a good thing listening to the vicar, and calling in on his poor wife,' Sarah muttered, wiping a tear from her eye.

'I hope the concert brings comfort for our community this evening. Seeing Mrs Rumbelow in such a terrible way made me worry all the more for my Alfie. What if he gets killed? And without once setting eyes on his son? Is it selfish to want my husband home? And Beatrice's Sam too? Why can't this horrible war end?'

Sarah spoke firmly. 'Ada Saward! Or should I say Ada Heath. No mother wants her son to go to war. But equally no mother wants her family to be taken over by the Huns. We fight for our freedom, for your son's future freedom and our alliance to the King and our country. God will guide us to victory.'

Ada shook her head. 'Mother, Mrs Rumbelow doesn't believe in God anymore. She's in a dark place right now and needs our patience, love and kindness to help her through her grief. We must help her, we must help each other when our friends' lives are destroyed by these senseless deaths.'

Chapter 26

That evening the Saward sisters dressed in some of their finest gowns, elegant yet demure, in keeping with the spirit of the concert. Ada wore her favourite pale blue silk dress trimmed with a fine white lace collar, Jessie's deep blue satin dress made her pale skin and violet eyes look even more radiant, complemented with a cream sash belt, while Beatrice glowed in a plum-coloured gown decorated with pink buttons down the front of her bodice. Sarah looked splendidly matriarchal in her finest white blouse and large cameo brooch at the neck, teamed with her smartest black skirt and jacket. Maria's face was fixed in a permanent beam as she flounced around the house in a green dress that Ada loaned her, a welcome change to the dark, practical colours she had been used to wearing before her arrival in Wolferton.

Ada and Beatrice both wore their lockets and smiled tenderly at the faces of their loved ones looking up at them, while Jessie's image of Jack's handsome face was firmly cemented in her head. Sarah lent her a pearl necklace that Harry had bought as a birthday gift. Maria clutched her locket, relieved that the sweet face framed inside was no longer a secret.

Ada was on edge, telling everyone that she had butterflies in her stomach and needed to leave.

'Have I ever told you how proud I am of you? And I know Alfie is too,' Harry said to her, taking hold of her hands. 'Good luck this evening. But I don't think you need it.'

Ada kissed her father on the cheek and stepped out of the front door, her ears ringing to the chorus of 'See you soon.'

Sarah straightened Harry's jacket pocket, her fingers sliding across the row of striped medals commemorating his services with the Norfolk Territorials where he held the rank of sergeant major.

'What about your Fabergé pin? Aren't you wearing it after all?' enquired Sarah.

'No, Sarah. You are,' he answered, getting the pin out of his pocket and pinning the precious jewel onto her lapel. 'You deserve to wear it as well as me, on account of your excellent work in the royal retiring rooms.'

'But . . .' she stuttered.

'It looks better on you, my dear. I insist! It looks too fussy with my medals.'

After a final glance in the mirror, Harry murmured under his breath, 'very good', with a smile in the corner of his mouth and a little nod. He stepped out of the front door arm and arm with his wife, who stroked the Fabergé pin and smiled, holding her head high.

Jessie and Beatrice followed, then Betty, who had dressed up in her best Sunday outfit, a dark blue suit, and Maria, who pushed a grinning Leslie in his perambulator.

Beatrice fingered the locket around her throat as she walked along the path leading to the church, wishing Sam could see how all the community was rallying together to support him and his comrades. It brought a lump to her throat and any wavering thoughts she had about her affections towards him disappeared at that moment. She nodded politely at Mrs Sparrow, the prim local teacher, who was holding the arm of her mother, Miriam, now almost blind, and slowly shuffling along the best she could. She noticed that the teacher gripped a photograph in her free hand of her uniformed brother Gerald, a tiny wispy moustache on his upper lip, his cap pulled down low.

The vicar stood at the back of the church, his tired eyes veiled in sadness, graciously greeting arrivals and pointing them to vacant seats. He courteously accepted condolences from parishioners for the loss of his son and enquired about the whereabouts and news of their men. Beatrice looked around, but there was no sign of Mrs Rumbelow.

Edith greeted her inside the church door, her face drawn. She showed Beatrice an official letter she received that day:

REGRET TO INFORM YOU THAT CORPORAL SAMUEL PETERS, 5TH BATTALION, THE NORFOLK REGIMENT IS REPORTED MISSING 12 AUGUST. THIS DOES NOT NECESSARILY MEAN THAT HE IS KILLED OR WOUNDED.

'What am I to make of it, Beatrice? Why can't they tell me where he is? How can he just be *missing*?' Edith croaked.

Florence took hold of her mother's shaking arm, clutching a photo of Sam close to her chest with her other hand. She looked pretty, dressed in her Sunday best dark-blue dress with white daisies, her hair tied back with a white ribbon.

Beatrice choked. 'I don't know, and I feel the same as you, Edith, but we mustn't give up hope. Would you like to join us? I asked Ada to reserve seats for us together.'

'And may I join you too?' a voice from behind asked.

Beatrice gulped. She recognised the voice and turned to see her friend Lizzie clutching a photograph of her and Wilf on their wedding day.

'I'm so pleased you could come, and that's a lovely photo of you both,' answered Beatrice, pointing towards their seats.

Edith and Florence shifted along the pew to make room for the lady farmer.

'I couldn't miss this concert, regardless of my feelings about Wilf. He is fighting for his country, after all. Besides, everyone's talking about it,' Lizzie whispered, taking her seat next to Beatrice. Edith sat on the other side of her and chatted to Sarah seated in the pew in front of her with the rest of the Saward family.

The church rapidly filled with parishioners taking up every spare inch on the seats. Mary Beck and her daughters arrived clutching their photographs, holding themselves with dignity, and took their seats at the front. Word had quickly spread as most arrived clutching framed photographs of their sons, fathers, brothers, uncles, nephews, grandsons and sweethearts, dressed either in their uniforms or Sunday best. The two sisters, Nancy Gates, whose peace-loving son Billy had been killed in battle, and Annie Fitch, arrived in full mourning, with black veils shielding their faces. They supported each other as they walked up the aisle and found seats, Nancy clutching a photo of an innocent-faced young soldier with a dimple on his chin.

Beatrice fingered the locket around her neck again and felt a surge of pride rise through her chest. She was proud to be part of a strong, united community. She was proud to be the station master's daughter, proud that her father was appreciated by royal families throughout Europe for his diplomacy and professionalism.

Soon everyone was seated, crammed close together on the wooden pews. Ada stood on a raised platform with the choir, with Clara in the prime central position, looking poised and elegant. She clutched a sheet of music in her hand and Ada was intrigued to know what surprise she had in store for the evening.

Magnolia sat behind Clara, arching her back and holding her head high as if trying to catch the audience's eyes.

Hubert, poised as always with an air of dignity and good breeding, sat erect at the piano next to the stage, his fingers gliding effortlessly along the ivories as he played hymns from memory. When he had finished, he shook his wrists and placed his hands in his lap, waiting for a sign from the vicar.

The chattering came to stop when Frederick Rumbe-low stepped forward and raised his hands. He cleared his throat. 'Ladies and gentlemen, please stand for their most gracious Majesties, Queen Alexandra, Queen Mary, and Princess Mary. God save the King.'

It was Hubert's cue and his fingers pressed down on the ivory keys with great force. The building was filled to the rafters with sound as the crowd belted out the national anthem. Heads turned to observe the royal family walk-ing slowly down the aisle, looking dignified, holding their heads high. Miss Charlotte Knollys walked behind them solemnly, courtier to Queen Alexandra who as well as being Lady of the Bedchamber, made history by being appointed the first woman private secretary.

They took their seats on the front pew. Their gowns were subdued; the Dowager Queen wore black lace while Queen Mary was in dark green and her daughter, Princess Mary, wore dark purple. Their necklines were adorned with pearls.

Beatrice sucked in a deep breath. Was she imagining it? Were the two queens clutching framed photographs of the monarch? It was a poignant reminder that their King was also a son, and a husband, like any another man. Being of royal birth did not change that.

All eyes swivelled towards the front of the church as the Reverend Rumbelow cleared his throat addressed the congregation from the platform. He put his personal grief aside for this very special occasion

'Your Royal Majesties, ladies and gentlemen, may I warmly welcome you to what I know will be a scintillating evening of music of unrivalled proportion. Our concert this evening comes at a time when we are anxiously waiting for news of the Sandringham Company, and our men serving under Captain Beck. We are united as one as we remember the countless sacrifices they make. We remember them all now, in our prayers and our hearts, and dedicate this evening to them, and to all of our brave and loyal servicemen, wherever they might be.'

He paused while the audience contemplated his words, some wiping away tears. His voice wobbled as he tried to continue, brushing away his own tears. The silence was broken by the sound of the church door opening and slow footsteps that came to a halt. A woman's anguished cries could be heard from the back of the church. All eyes were fixed on the vicar as he stepped down from the platform and walked slowly down the aisle, his chest heaving with sobs. At the back stood a forlorn figure dressed in black. Jane Rumbelow was fighting back tears. She lurched forward and gripped the side of the pew to steady herself. She straightened herself, clutching a photograph of Piers, her face fixed intensely on her husband's. Her jaw wobbled as she raised the photograph and held it out towards him. The church was hushed and Beatrice welled up as she watched the vicar take his heartbroken wife in his arms and hold her tight, stroking her hair. He took her hand in his and led her along the aisle, directing her to a reserved seat behind the two queens. Their faces showed kindness and sympathy. There was barely a dry eye as Jane's grief and rawness touched the hearts of everybody present; even Queen Alexandra was seen to dry her eyes.

The vicar returned to the platform and cleared his throat. His voice was soft at first and his eyes were on his wife as he told the gathering, 'My wife and I would like to thank you for your kind thoughts and heartfelt condolences. Our loss is almost too much to bear, but we hope with God's guidance, and your love too, that we will get through this.

'There may be moments when we question how God could love us if he takes away what we love the most. But he gave his only son Jesus for us. It is a sacrifice that some of us have now experienced. Please, I beseech you, do not give up on God. Our loyalty to our King and country, and our God, must always be uppermost in our minds and hearts.'

Reverend Rumbelow paused, looking towards his wife, who was being consoled by the lady next to her, Miss Potts, the Sunday school teacher whose brother was missing in Gallipoli.

He continued, his voice becoming stronger. 'Nations may rise and nations may fall. Let an outsider come and dictate and they will see that we are united. The moment the enemy appears at our gate we are as one man. And so it will also be in our great nation.'

A few people stood to applaud, followed by others. The vicar raised his arms, indicating for them to sit.

'This evening we unite here, bringing images of our beloved men who are always in our hearts and minds. From the heartache of this separation, we must take inspiration from our actions tonight to raise money for our troops. We are indeed most fortunate to have the celebrated Miss Clara Griffin join us from London where she is in much demand. She is most graciously here with us this evening in a voluntary capacity to support our cause, the Red Cross. She has kindly offered to sign photographs of herself afterwards for the price of a shilling. Every farthing raised will go towards supporting our men at war. God save the King.'

'God save the King,' chorused the audience.

The vicar signalled to Clara and Ada nodded. She sat anxiously at the front, twisting her fingers in her lap, wondering nervously about the surprise that would now unfold. Clara had never looked more beautiful, with her finely chiselled cheekbones and flawless white marble skin, her rosebud lips slightly parted. Her cream satin gown sat off the shoulders and was decorated with delicate flowers down the bodice. Her soft loose corkscrew curls hung down the sides of her cheeks like trailing golden laburnum.

Clara glanced at the royal gathering as she introduced her surprise solo, holding her arms outstretched towards them as she spoke. 'Your Royal Highnesses, ladies and gentlemen, it is my greatest pleasure to perform for you this evening some music composed by Gilbert and Sullivan that has not been performed for a number of years.'

As she paused Ada's hand flew up to her throat. *Gilbert and Sullivan?* What could it be? *The Mikado?* *H.M.S. Pinafore?* *The Pirates of Penzance?* Why the need for secrecy? These were all popular comic operas that were well known and loved.

'I've chosen to revive a small piece of this wonderful *libretto* because I feel it is particularly pertinent for women today, and for all the women here this evening headed by our beloved Dowager Queen Alexandra, Her Majesty our Queen Mary, and her daughter Princess Mary – three generations of royal women whose graciousness and generous care towards the community around Sandringham and Wolferton is well known to everyone here in this church.'

'Aye, aye!' thundered the approving congregation, some standing to clap their hands enthusiastically.

'I dedicate my song to all women, from all backgrounds. You have big hearts and minds. Some of your hearts are broken while you grieve terrible losses. War has tied us women together with a bond that nobody can destroy. This is why I have chosen to sing from the opera *Princess Ida* this evening. It has inspired me so much, and I hope it will do the same for everyone here this evening.'

Ada raised an eyebrow? *Princess Ida?* It was hardly well known. Why did Clara choose that opera? Ada glanced around and could see puzzled expressions on people's faces.

Clara continued. 'Please, let me explain, and then all will be clear. The story behind *Princess Ida* tells how she was married off in babyhood. However, she sets up a college for women, showing the strength of them against adversity. It's a farce about women rallying together, as we are now, though in this story the princess ends up happily with her childhood prince. I dedicate this music to all women here this evening, each and every one of you, who face losses of the greatest magnitude, and to believe we will come out stronger at the end, even though it may not seem possible at this moment. I hope you enjoy it.'

Ada glanced in the direction of the royal party. The two queens frowned, both had pursed lips and exchanged questioning glances, while the young Princess Mary, just eighteen years old, stifled a giggle behind her hand.

As Hubert belted out the music, Clara's crisp, crystal clear voice rose higher. She moved across the platform, pressing her hands against her chest, then gripping the sides of her head, before raising her hands high above her head as she expressed the drama and emotion of the song.

When she finished, and then curtseyed to the royal party, there was silence. Ada bit her lip as a feeling of panic gripped her. What if nobody liked it? For her, it was a wonderful chance to hear a lesser known piece of music from two great masters, but would Clara's choice be deemed controversial by the two queens?

The silence was broken when Princess Mary stood up to applaud enthusiastically. Within seconds, she was joined by others in the congregation. Clara bowed, and her face broke into a smile as the applause rang around her ears.

The programme continued as Hubert returned to the piano keys and Clara burst into song once again, joined this time by the choir. It was a moving rendition of the Irish ballad 'Danny Boy' which the congregation hummed along to. The applause was thunderous as the song came to a close. It meant a lot to many, conveying a message from a parent to a son going off to war. This was followed by a selection of more popular and lively Gilbert and Sullivan renditions from *The Pirates of Penzance* and *The Mikado*, musicals known to be favoured by the royal family. Magnolia's moment of glory came towards the end when she joined Clara for a jolly duet from *The Gondoliers*, with the audience spilling tears of laughter.

Hands clapped wildly and broad smiles replaced sad expressions. The audience were invited to join in the final song, which raised the church roof, 'It's a Long, Long Way to Tipperary'.

'Again', they cheered loudly, clapping furiously. 'Again. More. More.'

After an encore, Queen Alexandra, poised and regal, walked onto the platform. The church fell silent as she raised her hands and spoke, her voice solemn.

Turning to Clara, she thanked her for her *interesting* choice of opening song from *Princess Ida*, and commented, 'If my memory is correct, wasn't there a war and Princess Ida was abandoned by her women and ended up with her prince?'

Ada noticed Clara blush as the older Queen added, 'Well, my dear, let's hope the women of Wolferton are more civilised!'

The congregation clapped louder and the Dowager Queen raised her hand to signal silence, thanking everyone involved for making the evening such an outstanding success.

'Many of you here this evening, if not all, will have loyal men serving under Captain Beck.'

Heads nodded, and tears welled up once again. Mrs Beck and their daughters dabbed their moist eyes.

'These men, every single one of them with the Sandringham Company, have shown bravery and valour and it is my utmost intention, and that of His Majesty, the King, to discover the truth about what has happened to them.'

'Hear, hear!' a voice cried from the back. 'But how much longer must we wait?'

All eyes swivelled around to see who dare question the Dowager Queen. It was Mrs Sprout, who had two sons, aged eighteen and nineteen, both gardeners on the estate. Both missing.

Queen Alexandra shook her head. 'I wish I could tell you, but I will not lie. You deserve the truth, and believe me, we will do everything we can to find out. I promise you this. The King has personally cabled Sir Ian Hamilton, stressing how anxious he was for news of the 5th Battalion Norfolk Regiment with the Sandringham Company and Captain Beck.'

Queen Alexandra glanced towards Mrs Beck, who nodded, biting her lip. 'I do have some news I can impart. I have been informed that Captain Evelyn Beck has written to his family, his letter was received today, so we are thankful that he survived the terrible battle on 12th August. However, he cannot throw light on the fate of our brave Captain Frank Beck or his nephew Alec. He says the last he saw of them they were just one field behind him. He doesn't know where they are, or the others, and thinks they must have been taken prisoner.'

Mrs Beck's shoulders shook and she was comforted by her daughters who were also distressed. Then Mrs Beck rose and faced the hushed congregation. 'In my heart we cling to the hope that Frank and Alec are still alive, and will continue to do so until I am notified otherwise. I know the King is doing all he can to discover the whereabouts of the Sandringham Company. We must pray for their safe return. Gold save the King.'

Her words lifted the heavy atmosphere and a steady applause broke out.

Queen Alexandra raised a hand. 'I have been greatly moved by this evening and the warmth and emotion it has aroused within us, the compassion we bestow on each other. This shows me clearly is how much we benefit by being together, by uniting and sharing our sorrows as mothers, wives and daughters. So I would like to make a proposal.'

The congregation glanced at each other. 'Yes, good ladies of Wolferton and loyal servants of the King, I have a proposal. I suggest we form a women's meeting group for our families for us to support each other in our moments of despair. Like this evening, bring your photographs with you and talk about your boys, your men, those who are doing you proud.'

The congregation turned to those next to them and nodded, a flicker of a smile curling on their lips. They felt heartened that their wonderful Dowager Queen was not only taking heed of their anguish, but acting on it. Instant sounds of approval echoed within the church. 'That's agreed then. My staff shall make the arrangements without delay.' The Dowager Queen smiled.

'God Save the King,' a woman's voice belted out. She stood up and clapped her hands.

'Yes, God Save the King and our Queens,' shouted another woman, who followed suit and stood up. Soon everyone was standing. Hubert's nimble fingers pounded the ivories for a rousing rendition of the national anthem, as voices increased to a passionate, roaring crescendo. Hubert furiously hammered down on the keys, before climaxing with a final flourishing sweep, then standing to face the throng, their eyes moist with tears, breaking into a final united, 'God Save the King'.

Heads bowed dutifully as the royal party swept down the aisle. Beatrice raised her eyes and swore that Queen Alexandra was fighting back tears. Oh, the Dowager Queen had such a good heart, often offering to help those in need who were tenants on her estate and along with the King sought to improve living and working conditions. She was suffering too, Beatrice could see. They all were.

Lizzie Piper bade farewell to Harry and Sarah, while Edith chatted to the blacksmith's wife in the opposite pew. At the back of the church a large throng had gathered around the Queens, eager to know more about the women's group. Queen Alexandra pledged to do whatever she could to learn the fate of their missing men captured in Gallipoli, and women thanked her, sobbing into their already soaked handkerchiefs.

Maria, who had sat at the back throughout the concert with Leslie, spellbound and in awe at being within a few feet of her Queen, as well her dutiful daughter Princess Mary, and the very poised Dowager Queen, became flushed with excitement as Queen Alexandra looked in her direction. Maria watched as they consoled Nancy and Annie mourning for the loss of Billy and embraced Jane Rumbelow, whose eyes filled with tears as she showed this fine Queen the photo of her beloved son. The Queen promised to call in on her the following week, as she did all those who were bereaved on the royal estate. Jane curtseyed and took the Queen's hand, kissing it and raising her face. 'Praise be the Lord for our kind-hearted Queen Mother.'

It was a poignant moment that seared into Maria's heart, making her think how insignificant her problems were compared to the families in this church. At least she would see her Joey and brothers again, she would get to hug them and love them, but not poor Jane Rumbelow, and others like her.

She gulped back her tears and turned her attention to Leslie, bending over him, teasingly squeezing his chubby cheeks and praising him for his good behaviour. A well-spoken voice behind her enquired, 'Is he your son? If so, you are a wonderful mother. He didn't make a sound all evening.'

Maria turned to see the young Princess Mary. 'Oh no, miss, I mean Your Highness, Your Majesty. I'm sorry,

I don't rightly know what to call you. I ain't, I mean, *I haven't*, ever met a princess before.'

Princess Mary's eyes twinkled and her mouth widened into a grin, showing her perfect teeth.

Maria fidgeted with her fingers and her cheeks coloured, and she chided herself for her gauche manners. She dropped into a clumsy curtsey.

'I don't believe we have met before,' said Princess Mary. 'But please don't worry about such formalities, it's not, well, with the war, we are all much more equal, don't you think?'

The young princess smiled at Maria, who felt herself relax at the warm words. She could barely believe she was in the company of a princess, who she greatly admired. As well as visiting hospitals and welfare organisations with her mother, supporting projects that gave comfort and assistance to servicemen and their families, she had inspired a Christmas appeal in 1914 that won the heart of the nation with her heartfelt message:

I want you now to help me to send a Christmas present from the whole of the nation to every sailor afloat and every soldier at the front. I am sure that we should all be happier to feel that we had helped to send our little token of love and sympathy on Christmas morning, something that would be useful and of permanent value, and the making of which may be the means of providing employment in trades adversely affected by the war. Could there be anything more likely to hearten them in their

348

struggle than a present received straight from home
on Christmas Day? Please will you help me?

Even Maria's ma had scraped a few pennies together to
contribute and the money was used to fill a brass gift box
with her profile embossed on the lid containing tobacco,
a photograph of Princess Mary and Christmas card from
King George and Queen Mary, while non-smoking servicemen were given a packet of acid tablets, a writing
case with pencil, paper and envelopes, together with the
Christmas card and photograph of the princess.

She's so young and she did all that, thought Maria, in
awe. *What a kind and wonderful princess she is. She don't
seem to have any airs and graces, she's a real lady.*

Ada rushed to Maria's side when she looked over and
saw her talking to royalty. She introduced Maria to the
princess and, a moment later, much to Maria's astonishment, they were joined by the elegant Queen Mother.

Ada stepped forward. 'Your Majesty, may I introduce
Maria. She is a relative staying with us for a while and
helping in the house and with Leslie. She has a wonderful
way with him.'

Maria's cheeks flushed and she curtseyed awkwardly,
her chest swelling with pride that Ada had acknowledged
her to royalty as a relative. 'Your Majesty, I—'

'He is a very lucky young man then and you have a wonderful way with him. I didn't even know there was an infant
in church. I'm afraid the same couldn't be said for my
young children when they were that age,' she said, smiling.

The sound of quickening footsteps and rustling of a satin dress brought her discussion to an abrupt end.

'Your Majesty, oh, Your Majesty. It was such an honour to sing for you today. I am at your service any time.'

The hem of Magnolia's dress swept the floor as she dipped into a deep curtsey, her high-pitched voice warbling with excitement.

The Queen Mother turned to acknowledge Magnolia, who fidgeted with her hands in front of her, raising her flat chest and standing erect.

'How very kind of you, er, Miss Greensticks, isn't it?'

Ada stepped forward to introduce her, but was interrupted by Magnolia, whose lips twitched nervously as she dropped into a deep curtsey.

'Oh, I am honoured that you to remember me, ma'am. I am the celebrated Wolferton Nightingale. I had the pleasure of singing for you once before, if you recall, at Sandringham Church last spring. You were so kind and complimented me on my voice afterwards.'

Magnolia flashed a broad smile that showed her big teeth, waving her hand in the air in a jittery fashion.

'Indeed, Miss Greensticks, I certainly do recall. You are widely known in these parts. Your offer of help is much appreciated. If you speak to my lady-in-waiting, she will put you down for the first tea rota at our women's meeting.'

Queen Alexandra turned to Ada. 'You not only did your husband proud, but the entire village of Wolferton. Thank you so very much for organising such a wonderful evening. I'm sure I speak for Queen Mary and Princess Mary too.'

Before sweeping out of the church, she turned to Maria once more. 'It was a pleasure to meet you, my dear.'

'Did you see that, Magnolia?' asked Maria, excitedly. 'Both the old Queen and the Princess spoke to me. I can't believe it!'

'So I see Maria, how splendid. You are well and truly becoming one of us. And if you allow me to take you under my wing, if Mrs Saward doesn't mind, I can teach you the etiquette required for mixing in royal circles,' offered Magnolia , her chin jutting forward.

Chapter 27

Maria pinched herself. She couldn't believe it. She couldn't wait to write and tell her mother how she had spent the evening with three royal ladies – two queens and a princess – and spoken to them as well. She couldn't help but marvel at the Dowager Queen's grace and care for the people of Wolferton. She could picture her mother's face smiling as her finger traced the words, and showing the letter to her sister. 'Fancy that, our Maria mixing with royalty,' she could imagine her mother telling Freda, her chest puffed up with pride.

Before the day could end for her, Maria had an important task to do. All day Maria had been mulling over what she could do to prove herself to Mrs Saward. She had finally came up with a daring plan – if only she had the courage. Now, after a wonderful evening, she had the confidence to put it into action. It would require bags of guts and she couldn't put a foot wrong if she was going to pull it off.

It was now ten thirty and everyone had climbed the stairs to bed, including Maria, after chatting together about the evening's success. Sarah had retired to bed earlier, fretting about Mrs Inglenook's inspection of the royal waiting rooms the next day and complaining that her headache had returned. Harry was the last to head up to bed, and Maria listened out for movements. She heard Sarah go downstairs ten minutes later. She made up her favourite headache remedy by soaking coarse brown paper in vinegar to place on the forehead and then took it up to bed with her.

Maria lay still on her bed – waiting. Her ears pricked, listening out for any sounds in the house. There was a tiny window looking out towards the front garden that allowed a glimmer of shimmering silver moonlight to filter through. It was the only light in Wolferton as the inhabitants obeyed the government's strict blackout order. She placed a chair under the window, ducking her head under the low eaves, and pressed her face against the glass. She looked up into the coal-black darkness, relieved there were no Zeppelins overhead tonight.

Gazing outside she saw the shadowy figures of a couple of older men wobbling past the front of the house, no doubt the worse for wear after a few drinks. She screwed her eyes towards the crossroads ahead, blinking when she thought she saw something move. She blinked and looked again, but there was nothing. She shrugged it off as the light playing tricks on her.

She stepped down from the chair by the window and lay on her bed, deciding to wait a few more minutes, urging herself that she must see through her plan. Maria was still wearing her green dress, her nightdress hanging over the back of a chair. It seemed ages since she heard Harry's bedroom door close, and there was no sound from the Saward sisters. It was time to leave, but her courage was failing her.

Maria pushed aside any doubts and rose. She climbed onto the chair once more and looked outside the window again into the quiet, dark night, with not a soul in sight, and knew she had to act now if she was going to. And quickly.

She stepped quietly off the chair and picked up a dark blue shawl that Jessie had given her and slung it across her shoulders. She tiptoed down the stairs as softly as she could, careful to avoid any floorboards that squeaked. She paused on the landing, waiting a moment to see if anyone had been disturbed. All she heard was snoring from Harry's bedroom. Her heart pounded as she continued down the stairs, holding her breath, and into the kitchen, then out into the hallway.

Every evening she had noticed how Harry hung the keys to the station on a hook inside a small wooden cabinet in the hallway just inside the front door. Maria would watch from inside the hallway, observing him lock the cabinet and place its key in the top pocket of his jacket.

She now reached for Harry's jacket and fumbled in his pocket for the key she needed. Her hands shook and she struggled to steady them enough so as to undo the lock.

When she finally succeeded, her stomach flipped and she froze, hardly daring to breathe, looking anxiously around her. Her nerves were getting the better of her. She spotted the brass keys to the royal station, looped together on a ring under a sign that read WOLFERTON STATION. Her heart beat like a drum as she quietly removed the keys, then locked the cabinet again and returned the cabinet key to Harry's jacket.

She glanced around and listened again. The silence was eerie. She reminded herself how appreciative Sarah would be of what she was about to do as she unlocked the front door and stepped out, closing the door quietly behind her and walking quickly down the path. Her eyes spun in all directions as she dashed across the street to the station, tightly gripping the bundle of keys.

She sprinted to the royal retiring rooms. The station was creepy in the dead of night, cloaked in darkness, with no passengers on the platform, no soldiers waving through the train windows as they departed, no chirpy nods and whistles from Eddie pushing his trolley, no shrieking sound of the whistle from Harry and no sign of smoke pillows in the sky or the screech of the brakes as a train pulled into the station.

She shook off her reservations, telling herself she was there now and should get on with it. She nervously fiddled with the keys, trying to fit different ones into the lock, before finally succeeding. First, she would sweep and polish in Queen Alexandra's waiting room, then she would give a good shine to the silver picture frames and candlesticks. She knew where the cleaning materials were kept in the store cupboard near Harry's office and equipped herself with everything she needed. She knew she was taking a huge risk coming to the royal waiting rooms, but she hoped Sarah would be pleased once she saw all the chores had been completed to her high standards – they could keep it a secret between them.

Maria glanced up at the night sky, thankful for the silver white moon that provided enough light for her to work. She knew she was a good worker, Betty had told her so that day, and she wanted to show her thanks to this kind family and help them in their hour of need. Where's the harm in that? she asked herself.

She rolled up her sleeves, sweeping the floor, cleaning and polishing from top to bottom, from the glass chandelier that sparkled liked diamonds, to the deep plush carpet and parquet wooden flooring. She was careful with every ornament that she picked up to clean, being sure to place them back in the exact spots she'd got them from; nothing was left untouched and she even dusted the tall glossy leaves on the aspidistra plants. She paused for the briefest moment to admire the smiling faces of the royal family in their silver frames.

She worked with great deftness and speed, moving on to the King's waiting room, imagining the delight on Sarah's face when she saw how well she had worked. She heard the clock strike midnight. She would be finished soon, all that was left was to clean the elaborate silver candlesticks. She held them in her hands and admired the skilled craftsmanship, which took her breath away. They were unlike anything she had seen before, standing two feet tall and decorated intricately with swirling scrolling foliage on the base and on the detachable arms.

'Blimey, they weigh a ton. They must be worth a fortune,' she muttered under her breath.

'I hope they are, 'cause I'm 'aving them,' snorted a man's voice behind her.

Maria quaked at its sneering tone. She spun around and shrieked. As she did so the candlesticks slipped through her fingers and were snatched by the man.

'It's you!' cried Maria, her eyes filled with terror.

Walter pressed his thick hand over her mouth.

'Were you expecting someone else?' he asked contemptuously. 'Perhaps your young lover boy from the station? I've seen yer together.'

Maria wriggled in his grip and he laughed, pushing her across the room.

'How dare you say such a lie? What do you want here, Walter Jugg? You've no right to be in these rooms. Why can't you leave me alone?' she cried, the words sticking in her throat.

Walter sneered, stuffing the candlesticks into a canvas bag. 'I think you're right. These little beauties must be worth a small fortune.'

Maria rushed towards him. 'Give them back, Walter Jugg. They ain't yours.'

'And they ain't yours either. I've been keeping an eye on you. I ain't daft. I know you shouldn't be here at this time either. So what mischief are you up to?,' he growled.

'I ain't done nothing wrong. I'm here to help Mrs Saward, so you can't threaten me. The police know all about you and I ain't scared of you no more. Now get out of here before I scream.'

Maria opened her mouth to show him she meant what she said but he grabbed her and covered her mouth with a thick coarse hand. She looked desperately around her for an escape route, but she was trapped. He pushed her against the wall and she felt his hands grab her breasts. She turned her head as she felt his hot booze-soaked breath on her face. She kicked out at him. She tried to bite his hand, but he increased the pressure until she was gasping for breath. Tears sprung into her eyes, her heart pounding. Every part of her body shook with fear.

Hatred for Walter Jugg filled her veins. He wanted to ruin her life. Her new life with the Sawards and Joey's future. She summoned every ounce of strength remaining within her and gave a tremendous push, making him stumble and lose his grip.

He rolled back, then steadied himself, a sneer covering his face, as he pushed his hand up her skirt.

'If I don't get me money I'll be back for more of this tomorrow, and I don't just mean the silver. And make sure you bring a handful of what you can grab from 'ere, I'm sure they won't be missed. That clock will do nicely, I'd swipe it now, but it won't fit in me bag.'

Maria pushed him away, her heart pounding. Walter smirked, greedily eyeing up an ornate domed gold pendulum clock on the mantelpiece. She felt sickened by his touch on her skin and the enormity of his words.

'Never. Never in a million years will I take anything from the Sawards or the royal family. And you'll never lay a finger on me again, or else–'

'Yeah, or else what?' Walter sneered.

'Please, go. Just go now, leave Wolferton and I swear I won't say a word.'

'You listen to me, and listen careful. It's me that decides when and where I go and I'm staying put for now. I like it 'ere. I'll make sure the police and everyone here get to 'ear about how you broke in to help yourself for yer bastard son. And I might even pay a visit to 'im, too as is me right as his father. I 'ave my ears to the ground. Nothing gets past Walter Jugg.'

'Nobody would believe you! You're a wicked liar and blackmailer, and you'll get locked up, Harry will see to that,' spluttered Maria. 'You keep away from me and my Joey!'

'Just try me and see. I'll be seeing you tomorrow then. This is just the start. Bring me the money and the clock, or else . . .'

The cold greedy glint in his thin slate eyes seared through her quaking body. He tossed his head back and laughed as he stumbled outside with his haul. She heard him clear his throat and cough, the phlegm cackling. He spat out a lump of creamy-coloured thick gloop from the back of his throat. She shook from head to toe, watching the smirk spread across his face as he disappeared in the darkness.

She watched until he was out of sight and crumpled into a heap on the floor, gulping back tears.

'I wish I were dead,' she wept. 'Nobody will believe I didn't take the candlesticks. What am I to do?'

Chapter 28

Maria's legs wobbled unsteadily as she entered the station master's house. She quietly hung up the keys to the royal waiting rooms, and then placed the cabinet keys in Harry's jacket pocket. She sneaked upstairs to her attic room, lifting her skirt and taking each step slowly and holding her breath so as not to wake the family.

She felt a knot twisting inside her stomach as she pictured Sarah's face when she discovered the missing candlesticks in just a few hours. She winced as she imagined Walter watching her, his shadow close and ready to pounce.

Maria couldn't sleep a wink, her mind on overdrive, wondering what would happen to her. How could she make anyone believe her? Could she confide in any of the Saward sisters? Should she take her chances and call Walter's bluff?

She wondered how thorough Mrs Inglenook's inspection would be, if it included checking all the possessions in the royal waiting rooms were in place. Would she bring an inventory with her? Would Sarah notice the disappearance straightaway? Maybe, just maybe, it might escape their attention.

By the time the sun rose her mind was made up. She decided to stay silent, letting the day run its course, bitterly regretting that she had set foot in the royal retiring rooms the night before. She could barely muster the energy to get up, her body sunk into the straw mattress and her eyelids as heavy as two tombstones.

She groaned as she slowly slid out of bed, shivering at the sensation of the cold water on her body as she washed, hoping it would wake her up. For the first time since she arrived at the station master's house, the lusty bawling from Leslie jarred her nerves and irritated her; she was in no mood to soothe him this morning. She heard Ada pick up her young son and calm him, and she guessed she would be waiting for Maria to go downstairs and take him off her hands.

She picked a dark blue dress with white collar and cuffs to wear, another cast-off from Ada that was her favourite, and swept her hair off her face, tying it back with a white ribbon. Her face was white and drawn and dark shadows under her eyes were evidence of her wretched night.

It was eight o'clock by the time she dragged herself into the kitchen and Harry was leaving for the station. Maria watched through the kitchen door as he picked up his jacket and reached into the cabinet to remove his keys to the station. She heard the front door close after him.

Beatrice left a couple of minutes later for her duties at the post office, taking charge for her mother during Mrs Inglenook's inspection. Sarah and Jessie had already left for the waiting rooms and Maria's stomach twisted in knots as she anticipated the surprise in store for them. She covered her mouth with her hand as she yawned for the umpteenth time, unable to hide her tiredness.

Maria declined the offer of breakfast and barely heard a word of Ada's excited chatter about the concert, merely nodding in agreement at the appropriate time.

Suddenly Beatrice burst into the house breathless with excitement. She clutched her chest, smiling and holding out a letter to Ada.

Ada took the envelope. Her lips trembled as she ripped it open. 'It's from Alfie,' she gasped. 'He's coming home on leave!' she exclaimed. 'Next week. He has three days leave!'

Ada's eyes were moist and her voice trembled. 'I can't wait to show him his beautiful son.'

Beatrice placed an arm around her sister's shoulder. 'I'm so happy for you. I only wish there was good news about my Sam . . .'

'I'm so sorry. It's so selfish of me when your Sam is missing. Please forgive me, Beatrice.'

'There's nothing to forgive. I'm truly happy for you,' Beatrice reassured her. 'It will be wonderful for him to see Leslie. What a moment that will be.'

'I shall look forward to meeting him too. I'm so happy for you too, Ada,' added Maria, whose spirits began to lift at Ada's joyous news.

Ada grinned from ear to ear and she looked up. 'I need to leave soon, after telling Leslie the wonderful news. I am meeting Magnolia and Aggie this morning to start planning our first women's meeting. You know Magnolia, she has to be at the centre of everything that happens.'

'They mean well, I'm sure. I can see they have good hearts underneath their fancy clothes and airs and graces,' mulled Maria.

Betty stepped into the room clutching Leslie, washed and dressed in a pale-blue cotton playsuit. 'What news is there? I could hear lots of excitement while I was upstairs with this young man.'

'Oh, Betty, Leslie is going to meet his father for the first time,' Ada exclaimed, taking hold of Leslie and smothering his face with kisses. 'You are going to meet your father,' she cried.

Leslie screwed up his face and punched the air with his arms, trying to free himself from his mother's tight grip.

Maria reached forward. 'Shall I take him from you? I'm sure Leslie would benefit from some fresh air after his breakfast. I was thinking of playing with him in the garden this morning.'

Ada stroked his plump cheeks and blew him a kiss. 'I'm sorry if I squeezed you too tight. I'm so thrilled you will be meeting your father next week. Oh, Leslie, your father loves you so much. We all adore you.'

Handing Leslie over to Maria, she told her, 'He'd love to play in the garden, I'm sure, and now is the best time – before it gets too hot.'

After Ada had left Maria picked up a ball and scooped up Leslie from where she had popped him down on the floor and made her way into the garden, holding him against her chest so he could see over her shoulder. She had a small blanket with her and spread it out on the grass. The garden smelt divine, the scent of sweet honeysuckle wafting under her nose, combined with the headiness of lavender.

'Catch,' she called out, throwing the ball to the end of the garden. The infant crawled after the ball on all fours, like a worm wriggling across the ground. He was grinning and chuckling merrily. Maria ran after it too, pretending Leslie had beaten her to it, throwing her hands in the air in mock delight. She watched as he chased after the ball again, which she'd tossed towards the flower border, pleading for a moment's peace and urging him to play on his own.

She sat on the grass, her arms gripping her raised knees, and her face pointed up towards the sky, inhaling the perfumed air. A warm breeze washed over her. She couldn't resist closing her heavy eyelids, giving way to an aching body and lying down. She half opened her bleary eyes and saw Leslie kicking the ball. Unable to resist the tiredness any longer she closed her eyes as swallows soared overhead. She could just about make out the padding sound of Leslie's crawl on the grass.

She was rudely awakened from her drowsy state by the force of the ball smashing hard on her cheek.

'Leslie. Not so hard,' she complained. 'You'll have me teeth out if you're not careful.'

Her eyes were half open and she sleepily looked around. She jolted upright and called out, 'Leslie, where are you?'

She recognised the sound of his cries from the distance. Panicked, she leapt up and hollered his name again. She expected him to appear from one of the bushes, but there was no response.

She heard his cry, this time louder. She spun around in circles, pressing her hands against her head as the sound of his voice seemed closer. And then she saw him, held in a tight grip by Walter Jugg, his bulky canvas bag slung over his shoulder.

'Give him to me this minute, Walter,' Maria demanded, reaching forward to grab the flailing child. 'Please, I beg you. Leave him be. He ain't done you any 'arm.'

Walter threw back his head and laughed coarsely. His forehead was beaded with sweat and he had a menacing air about him that frightened her.

'Well, my pretty little thing. That depends on you. Have you thought over what I said?'

Tears filled Maria's eyes. She choked on her words. 'Just give me the boy, and you can go. I won't tell anyone about this.'

'I asked you to bring me that pretty clock. I could make a bob or two from it. And where's me money you thieved from me?'

Maria trembled as she rose and faced her tormenter, feeling hatred for him well up inside. Her eyes bored into him. She spat out her words, 'Never. Never. Never. I ain't stealing a farthing for you, Walter Jugg. I'm a decent, honest girl. Now give me back the boy.'

'Well, think again,' Walter hissed. 'Maybe yer posh Saward family will cough up for this little 'un. I need that money now, otherwise I'll be thrown out of me pub if I can't pay me debts. And I ain't giving that up without a fight. I'll do whatever it takes. But I'm prepared to be reasonable, if you need another day or so, so tell them that.'

Maria was enraged and lurched forward to grab Leslie from Walter's grip. The boy's arms reached out to her and he cried out for her, his cheeks crimson, but Walter shoved her to the ground and ran out of the front gate carrying Leslie under his arm, the baby's screams becoming louder and more desperate, and a canvas bag in the other with his stolen loot.

Maria picked herself up and chased after them, scalding tears streaming down her cheeks. She saw Walter dash towards the crossroads and summoned all her energy to chase after him, promising herself she would get Leslie back.

She saw Walter scramble over a grassy bank and down the railway track, her heart filled with dread. She became breathless and gripped her chest, screaming for him to stop.

Her cries attracted Harry's attention on the opposite site of the station. He was outside the royal waiting rooms and she yelled out to him for help. Sarah heard the commotion and joined him on the platform with another woman, who Maria assumed to be Mrs Inglenook. Eddie saw her too.

'It's Walter. He's got Leslie. He's taken him. Please do something,' Maria cried, cupping her hands to her mouth.

Eddie immediately leapt onto the track and ran along it until he reached Maria. She pointed ahead to Walter and the child and Eddie ran after them at breakneck speed, with Maria behind him trying to keep up.

She saw Walter pause for breath in the middle of the track, and she quickened her pace, desperate to grab Leslie. She heard the panic in Harry and Sarah's cries behind her, but continued running on the stony track. She would never forgive herself if anything happened to Leslie. Nobody would ever forgive her. Her heart thumped hard inside her. Her legs that had seemed so tired earlier galloped along the track as fast as a winning racehorse about to cross the line. There was a fire in her heel that edged her forward, giving her renewed energy.

Walter's pace was slowing and he seemed to be struggling. He paused again, bending over and gasping for breath. He shifted the bag with his stolen haul from one arm to the next, still clutching the screaming child over his shoulder.

Eddie was much younger and fitter than him and he was rapidly catching up. Maria tried her best to keep up as well, leaping over the railway sleepers and narrowing the gap between them.

The sight of plumes of thick black smoke billowing in the sky in the distance made her stop. She cried out to Eddie, who turned and looked up as she pointed towards it, moving closer towards them. She knew once the train turned the bend it would only be a couple of hundred yards away. Blood was pumping in her ears as the engine inched closer, sounding its horn to announce its imminent arrival at the station.

Eddie carried on running and she followed. 'Stop, Walter,' she screamed. 'Stop. Look ahead, there's a train coming.' Her cry was filled with sheer terror.

Walter stared up at the smoke and spun around, gripping his side and breathless. The pause was long enough for Eddie to lurch forward and grab Leslie, his face purple from crying, and pass him to Maria, who had now caught up and she immediately jumped off the track.

'You bastard. You filthy bastard,' Eddie screamed at Walter, raising his arm to punch him.

'Quick, Eddie. Quick. The train's coming. He's not worth it,' Maria hollered as she climbed up the bank, gripping Leslie tightly in her arms, the sound of the engine inching closer.

Eddie grabbed Walter around the collar of his jacket and dragged him to the side of the track just as the train approached the corner. They both fell in a twisted heap on the ground, grappling with each other. Eddie grabbed hold of Walter's bag and tossed it away, the candlesticks spilling out onto the grass.

Walter tried to sit astride Eddie, but the younger man managed to grip the burly man's neck. His eyes were bulging as he went to strike Eddie across the face, but missed. Eddie gritted his teeth and fought back ferociously, grabbing Walter's arm with both hands to push him off, both uttering foul oaths, their eyes full of rage.

'I've had enough of you buggers. I'm off,' he swore at Eddie. With one big push, he shook his body free from his jacket, leaving Eddie holding it in his hands, releasing him from Eddie's grip.

Maria's knees buckled and yelled out, horrified to see the smoke billowing closer. 'No, Walter. Stop!' she screeched.

Walter tried to jump across the track, but crashed face down onto the ground. Maria couldn't tell if his foot was trapped under the track, or he had injured himself falling, and was struggling to get up.

'Help him, Eddie. Do something!' she yelled.

'I can't move. Help me,' screeched Walter, trying desperately to free his trapped leg.

Eddie sprinted towards him, his eyes fixed on the train as it edged closer and closer. He saw driver Dobson's face, the alarm and desperation as he hurtled around the bend and was within a few feet of them.

He yanked desperately at Walter's leg, but it wouldn't budge, having become wedged under the metal railway track. Walter's eyes filled with terror as the train hurtled round the bend straight towards him.

'No!' she shrieked. 'Oh no! Walter. Eddie! Move, quickly!'

She looked away, scrunching her eyes shut as the brakes screeched to a halt, as Walter's last piercing cries rang out. A moment later, a hazy figure staggered towards her through the smoke.

'I'm sorry. I did everything I could.'

'Oh, Eddie. You're alive. I thought I'd lost you,' wept Maria. 'I couldn't bear to lose you.'

Chapter 29

Four days later, towards the end of August, devastating news began to filter through to Wolferton. The Sandringham Company had suffered terrible losses in Gallipoli. The Sawards devoured newspaper reports told by the few survivors. It became clear that their lads were out manoeuvred, suffered poor leadership and didn't stand a chance.

Beatrice held a letter in her shaking hand as she knocked on Edith's door. Their worst fears were confirmed.

IT IS MY PAINFUL DUTY TO INFORM YOU THAT A REPORT HAS BEEN RECEIVED FROM THE WAR OFFICE NOTIFYING THE DEATH OF PRIVATE SAM PETERS.

'Oh no. Not Sam too,' wailed his heartbroken mother.

Beatrice and Edith collapsed into each other's arms. Florence was inconsolable. She later took charge, though, making tea for her grieving mother and Beatrice, before calling on the doctor, saying her mother needed something to calm her nerves.

'She returned home with the doctor who attended to Edith.

Florence asked Beatrice, 'Do you think Sam suffered? I can't bear to think of him like that.'

'We mustn't allow ourselves to think that way. Sam was with Captain Beck. I know he would have done his best for his boys.'

'Do we know what happened?' asked Dr Fletcher softly.

Beatrice answered. 'Just that he was surrounded by snipers and gunfire. He didn't stand a chance. None of them did. And what for? There was no victory, it was a waste of a good honest, life, of so many young lives.'

Florence's voice shook. 'Ma keeps asking what's going to become of us. Are we going to be thrown out of our home, seeing as it's a tied cottage? Maybe it will be needed for whoever takes on Sam's job. She fears we won't be able to stay here. She says she's heard it's happened to other estate workers and she worries we'll end up living off charity or in the workhouse.'

Beatrice dried her eyes. She knew how much this worried Edith and she promised to ask Harry to speak to the royal estate agent on their behalf. She fumbled with her locket and opened it, her lips curving into a smile at Sam's happy face looking up at her.

'I will never forget you, Sam Peters,' she murmured through moist eyes, leaning down to kiss the photo tenderly.

Beatrice took Florence's hand. 'This terrible war will end, it cannot last for ever. We'll get through this somehow, we have to. I know how hard it feels right now, thinking of a future without Sam. But he has given his life for us to be free. He would want us to be happy. And you will one day, I promise you that. Remember too that you and your family will always be dear to me.'

Florence's voice wobbled. 'I never thought of it that way, but I suppose that's true. Our lives go on, but I miss him so much, Beatrice.'

'We all do, but he will always live in our hearts.'

'There's something else. The letter mentioned that some of Sam's personal effects were being returned to us, including Ted the tortoise. They found him alive in his tin. Ted is coming home. Only he was meant to bring Sam back with him,' Florence gulped.

∽

Jessie's heart ached at the latest devastating news. She resigned herself to not hearing from Jack. 'No news can be good news at times like this,' the vicar had told her when she confided in him her fears for Jack's safety.

'Jack's duties as the King's Messenger are highly secret and he never knows himself where he is going until the last minute. You must continue to be patient. Please pray and believe that God has not deserted us, even though it might seem that he has. Use your faith and belief in him to help you through the worst moments.'

Later that afternoon Jessie went to the church to pray for Jack's safe return. She saw a woman dressed in black seated in one of the pews, her head bent low in prayer, her back heaving up and down with heartfelt sobs.

She looked up at the sound of Jessie's footsteps on the stone floor and rubbed her eyes. 'I'm so sorry, I didn't mean to interrupt you,' Jessie whispered.

Jane Rumbelow wiped her moist eyes. 'I'm trying to believe in God. But all I ask him is why he has forsaken us? I can't help it. I'm so sorry to hear about Sam's death, I know only too well how painful this is for his family and Beatrice. I can't bear to hear about all our men dying. There soon won't be any young men left in Wolferton.'

Jessie sat next to Jane on the pew. She took the vicar's wife's hand. 'We must never forget they have given their lives so we are not ruled by another nation. I wish I could do something. I think it's a war we have to fight. If only we knew when it would end.'

Jane asked. 'Do you know what came for us today? A package of Piers' belongings returned to us as his next of kin. He'd kept all our letters, our Christmas card and . . .'

Her body shook, the words sticking in her throat. Jessie reached over to hold her. Jane pulled away, gripping her hand tightly, her jaw clenched.

'They can't send us his body for burial, just his bloodied uniform. They returned his uniform to us soaked in his blood. How could they be so heartless as to send that?'

Jessie did her best to offer words of comfort, but felt they were shallow in the face of the poor woman's unbearable suffering. They sat in companionable silence for a few moments until the church door creaked open and the vicar walked towards his grief-stricken wife, holding his arms out for her. His eyes were filled with compassion and love. Jane stood and nodded to Jessie, grabbing the side of the pew for support as her knees suddenly buckled. After steadying herself, she turned and walked out of the church, the vicar's arm held protectively around her shoulders to steady her.

∽∽

Jessie returned to the station master's house with a heavy heart, noticing that more and more women were dressed in black. It was now four days since Leslie had been snatched by Walter Jugg and the Saward sisters and their mother took it in turns to keep an eye on Maria from where she slept on the sofa in the front room. She had been there since she had returned to the house. She was still wearing the same clothes, with a blanket wrapped around her and a pillow under her head.

When Maria had first returned home following the drama on the railway she was in a highly anxious state. She repeatedly called out Eddie's name and burst into tears. Dr Fletcher told the Sawards that Maria was in deep shock and gave her a strong sleeping draught to help.

Maria's eyes flickered open and she saw Jessie and Sarah's faces looking down on her. Sarah's expression was one of concern and her eyes lit up as Maria pushed herself up, looking confused.

'What's happened? Why am I lying here?'

'Can you remember anything?' asked Sarah.

Maria shook her head. 'Nothing. Except . . . Walter . . .'

'You have no need to worry about him anymore, my dear, he won't be causing you any further trouble,' she said, fluffing the pillow.

Maria rubbed her eyes and stared blankly at her. 'What do you mean? I know he was here to cause trouble. What's happened to him?'

Jessie and Sarah exchanged anxious glances. 'Tell her, Mother. She needs to know?'

'I don't understand. What do I need to know?'

'He's dead, Maria. He died on the track. He fell and couldn't get up and a train . . .'

Maria interrupted the station master's wife. 'It's coming back to me now . . . the train . . . Eddie chasing after Walter . . . and Leslie. Where is Leslie? Is he safe?'

'Shush, you have nothing to worry about. Leslie is safe, and so is Eddie. Leslie is playing up Betty and Eddie is a stubborn lad. He refused to take time off work, not even a day, despite suffering from shock. It's been four days now since Dr Fletcher gave you a sleeping potion and it really knocked you out. He said it would do wonders for you, help you feel calmer when you woke up. You've had a terrible shock, Maria, but it's over now.'

'But I should have done something. I should have stopped Walter. You must hate me for all the trouble I have caused,' cried Maria.

Sarah took Maria's hand. 'Of course we don't and you mustn't blame yourself. There was nothing you could have done. We have our Leslie back, and not a hair harmed on his head. Just imagine what could have happened if Eddie hadn't . . .'

'I can't believe Walter has gone. I know he was a wrong'un, but I just wanted him to leave me alone, and now he's dead. Why do so many terrible things happen to me? I've brought you nothing but trouble.'

'Stuff and nonsense,' retorted Sarah, handing her a handkerchief. 'You've brought happiness to us all, and I never thought the day would come when I said that, but it's true. Everyone you meet takes you to their hearts.'

Jessie smiled. 'We've got used to you being here now, haven't we, Mother?'

'What? You really mean that?' asked Maria, raising her eyebrows. 'Does that mean . . . ?'

Ada had walked into the room at that moment. 'Oh, yes, it's true,' she said, having heard the tail end of her mother's words. 'There's Eddie to start. Anyone can see he is smitten. Little Leslie adores you. Betty says you are the best house worker ever, the Greensticks sisters have taken a shine to you for some reason, and even Queen Alexandra enquired after you when Mrs Inglenook informed her about what happened.'

Jessie moved to the window and spotted Florence walking past. She was a forlorn figure dressed in black, which made her face look ghostly white. Jessie rushed out to invite her in, remembering that Betty had baked a cake for Edith that morning, and offered it to Florence to take home.

The family gave their sincere condolences, and promised to call in very soon, now that Maria had awakened. Beatrice spent all of her free time with Edith, the two women comforting each other, at the end of her working day.

Maria said, 'I'm so sorry for your loss, Florence. I've heard what a grand lad Sam was. Beatrice is so cut up.'

Florence dabbed her damp eyes and thanked her, telling Maria how she admired her courage in chasing Walter. She was about to leave, with the cake wrapped up in brown paper under her arm, when she turned to Maria. 'You're the bravest girl I know. I heard what happened on the track. I'm so glad no harm came to you, or Eddie'

'I did nothing,' Maria scoffed. 'Eddie is the hero of the day. He is, well. . .'

Maria struggled to find the right word. She wanted to say *special*. He had shown her that he was very *special*.

Florence spoke softly. 'I hope you don't think I am speaking out of turn, Maria, but you will be kind to him, won't you? To Eddie?'

'What do you mean? Eddie and I are just friends.'

'Oh no, Maria, you need to open your eyes. And soon, before he enlists. Knowing him, he'll lie about his age and be off. I must go now. And I hope we can be friends.'

'Of course we can. At times like this we need all the friends we can.'

After Florence had left Maria turned to Sarah and asked what Florence meant about Eddie.

'Well, you did call out his name in your barely conscious state a number of times. Perhaps she can see he has

377

a soft spot for you and is trying to drop a hint,' suggested Sarah, with a faint smile.

The station master's wife picked up a blue shawl from a chair. 'Is this yours?'

'Oh, Mrs Saward, it ain't what you're thinking. I swear to you.'

'We found it in the royal retiring rooms and I—'

Maria interrupted her, her heart racing as the words spilled out. 'Please hear me out. I only wanted to help you. I wanted to clean the royal retiring rooms nicely as a surprise to show my thanks to you for your kindness. And then . . . then Walter saw me there. I didn't know he was following me, and he tried to make me steal for him, but I wouldn't do it. I swear to God I wouldn't take a thing that weren't mine. He stole the candlesticks to pay off his debts and wanted me to take the pendulum clock, but I refused. That's why he snatched Leslie and made up those lies about me as well – to blackmail you.'

'We believe you, Maria. We found the candlesticks in Walter's bag. They were extremely valuable, a present, to Queen Alexandra from her mother, the Queen of Denmark. She is extremely grateful they have been returned, and would like to thank you herself when you are well enough,' Sarah responded gently.

'And that's not all. Mrs Inglenook was most impressed with the high standard of your cleaning in the royal waiting rooms. And that is praise indeed coming from her.'

Maria's face brightened instantly. 'Really? That's very kind of her to say.'

'In fact, she said one of their maids at Sandringham House is leaving soon to have a baby, and she wondered if you would be interested . . .'

Maria's eyes widened. 'Oh yes. Tell her I am *very* interested.'

Sarah continued, 'There's more, Maria. If it works out well Mrs Inglenook will enquire with the estate manager if there is a small cottage on the estate you can live in with your mother and Joey.'

Maria's face could not hide her excitement. 'Oh, I'd love that. I really would. I will work like a slave from dawn till dusk, I promise you.'

Her face dropped a moment later. 'But what about Freddie and Archie? I'd give anything to have them here too.'

Sarah smiled. 'I'm sure that can be arranged. Harry's looking into it. There is always plenty of work on the estate for two strong young lads, especially with so many of our men away at war.'

Maria's lips quivered. The words stuck in her throat and tears sprung to her eyes. 'I don't know what to say. I ain't ever been this happy before. I feel part of a proper family now. How can I ever thank you?'

'Oh, I'm sure we can find a way,' Ada, who had remained quietly in the corner of the room, said with a smile.

Maria freshened herself up and found she could move around the house like her old self. She gulped back the best part of a whole pot of tea and devoured a couple of fried eggs – kept specially by the Sawards to help her regain her strength – piled on top of a thick slice of bread. Feeling her strength was restored, she announced she wanted to go out for some fresh air.

Her mind turned to Eddie and she felt a stirring inside her. Florence's words rang in her ears and she realised she must have a soft spot for him. The thought that he laid his life on the line for Leslie sent her head into a spin. She'd already seen his kindness towards Robbie, and now after his latest heroics, she felt her heart warm towards him even more. The realisation too that his cheery wave, his jaunty smile, his tuneful whistle and his cocky ways that she had taken for granted might soon vanish from Wolferton filled Maria with sadness. She found herself wondering if Eddie could become more than a good friend, if she needed to open her eyes, as Florence had suggested. But part of her could not believe that he would want anything to do with a girl like her.

She knew she must speak to Eddie face to face and thank him for his bravery for saving Leslie from Walter's clutches. The next day, feeling revived from her ordeal, she found herself pacing along the platform, intending to wait for him to finish work.

She saw that he was helping two pretty young girls with their bags. She was shocked to feel a twinge of jealousy stirring inside as she observed him teasing them as they giggled at his jokes.

Maria had seen the girls at the concert, and as their faces turned towards her, still laughing, she changed her mind about talking to Eddie and turned away. She strode quickly towards the station garden favoured by Queen Alexandra and leant her back against a shed next to it, her pulse soaring.

A moment later, Eddie appeared, a broad grin on his face. 'Hello, Maria. How are you feeling? Why did you run off like that? I would have introduced you to Lucy and Lavinia, they are cousins on Ma's side and visiting for a few days, staying with relatives in Snettisham.'

Startled, Maria jumped back. She sensed that her feelings towards Eddie had grown into something more than just friendship and she struggled to find the right words.

'I just came here . . . just wanted to say—'

Eddie took hold of her shaking hands in his and held them, smiling reassuringly at her. A warm sensation rippled inside Maria as she glanced at his handsome face, his open, honest face and wished she was running her hands through his thick dark hair, the fringe hanging over his eyebrows. He gently stroked her cheek and she rested her face against the palm of his hand, enjoying the warm tingling sensations it aroused within her.

'Is it true? Are you enlisting?' she asked, her voice hoarse.

Eddie cupped Maria's chin in his hands. She didn't mind that they were dirty. The sensation of his touch made her tingle all over.

'As soon as I can, when I'm seventeen, I'll be off with the Territorials, or I'll lie about my age and sign up with the Army. I can't wait until I'm eighteen to be called up. Kitchener's asking for volunteers and I'm no coward. I'm not staying here and being given a white feather.'

Maria shook her head. 'I just came to say thank you . . .'

'Shush, you don't have to thank me for anything. As long as you are okay that's what matters to me. I would do anything for Harry and his family. They are some of the best people I know. And that includes you, Maria.'

Maria's body tensed and her eyes moistened. 'But you wouldn't say that if you knew the truth about me. I ain't who you think I am, Eddie.'

'What are you talking about? I know you're a Saward, that's more than good enough for me.' Eddie smiled.

Maria shook her head. 'It's not as straightforward as that. Is there anywhere private we can speak for a moment?'

Eddie led Maria into the gardening shed, his eyebrows furrowed. The shelves were filled with clay flowerpots and a spade and rake were propped against the wall. Half a dozen egg trays were piled up on the side in the shed, ready to be dispatched to a hospital treating wounded soldiers on the Western Front. Some had the names of the donors written on the shell, with a heartfelt message of encouragement. She spotted a large white egg with Florence's name and screwed up her eyes as she read the tiny words written in ink: *I pray for your safe and speedy return home.*

'Can you hear something? What's that sound?' asked Eddie, staring around him.

Maria spun around. She cupped her hands to her ears and smiled. 'It sounds like a cat. I'm sure I can hear meowing,' she blurted, a surprised look on her face.

'It sounds like more than one cat to me. If you listen hard, there are some tiny meowing sounds too,' Eddie exclaimed. 'Where's it coming from?'

They followed the sound to the corner of the shed where there was a pile of newspaper.

'I don't believe it! It's Oscar,' yelped Maria. 'He belongs to the Greensticks sisters and went missing. They'll be over the moon when I tell them I've found him.'

'It can't be a him,' pointed out Eddie. 'Look behind Oscar, there are three kittens!'

Maria knelt down in front of Oscar, his green eyes as startled as hers. Sure enough, there behind him were three tiny bundles of ginger fluff no bigger than the size of her hand, their eyes tight shut, and cuddled up against the plump ginger cat. Oscar shifted protectively towards his young brood and hissed, baring his sharp white teeth, standing up on his hind legs, when she reached out to touch them.

'I can't believe it. I mean, I'm sure it's Oscar, but Oscar's a tomcat. I can't wait to tell Magnolia and Aggie, to see the shocked looks on their faces.'

Eddie scratched his head. 'Well, that's a strange thing for sure. There is one simple explanation though.'

'Oh yeah, what's that?' enquired Maria, feeling more at ease with Eddie.

'Well, Oscar was never a tomcat. He's a girl, I mean, she's a girl.'

Maria threw her head back and laughed. 'Of course, how silly of me. You would think they'd know the difference after having so many cats. How could the Greensticks sisters have got it so wrong?'

Eddie shrugged. 'Who knows? I guess these mistakes happen. You'd best let them know that Oscar is safe and sound and has her own family to look after now.'

Maria and Eddie stood inside the door smiling down on Oscar and the sleeping kittens. Taking a deep breath, she blurted, 'Oscar's not the only one with a family. I want to show you something, Eddie.'

She fumbled under her blouse and unclasped her locket. 'This my Joey.'

Eddie looked at the picture and smiled tenderly at Maria. 'He's a bonny boy, and good looking too, just like his ma. It must have taken you some courage to show me, Maria.'

Maria gulped, and wiped away a tear. Eddie took her hand. 'Please, let me put your mind at rest. I know all about Joey. Mr Saward told me the day Walter died. I couldn't make sense of why a nasty man like him should turn up out of the blue and snatch Leslie. I couldn't work out his interest in you. I know he's Joey's father, and how it came to be.'

Maria's face burned. 'Mr Saward told you? But he promised me . . .'

'He felt I was entitled to know after what happened, and he swore me to secrecy. But it don't matter a fig to me. Your Joey, he's such a dear looking chap.'

'Oh, Eddie,' sobbed Maria. 'I promise you I'm a good girl.'

'I know you are. I saw how you cared for Robbie. He was nothing to you, yet he told me how you comforted him and he is looking forward to meeting your brother Archie. He said you mentioned him.'

'I did, and I will. How is Robbie doing?'

'He is getting stronger day by day, and I found out yesterday who his benefactor is, the mystery stranger paying his doctor's fees. He called in to see Robbie one day and Ma told me.'

'Oh tell me, who is it?' asked Maria.

'It's a solicitor from King's Lynn. The one who spoke up for him in court. I think he said his name was *Perry* something. Ma says a kinder man you couldn't wish to meet,' Eddie replied.

'I can't wait to tell Beatrice. She'll want to know and to thank him personally as she has taken an interest in Robbie's well-being. She said he was such a kind man.'

'Ah yes, I remember his name now, it's Mr George Perryman, he has family nearby. He was visiting them when he called in.

'It's my turn to ask you something now, Maria. There's something about you that draws me to you like a bee to the brightest flower. I admire your gutsy spirit and I can see that you want to better yourself in life, just as I do. We're both young now, I know that, but, after the war, hopefully we will have our whole lives ahead of us, with your Joey. I'll be a man when I come back and will be able to look after him.'

Maria gulped; her eyes filled with tears. 'I hope you won't stay away that long, Eddie Herring.'

'Here, let me,' Eddie offered, tenderly wiping her cheeks dry. 'I don't want to make you sad. I don't ever want to make you cry.'

Maria flung her arms around Eddie's neck and kissed him hard on the lips. He placed his arms around her waist and pressed her body close to his. Their lips locked into a slow gentle kiss. It sent a fizzing sensation throughout her body and she wished it could last for ever. Maria felt her heart was beating so loudly it would burst out of her chest and her body weakened in his tender hold.

She pulled herself away, her face flushed. 'Eddie Herring, I feel quite giddy. I ain't ever been kissed proper before.'

'There's plenty more where that came from,' he smiled. 'Well?' 'What's your answer? Will you be my sweetheart?'

'What do you think, you big tease?'

'I want to hear it from your own lips, Maria Saward.'

He pressed his body against Maria's again, pinning her against the wall. He stroked her hair and cheek, rubbing his finger along her lips.

As she opened her mouth to reply, Oscar meowed loudly. 'Oscar's answered for me. And yes, Eddie Herring, I will be your sweetheart.'

Eddie pressed his lips against Maria's and they sealed their commitment to each other, a hungry insatiable desire rising within Maria.

'I must go, I can hear Mr Saward calling for me.'

Maria watched him leave, her heart singing. She felt Oscar nuzzling her ankles and bent down and gently stroked the new mother cat. 'You are a clever cat. And full of surprises. We'll have to think of a new name for you now. I'm sure Eddie will find a box to take your babies to their new home. Wait until Magnolia and Aggie see you. They won't believe it!'

She closed the shed door behind her, leaving it slightly ajar so Oscar and her brood had plenty of fresh air, placing a large stone against it. Then she left the station, her heart fit to burst, walking on air to Kitty Cottage.

She lifted the feline-shaped door knocker and banged it down impatiently, shifting from foot to foot as she waited for one of the sisters to open the door.

Aggie opened up, releasing the inside latch and chain and apologising for keeping Maria waiting. 'We have to make sure our cats are secure before we answer the front door. We can't be too careful, especially since Oscar ran off.'

'That's why I'm here Aggie. I've found him! I mean, her.'

Maria could barely contain her excitement and the words gushed out of her mouth. Instead of ogling Aggie's eccentric dress, the white blouse with big puffed sleeves and the largest pink bow tied around her neck, Maria couldn't wait to tell her everything.

'You've found him? You've found our baby Oscar? That's wonderful news! Where is he?'

'Who is it?' called Magnolia's voice from the back room. 'Did I hear someone mention Oscar?'

'Yes, Magnolia. I've found Oscar. You're never going to believe what I have to say. May I come in? I have some wonderful news to tell you.'

'Oh, my dear, do step inside. But why don't you have him with you?' she asked anxiously, while Jasper wriggled in her arms.

Maria was ushered into the back room. Two of the cats sat in their baskets washing their paws, looking up briefly and making faint meowing sounds, before flicking their tails and settling down contentedly. Magnolia sat down in a chair stroking the tabby cat on her lap.

'Poor Jasper, he hasn't been himself since Oscar disappeared. I had no idea they were so attached,' mumbled Magnolia. She wore exactly the same dressy blouse as her sister, but a royal-blue bow was tied around her neck, the satin fabric hanging down to her waist.

'It's true, I've found Oscar. He's at the station, in the potting shed, and he's safe. You've no need to worry,' Maria explained, her face brimming with excitement.

'I'll take a lead and go now and bring him home. Thank you for finding him, Maria, you are such a good girl. I always said that, didn't I, Aggie?' said Magnolia, placing Jasper down on the floor.

'Before you go there is something else you must know. You won't believe this, but Oscar, well, Oscar isn't a boy cat, he's a girl. I mean she's a girl.'

'What are you talking about? Have you taken leave of your senses?' Aggie spluttered.

'Oscar has had kittens. That's how I know, and he's looking after them now. He's had three little ginger kittens! They are so fluffy and sweet.'

The sisters gasped, their eyes as wide as saucers as they stared at each other. 'I can't believe it. This is the most wonderful news, though I never expected such a happy surprise,' gushed Magnolia, her jaw falling to the ground.

Jasper purred from Magnolia's lap. 'Did you hear that, Jasper? Now I wouldn't be at all surprised if you were responsible for Oscar's condition. I do feel foolish, fancy not knowing Oscar's a girl.'

Aggie took Maria's hand in hers. 'We can never thank you enough, my dear. You don't know how much Oscar means to us.'

Maria bent down to stroke Maud as she rubbed the side of her head against her leg, demanding her attention.

'She's taken to you.' Aggie smiled. 'Look, there's Helena now, she wants some attention as well.'

'What are you going to do with Oscar's kittens? Have you got room for them here?' asked Maria, her eyes scanning the room, which seemed full to capacity.

'That's a thought,' piped in Aggie, casting a sideways glance at her sister. 'Perhaps you would like one. You could have first pick, though I'm sure they are all equally adorable.'

'Really! That would be wonderful. But I'd have to ask Mr and Mrs Saward first. I'm sure Leslie would just love to have a kitten to play with. You really are the kindest people. Thank you for accepting me into your lives.'

Maria lowered her eyes, biting her lip, wondering if they would feel the same way about her if they knew about her Joey. She prepared to leave, stepping towards the door.

'My dear, before you go, there is something we would like to tell you,' said Magnolia.

The sisters exchanged glances. 'You tell her,' urged Aggie.

'Tell me what?' asked Maria, perplexed.

Magnolia gulped. 'Now we know you better, I feel we owe you an explanation. I know we can come across as snooty busybodies who put on airs and graces and sometimes we seem harsh, not thinking before we speak. Or at least I do.'

Maria nodded. 'It's true, I used to think you were so snooty. I ain't posh like you, but I know better now and can see you both have kind hearts.' She paused. 'I thank you kindly for accepting me, but I feel it's under false pretences. There are things about me you don't know, and if you did you would shun me.'

'Ah yes, are you talking about little Joey? We know all about him, my dear, and we can't wait to meet him,' the two sisters said in unison.

'But how do you know? And why are you being so kind to me?' Maria gawped. She could scarcely believe her ears.

'Shall we tell her?' asked Magnolia, glancing at her sister, who nodded.

'Because we are more like you than you think. You see, we weren't born posh.'

'I don't understand. What are you saying?'

Magnolia huffed a deep breath and exchanged a glance with her sister, who nodded. 'Our mother was a maid in Sandringham House and found herself with child. She would never tell us who the father was, except that he was connected to the royal family. He was very generous to her, and by all accounts he loved her. He found a house for her to live far away so nobody would gossip. They had another daughter. When he died suddenly she found he had made arrangements to have her taken care of for the rest of her life – and their children, too.'

'So you mean to say, this is your story you are telling me. You are both . . .' Maria started, unable to finish the sentence.

'Yes, bastards. That's the word you're after, isn't it,' retorted Aggie.

Maria turned crimson. 'I didn't mean to offend you, only I can't believe this.'

Magnolia nodded. 'Every word is true. We were told by our aunt, who brought us up once our mother had died when we were young.'

'I don't know what to say. I feel as if one life is behind me and I have a new one to look forward to, with my ma and Joey. It's as my ma always says, "Whenever something bad happens, you will always find some goodness in it too."'

∽

Maria made her way back to the station master's house with a lightness to her step. As she reached the station, the sound of the signalman's whistle ringing in her ears and plumes of smoke alerted her to the imminent arrival of a train. She spotted Ada running quickly across the path pushing Leslie in his perambulator. She had never seen her so excited.

'Alfie's here. He's on this train! He managed to take an earlier leave and is here sooner than expected.'

Maria could scarcely believe her ears, thrilled there was some good news for the Sawards after the heartache of Sam's death. She momentarily forgot the terrible sadness and grieving that pierced the hearts of almost all families in Wolferton. Alfie would be here any minute, to hold his wife and see his beloved son for the first time. She felt her chest was bursting, so great was her happiness.

As the train steamed into the station and screeched to a halt, billowing clouds of smoke from the engine, she stood back on the crowded platform and watched families pushing through, looking for their sons, husbands and loved ones, returning home on leave. She spotted Ada darting between families, waving a white handkerchief. She heard her cry out, 'Alfie! Alfie!'

A handsome fair-haired soldier leant out of a carriage window.

Maria recognised his kind face from photographs at the station master's house.

'Ada. Oh, Ada! Over here!'

Within seconds, a soldier carrying his military rucksack burst out of the carriage. Ada ran towards him and they crashed into each other's arms, tears streaming down their faces, clinging tightly to each other.

Maria gulped at the passion of their emotional reunion and she looked away for a moment, not wanting to embarrass them. Unable to resist peeking, she watched Alfie squeeze the breath out of his ecstatic wife. He kissed her face tenderly until they were both breathless, stroking her cheek and brushing away a loose strand of hair as he pulled away. Ada's small hand reached up to Alfie's face to brush away a tear in the corner of his eye and he grabbed it and pressed it to his lips, his loving eyes never leaving her flushed face.

'Thank God you are home safely. And earlier than I thought too. What a wonderful surprise, my darling. I wouldn't want to live if anything happened to you,' Ada blurted.

Alfie placed a finger over her lips. 'Shh, I told you I would return. It might only be for a few days, but I am a man of my word.'

Harry appeared at that moment, his face beaming. He opened his arms and embraced his son-in-law, patting him on the back. 'Welcome home, Alfred. Oh God, it's good to have you back.'

Turning and pointing to the perambulator, which Ada had parked up against the wall, Harry grinned. 'I think there's someone you should meet.'

Alfie's jaw dropped and his face lit up as he glanced at his wife. Ada nodded. 'Oh yes, I'd almost forgotten . . .'

Alfie made his way over and looked down at his son, grinning from ear to ear. As he reached down to scoop him in his arms, his face lit up with joy.

Maria bit her lip and half looked away. She felt a bittersweet pang inside her, thinking of her Joey, an innocent child who had no father's love to guide him through life.

'He's such a bonny little chap. I feel the luckiest man in the world.' Alfie beamed, pinching his son's plump cheek.

Harry reached for his pocket watch and glanced at the time. 'All aboard,' he shouted out.

Leaning backwards, he blew the whistle and passengers clambered aboard before the train resumed its journey, chugging along the winding track towards Hunstanton, belching out thick smoke as it went.

Through the haze, Harry spotted a woman's shape loitering on the platform. Her back was turned to him, yet there was something familiar about it. When the smoke had cleared, she turned round, nervously twisting her hands, her shoulders stooped. She had a weary expression on her face and looked older than her forty years.

'Mollie? Is it Mollie Bucket?' he queried.

Her mouth twitched nervously and she avoided looking the station master's in the eye. 'Yes, Mr Saward, it is. I've come to see me boy. How is my Robbie?'

'Well I'll be damned. We'd given you up for dead. It's been three years or more since you were last seen. Where have you been all this time? Not even the police could find you.'

Mollie raised her face. 'I know I did wrong going off like that and me name must be mud, but I did what any woman would do if she felt 'er life were in danger and had had one beating too many. What good would a dead mother be for her child? I do wish I'd taken me Robbie with me though.'

'So where have you been all this time?'

'I've been staying with me cousin Fanny near Norwich, working as a cleaner, taking what work I could. But Fanny, she came down to Wolferton twice to go to the Horticultural Show at Sandringham an' asked after Robbie with his teacher who she bumped into there, so I knew 'e was all right – well, as right as he could be. I would 'ave sent word to him, but I were scared his father would come for me. I was always intending on coming back for my Robbie.'

Harry told her, 'He's not had it easy, Mollie. Have you heard what happened to him and Sid?'

'I only just 'eard, Fanny saw their names in the paper an' I couldn't believe it. My poor Robbie. It broke me 'eart to read about the trouble 'e got into. There weren't a day go by when I didn't think of my Robbie an' the brute I left him with. I always intended to come back for 'im when I'd saved enough for the two of us. With Sid locked up, I knew it was safe for me to come back now.'

A small audience gathered around Mollie and Harry as word spread. Some were pointing to her as they recognised her, shaking their heads and muttering under their breath. *She's got a nerve, after leaving her poor boy like that.*

Mollie pleaded. 'Please don't judge me harshly, Mr Saward. I never went with other men, never did anything dishonest, I just kept me head down an' worked 'ard. Where can I find Robbie?'

Eddie rushed forward. 'Is it true, Mrs Bucket? You've come back for Robbie?'

395

Mollie nodded. 'I 'ave. An' this time I'm 'ere to stay. If 'e'll let me. Maybe we can make a fresh start in Norwich, well away from Sid when the time comes for him to be released.'

'Perhaps it's best to take just one day at a time for now, Mrs Bucket. He's doing well, he's getting his strength back. I can take you to him. He's staying with me and my ma, she's looked after him like her own. I know he'll be that pleased to see you. That's if I can have a moment's leave, Mr Saward.'

The station master assented with a smile. 'Of course, you must take her, but come back quickly.'

Mollie took Eddie's hands and clasped them in hers, her eyes moist. 'It sounds like you've been a very good friend to my Robbie. And yer ma. How can I ever thank yer?'

Eddie's face reddened as he muttered that it had been nothing. Maria grinned at him as he strode off up the plat- form, with Mollie quickening her step to keep up.

Her heart was gladdened knowing that Robbie's mother had returned for him; she could imagine how overjoyed Robbie would feel to see her again. Soon Maria would have her son with her too, and she swore to herself that she would never be parted from him again either.

She smiled as she glanced at Ada, who beckoned Maria over. 'Alfie, there is someone else you should meet. May I introduce you to Maria. She is a Saward from Audley End and her side of the family is coming to live in Wolferton.'

Maria opened her mouth to speak, but Ada contin- ued quickly, gushing, 'And she is absolutely wonderful with Leslie. I don't know how I would have managed without her.'

'I'm very pleased to meet you, Maria, and I'm very grateful for everything you have done for Ada and our Leslie. It looks like I have lots to catch up. I'm always pleased to meet another Saward.' Alfie smiled warmly, his eyes twinkling, and shook Maria's hand tightly.

Maria's face beamed, she gulped back a tear and raised her chin. 'Yes, I'm a Saward too, and proud of it. Everyone knows it now, even the queen.'

As the words spilled from her mouth her heart was singing. For the first time in her life, she really believed it was true.

Maria could scarcely believe what a day it had turned out to be. She glanced around the station and felt truly contented, knowing she was where she really belonged. She caught sight of Harry's face as she passed him. Did she imagine it, did Harry really wink at her while whistling a tune under his breath?

Acknowledgements

I would like to shower a thousand thanks on my editor at Bonnier Books UK, Claire Johnson-Creek. From the moment she commissioned my books it was clear she shared my passion for *The Royal Station Master's Daughters*. She has given me terrific support and her forensic editing is exceptional. It's been a great joy and privilege to work with Claire.

My wonderful agent, Hannah Weatherill at the Northbank Talent Agency, was behind me all the way providing insightful suggestions. I am also thankful to Diane Banks and the Northbank team for their faith in me and encouragement.

This book would not have been written if I had never encountered Brian Heath. He introduced me to his incredible great grandfather, Harry Saward, and put me in touch with his cousin, Penny Coe. Brian has been incredibly generous in sharing his family's unique history and I hope I have done justice to Harry's memory, a story Brian wanted to be told. Thank you, Brian, I am so grateful to you, and Penny too.

Special thanks must go to Richard Brown who bought and restored the royal station at Wolferton. We bonded over our shared passion for its royal history and he kindly showed me around the exquisite suite of rooms once graced by European royal families.

I doubt anyone can know more about Sandringham's royal history than Ben Colson, who resides in the splendid royal retiring rooms opposite Richard's; there are two sets, one on each platform. He fired my imagination by recounting so many wonderful royal anecdotes. I thank you both with all my heart for your many kindnesses.

Historical accuracy is key to me, and I am indebted to Norfolk historian Neil Storey for casting his sharp eye over my draft. I first met Neil when he spoke at a lunch in Kings' Lynn for Gallipoli & Dardanelles International. His talk was gripping and heart wrenching and I knew I had to include this tragic period of Norfolk's history in my book.

I would like to thank the readers of the Eastern Daily Press and Lynn News who responded to my appeal and shared stories of their families' experiences back in those dark days of Gallipoli, stories that will live on through the pages of my book, if not this one, then in either book two or three of this series.

These kind people, and others who have helped me along the way, include Michael Vawdser, Pearl Richardson, Alexis Brand, John Crowe, Graham Beck, Jane Chater, Steve Smith, Alan Coleby, Evelyn Sainty, Roger and Ann Kerrison, Betty Woodhouse, John and Sally Godfrey, Dick Melton and Kate Thaxton of the Royal Norfolk Regimental Museum.

I thank my author buddy Di Redmond for our many enjoyable evenings nattering about this book in Cambridge restaurants and for her support. I am sad my dear friend Diana Lloyd did not live to see it come to fruition as she so enjoyed hearing about it.

And lastly, I must thank my husband Stephen for accompanying me on many trips to Sandringham and Wolferton and sharing this journey with me, and my family, David and Fiona, and James and Beth, who encouraged me all the way. I am so lucky to have you!

Dear Reader,

Welcome to the first book in my new series, *The Royal Station Masters' Daughters*. I am thrilled to share their special stories with you that take us on a journey back in time to when royals travelled regularly by rail.

Jessie, Beatrice and Ada were in real life the daughters of Harry Saward, Station Master at Wolferton, close to Sandringham House in Norfolk, the much-loved country retreat of the royal family since 1862.

Harry's position and unique glimpses into royal life span forty years starting from 1884 under the reign of Queen Victoria, King Edward V11 and King George V. Whilst I have retained real names for Harry and his family in this book, the stories are fictitious, as are the other characters I created, while trying to stay true to historical facts.

Today this small rural station that once welcomed Europe's royal families and leading political figures of the day is closed. In its heyday Harry recorded an astonishing 645 royal trains steaming in and out of the station between 1884 and 1911 alone. He would greet the distinguished arrivals and ensure they were comfortable, including, Maria Feodorovna, Dowager Empress of Russia, sister of Queen Alexandra, the Kings and Queens of Spain, Portugal, Denmark, and the King of Greece, and also German Emperor Kaiser Wilhelm II, cousin to

King George V who would go on to drop bombs close to Sandringham in WWI. Even Rasputin is said to have arrived out of the blue at Wolferton to see King George on matters of war, but was sent packing, most probably by Harry on instructions from the King's courtiers. Now you can see why I was hooked!

This is the first in a series of three books and is set during August 1915 when loyal estate workers from the Sandringham estate, the gardeners and gamekeepers, the dairymen and farm workers, rallied to pledge their support to King and country and were posted to Gallipoli to fight the Turks. The outcome for the Sandringham Company, who made up the 5th Battalion of the Norfolk Regiment, was catastrophic. There was a terrible loss of life. News trickled home about the scores of deaths and reports of missing men too, their unknown fate providing a glimmer of hope to families that they might still be alive. However, many families faced a lengthy and agonising wait until after the end of the war when the remains of more than 140 Norfolks were discovered, including Captain Frank Beck, the estate agent who in a speech made to families before their departure poignantly promised to bring his men back home. It's a desperately sad story that captured the public's imagination in the film *All The Kings Men*, starring David Jason as Captain Beck, their fate shrouded in myths.

I wondered about the fate of the women left behind and wanted to tell their story. A whole community bereaved, mourning the loss or disappearance of fathers, husbands, sons and brothers as they continued with their daily lives. How did they cope not knowing whether their loved one was dead or alive, stoically refusing to wear black arm bands until receiving official confirmation from the War Office that their loved one had died?

My affection for Wolferton goes back many years. I first visited the royal station with my parents as a child. A previous owner had opened it as a museum and when I stepped inside the royal retiring rooms, comprising of separate suites of rooms for the King and Queen so they could relax in comfort and elegance before travelling on to their destination – I am told royals do not wait, like us commoners, they *retire* – I glimpsed an Aladdin's cave of royal treasures. I can recall my sense of awe as I gazed into the display cabinets crammed with royal memorabilia. The station heaved with jaw dropping visitors whose imagination, like mine, travelled back in time. I could scarcely believe I was standing in the sumptuous rooms once graced by five generations of monarchy.

The last royal train ran in Wolferton in 1966 and the station finally closed to public use in 1969. It was much loved by Queen Elizabeth and her young family, with a five-year-old Prince Charles once blowing the guard's whistle when his great grandmother, Queen Mary, departed from Wolferton, setting off the train ahead of time!

Today the royal station and downside platform is owned by Richard Brown, a railway enthusiast who lovingly restored it to its former glory. He generously and genuinely delights in welcoming guests to step along the platform where countless royals once trod and speaks with great passion about its history.

On the opposite side of the track Ben Colson lives in his exquisite royal suite of rooms, the first to be built at Wolferton station. Ben is one of the most knowledgeable guides at Sandringham House and thrilled me with his royal stories. His rooms retain their original features, including an oak vaulted ceiling, a replica of what is in the Great Hall, Windsor. It's easy to imagine Queen Alexandra and her ladies sitting there sipping tea from delicate bone china cups. Richard and Ben opened my eyes to a very special world from a bygone era and excited my imagination, for which I am extremely grateful.

I mentioned earlier how I endeavoured to stay true to historical facts that I could weave around my character's lives. One example was discovering the National Egg Collection. I read many headlines about it in newspapers of the day. It aroused my curiosity and I was amazed to learn about the national public appeal for newly laid eggs during WWI. They were despatched to British wounded servicemen in Base hospitals in France and Belgium. Over

41 million eggs were collected, of which 32 million were shipped to these hospitals. Queen Alexandra was patron and donors were encouraged to write their name and address on the eggs with a message for the wounded. Local groups were set up and free transport was provided by the railways, so it's not unreasonable to assume that boxes of eggs were collected in Wolferton and would have been despatched from the royal station which I describe in the book.

I'm delighted that *The Royal Station Master's Daughter's* is part of the Memory Lane community. My second book, *The Royal Station Master's Daughters at War*, is set two years later in 1917 and will be packed with more royal stories and dramas for Jessie, Beatrice and Ada and their impoverished relative, Maria, who has since flourished as a royal maid. There will be more wartime heartache and unexpected revelations, culminating in a terrible tragedy at the station.

As we approach the Queen's Platinum Jubilee in 2022, this is the perfect time to enjoy royal stories. As Harry Saward and his family would say, *God Save The Queen!*

With much love,
Ellee xxx

A Recipe for Trench Cake

This official recipe for trench cake was released by the government during WWI. It was a popular traditional cake that could be baked at home and posted by families to their men serving on the front line.

The recipe required no eggs as some ingredients were hard to come by and people were encouraged to donate eggs to the National Egg Collection. Vinegar was used to react with the baking soda to help the cake rise.

Ingredients

- ½ lb plain flour
- 4 oz margarine
- 1 teaspoon vinegar
- ¼ pint of milk
- 3 oz brown sugar
- 3 oz cleaned currants
- 2 teaspoons cocoa
- ½ teaspoon baking soda
- ½ teaspoon nutmeg
- ½ teaspoon ginger
- Grated lemon rind

· MEMORY LANE ·

Method

1. Pre-heat the oven to 200ºC/180ºC fan/gas mark 6.
2. Grease a cake tin.
3. Rub margarine into the flour in a basin.
4. Add the dry ingredients.
5. Mix well.
6. Add the soda dissolved in vinegar and milk.
7. Beat well.
8. Turn into the tin.
9. Bake for about two hours.

Why not give it a try and post your photos on our Memory Lane Facebook page.

Look out for the next book in *The Royal Station Master's Daughters* Series . . .

The Royal Station Master's Daughters at War

Life is going well for Maria. Welcomed into the Saward family, she has secured herself a job as a maid for Queen Alexandra and is living with her family in a beautiful cottage on the Royal Sandringham estate. The luxuries and privilege associated with the royal family are a far cry from the poverty and suffering she endured before, though the royals, like the nation, are tightening their belts. But when a mysterious relative turns up, seemingly on the run from the law, Maria's new-found happiness could be under threat.

Meanwhile, World War I is still raging, and the daughters of Harry Saward, the royal station master, are doing their bit for the war effort. Ada's beloved husband Alfie is away on the front line, leaving her to care for their young son alone. Beatrice, a nurse in a local cottage hospital, is faced with the daily horror of young men wounded in battle, whilst mourning the loss of her first love, Sam. And Jessie is transforming Queen Alexandra's flower garden at Wolferton Station into a vegetable plot to help with food shortages, all the while longing for the return of her sweetheart, Jack.

In a village torn apart by war and tragedy, how will the family survive the many challenges that war brings, and find the happiness they're all searching for?

Coming in ebook in 2022 and paperback in 2023. Pre-order now.

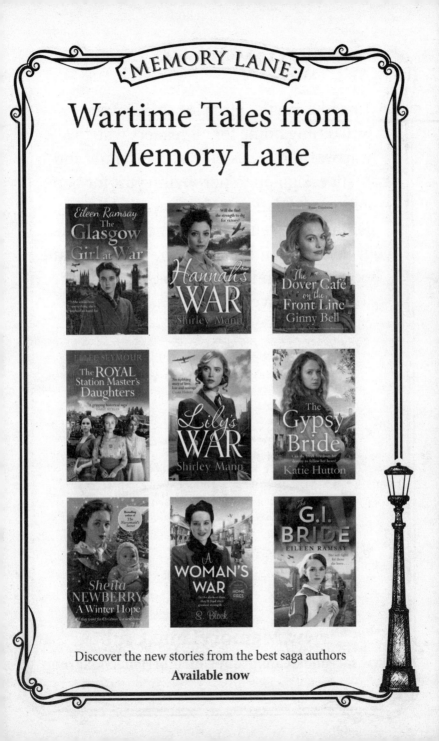